Published by ECW Press
665 Gerrard Street East
Toronto, Ontario, Canada, M4M 1Y2
416-694-3348 / info@ecwpress.com

LIBRARY AND ARCHIVES CANADA
CATALOGUING IN PUBLICATION

Masson, Cynthea, 1965–, author
The flaw in the stone / Cynthea Masson.

(The Alchemists' Council ; book 2)
Issued in print and electronic formats.
ISBN 978-1-77041-274-3 (softcover)
ALSO ISSUED AS: 978-1-77305-147-5 (PDF),
978-1-77305-146-8 (EPUB)

I. TITLE.

PS8626.A7993F53 2018   C813'.6
C2017-906210-7   C2017-906211-5

Editor: Jen Hale
Cover design: Michel Vrana
Paper texture © Kamyshko/Shutterstock
Honeycomb © sauletas/Shutterstock

The publication of *The Flaw in the Stone* has been generously supported by the Canada
Council for the Arts, which last year invested $153 million to bring the arts to Canadians
throughout the country, and by the Government of Canada through the Canada Book Fund.
*Nous remercions le Conseil des arts du Canada de son soutien. L'an dernier, le Conseil a investi 153
millions de dollars pour mettre de l'art dans la vie des Canadiennes et des Canadiens de tout le pays.
Ce livre est financé en partie par le gouvernement du Canada.* We also acknowledge the Ontario
Arts Council (OAC), an agency of the Government of Ontario, and the contribution of the
Government of Ontario through the Ontario Book Publishing Tax Credit and the Ontario
Media Development Corporation.

Ontario
Ontario Media Development
Corporation

ONTARIO ARTS COUNCIL
CONSEIL DES ARTS DE L'ONTARIO
an Ontario government agency
un organisme du gouvernement de l'Ontario

Canada Council
for the Arts

Conseil des Arts
du Canada

Canada

PRINTED AND BOUND IN CANADA   PRINTING: MARQUIS   5   4   3   2   1

RECYCLED
Paper made from
recycled material
FSC
www.fsc.org   FSC® C103567

THE ALCHEMISTS' COUNCIL
BOOK TWO

THE FLAW

IN THE

STONE

CYNTHEA MASSON

FOR

ANITA YOUNG
AND
TAMI JOSEPH

IN GRATITUDE FOR THE TRANSFORMATIONAL
ALCHEMY OF FRIENDSHIP

The Rebel Branch urges
you to read this book.

Prima Materia

Long before Jaden witnessed the mutual con-
junctions of Sadira with Kalina and Arjan with
Dracaen, the Alchemists' Council and the Rebel
Branch had worked for millennia at cross purposes.
The Alchemists' Council aimed to perfect the
Lapis by vanquishing its Flaw, whereas the Rebel
Branch sought to increase the Flaw and thereby
regain control of the Lapis. According to sacraments of the Alchemists' Council, perfecting the
Lapis culminates in eternal union as the communal
One. According to decrees of the Rebel Branch,
maintaining the Flaw preserves free will throughout
the dimensions. Until the war over the Lapis is ultimately waged and won, Council holds responsibility
for maintaining the elemental balance of the outside world through the quintessential power of the
Lapis. To increase this Quintessence, alchemists in

Council dimension participate in the Sacrament of Conjunction, a ritual wherein two beings fully merge into one body and mind. Meanwhile, in Flaw dimension, rebels seek the means to alter this sacrament through blood alchemy — the means to ensure conjunction becomes mutual: two minds, two essences, two beings, each sustaining free will within one body fused through the ancient bloodline.

We are the Blood of the Dragon! We live as the Flaw in the Stone!

PROLOGUE
fflaw Dimension — 1848

Genevre had merely wanted time to herself to contemplate matters. Within months, she would turn thirty, thus reaching her Day of Decision. Like all who resided in Flaw dimension — whether rebel alchemists or outside world scribes — she would formally announce her choice on that day. She rehearsed both options repeatedly: *I, Genevre, outside world scribe, in choosing to ingest Dragonblood Elixir, hereby commit myself to the Rebel Branch. I, Genevre, outside world scribe, in choosing to reject Dragonblood Elixir, hereby reject the Rebel Branch.* What would become of her, she wondered, if she chose to reject those who had sheltered her?

She needed time and space alone to think. The caverns of Flaw dimension were spacious, but rarely empty of rebels, attendants, or miners performing one task or another. Her own quarters, while private, felt too confining of late. As she was still officially training with the Rebel Branch, she could not venture into the outside world without accompaniment. So only one choice remained. Thus, despite her trepidation, she entered the rickety lift and manoeuvred its mechanisms without assistance to lower herself into what she assumed were the deepest archives.

Genevre walked slowly along the main passageway, intermittently peering into the dimly lit archival rooms along the way. She saw no one in the first five rooms. In the sixth, brightly lit with large, low-hanging luminescence lanterns, she noticed Azoth Fraxinus struggling with the weight of a large manuscript. She considered helping him, but decided doing so would defeat her purpose of removing herself from the company of others, and continued past the room unnoticed. The remaining four rooms along the passageway were empty. She stood a few steps beyond the tenth room considering whether to wander down the dark narrow passageway to her right. She regretted not bringing her portable luminescence lantern; she had not realized the secondary passageways would be completely unlit. In her decade with the Rebel Branch — even during official lessons as an apprentice — she had never had reason to explore the archives beyond the main corridor.

Just as she was about to turn back, she was startled by a flash of light quite a distance down the dark passageway. A second flash quickly followed the first, then a third, fourth, and fifth. The flashes seemed to be approaching her, lighting a pathway along the ground. In the growing light, she noticed a robed figure likewise approaching her. Not wanting to be found lingering with no assigned task, Genevre slipped into the tenth archival room, tapped a hanging lantern to activate its luminescence, pulled a random manuscript from a shelf, and sat at a table pretending to read. A minute or so later, Senior Scribe Thuja walked past the archival room window, paying Genevre no notice. When she heard the clanging of the lift mechanisms in the distance, Genevre replaced the unread manuscript, tapped off the light, and ventured out of the room into the dark secondary corridor.

Genevre watched the passageway light up with each step she took. Miniature luminescence lanterns were affixed to both walls just above the ground. Similar lanterns lit up above intermittent archways leading to small archival rooms or narrow tertiary passages. The lanterns appeared to be alchemically rigged to coordinate with one's footsteps and movements. But the effect seemed magical to her. She slowed her pace, then quickened it; she jumped, she hopped, she ran. Genevre was overcome by a spirit of youthful play, something she had not experienced since her arrival in Flaw dimension. She laughed aloud amidst the flickering lights as she moved up and down the secondary passage, her purpose for descending into the archives forgotten.

Genevre would have been quite content to spend

the remainder of the afternoon playing with the lights if not for her unceremonious fall during a manoeuvre better suited to a ten-year-old. She lay face down for a few seconds as she recovered from the shock. As she turned her head and began to push herself up, she noticed yet another unexpected light — this one thin and narrow as if emanating from under a door located down one of the dark tertiary passages. Though luminescence lanterns no longer lit her way, this new path was so narrow she could navigate its darkness by running a hand along each wall as she cautiously made her way towards the light one step at a time.

When she reached the wall at the end of the passageway, she ran her hands along its smooth surface looking for a door handle. She found none, nor could she see or feel any further evidence that an entrance existed beyond the door-width light near the ground. Kneeling by the wall and attempting to peer into the light proved useless, as did lying prostrate slightly farther away in an effort to provide herself with a better vantage point. She could not see into the room — the room she presumed existed — behind the wall. Standing up again, she placed both hands flat against the wall and pushed. She felt nothing beyond the apparently solid stone surface. The light was inexplicable. Finally, she made her way back to the lift and returned to her quarters inspired to find the answer to this mystery.

Whenever possible over the next several weeks, Genevre would descend into the archives and make her way to the *door-not-door* — the name she dubbed the area upon her second visit. In the rare event that she ran into a rebel in the main passageway, she made up an excuse for her presence. On one such occasion, her lie cost her an unexpected two hours of note-taking. Azoth Fraxinus led her to an archival room after she had feigned a need to distinguish Dragonblood from Dragonsblood ink. *Oh*, Fraxinus had said, *the differences extend far beyond the letter "s" — they are eminently fascinating!* He not only escorted her into the room but located a variety of documents and gave her a long, detailed lesson, ensuring she understood each of the subtle but numerous differences in the inks. After the lesson, he suggested they walk together to the main dining hall for a much-deserved glass of ruby liqueur before dinner. When High Azoth Dracaen happened upon them, Azoth Fraxinus sang Genevre's praises.

"Your protégé is admirably dedicated! What a pleasure providing her with an impromptu archival lesson!"

Dracaen smiled and said to Genevre, "I had been wondering where you were spending your time."

"I look forward to the next lesson," she said. Thus began a pattern of enduring a few hours with Fraxinus each week in order to have a valid excuse for descending to the archives regularly. *I need to study for my next lesson*, she would say to anyone who asked.

Of course, Genevre spent the majority of her time in the archives *not* in lessons with Fraxinus but at the end of the tertiary passage investigating the *door-not-door*. She refused to accept that the mystery was unsolvable. As was her custom, she would persevere until she found an answer. The process of moving her fingertips over the surface was meditative. The sensation of slamming her hands against the stone, oddly satisfying. The act of leaning her back against the wall, restful. On days that she was certain she was alone in the archives, she unveiled her portable luminescence lantern and visually inspected details of the wall's surface. Despite her hours of purposeful investigation, in the end it was a moment of carelessness that unlocked the mystery.

She dropped her lantern. Its luminescence immediately dispersed and extinguished as its glass ampoule broke into pieces. Not wanting to leave evidence of her presence, she felt around in the darkness to collect the glass. The pieces were large — the ampoule had fractured rather than smashed. She found three pieces easily and placed them carefully into the pockets of her robes. The fourth not only took longer to locate but had a sharp edge on which she cut herself. In pain, she shook her hand, splattering blood onto the floor and wall. That gesture was her fortunate accident. Genevre jumped, startled, as the wall opened to reveal a door. Heart pounding, she pushed against it.

Blood alchemy. She remembered the term from her first lesson with Fraxinus. Her own blood had been the key to the door. She would have contemplated this phenomenon further if not for the greater marvel that met her as she stepped over the threshold: a small, brightly lit library, shelved floor to ceiling with leather-bound manuscripts. As hidden as Flaw dimension already was, what sort of manuscripts would the rebels need to secret away? Her desire to remain with the Rebel Branch was no longer a question; she needed time — decades, centuries — to investigate these manuscripts. For now, she walked towards a door on the other side of the room. Upon touching *that* door with her blood-stained finger, it too opened. Across its threshold was yet another library, just as bright but substantially larger. The door on the other side of *that* room led to yet a larger room, and then a larger, and a larger. The ninth library was so astonishingly vast, Genevre could barely breathe amidst its magnificence.

From her position immediately inside the door, the shelves of manuscripts appeared endless. They both ascended and descended multiple levels, each level accessible by a spiral staircase, each shelf accessible by a ladder connected to a metal track. She moved to the room's centre, turning around slowly, absorbing its splendour. Even if she were to live as long as the oldest recorded High Azoth of the Rebel Branch, she would have time to examine only a fraction of these myriad manuscripts. Thrilled yet overwhelmed, Genevre walked to the far side of the room and touched her finger to the tenth door. When nothing happened, she took one of the ampoule pieces from her pocket and cut herself to draw additional blood. Then, when she pressed her bloody finger against the door, like the others, it gave way.

She closed her eyes as she crossed the tenth threshold. She tried to picture a library more spectacular than the one from which she had stepped. Her disappointment was palpable when, upon opening her eyes, she found herself in a circular room smaller than her own quarters. Only a single table flanked by two chairs stood in the room. On the table was a wooden stand holding a large manuscript. It was the grand finale in a sequence of hidden treasures.

Genevre opened the non-descript leather cover to find a blank page. One after the next, she turned the pages. All were blank. Were these empty folios meant to be inscribed? Was she the one who would fill them one day? Most likely not. Though she had stumbled upon it, she could not bring herself to believe this manuscript was *hers*. She was, after all, merely an outside world scribe with no alchemical abilities beyond those of her meagre training. Not even her private tutoring with Fraxinus—

She remembered something.

Dragonsblood ink is made from the dust of the Dragonblood Stone, mixed with water from the cavern pools, Fraxinus had explained. *Its power rivals that of Lapidarian ink — transforming presence through absence. But Dragonblood is something else altogether — blood born of fire.*

Fire? Genevre had asked.

A metaphor for a very particular form of bloodline blood.

The bloodline — Dracaen speaks of it often. He expects much of me because it flows through my veins.

Yes, Fraxinus had said, *but as rare as the bloodline is among those destined to be alchemists or scribes, an even rarer form existed once upon a time. According to our most ancient scriptures, a manuscript exists that some believe to be written in ink comprising dust of the* Calculus Macula *mixed with the blood of Osmanthus. As one of the scriptural enigmas states, "Only one born of three can make the invisible visible."*

Genevre trembled. Once again, she removed a piece of glass from her pocket, reopening her wound for the second time. She held her bleeding finger above the first folio while applying pressure with her thumbnail to ensure the release of large drop of blood. At first nothing happened as the blood hit the page, and she suddenly feared the repercussions if anyone were able to trace the manuscript defacement to her. But, as the minutes passed, the folio began to bear forth its message. The illumination emerged first, rendered in dark crimson and gold. It featured what appeared to be a small being within an ancient alembic, or some kind of transparent vessel. Shortly thereafter, a few words appeared above the image. Their size, style, and placement suggested they formed a title, but Genevre could not read the ancient script in which the words were written.

"Congratulations."

Genevre spun around. Dracaen stood directly behind her.

"You have done what no High Azoth, including me, has ever managed to do. Your bloodline alchemy truly is extraordinary."

Genevre blushed, ashamed at being caught but simultaneously proud of her accomplishment.

"You are no mere outside world scribe," continued Dracaen. "But neither are you, as yet, an alchemist — rebel or otherwise. Thus, as High Azoth of the Rebel Branch, I must ask you to leave this chamber immediately."

"But—"

"We will return here together one day, but for now — for your own safety and that of the entire Flaw dimension — you must leave and allow the manuscript to mature."

"I don't understand."

"One by one, over the years — three decades if the scriptural enigmas have been correctly interpreted — the words and illuminations on each folio will emerge. We cannot risk contaminating the sacred process with our impatience."

"At least tell me what these words say." She pointed to the letters inscribed above the image of the alembic, now fully revealed and spectacularly vivid on the first folio.

Dracaen moved closer to the manuscript. He smiled and sighed. "Finally."

"Finally?"

"*Finally*, the Rebel Branch has gained an advantage over the Alchemists' Council. Even if you choose to leave us on your Day of Decision, today you have repaid our hospitality beyond measure. The Rebel Branch will be forever grateful. With this manuscript, our greatest potential has begun to manifest."

"What do the words say?"

"Roughly . . ." Dracaen began but then paused as if pondering the best translation of the manuscript's title. He announced it solemnly: "*Formula for the Conception of the Alchemical Child.*"

I
Council Dimension — 1695

"It tastes different," said Ilex.

"I do not believe so," responded Melia.

"But it does. I am certain. You have most likely forgotten — too long removed from the outside world."

"One's sense of taste is not affected by time spent in Council dimension."

"Respectfully, I disagree," insisted Ilex. "In my experience, senses are enhanced by proximity to the Lapis and its Quintessence. As far back as my Initiate days, I recall my sense of touch becoming heightened whenever I immersed myself in the channel waters." Ilex moved a pot of honey towards Melia. "And with the maturity of Elixir years, Lapidarian honey most certainly feels more sensuous against one's fingertips and tongue."

Melia laughed. "I have not progressed much further into my Elixir years than you, Ilex. Surely our experiences would be similar."

"On that point, I agree. What possible difference could a few Elixir years make between alchemists? We are both Magistrates after all, even if you are officially my senior."

Melia, smiling, lifted the small wooden spoon out of the pot, positioned it over her left hand, and allowed the golden nectar to drip slowly onto two outstretched fingers. She then moved her fingers to her mouth, savouring the honey from each.

"Your verdict?" asked Ilex.

"No difference," she announced. She laughed and then insisted, "Give me your hand."

"I do not recall this requirement as part of the official lesson we are to rehearse."

"This part is a private, unofficial lesson."

Ilex hesitated before allowing Melia to cup his right hand in her left. She then reached for the spoon again, this time allowing the drops of honey to fall onto his fingers. But instead of encouraging him to move his hand to his own mouth, she pulled him towards her own. She moved her tongue gently along each of his honey-laden fingers. In this moment, Ilex thought of only one thing: conjunction, in every sense of the word.

"I've changed my mind," Melia said.

Ilex tilted his head, taken aback.

"I agree with you after all," she clarified. "Council

dimension honey *does* taste different to me today than it did in my youth. And alchemical factors do indeed appear to be affecting my sense of touch."

"What are you doing?"

Ilex and Melia, startled by the sudden intrusion, jolted away from one another.

"Cedar!" said Melia. "Have you no sense of protocol? A Junior Initiate does not simply walk unannounced into a Magistrate's chambers."

"What is the protocol for an Initiate walking into an Initiate classroom?" Cedar lowered her eyes, but her attempt to repress a smile belied the deferential gesture.

Melia did not respond. She gestured to Ilex, subtly implying he clean up the honey she had spilled when interrupted by Cedar. His attempt to comply was ineffective.

"My apologies for interrupting your . . . classroom preparation. I certainly understand how such intense focus on an Initiate lesson could lead you to forget that Initiates would be attending," said Cedar.

Melia nodded, ignoring the edge of sarcasm in Cedar's voice.

"Whom are you planning to choose as *your* partner?" Ilex asked Cedar.

"For what?"

"Today's lesson on Lapidarian honey."

"I offer my services," proclaimed Ruis, appearing beside Cedar. "What will be required of us?"

"It seems we are to spill Lapidarian honey on

the table and then attempt to wipe it up," replied Cedar, no longer attempting to hide her smile.

"You have certainly become rather forthright since the day I brought you to Council dimension," observed Melia.

"A lot has changed in two years."

"We had just been speaking of the effects Council dimension can have on an individual. You may be pleasantly surprised once you reach Elixir years."

"I look forward to the honour of receiving Elixir," replied Cedar.

A few other Initiates wandered in, followed by Obeche, who made his usual dramatic entrance.

"Senior Initiate Ruis," he called. Obeche had a habit of challenging certain students whenever the opportunity presented itself.

"Yes, Junior Magistrate Obeche."

"Please illuminate for me three characteristics of—" He broke off suddenly when he noticed the remains of the spilled honey.

He turned away from Ruis to address Ilex and Melia. "Have you discerned a new method to differentiate Lapidarian honey from the honey of the outside world?"

"Certainly, the occasional alchemical experiment is warranted in preparation for a joint Initiate session," replied Melia.

"Certainly," said Obeche.

Though several other Initiates had by then gathered around the table, Obeche once again addressed

Ruis, "Senior Initiate Ruis, can you discern which of these three pots holds in its belly the metaphorical gold?"

"This one," Ruis responded without hesitation, pointing to the pot farthest from him. He exuded confidence, suggesting he had gleaned sufficient details from his preparatory reading.

"Why that one?"

"The honey in that pot has a sheen to its surface — a golden sheen."

"All that glitters is not gold," said Cedar.

Ruis turned to her and smiled.

"Impressive, Cedar. And disappointing, Ruis," concluded Obeche. He walked to the front of the classroom to take his position behind the lectern. Ilex placed the pots on a silver tray, which he then carefully carried to the front of the room. Melia likewise stood and moved to a position between Ilex and the classroom alembic.

"Initiates, take your seats!" instructed Obeche. "As you will have already ascertained, during this joint Initiate session, Senior Magistrate Melia, Junior Magistrate Ilex, and I will elaborate on the characteristics and life-enhancing properties of Lapidarian honey. Needless to say, you are to exhibit the utmost maturity and cautionary behaviour throughout the lesson, as you would when you handle any volatile alchemical substance."

"Honey is volatile?" asked Cedar.

"Not generally," responded Melia. "Not literally.

But Lapidarian honey has been known to mitigate . . . inhibitions. This," she held up the pot whose contents she and Ilex had most recently sampled, "is the vessel containing the Lapidarian honey. Regular honey — honey from the outside world — merely sweetens the palate. Lapidarian honey tantalizes the senses like a fine aged wine. Or so I recall from my youth."

"Youth, of course," Obeche added for the sake of the Initiates, "is no excuse for disreputable behaviour. Any Initiate who partakes of excessive honey today or, more specifically, who illustrates lack of control over its effects will be reprimanded accordingly."

"'The quality of mercy is not strain'd,'" quoted Ruis.

"It droppeth as the honey upon the page beneath," replied Cedar, softly laughing.

Council Dimension — 1785

Melia climbed up onto the gnarled, tangled, and expansive trunk of the ancient wisteria tree. She balanced herself by holding a branch with one hand and extended the other to Saule.

"Sit here," Melia suggested, gesturing towards an indentation in the trunk's expanse that would welcome Saule in perfect comfort. Though Ilex had brought Saule to Council dimension, Melia had been the one who had grown to cherish her over the years. Now, as Saule settled into the naturally formed seat in the tree, Melia found it hard to believe her young friend had already become a Magistrate. In watching Saule now, Melia was reminded once again to acknowledge that, as slowly as one aged in Council dimension, time nonetheless continued to pass. Melia herself was proof of that, having reached Novillian status only a few months ago. She still remembered crossing the threshold of the Initiate classroom for the first time all those years ago; now she was one of the nine Elders. Yes, alchemists could live for hundreds of years — for an eternity given a fortuitous alignment of circumstances and Quintessence-infused Elixir — but the threat of conjunction or erasure or even Final Ascension effectively quelled taking time for granted. How could she predict the number of years or months or mere hours she had left to share simple joys with friends?

"Oh! Melia," said Saule, "this tree is stunning — even more majestic than your description last week led me to imagine."

Melia positioned herself beside Saule. She leaned her head back as far as she could to gaze in awe at the masses of cascading purple blossoms.

"Yes, I heartily agree. Spectacular, unparalleled beauty!" Melia confirmed. "One unmatched even by the most radiant of trees in the Amber Garden."

Saule laughed. "I would not hazard such a comparison. I cherish the Amber Garden above all landscapes in Council dimension — gardens and forests alike. Yet I'm astounded by the splendour here. The sight, the aroma, the softness of the petals, the roughness of the bark — I feel bathed in sensation. And I'm grateful for your generosity in bringing me here."

"One attains certain privileges as an Elder, unlimited portal transport being one."

"Are we in an ancient garden of the outside world? Japan, perhaps?"

"Most certainly not. We remain within the confines of Council dimension. Even the most revered wisteria trees in Japan cannot rival the expanse and beauty of this one. Azoth Magen Quercus once told me that this particular tree is more than three thousand years old."

"Three millennia — how is it possible?"

"We are sitting in the first wisteria tree of the original Lapidarian garden, one created through manuscript inscription many Councils ago with sacred inks gleaned from the Lapis: a sacred grove to house the bees, centuries before the majority were transported to the lavender fields of the primary apiary. Like the fields, this garden exists in a subspace of Council dimension, accessible only by portal. Of course, you may return whenever you'd like — you need only attain permission from an Elder for transport."

"Portal transport is granted only if the reason is warranted. I am not certain 'desire to immerse my senses in the ancient wisteria tree' would count as valid grounds for travel."

Melia laughed. "You need permission from an Elder. I will grant you permission. I cannot think of a better excuse for travel than sensuous pleasure. If you listen carefully, you can still hear a few Lapidarian bees. Whenever the Elders deem it necessary, a few hundred bees are returned to this ancient garden from the lavender fields to maintain the wisteria tree along with the other trees and plants. If no one finds pleasure in this garden, no one will think to ensure its maintenance through future rotations. I am grooming you for your future on Elder Council, my friend."

"A few centuries away, I should think."

"Stranger things have happened in the history of the Alchemists' Council."

"Well, if I am to become an Elder one day, I hope to be like you. You're different from the others," observed Saule. "You treat me differently. I confess, sometimes I do not understand your intentions. What interest has a Novillian Scribe in fraternizing with a Junior Magistrate?"

"I cannot speak for the other Novillians, but I, for one, enjoy your company. The Orders of Council mean little to me in the arena of friendship. After all, we may end up spending hundreds of years together. What difference could a few orders of separation make within such an extended time frame? Or, if we have only a few years together, why not create memories to last an eternity? Just don't get yourself erased or chosen for conjunction."

"Ha! Another difference — you are the only Elder who makes me laugh."

"And who from the Council at large makes you laugh, Saule? If you say Obeche, I may fall from the tree."

"See," laughed Saule, "I appreciate your sense of humour."

"So does Ilex," said Melia.

Saule paused, observing Melia before venturing her next remark. "You don't have to remind me of your love for Ilex, Melia. I know you're committed to him alone. The entire Council is aware of the depth of your love for one other."

"Yes. Ilex and I are indeed bound eternally by love. But I was not purposely reminding you of my relationship with him. I was simply stating a fact of my current life."

"Apologies, Melia, I—"

"Wait. I must interject. You needn't apologize. I consider you one of my closest friends. I trust that you reciprocate my feelings of friendship and will be honest with me if you do not."

"Then I must confess to you, I am indeed finding it difficult to navigate this friendship — to locate its boundaries. Perhaps I would better understand the intimacies of friendship if I too had a beloved, someone in my life to love, as you have Ilex in yours."

"You are a member of the Alchemists' Council, Saule. You're not limited to the confines and misguided morality of the outside world. You are certain to find love one day. In the meantime, we will navigate this friendship together, most likely into uncharted territory."

Saule smiled. "Even an eternity may not be long enough for me to find happiness in love. You do not yet know my tattered history. I have experienced one failure after another in that realm, both inside and outside Council dimension."

"Then begin at the beginning. We have all the time in the world — and that may not be an exaggeration. What better way to bring closure to your failures than by speaking them aloud to a friend in this brilliantly soothing arboreal landscape? Tell me your story, Saule."

"Once upon a time . . ." began Saule, taking her first step towards her unmapped future.

Council Dimension — 1800

Melia stood on the balcony of her residence chambers overlooking the landscape. The rising sun made the ancient stone of the grand Council buildings appear to glow. She knew she was fortunate to have lived so long — indeed, for almost four centuries now — amidst the beauty of Council dimension. Her earlier years as a Magistrate preparing Initiate history lessons served well to remind her that certain periods of the Alchemists' Council had been far more tumultuous than those of her tenure. Would she and Ilex have had the luxury of falling and remaining in love if, for example, they had been Council members during the period of the Second Rebellion? Yes, Melia had witnessed various outside world conflicts over the centuries; yes, she had known strife among Council members — especially since Quercus had become Azoth Magen — but overall she and Ilex had enjoyed years of relative serenity together: a state of being epitomized in the sunrise she watched as Ilex slept soundly in her bed. She considered abandoning her view of the horizon, moving back into the room to wake Ilex by positioning herself on top of him — her morning reveries moving her from a state of calm nostalgia to arousal within moments. But she was distracted by Ravenea, who was walking alone along the channel path below the residence building. Could she be headed this early to the Scriptorium?

"Ravenea!" she called out softly, aiming to attract her friend's attention without waking Ilex or anyone in nearby chambers. When Ravenea did not respond, Melia tried again, this time with pendant in hand. Whether influenced by pendant proximity or not,

Ravenea turned and looked up to the third-floor balcony where Melia stood waving. Rather than replying aloud, Ravenea gestured for Melia to join her. Melia returned to the room, changed quickly from her nightclothes and shawl to her cotton gown and silk day robes, and moved swiftly and quietly through the corridors and out into the courtyard, temporarily forgetting about Ilex and what she might otherwise have shared with him that morning.

Ravenea awaited her on a small bench beneath a large oak tree.

"Good morning," said Melia. "Were you headed to the Scriptorium?"

"Yes. I could no longer lie in bed. The night was . . . restless. I saw no purpose in wasting time when I could get an early start on work."

"On this beautiful day, could you find nothing to occupy your leisure hours beyond Novillian duties?"

"As you know, Melia, ascension becomes less frequent — indeed, is no longer assured — once one reaches the higher orders. I must prove myself worthy should a rotation commence."

"True," Melia nodded. "But you have certainly earned yourself time to relax on occasion, even if such occurrences are rare."

"And take the risk that Obeche will outrank me one day?"

Melia laughed loudly then, prompting Ravenea to grab Melia's arm and suggest they move elsewhere so as not to disturb anyone still asleep in the residence chambers.

"I welcome time with you before commencing today's duties," Ravenea said as they walked along the path together. Melia sensed a note of sadness behind Ravenea's decorum.

They opted for a small alcove of trees and benches surrounding the pond referred to as the Wishing Well by those who had arrived in Council dimension prior to Quercus's edict as Azoth Magen of the 17th Council: "Alchemists will no longer use Lochan Pond to practise outside world folkloric nonsense." Tossing in a coin was thereafter strictly forbidden; thus — wish or no wish, belief or indifference — doing so had become a means of quiet rebellion by Council members who had experienced conflict with Quercus over one matter or another. Melia was particularly fond of peering into the water for outside world coins that she could add to her growing international collection.

"There's at least one to be found today," said Ravenea, knowing of Melia's habit and pointing towards the pond's centre.

"I can't see it."

"Neither can I, but I threw one in myself just last night, so it must be somewhere."

Melia laughed again, imagining what had sparked Ravenea to risk censure this time. Her previous coin-tossing incident had followed a reprimand by Quercus on the state of her apparel:

Ravenea! An alchemist who aspires to Azoth should not don wrinkled robes. Melia had been in earshot on that occasion and was rewarded later with a gold coin that looked like it hailed from ancient Greece. Melia did not ask Ravenea if the coin had been hers; she had merely dried it off and tucked it away in her coin box to admire on another day.

"In all seriousness, Ravenea, you have no reason to doubt your abilities to ascend to Rowan on the next rotation. Azothian status will then be well within your grasp. You could afford to spend more time with friends or, dare I suggest, a lover. Scribe Esche seems fitting."

"Melia!"

"Well, if not Esche, then perhaps Magistrate Saule could—"

"Melia! Stop!"

"But she is lonely too!"

"I am not lonely! A choice of lovers is readily available to me, if I should be overcome by unquenchable thirst. For now, I am content to let this situation — and discussion — rest. I do not need distractions on my path to Azoth."

"So you plan to remain celibate for several decades?"

"If need be."

"Ravenea! Be sensible."

"I am being sensible. I am sensibly saving myself from distraction and heartache."

"Lovers come and go. Heartache comes and goes.

If I were not bound to Ilex, I would be taking advantage of Council benefits: hundreds of years, dozens of lovers, no risk of pregnancy or disease. On this subject, I truly do not understand you, Ravenea."

"And I do not understand you, Melia. Really, it's a wonder we're friends at all."

Melia smirked. "Really, it's a wonder we have never been lovers."

"You're incorrigible!"

"And you love me for it."

"I do love you." Ravenea paused, staring into the pond. "And that is the reason that what I am about to say is so difficult for me."

Melia turned to her, worried by Ravenea's expression as much as by her words. The sadness Melia had sensed earlier was now clearly manifest.

"I noticed something in a manuscript a few days ago," continued Ravenea. "And my inquiries on the matter led to a swift flurry of activity among the Readers. Their discoveries and interpretations were sent last night to the Azoths for validation. Elder Council will likely convene later today. I was, of course, advised by the Azoth Magen not to say anything to anyone — least of all *you*. You were to learn of the news at Elder Council. But sitting here with you now, having this particular conversation, I have concluded I cannot keep both our friendship and my silence."

"Ravenea, you're frightening me. What is the problem? Am I to be erased?"

"Erased? Of course not! Why would you even suggest such a possibility?"

"As I said, you are frightening me. Exile to the outside world inevitably comes to mind."

"You are not about to be erased." Ravenea paused. "You are about to be conjoined."

Melia understood in that moment what it meant for one's heart to sink. Utter dread moved through her in a rush of sensation that she had not experienced in all her years. Only minutes ago, she had been revelling in her good fortune, and now the wheel had turned. She should have known better than to tempt fate. Quercus would reprimand her for indulging in such worldly considerations as an Elder of the Alchemists' Council, but Melia had read too much outside world literature not to question the timing of this news.

"If I am not the victorious one, Ilex will lose me," she said. Not until she heard her own words did she realize that she feared as much for Ilex's future as she did for her own. She could no longer hold back her tears.

"Conjunction is a sacrament," said Ravenea. She sounded authoritarian, as if she were already an Azoth. "You must remember this primary truth of alchemy. You must believe that by fulfilling the sacrament, you will strengthen the Council in maintaining both Lapis and Quintessence."

Melia fell to her knees, purposely allowing her tears to fall into the pond. "Accept my tears in place of the coins I have removed from your waters," she whispered. "Grant me one wish and one wish only: May I never be separated from my beloved Ilex."

"No!"

But Ravenea was too late. The wish had been made — salted tears to fresh water, spoken with true intention. And, though Melia knew the pond could not grant wishes in exchange for either coins or tears and that her wish could hold no influence over the conjunctive pairing determined by the Council Scribes and Readers, she could tell from the intensity of Ravenea's interjection that she would soon regret speaking aloud her desire.

"Melia, you do not understand."

Melia looked up at Ravenea, waiting.

"Your partner for the conjunction has already been determined," said Ravenea gently.

"Please tell me I have been paired with someone from a lower order. Please tell me I have a chance to be victorious."

"Yes. On both counts. But those details make little difference in this particular case."

"Who is it? Tell me, Ravenea. Please."

"You are to conjoin with Ilex."

And Melia pounded her fists on the ground so fiercely that Ravenea could feel the vibration under her feet.

Ilex and Melia sat together at the cliff face — one of the few places they presumed privacy could be attained, even if only briefly.

"They will come looking for us," Ilex said.

"Stop being like this," replied Melia, annoyed with him in this moment yet still wiping tears from her cheeks.

"Being like what?"

"Stop worrying about the most trivial of matters!"

"Perhaps I simply cannot bear to think of the most distressing matter."

"Nor can I," said Melia softly. She laid her head against his shoulder.

Ilex repositioned himself to hold her as she cried. For the next few minutes, they remained still and silent in each other's arms.

"We can't continue in this manner," Melia finally said, pulling herself up. "We cannot spend our remaining time together wallowing in despair. The Readers made the discovery only a few days ago. The official Announcement of Concurrence is unlikely to occur for a few more weeks, and the Sealing several weeks thereafter. The Sacrament of Conjunction itself could be a few months away."

"Let us hope for several months."

"Let us *think* during these months, Ilex. Let us not waste even a day. We cannot resign ourselves to the apparently inevitable. Surely we can together find a feasible solution."

Ilex paused before responding. "We could leave. We could leave Council dimension, live together in the outside world, refuse to conjoin."

"For how long, Ilex? How long would we survive without an influx of Elixir?"

"We are powerful alchemists, Melia. Our Elixir would run strong in our blood for decades, centuries even. And we have powerful allies."

"If you're referring to our friends here in Council dimension, you must wonder who would remain allied with us when we are no longer Council Scribes, when we are instead two deserters — two defectors who fled Council dimension rather than following our prescribed destiny and observing the Sacrament of Conjunction."

"I refuse to believe no one would help us — if not with a supply of Elixir, at least with a few jars of Lapidarian honey each month."

"Ilex! Even if someone — and I cannot imagine who — offered to take such a risk for us, that person would then be in jeopardy of erasure. We could not possibly ask or accept such assistance. As strong as is our love for one another, it can't take priority over another alchemist's life."

"Then we will carry with us as many jars of Lapidarian honey as possible — the entire store cupboard in our satchels!"

"Be sensible, Ilex. At most, we could escape with a half-dozen jars each."

"Melia, you suggested we spend our time seeking

a solution. To find one, we will need to be much more than sensible."

She remembered something then. Years ago — a hundred years ago or more — back when they had first become intimate, first sworn their love to each other, they had fantasized about the possibility of their conjunction. *Someday we will conjoin as one body for eternity*, Ilex had said with glee. Even then she had reprimanded him for his naïveté. *If we were to conjoin with one another, one of us would achieve victory over the other. Is that what you want, Ilex? Victory over me?* She could still picture his face, crestfallen. *No — no, of course not. We would be like the Rebis of the outside world manuscripts: mutually conjoined.* They had laughed then, picturing themselves as one body that diverged at the torso into two. And they had joked of all the possibilities such a state could afford them. But ultimately, they had agreed that the physical challenges of living as one would likely prove overwhelming. Conjunction as they had witnessed it in Council dimension certainly had its advantages over the sort illustrated in manuscript depictions of the Rebis. *Still, there must be some truth to the matter*, Ilex had insisted. *Illuminations of the Rebis are far too frequent not to be grounded in some fragment of truth.* She now grasped onto this fragment.

"Mutual conjunction," she said aloud.

"What?" asked Ilex.

"What if it truly were possible? What if we could conjoin *mutually* as two into one?"

"Physically, you mean — like the Rebis? Did we not decide decades ago how impractical such a conjunction would be?"

"Not like the Rebis in its literal illustration on the page but in its figurative representation: two bodies mutually conjoined into one. One body housing both of us — neither of us victorious. What if together we could find a means of re-enacting the primordial myth?"

"Are you suggesting we become the next Aralia and Osmanthus?"

"So to speak."

"This plan is one you see as more sensible than my plan to escape from Council dimension with a few jars of Lapidarian honey?"

"Yes. As members of the Alchemists' Council, we're connected to the Aralians. What if we were to seek the aid of the Osmanthians?"

Ilex stared at Melia, clearly uncertain whether she intended her remarks to be taken seriously. "Surely, you're not suggesting we ask for assistance from the Rebel Branch?"

"Do you remember what I told you of that conversation with the High Azoth — when I first met with him to attain a seal of erasure?"

"You mean when he tricked you into confession?"

"He didn't trick me. He merely asked if I were pleased that, as a Novillian Scribe, I would no longer be subject to forgetting the ones erased."

Ilex nodded. "Yes. And then — inexplicably

— you confessed to him that you had always maintained certain memories of the ones erased."

"My admission wasn't coerced, Ilex. I offered it willingly, intuiting he could provide an explanation. And he did: *You have the fire of Dragonblood in your veins.*"

"And what does that mean to us now, Melia? What does Dragonblood mean for the conjunction?"

"I do not yet know. But I sense that the High Azoth might."

Santa Fe, Rebel Branch Stronghold — 1800

When High Azoth Dracaen first set the nondescript manuscript in front of her and opened it to a folio housing an equally unremarkable image, Melia had shrugged. Folio 8 recto depicted a pendant-bearing young man with black hair and brown skin. He wore turquoise robes and wielded a gilded sceptre. Certainly, the gilding was pristinely crafted; indeed, the sceptre sparkled brightly despite the age of the manuscript — one of the oldest in Rebel Branch archives, she assumed from its physical characteristics. But she had worked with numerous manuscripts with similar features, and she had seen all too many images of sceptre-wielding young men, so she could not understand why Dracaen had requested she make the journey today from

Council dimension to meet him and Ilex in a Rebel Branch stronghold near the Santa Fe protectorate. Given her growing anxiety about the approaching conjunction, the last thing Melia wanted was to waste time travelling, and she told Dracaen as much without glossing her point to spare his feelings.

"As much as I've missed Ilex during his Santa Fe tenure, I do believe my time would be better spent researching in the North Library. At most, we have only one month remaining. Today, I had been planning to continue my work on Aralia and Osmanthus."

"You will not regret your choice to journey here once you comprehend the significance of this manuscript," Dracaen responded. Ilex had his back turned to her, standing at a sideboard where he was busy fitting a Lapidarian candle into a silver holder.

"We do not need the Lapidarian light, Ilex." Her tone hinted at sarcasm. "The regular candlelight is ample — look how the man's sceptre shines!"

Ilex ignored her. He brought a luminescence lantern and the candle to the table, lighting both before extinguishing the flames of the regular beeswax candles.

"Look again with new light," Dracaen suggested as Ilex moved the Lapidarian candle closer to the manuscript. "You will soon appreciate the brilliance not only of this particular folio but of the manuscript itself."

Melia looked again at the image of the man and his sceptre. When she returned her gaze to Ilex, he gestured back towards the manuscript. She sighed and told herself, as she had repeatedly on the journey to the Santa Fe stronghold, that Dracaen and Ilex must have their reasons for their behaviour. But no matter how often or at what angle she regarded the image, no matter how much light she directed upon the manuscript, she could see nothing of the brilliance they praised.

"Turn the page," Dracaen instructed.

Melia turned the page. Unlike folio 8 recto, folio 8 verso was completely blank, leaving her momentarily mystified. What ancient Scribe of either Council or Flaw dimension would dare waste sacred manuscript space? *Use every available segment*, her Novillian tutors had instructed repeatedly when she had first ascended to Lapidarian status. She shook her head and sighed again before turning the folio back to the image of the young man.

And in that instant, she began to understand. In fact, she was so startled that she froze, speechless, staring at the image on folio 8 recto. She no longer saw a young man with dark hair and skin and a golden sceptre. Where he had stood appeared instead a young woman with golden hair and pale skin. She wore bright green robes and carried an open book in her right hand. Though Melia knew for certain she had turned back only the one folio, she second-guessed herself and turned to another folio and then another. Nowhere could Melia find the man with the sceptre whose image she had seen.

"Where did he go?" she asked. Dracaen and Ilex simply stood watching her, smiling broadly.

Saying nothing, Ilex reached forward and turned folio 8 to the blank page on its reverse side and then back once again to the illuminated page on its front side. There he was — the young man holding the sceptre. Ilex then moved from folio 8 recto to folio 8 verso to folio 8 recto again. There she was — the young woman.

"What? How?" Melia was dumbfounded.

She herself began to turn the pages. *Recto, verso. Recto, verso. Recto, verso. Man, woman. Man, woman. Man, woman.*

"What sort of magic is this?" she asked.

"Not magic. Alchemy," Ilex responded.

"This cannot be mere alchemy," she insisted.

"*Mere* alchemy? My dear Melia, how can you — how can any member of the Alchemists' Council — utter such a phrase?" asked Dracaen.

"What I mean is that I have never in my hundreds of years with the Council witnessed such a spectacle within an alchemical manuscript, Lapidarian or not. How did the Scribe of this manuscript accomplish such a feat?"

"I cannot answer that question, as I have not yet even determined the name of the Scribe, let alone the techniques involved," explained Dracaen.

"You said I'd come to understand the brilliance of both the image and the manuscript. Do all the folios function similarly to the eighth?" Melia asked, proceeding carefully and repeatedly to turn folio 7 back and forth. She was not disappointed.

"All but one," Dracaen said. "Turn to the final folio."

Her doubt about the importance of this visit to Santa Fe extinguished, Melia did as Dracaen requested.

The final folio contained a single image of a woman in a beautiful Azadirian shawl, the multi-coloured intricacies of which were dazzling. Of the various images she had noted thus far in the man-uscript, this one was by far the most exquisite. She turned the folio back and forth twice, but the image remained the same.

"Strange," she said, "that the most elaborate figure in the manuscript is the one that remains constant."

"You are mistaken, Melia, as was I initially," said Ilex. "I can assure you, the image does not remain constant. Its method for transmutation is simply different than for the other images."

Curious now, Melia changed her perspective. At first, she tried tilting her head to look at the manuscript from a different angle. Then she slowly turned the manuscript upside down.

"Subtlety," said Ilex.

"What?"

"The method for transmutation requires more subtlety."

Melia adjusted the manuscript back to its upright position. She then held it in two hands, lifting it slightly off the table and closer to the luminescence lantern. She then began to move it gently from side to side as she watched the figure. Finally, she witnessed the transmutation of the image. Held at one angle, in a certain slant of light, the image of the woman in the Azadirian shawl shifted to a second woman with different hair, skin, and clothing. As Melia continued to move the manuscript from side to side in the brightness and shadows cast by the light of both the luminescence lantern and Lapidarian candle, the image shifted from one woman to the other.

"I see what you wanted me to see, Dracaen. I see the most remarkable manuscript I have ever beheld. But I do not understand. I do not understand how the image — how any of the images — were created. And, more importantly, I do not understand *why* they were created. What was the intention of this Scribe? What is the purpose of this alchemical magic?"

"The purpose?" echoed Dracaen. "Melia, its purpose is the most obvious, factor — the most pressing reason I have brought you here. Do you truly not understand what this manuscript means for you? For Ilex? For the future of both the Rebel Branch and the Alchemists' Council?"

"I truly do not."

"Have you neglected the title inscribed on the front piece?"

Cautiously Melia manoeuvred the manuscript and turned to the first inscribed folio. "*Chimera Veritas*," she pronounced. And in that moment — a moment she would never forget for the rest of her existence — she shuddered.

"It *is* possible," she said. "The chimera is real."

"Yes."

"And if the chimera is real, then we can succeed. We can learn. This remarkable Scribe has shown us that the seemingly impossible is indeed possible. In the manuscript images, this Scribe has shown us what we can replicate in human form."

"Yes, my love," said Ilex. "I do believe human replication of this transmutation is indeed the intention of the Scribe."

Over the hour that remained before she was scheduled to return to Council dimension, Melia stared from various angles at the shifting image on the final folio. The physicality of it, the literal ink on the page of it, fascinated her. How had the Scribe, whether Lapidarian or Novillian — whether from the Rebel Branch or the Alchemists' Council — rendered such a perplexing figure onto parchment? As a Novillian Scribe herself, Melia could not fathom the technique involved. Beyond measure, the image in and of itself illustrated a new level of complexity and possibility for the wonders of Lapidarian ink, let alone the transmutation it represented theoretically. Why had she not been introduced to such revolutionary concepts years ago in an Initiate lesson? Perhaps only the Rebel Branch manuscripts held such knowledge. Regardless, had she known of this particular manuscript's existence, she would have been saved from decades of apprehension about the Sacrament. Melia now held in her hands a visual embodiment of the truth its Scribe intended to share: mutual conjunction existed.

ꬍlaw Dimension — 1800

The following week, Melia learned that the Rebel Branch, like the Alchemists' Council, had also maintained archival libraries through the generations. From one such chamber had come *Chimera Veritas*. The archives were housed deep within the Flaw dimension — seemingly farther beneath the surface than the catacombs in Council dimension. Though accessing them by a series of staircases was possible, the time needed to descend and, worse, *ascend* was prohibitive for daily work. Thus the rebels, so long ago that even Dracaen had no living memory of the event, developed a lift of sorts, manoeuvred by a series of chains and pulleys.

"After you," said Dracaen.

Melia stepped into the small wood and metal chamber with trepidation. What if the cables were to break and she were to plunge to the archival depths? Would immersion in a catacomb alembic suffice to revive her?

"Do not fear, Melia," Dracaen advised. "The system is well maintained by our miners — outside world workers who help us with dimensional main-tenance."

"Trustworthy in their duties, I presume?" She peered through the metal bars surrounding her into a dimly lit abyss.

"Of course. As are your labourers in Council dimension — the gardeners, the cooks, the librarians."

"Keepers of the Book," replied Melia.

"Yes, as trustworthy as Keepers of the Book."

The lift shook and began to descend. Melia grasped onto one of the bars, trying to convince herself she was safe. "What do your miners *mine*?"

"Nothing — so to speak. Generations ago, they were employed to clear this area. They mined the rocks and minerals to create *nothing* — a space for our archives. You must recall, Melia, that *nothing* is indeed something in the Flaw dimension. Nothing *is* the Flaw. Our realm exists as the opposite of yours — as a necessary coincidence of opposites that must be maintained for both dimensions to sur-vive." The lift creaked and groaned so loudly that she had to strain to hear Dracaen. "The Alchemists' Council revels in forgetting that detail; thus, they aim to destroy us. The Rebel Branch, on the other hand, knows that in destroying the other we would destroy ourselves. Our goal is and always has been co-equivalency, mutual conjunction for all."

"And yet you appeared to have forgotten that mutual conjunction was possible. You seemed as surprised as Ilex and I were by the *Chimera Veritas*."

"The Rebel Branch has never forgotten the possibility of mutual conjunction. We simply had no means to reproduce it, to enact it, to ensure it. We knew the missing . . . ingredient, so to speak, was blood from the conjoined bloodline — blood that combines the rebel and the alchemist, blood of our primordial ancestors. We have tried to recreate the blood chemically — *alchemically*. But the tincture we developed, Sephrim, proved only to increase one's chance of victory in conjunction rather than to ensure co-equivalency."

The lift came to a screeching halt, and Melia released the bar. Her hand ached.

"But you and Ilex appear to have confirmed it again for us, Melia. Your bloodline will enable our future." Dracaen opened the lift's sliding door and gestured for Melia to step out.

"It's too dark," said Melia.

"Your eyes will adjust as the luminescence lanterns guide our way," replied Dracaen.

He was correct — again. Her vision grew accustomed to the luminescence. She required only a few minutes before the cool temperature and soft lighting relaxed her. By the time they crossed the threshold into the archival room, Melia felt completely calm for the first time since the day Ravenea had told her about the conjunction. High Azoth Dracaen was not to be feared. Melia believed his intention in helping her and Ilex was for the greater good.

Two other rebels awaited them in the room.

A variety of scrolls, manuscripts, and papers was spread on the table.

"I am Larix," said the one with the lighter hair. "Senior Reader of the Rebel Branch of the Alchemists' Council. I have carried my Dragonblood pendant for two hundred and three years."

"I am Thuja," said the one with the darker hair. "Senior Scribe of the Rebel Branch of the Alchemists' Council. I have carried my Dragonblood pendant for two hundred and ninety-four years."

"I am Melia, Novillian Scribe of the Alchemists' Council. I have carried my pendant three hundred and sixty-two years. On the final day of the Aurora Consurgens of the 17th Council, I am to conjoin with Ilex."

"Three weeks from now, I understand. What a glorious day that will be," said Thuja.

"Provided your bloodline and our alchemy coincide as predicted," added Larix.

"With your permission," said Thuja, "we will subject you to a series of trials today."

"For what purpose?"

"To ascertain the validity of your bloodline," explained Dracaen. "Larix and Thuja will conduct the same tests on Ilex tomorrow. If the results are as predicted, you can both begin ingesting the Sephrim within a few days — well in advance of the conjunction."

"You said the Sephrim didn't work the way you intended," said Melia.

"It did not work as intended on those outside the bloodline. On those within the bloodline, we are anticipating a much superior outcome."

"An outcome," added Thuja, "that may well change the future of both the Rebel Branch and the Alchemists' Council."

Larix pulled a chair away from the table and gestured for Melia to sit. He then handed her a small scroll and asked her to read it aloud. As she unfurled it, she inexplicably felt her fingertips go slightly numb. The lettering on the scroll appeared unfamiliar to her — she assumed it to be an early alchemical script of the Rebel Branch that she had not had the opportunity to study within Council dimension. She shook her head; she could not comprehend the scroll's content.

"Tilt back your head," said Thuja. She approached Melia holding a small bottle.

Melia looked at Dracaen. He nodded his approval. She tilted her head back and allowed Thuja to place a few droplets of liquid into each eye. She blinked and pulled herself upright.

"Try again," said Larix, pointing towards the scroll.

Melia tried to focus. "Now I cannot make out the letters at all — they are blurry. Before the eye drops, I could at least see, if not comprehend, them."

"Patience," advised Dracaen.

Yet again, he was correct. Within a minute, the letters not only became clear on the page but comprehensible to her mind. She read several sentences aloud before Larix indicated she could stop. The passage itself — an alchemical recipe involving copper and salt — seemed irrelevant. The fact that the eye drops had changed her vision so drastically that it had affected her ability to understand a language inaccessible only minutes earlier seemed fantastical. Surely an alchemical concoction, even one distilled in the Flaw dimension, could not infuse one with new knowledge.

"How is such a transformation of my vision possible?"

"The drops contain a diluted form of Sephrim. It did not transform your vision. It allowed alchemical knowledge lying dormant in your blood to be reawakened. You have passed the first test."

The afternoon proceeded with a series of similar tasks, the majority involving manuscripts featuring images of the chimera — some visible merely by adjusting the viewing angle; others transformed by the addition of a few more drops of Sephrim to her eyes.

"Why not simply have me drink the contents of the bottle?" asked Melia after the third infusion.

All three rebels laughed.

"Sephrim, even in its diluted form, has been known to result in unpleasant side effects. We're merely taking precautionary measures," explained Larix. "Though our tests indicate that you are indeed of the primordial bloodline, we can only hypothesize rather than know with certainty how your body and mind will react to such a powerful drug."

Melia momentarily worried that the negative effects of the Sephrim would manifest in her later, perhaps after she returned to Council dimension. But to calm her fears, she simply reminded herself that the potential conjunctive results were worth the risk. Thus, after a few hours of testing and one additional hour of precautionary observation by Dracaen, Melia stepped onto the lift and ascended out of the Rebel archives with a contented smile. She was certain in this moment that all would be well, that she and Ilex would indeed be mutually conjoined for eternity. Only then, and only briefly, did she allow herself a moment of concern about the extent of eternity.

Council Dimension — 1800

Three weeks later, on the final day of the Aurora Convergens, Ilex and Melia stood at the cliff face listening to the ritual chanting of the Elders. Melia could feel Ilex trembling. She understood his concern. She had attempted to comfort and reassure him repeatedly the night before. Knowing that regardless of the conjunctive outcome their final night together would be their last as separate entities, their sexual

48

intimacy was more passionate than ever before, even their earliest days of love.

"You will never be inside me again," Melia had whispered.

"I will forever be inside you," Ilex had replied.

Their laughter had been immediately followed by tears. Their sorrow now was as intense as their sexual passion had been the previous night. Their recent intimacy would soon seem a distant memory. She looked at Ilex and he at her, both uttering "I love you" as the Elders began their chanting.

The pain was sudden, harsh, and almost unbearable. Melia felt as if she would lose consciousness. The sensation of falling into an abyss initially startled her, yet she relaxed shortly thereafter, allowing herself to savour the peacefulness that accompanied a gentle descent into nothingness. *Ilex*, she called out to him. *Ilex!* But he did not respond. *Perhaps he is gone*, she thought. *Perhaps I am alone now.* For as much as she loved him, for as much as she would mourn his loss for an eternity, in that brief period of feeling utterly alone, she was surprised at her contentment.

The stabbing pain that jolted her from her reverie must, Melia realized instantly, be the Sword of Elixir wielded by Azoth Magen Quercus. Based on everything she knew of the Sacrament of Conjunction — from early Initiate lessons to the multitude of pairings she had witnessed herself — the piercing of the sword brings forth the Rebis.

She expected a brilliant flash of light, the removal of the sword by the Azoth Magen, and a return to solid form at the cliff face. Despite their weeks of preparation with Dracaen and the rebels, she expected to stand alone and victorious. Of course, she should have realized her conjunction with Ilex would defy expectations.

Various Elders had voiced their concerns during the months leading to the conjunction: *You two are in love. Conjunctions of love are unable to bind. Council archives record four precedents of such failure.* And so on and so on. Even after the Azoth Magen condoned their conjunction based on Elder Council proceedings, the caveats continued. Indeed, the most grievous was uttered to Melia by the Azoth Magen himself during a private conversation after the Sealing of Concurrence.

"The dominant element in your essence is fire, Melia," Quercus had said. "Ilex is water. Fire and water cannot conjoin. Thus, I advise you to prepare for failure. Though I have officially sealed this conjunction out of respect for the Elders and the manuscript prophecies, I cannot help but wonder if we have been misled. Manuscript manipulation is well within the repertoire of certain rebels."

"Accomplishing the seemingly impossible is well within the repertoire of certain alchemists," she said to reassure both the Azoth Magen and herself.

"Regardless, be cautioned. Success entails its own dangers. Water can drown fire."

"Or quench its thirst."

But now she was gasping — not as she had while falling into the abyss, not as she had while being pierced by the Sword of Elixir. No. Now, she gasped for breath. Instead of standing on the earth, solid in her victory at the cliff face as she had anticipated only moments ago, she flailed in the sea — literally. All she could see was water, all she could feel was water, all she could taste was water, its saltiness pungent and callous in her throat. She was drowning.

Ilex! She cried from within, not able to vocalize. *Ilex! Stop!*

But the waters swelled, engulfing her, pushing her beneath their raging depths. She could no longer see. Darkness prevailed. She longed in that moment not for earth or even air, but for light. She screamed for light. And in doing so, she reignited her essence, lighting the spark that was to become her salvation. She imagined herself as a flame — at first only that of a Lapidarian candle. But her fire grew, from candle to campfire, from campfire to bonfire, from bonfire to forest fire, from forest fire to volcanic lava, destroying everything in its wake. And the waters receded.

Melia cried out in victory across the parched seabed until her rage subsided and she bore witness to the power of her own essence as she struggled to rein in its fires. All that remained of the waters was a small vibrant pool of aquamarine — liquid crystallized against annihilation. *Ilex*, she whispered. *Ilex!* Transforming herself out of love into a single flame, she knelt beside him. *I . . . I did not mean . . . I did not know my own strength*. And she wept. She wept and wept until her flame turned to tears, until her tears fell onto the pool, until the crystalline waters absorbed the molten fires, and the two became one ever after.

Against all predictions of failure, Ilex and Melia had succeeded. Victorious before the Elders, before the entire Council, they stood together mutually conjoined. They had conjoined despite their love and despite their elemental opposition. Or, as they would come to explain their circumstance over the years to anyone questioning their conjunction within Council dimension, they had succeeded *because* of their love and elemental opposition. Though they were elated in their success, the alchemists surrounding them in the immediate aftermath of the ritual clearly were not. Rather than raising their voices in congratulations, which would normally cause a ripple effect of cheers throughout the orders, the Elders standing directly in front of them simply stared agape. Instead of seeing one alchemist reigning in victory, they saw two alchemists alternating dominance within one body. No one knew what to do or say since no one had observed such a spectacle within Council history — at least not within living memory of Council history.

"Who are you?" asked Azoth Magen Quercus finally.

"I am Melia, Novillian Scribe of the Alchemists' Council. I have carried my pendant three hundred and sixty-two years. On the final day of the Aurora Consurgens, I conjoined with Ilex."

"I am Ilex, Lapidarian Scribe of the Alchemists' Council. I have carried my pendant three hundred and forty years. On the final day of the Aurora Consurgens, I conjoined with Melia."

Beyond the sounds of the forest — the crows and toads of the ritual — the cliff face was silent. *We will wait*, Melia said to herself and, she hoped, to Ilex. But he did not respond to her words — at least not in any perceivable way. She had heard his voice only when he had spoken aloud. She knew he was there. She could feel him — acutely aware of his presence and emotional state — but she could not *hear* him inside; she could not read his thoughts beyond their intensity. She thus assumed they would have to speak aloud to each other to communicate details. But she certainly could not speak aloud the words she would like to say to him right now: *We are as Dracaen promised we would be — the* Chimera Veritas *made flesh*. She simply stood silently waiting, refusing to say another word even to the Elders until the Azoth Magen gave his directions or verdict. Ilex likewise remained silent.

Meanwhile, as they waited, Melia experimented physically. She shifted her body from side to side, acclimatizing to her new form. The sensation was unusual, to say the least. For as much as she had known Ilex in every conceivable way, and for as much as she longed for mutual conjunction, *being* one with him — one with his body — was unsettling. Traditional conjunction would have been much easier. Within less than a minute, she understood that the most disconcerting aspect was not the sensation of Ilex's body in and of itself, but the continual shifting between the conscious sensory perception of parts of her own body and the perception of parts of his. A few seconds would pass in which she would feel completely herself in every physical aspect; a few seconds later, she would feel some aspect of her body was *not* herself — the twitch of an arm muscle, the movement of fingers, a slight arousal in sexual organs not her own. Or were they? Were his now *hers*? How would she adjust to these fluctuating sensations? It then occurred to her that she was not the only one experiencing these shifts. She could sense Ilex's feelings. Though she could not know his precise thoughts, she could tell that he too was unnerved.

"Do you not see?" called Ravenea into the silence from her place among the Elders. "Do you not see the glorious phenomenon before our eyes?"

Everyone began to murmur, no one completely sure what they were witnessing. Though individual voices were not distinguishable, Melia sensed through their intonations a mixture of excitement, fear, and anger. "Erase them!" someone suggested loudly. As her anxiety heightened, she felt Ilex's right hand reach over to hold her left. The gesture comforted her, prompted her to focus not on the threat of erasure but on their exceptional physicality. How would they coordinate physical movement? How would they manage the walk back to their chambers? And to whose chambers? Concentrating on the minutiae of practical details allowed her, temporarily, to suppress her fear.

Azoth Magen Quercus raised his hand, gesturing for silence. He moved closer to Melia — to Ilex and Melia — observing them at various angles, as Melia had done with the image on the final folio of *Chimera Veritas*. She and Ilex were now a living embodiment of that manuscript illumination, one she assumed by his ongoing skepticism even the Azoth Magen had never seen. Though more anxious with each passing minute, Melia realized she could not expect Quercus or anyone on Council to understand the complexity of the situation immediately. She also soon realized that neither she nor Ilex could ever fully explain how they had achieved mutual conjunction. Doing so — admitting they had collaborated with the Rebel Branch — would put them at an even greater risk of erasure. As problematic as the initial reaction was proving to be, living among alchemists as a conjoined pair would surely be preferable to living out their mortality among people of the outside world.

"Scribe Ravenea!" called Quercus. "Approach."

Ravenea stood directly in front of Melia and smiled. Melia could not ascertain whether she was seeing Ravenea through her own eyes or through Ilex's. Either way, her memories of Ravenea remained her own — none of Ilex's thoughts overran or interfered with hers. This realization was as comforting as it was perplexing.

"Did the manuscripts show any potential anomalies?" asked Quercus.

"No. None whatsoever," replied Ravenea. "I assure you now, as I did weeks ago, everything aligned as it always does with conjunctive pairs."

"Then," Quercus addressed Ilex and Melia, "what have *you* done? How do you explain this . . . this . . . blasphemy?"

"Forgive me, Azoth Magen," said Ravenea before either Ilex or Melia could respond, "but I do not believe this conjunction to be blasphemous. It is . . . unorthodox, perhaps. But I would contend that Ilex and Melia have enacted the Sacrament of Sacraments. They have become the living embodiment — the Quintessence, if you will — of the Primordial Myth. They have re-enacted the First Conjunction, that of Aralia and Osmanthus. Their achievement is to be honoured, revered even. Certainly not scorned."

"Your opinion is noted, Scribe Ravenea," replied Quercus dryly. "Whether or not it will be the official reading of the conjunction will be decided among the Elders."

Instead of signalling the traditional, celebratory procession from the cliff face back to the main Council grounds, Azoth Magen Quercus requested that all Council members, other than the Elders, return immediately to their chambers.

"Have you nothing to say?" asked Quercus.

Melia shook her head.

"Perhaps . . . she . . . he . . . *it* has something to hide," suggested Azoth Ailanthus.

Melia grimaced. As dreadful as she felt being scrutinized by the Elders at the cliff face, she suspected the worst was yet to come. She and Ilex were escorted through the forest to Azothian Chambers. Despite the discomfort of being grasped on each arm by an Azoth, the process of walking was easier than anticipated. Melia had feared having to coordinate one of her limbs with one of Ilex's. Instead, she simply focused her intention on walking, and they managed to move forward together without incident, as if both legs were her own. Perhaps Ilex's attention was likewise focused on moving along through the forest. After all, though they had been conjoined for less than an hour, she recognized that a shared intention would in all likelihood result in a shared success, whether the goal was to walk or otherwise.

Moments after being confined to her chambers, Melia lit a Lapidarian candle, and then walked it and her newly conjoined body to the large mahogany wardrobe on the opposite wall, slid one of its panels to the side, and stood before the exposed mirror. She gasped . . . or at least she felt like she had. But now, looking into the mirror, she saw Ilex reflecting back at her; *he* had been the one to gasp. She moved closer to the reflected image and held out her hand. Against the glass, she held her hand to his. She touched him — a cold, smooth mirage of reality.

"Can you see me?" she asked him.

"No," his reflection responded. "I can hear you, but I see myself."

"Then why did you gasp upon seeing yourself?"

"I didn't gasp. You did," he said.

"No. Yes. I suppose I did."

"I think you are in control of my — *our* — body."

"Then how are you speaking?"

Melia watched Ilex shrug and shake his head. "I don't know," he said.

"I didn't shrug," she said.

He looked confused.

"I didn't shrug, but I saw you shrug," she explained. "Your shrug suggests I am not in complete control of our body."

"No. Yes. I suppose not."

Melia tilted her head. She watched Ilex's reflection tilt his head simultaneously.

"Did *you* do that?" she asked.

"No. I simply allowed my body to . . . react, to *follow* you."

"Interesting," she said. "That certainly holds potential."

He laughed. *She* laughed. Melia watched his face. She held her fingers up to her own cheek and watched his reflection turn his head to kiss the palm of her hand. They smiled, eyes glistening.

"Let me see you," he said. "Let me see you in the mirror."

"How? Perhaps your appearance is to dominate. Perhaps I am simply to exist within your body."

"No. They saw you earlier. Ravenea and Quercus and the others. They saw us — both of us, each of us."

"Yes. Of course. I'd forgotten. But *how*?"

"I don't know. Apparently, we have much to learn, my love."

"Much to learn."

Thus, they spent their first night together, hour upon hour in the candlelit darkness, enchanted by one another and by the possibilities that awaited them.

Neither Melia nor Ilex revealed anything regarding the Sephrim or the rebels during the six-week period dubbed later by Ravenea as the Inquisition of Conjunction. They were questioned relentlessly. When not being interrogated in Elder Council sessions — which lasted several hours per day — they were set upon by Council members with count-less questions and comments. Lapidarian Scribe Obeche was particularly ruthless, seemingly unable to abandon the notion that Ilex and Melia were in alliance with the Rebel Branch. Obeche found sup-port for his cause through fellow Lapidarian Scribe Ruis, who had organized a schedule of alchemists to keep watch over the Lapis. *I fear Ilex and Melia will attempt to increase the Flaw*, he reportedly told Obeche and his allies. The Initiates, meanwhile, tended merely to stare, moving cautiously to the side if Ilex and Melia passed by. "Good morning, Scribe Melia," one of them would say. "Good morning, Initiate," Ilex would respond, purposely attempting to startle them.

One evening, as they strolled amidst the glis-tening trees of the Amber Garden, Melia con-fronted him. "Why do you continue to do that?"

"Do what?"

"Frighten the Initiates."

"They are not frightened, Melia. They are amused, as am I. They have dubbed us Meliex, and it has already caught on among the orders. What do you think?"

"I am Melia," she responded, adamant.

After hours of questioning over the weeks by the Elders, pendant reading by the Azoths, man-uscript consultation by the Readers, and research by the Senior Magistrates (into the phenomenon of mutual conjunction, about which little beyond the Primordial Myth could be ascertained), Azoth Magen Quercus announced at a general assembly of Council that Ilex and Melia had been cleared of all suspicion and would be returning to their duties as a Novillian Scribe. The vast majority of alchemists — including Cedar and Amur — accepted this proclamation. For them, Council business, including finding a new Initiate, continued as usual. A few — such as Obeche and Ruis — continued to voice dissent or, alternatively, silently stare at them as one might eye an enemy or traitor. A few others — in particular, Ravenea and Saule — became even closer friends with Melia, spending hours away from Council business to chat about existence and eternity while walking along the garden paths or sitting in the branches of the ancient wisteria late into the evenings. At other times, Melia would purposely and willingly enter the shadows — as they had come to refer to a phenomenon of mutual conjunction which allowed one person to dominate and one to retreat — when Ilex desired time alone with his friends, especially with Amur or Wu Tong. Melia had little interest in observing the activities they pursued in her virtual absence.

What was now their chambers had been Melia's alone before the conjunction. Since she had been of a higher Order than Ilex, the Elders agreed that together they would occupy a spot on Council as Novillian Scribe and thus reside in the Novillian section of residence chambers. A rotation in Orders of Council would soon ensure that Ilex's former chambers among the Lapidarian Scribes would be filled by an ascending Reader. Ilex vacated his chambers and moved his possessions into Melia's. A room once tidy and minimalist in its decor was now a cluttered mess of Ilex's paraphernalia. This inconvenience was one of the many aspects of mutual conjunction that tested Melia's patience.

"Why do you need this?" she would ask, picking up an obtrusive and seemingly useless object that Ilex had placed on one of her bookcases. "I like it" or "That could prove useful someday" became Ilex's stock phrases. Melia sighed. "I will forgo this if you will forgo that," he would interject on occasion, holding an object of his in one hand and an item of hers in the other. She would then consciously take control of the hand holding her item and alternately place it back in its original location or place it in a box of their belongings that eventually would be removed from the premises, if not from Council dimension altogether. Perhaps it would have been better after all if the Elders had simply seen fit to banish them from Council dimension. Then she and Ilex could have started again with only a few possessions each rather than having to negotiate over every object. But such practical considerations were not the concern of the Elder Council. *I am sure you will come to a compromise*, Azoth Ailanthus repeatedly said whenever Melia or Ilex approached him on matters not directly affecting Council business. Thus, they worked out all such details through necessity or concession.

"Why do you think they could sense nothing of Dracaen or the others in our pendant?" Melia asked Ilex as they lay in bed one night. She had been waiting quite a while to ask him this question, afraid that doing so aloud during the Inquisition or its immediate aftermath might affect their conjoined pendant.

"How can we know the intricacies of our bloodlines and the effects of Sephrim?" responded Ilex.

"Until we can safely meet and consult with Dracaen, we must discover its intricacies as we progress," said Melia, more as a promise to herself than advice to Ilex.

The days and weeks thereafter went by filled primarily with Council business. For their part, Ilex and Melia required several months to adjust to one another in ways they had never had to do before. Melia fulfilled most of the Novillian duties during the first months as a conjoined pair — Ilex merely observing as if in apprenticeship. Ilex, meanwhile, would dominate during intervals that Novillian knowledge was not specifically needed, such as when a Magistrate required help on an Initiate lesson. Day-to-day physical adjustments ranged from the trivial to the complex, involving everything from pouring tea to manuscript inscription, from mixing ink to making love. The latter took extensive practice since two sets of sexual organs could not be physically present at the same time. Achieving a level of sexual intimacy that satisfied both Ilex and Melia took some creative manoeuvring that involved shifting from one body to the other repeatedly. This constant shifting was difficult work, ultimately detracting from any pleasurable results. Eventually, self-satisfaction became their norm — one body and mind prominent while the other merely observed from varying degrees of dormancy.

"I could help," Saule suggested to Melia one evening during a conversation in the wisteria tree.

Melia laughed, "Someday perhaps, but we are doing just fine on our own for now."

She could feel Ilex stir slightly from his dormant state in the shadows, to which he had retreated out of politeness — etiquette they had firmly agreed upon to allow them each a certain level of privacy within individual friendships. Clearly the thought of engaging sexually with Saule had momentarily appealed to him. But Melia had no interest in pursuing the matter. She had no intention of sharing Ilex with anyone, let alone sharing herself. She was not about to let their mutual conjunction become the breaking point for a promise they had made to each other over a century ago to be different than most other alchemists of Council dimension. Of course, like any other alchemist, Melia knew that time passing within an eternity could lead one, or in this case two, to a change of heart and its inherent desires.

Council Dimension — 1816

For the century or so that progressed between the day they first held hands to the glorious night of passion before the Sacrament of Conjunction, Ilex and Melia had shared an intensity of physical and emotional intimacy enviable to all who knew them. Their friends both on Council and in the protectorate libraries would marvel aloud at the constancy of their love, seeking advice on their own relationships. In this sense, Ilex and Melia had become counsellors of a sort — listening to problems and proffering suggestions on all manner of situations. Regardless of their places in the orders, they had achieved an impressive reputation for their generosity and kindness and sound advice.

After the conjunction, everything changed. In the immediate aftermath, Council members seemed either fascinated or repulsed. Ilex and Melia moved between one state and the other at intervals of seconds or hours or days, depending on a variety of factors. One such factor included the rank of the individual or groups with whom they interacted. Those alchemists newest to the Council exhibited pure curiosity; indeed, the new Junior Initiate — Linden — would stare at them outright, smiling satisfactorily when Melia would shift to Ilex or vice versa. Those in the higher orders showed far more concern — worry about the precedent this mutual conjunction might set; fear that if such conjunctions became the norm, the entire structure of the Council would change. Even after the Inquisition, the Elders had expressed concerns regarding the standard of one hundred and one members, questioning how to remain stable when two minds — two beings — existed in one body. On a practical level, after ranking Ilex and Melia as one Novillian Scribe, they set about filling the spaces left in the Orders of Council from Lapidarian Scribe downward. On a philosophical level, however, they discussed whether the Alchemists' Council comprised the bodies or minds of its members. How could two be separated into one or the other when both mind and body are mutually conjoined? Several Elder Council sessions were called to debate these and other such questions over the initial few years.

Of course, the Council need not have worried or debated. In the sixteen years since the conjunction, no conjunctive pair had been able to replicate the results. Granted, the Sacrament of Conjunction had occurred only three times in those sixteen years, but hundreds had occurred over the millennia. Thus, the Elder Council concluded the virtual impossibility of mutual conjunction, decreeing Ilex and Melia the exception. And as the declared exception, they endured increasing hostility, especially from the growing faction who believed them to be associated with the Rebel Branch simply by virtue of their difference from other conjoined pairs. Dracaen himself appeared unconcerned; indeed, he required little from them beyond the occasional drops of blood and reports on their well-being. *In good time*, he said repeatedly, *the enigmas of bloodline alchemy will eventually be deciphered thanks to your conjunction. For now, simply be yourselves.*

"Obeche has been especially vocal of late," complained Melia to Ilex. They were standing on the balcony of their chambers overlooking Council grounds. The sun was setting, the sky, as always in Council dimension, splendid in its array of colours.

"It makes no difference. His track record is not exactly stellar," replied Ilex. Though they were alone and at no risk of being overheard by Obeche, they spoke softly. They could not take the chance that anyone on a nearby balcony or close to a window might overhear.

Melia sighed. "Though I would not have wanted to lose you, sometimes I wish we'd never had the bloodline confirmed, never succeeded at mutual conjunction. I am weary of the ongoing suspicion."

"I cannot agree with you, Melia. Enduring the occasional insult — or even outright condemnation by Obeche — is nothing to bear in comparison to what I would have suffered with the loss of you. We made the only reasoned decision."

"We made the only impassioned decision," responded Melia. "Reason did not prevail."

"Even so, I would not choose otherwise, my love. I would not make a different choice despite my anguish."

Melia immediately felt Ilex begin to retract himself into the shadows.

"Wait! I don't understand," said Melia. "What anguish?"

Ilex remained silent.

"Ilex, talk to me. What is the matter? What anguish? Are you exaggerating your feelings to spare mine? Is your love for me waning?"

"How can you ask that?"

"How can you retreat from me in this moment?" She could sense his discomfort.

"I do not want you to feel the grief I feel."

"What grief? What are you saying?"

"I miss you," he said.

"But I am here, closer than ever."

"No. I miss *you as you* before *you were us*. I want to touch you — physically — the way we used to do. Do you remember those first few times we dared to touch? Do you remember that day in the classroom with the honey?"

"Yes!" Melia laughed. "And the expression on Cedar's face!"

"I remember! I tease her about that on occasion. She still blushes."

"Someday she will no longer blush. Someday she will barely remember her early days as an Initiate. Time passes, Ilex, even in Council dimension. No one can go back to being the individual who existed before being influenced by others. Even without the conjunction, our effects on one another over all these years could not be erased from our sense of being — well, not without an actual erasure, I suppose. And we're safe in that regard: conjoined, we can never forget one another, even if the Elders erase us for suspicion of rebel activity."

"Do not even utter such a proposition!"

"I apologize for my poorly timed attempt at wit."

"I am not in the mood for humour, Melia."

"If you want, you can—"

"No! I want to touch *you* without touching *myself*. I want to touch *you*, to kiss *you*, to share intimacy with *you*. I want to forgo this sacred conjunction only for tonight so that we can conjoin sexually — man and woman, as we used to be, as we used to do."

Melia did not reply immediately. She needed to think through the repercussions, the possibilities, the alternatives. Ilex must have been following her emotional trail, intuiting her thoughts as they reached their conclusion.

"We could ask—"

"No!"

"Yes," she insisted. "You're missing physical sex with another, which neither of us has experienced since our conjunction. I understand. How can I not when we share one body?"

She moved from the balcony into their room,

despite Ilex's protests. She removed her Azadirian shawl and donned her outer robes, moving towards the door. He tried to resist, tried to move their body to the bed, but over the years Melia had become stronger in that regard, especially when determined. He knew as much. And he knew their journey through the corridors of residence chambers would be easier on both of them if he stopped resisting.

"Where are we going?" he asked. But he need not have bothered asking since, by that point, they were only seconds away from their destination.

Melia stopped and knocked on the door in front of her.

"What's wrong?" asked Saule, surprised by their late-night appearance.

"I have a proposition. May we come in?"

"Yes, of course."

Ilex did not interrupt or again attempt in any way to dissuade Melia. She was determined in her pursuit. What she proposed, she proposed out of love for both Ilex and Saule. At least, love was the excuse she had used to convince each of them to accept her suggestion that night. Later, she understood that her own desire played more of a role in her decision than she had been ready at the time to admit.

Within the hour, they were lying side by side on the bed. Several minutes passed merely listening to each other's breath. Their physical intimacy began slowly but decisively with a kiss by Melia. Ilex progressed quite tentatively at first, as if not certain of himself after all these years of being with Melia exclusively. They alternated in a sophisticated dance — Ilex and Melia each moving in and out of the shadows briefly to allow the other to emerge and be present alone with Saule. Ilex ran a hand over Saule's breasts, Melia ran her tongue along Saule's neck, Saule moved her fingers along Melia's thigh. Thus, the night progressed moment by moment, touch by touch, kiss by kiss, caress by caress, until Ilex begged to be inside Saule, and Saule pleaded to be inside Melia. And in that simultaneous instant of mutual penetration — in what seemed in retrospect to be a corporeal impossibility — when Ilex entered Saule, and Saule entered Melia in precisely the same movement at precisely the same time, something happened that could only be described as *alchemy* beyond anything any of them had experienced in their years as alchemists. Alchemical transmutation turned three into one that night, in a way that none of them would ever be able to describe effectively but that each would remember as the concurrence that transformed their lives ever after. Not until almost a century later did Melia realize this concurrence was precisely the bloodline alchemy for which Dracaen had been patiently waiting.

II
ꜰlaw Dimension — 1878

"Are you certain? Are you certain our choice is prudent?" asked Genevre.

"Any decision on which we concur is in this moment the wisest choice we could make," Dracaen responded.

She stood beside Dracaen, close enough to touch but far enough to preserve some sense of decorum, even if they both knew perfectly well what remained unspoken between them. Genevre shifted her stance slightly as she lay a hand tentatively against Dracaen's shoulder. She shivered as he placed his hand against hers. They stood now, face to face, hand to shoulder, touching. He could lean forward and kiss her. But he did not, of course. He was, after all, the High Azoth of the Rebel Branch of the Alchemists' Council, and each step he took — literally or figuratively — moved him towards one ultimate goal. He had too much pride to let personal desire, even at the height of arousal, cause him to stumble.

"Close your eyes." He directed her, as if in a stage production. "Move closer to me. Let me feel the length of your body against mine."

Genevre breathed slowly and deeply as she pushed herself against him, her bare breasts resting against his naked chest. She herself felt a surge of arousal as his body reacted swiftly and willingly, and his breathing quickened. She wanted him. She wanted to fall to the floor, to lie back, to open herself to him. Evidently, she did not share his sense of duty in and of itself. Why could they not be both lovers and rebels, attempt to create both a biological and an alchemical child?

She remembered the day he first proposed to her. They had been sitting in the caverns near the pools after a long day of manuscript revision. The work had been arduous, a series of painstaking illuminations infused with both Lapidarian and Dragonsblood inks — undetectable palimpsests whose details were meant to distract the attention of Council Readers the following century. *We have a plan*, Dracaen repeatedly said. *And you are part of that plan*. The alchemical phosphorescence was so bright in the pools that day that Dracaen himself appeared to be glowing. The blue-black sheen of his hair reminded her of the brilliant obsidian pieces stored in the calligraphy room. Framed by such thick, dark brows and lashes, the shimmering emerald green of his eyes seemed out of concordance yet stunningly magnificent. *His eyes are otherworldly*, she recalled thinking. Perhaps Dracaen had been so long removed from the outside world that he had lost all semblance of it. Amidst such thoughts, she should not have been surprised at his request or at the gift he proffered simultaneously: a beaded raven feather.

"Genevre, now that you have reached the threshold of your sixtieth year, now that you have been granted Dragonblood Elixir for thirty years, the time has come for me to request your hand in marriage."

In retrospect, she considered his turn of phrase cruel. She could not have known for those few seconds before his next words that, like his eyes, his proposal was not of the outside world.

"I refer, of course, to a chemical wedding as described in the fully matured *Osmanthian Codex*, which Fraxinus and I have been interpreting over the past year. Who better than you to take such a crucial step in the plan with me than the person who awakened its words?"

"What is a chemical wedding?"

"The ritual bonding whose purpose is the creation of the alchemical child — the homunculus, created in an alembic from the elemental conjunction of opposites."

"I am not an alchemist. I am an outside world

scribe. I am not . . . adequate," responded Genevre, her words unusually slow.

"You are one of the most powerful alchemists ever known to the dimensions — even if I am one of the few who currently understand your potential. You yourself have only begun to recognize your bloodline powers. As I have always assured you, you are extraordinary — one of a kind, truly. Your abilities to inscribe and erase immaculately are innate and invaluable. Your skills with both Dragonsblood and Lapidarian inks are unparalled. You have already proven to be more of an asset to the Rebel Branch than you can fathom. If we were to combine our powers — our alchemical genetics — our progeny could change the worlds."

Genevre sat transfixed. Emotionally, she fluctuated between fascination and revulsion, joy and anger, pride and humiliation. Dracaen spoke as if their child was destined to be a messiah among dimensions. How long had he been waiting for this moment? How long had he been grooming her to play this role in his alchemical pageant? She thought back to her first day in Flaw dimension, her belief at twenty that she had been saved. And she thought back to the broken luminescence lantern, to the moment thirty years ago when her blood had opened the door to her future.

These and other memories came unbidden as she now stood chest to chest with Dracaen, the Rebel Branch Elders encircling them and chanting as if they were about to conjoin rather than marry. While the other Elders intoned the ritual words, Thuja, Larix, and Fraxinus acted as Purification Attendants, encircling the couple, waving censers filled with the essence of *Juniperus osteosperma*. The fragrant smoke stirred something in Genevre, something she could not quite remember, something that brought her comfort at this moment of trepidation. Calmed, she watched the purification of the sacred vessel — a delicate clay urn, crafted by the rebel Azoths from the wet mineral sands of the deepest cavern pools, painted with Dragonsblood and Lapidarian inks, fired in the smoke-filled kilns of the obsidian quarries.

"Accept the sanguine salt," said Dracaen. He removed the lid of a small bejewelled box and emptied its contents — a powder made from his own dried blood — into the sacred vessel.

"Accept the sanguine salt," echoed Genevre, emptying a similar box filled with her own powdered blood.

"Accept the seed of the Flaw," said Dracaen, pouring a small flask of Dragonblood Elixir onto the mixture of powders.

"Accept the seed of the Flaw," said Genevre, doing the same.

"Accept the egg of the Lapis," said Dracaen, moving a tiny egg-shaped Lapidarian fragment from a glass phial to the sacred vessel.

"Accept the egg of the Lapis," said Genevre,

wondering how the rebels had procured such a sacred ingredient as she placed it into the mix.

"I will be King," said Dracaen. "And you will be Queen."

"I will be Luna," said Genevre. "And you will be Sol."

"And thus," declared Fraxinus, "have your destinies crossed in the sanctified bond of the alchemical chiasm, in the consecrated union of *Conjunctio Oppositorum*, in the Quintessence of elemental balance. In both the absence and the presence, so be it!"

"So be it!" replied all the rebels.

Dracaen sealed the sacred vessel and handed it to Genevre, who carefully climbed the steps to the lip of the alembic. She held the sacred vessel as far above the opening as her arms could reach and then, upon Dracaen's cry and in one swift movement, plunged the vessel into the alembic, gasping as it crashed and shattered onto the glass floor. She remained motionless momentarily, only beginning her descent of the steps when the vapours emanating from the alembic began to overwhelm her senses. Moments later, standing beside Dracaen, watching the churning fluids within the glass of the alembic, Genevre felt nauseated. Even after closing her eyes, the sounds and scents continued to disturb her equilibrium.

"I must go," she whispered urgently.

"Larix!" Dracaen called out, steadying Genevre.

She must have lost consciousness then. Her mind shut down.

Later, lying under the blankets in her dark and silent chambers, she awakened to searing pain unlike anything she had previously experienced. She writhed in so much agony that she could barely breathe, let alone call out for help. Minutes, hours — she could not tell — passed in fear, pulling her closer to a certain death.

But then all was well. Suddenly, she sat up, pain free and perfectly content, inhaling the cool air of the room and calming fragrance of juniper still lingering in her hair. In the weeks leading up to the chemical wedding, she had doubted their union could result in an alchemical child. If such a feat were so easily attained, why would the practice have lain dormant for so many centuries, secreted away in a single manuscript? Why would Dracaen not have conjoined necessary opposites between dimensions with some other outside world woman? She could not fathom that she was by some means *special*, despite her inherent ability to have activated the inks of the *Osmanthian Codex*.

Now she reached clarity. Now her opinion changed. Now no doubt remained that they had indeed conceived a child, her body having mimicked the contortions of the sacred seed and egg as they conjoined and embedded themselves into the alembic waters.

Weeks had passed. Surely the embryo would by now be visible in the *sacred alembic*. Genevre could not bear another day of disappointment. Though she had hesitated even up to the moment that the chemical wedding had been sealed, though she had questioned the mere concept of the homunculus until the darkest hour on the night of conception, she could not help but hope to witness the spark of life in the alchemical being that would become her child. She descended the steps slowly, delaying the possibility of another day passing with no visible result.

But she knew immediately upon stepping into the chamber that this day was different. The colours swirling in the alembic fluids had changed. Before, they had been murky as if a blend of clay and mud, water and phlegm; today, they were brilliantly vivid, a rainbow of gemstone shades rhythmically pulsing as if they themselves were about to give birth. For better or worse, she would have her answer today.

"Fetch Dracaen," she yelled back to the young attendant at the top of the staircase. His job was to guard the entrance to the chamber from prying eyes. She could tell he hesitated to leave his post. "Call for him! Now!"

She waited at the bottom of the steps, mesmerized and immobilized as she watched the colours swirl — ruby and sapphire, emerald and amethyst. She swore later that the pulsing echoed her own heartbeat. She could not tell how much time passed before Dracaen arrived. He stood fleetingly at her side, grabbed her hand, and guided her along with him as they walked from the landing to the alembic platform to peer inside. The fluids were now so bright — the alembic glass only inches in front of her — that watching them caused her eyes to burn.

"We have succeeded," said Dracaen, still holding Genevre's hand.

"Are you certain?"

"The conjunction of the colours — a sure sign of embryonic coagulation."

"How long now? How long until we will see our child?"

But she did not need to wait for his answer. As if on cue, the fluidic movement suddenly ceased — utterly, completely stopped as if it had turned to solid, crystalline rock. Genevre watched aghast, fearful that her child-to-be was to be nothing at all.

She was wrong.

"The anvil!" Dracaen cried. "Larix! Larix! Fetch the anvil!"

Emerging from a door on the other side of the chamber, Larix passed the anvil to Dracaen. Its handle appeared crafted of marbled mahogany, its head of iron and Dragonblood Stone.

"When the water of the fluid turns to the earth of the rock, the fire child shall be born into the air!" Dracaen intoned. With each name of an element — water, earth, fire, air — Dracaen hit the alembic wall with the anvil. The noise was deafening, resounding through the chamber. Again, he uttered the chant, each word of the alchemist intoned to match elemental vibration and thus activate transmutation. Again, he smashed the anvil against the glass of the alembic. On his fourth iteration, upon the word *fire*, a crack — loud and long — broke open the glass.

"Close your eyes," yelled Larix.

But Genevre could not obey. She alone was witness to the alchemical birth. The glass and the rock formation shattered completely, fragmented into pebbles that exploded like shrapnel throughout the room. She remained standing and unharmed, able to step forward and catch them in her arms. *Them.* The homunculi. A boy and a girl. One as dark as a raven, the other as bright as the sun.

They did not resemble outside world newborns. Instead, each child looked as one might expect a fully developed two-year-old — the girl only slightly smaller than the boy. Genevre clasped them to her, only releasing her grasp when Dracaen suggested she must let them breathe. He then picked up the girl, and Genevre the boy. Together, they ascended the staircase to emerge into the mists careening rapidly across the Dragonblood Stone as if in welcome to the newcomers.

"Sound the chimes!" commanded Dracaen.

Why should the Elders not rise up to greet these children — the only children to have been brought forth from the Flaw in generation upon generation? Even Dracaen could not remember such an event, outside its references in a few ancient manuscripts.

The other rebels gathered round, proffering their congratulations and astonishment.

The children merely stared ahead, not catching the eyes of anyone in particular though they appeared on occasion to be taking note of their environment. The boy, in particular, showed little interest in his new world until a band of mist brushed across his face and startled him. He held out his hands thereafter, gesturing in an attempt to call the mists to him. Eventually, seemingly frustrated in his failure to do so, he hung his head against Genevre's breast. The girl was the first of the two to smile, a result of Thuja's efforts to entice her with a shiny piece of onyx shaped like an egg. She held the egg in her small hand, observing it first, then smelling it, then holding it against her mouth as if reading a pendant. Perhaps this child would eventually participate in Dracaen's plan. But what of the other one? What of the boy who hid his eyes from the world, seemingly unwilling to engage?

"The naming will occur in three nines," announced Dracaen. "Until then no name shall be written or spoken."

Genevre momentarily turned her attention from the boy to Dracaen. She did not understand the decree. Though she knew more about alchemy and its dimensional laws than the average outside world scribe, she did not have the vast historical knowledge held by Dracaen and other Rebel Branch Elders, all of whom had nodded in agreement. She was about to ask Dracaen for clarification when Thuja stepped forward reaching for the boy.

"What are you doing?" asked Genevre, holding the boy closer to her chest.

"Larix and I will take the children to their chambers." She noticed then that Dracaen had already let Larix take the girl, who reached out to her brother. Larix reined in the girl's hand, attempting to quell her instinct to bond with the child in Genevre's arms.

"Their chambers?"

"We took the liberty of preparing chambers for feeding and rest."

"When? Why was I not consulted?"

"We chose not to distract you from your duties," replied Thuja sweetly.

Genevre winced. She understood, hearing Thuja's gentle tone, that the Elders expected her merely to acquiesce. She had played her role and was now to return to her regular scribal duties as if nothing had happened, as if she had not contributed her blood and essence to these young beings, as if she were not their mother.

"No. They will stay with me," Genevre insisted.

"No," said Dracaen. "They are best left with Larix and Thuja. You do not know how to care for them."

Genevre felt stung. Thuja and Larix nodded, as the remaining rebels shuffled into the darkness and departed.

"They're my children," said Genevre. "Like any new mother, I will learn to care for them."

"No, Genevre," said Dracaen, "they are not *your* children. They are *our* children. They are children of the Flaw. And, as children of the Flaw, they will be raised by no one and by all."

"Am I not one of the *all*?" she asked. "Or are you about to toss me back into the outside world without the children that you and I created?"

"Perhaps she could stay with them throughout the three nines," suggested Larix.

"Yes!" replied Genevre immediately, though she still was not certain what three nines meant or what she could do between now and then to ensure a life-long bond with her children.

"Are you certain?" asked Dracaen.

"Yes."

"And do you agree to return to your scribal duties after the naming?"

"When is the naming?" she asked.

"Three times nine days," Dracaen responded.

"Twenty-seven days? I have twenty-seven days to bond with my children?"

"You have twenty-seven days to nurture them, to meet their needs, to observe their development and their behaviours. Thereafter — after the naming — you must be prepared to let go, to return to your duties."

Despite her hesitation ever to relinquish her children to Dracaen, Genevre agreed to his conditions. She would make the most of each minute of her twenty-seven days, and she would find a means to maintain contact thereafter.

"Fine," said Dracaen. "You may stay with the children in their chambers."

"Can they not . . ." she began, but she stopped herself upon seeing a flash of anger cross Dracaen's face. "Yes, I will move for the three nines into their chambers."

On the walk to the chambers, she held the boy in one arm, softly stroking his hair with her other hand. She smiled at the girl, who looked quizzically back at them from her position against Larix's shoulder. But the girl did not smile in return; instead, she squinted her eyes and wrinkled her nose as if as uncertain as Genevre what the days ahead would offer.

To Genevre, the boy was as precious as the crystalline structure from which he had been born — beautiful yet fragile. The girl was quite the opposite — rough-edged and sharp, determined to succeed no matter what the challenge. Genevre had reached this conclusion by the end of the first day. A child born of the outside world would show little personality beyond its discomfort or contentment during its first few weeks. But an alchemical child — at least one born of the Flaw — developed at an astounding pace. By the morning of the second day, an outside observer would surely think the children were nearing three years old, though such an onlooker might wonder why they could not yet speak.

"During the twenty-seven days," Thuja explained on the morning of the third day, "the alchemical child can develop to initial maturity."

"Maturity!" Genevre exclaimed in response. She glanced at the children who sat across from one another, rolling the onyx egg back and forth. The girl laughed and squealed. The boy, head tilted, watched his sister as if wondering how she made her sounds.

"If all progresses as recorded in the most ancient Draconian accounts, after twenty-seven days, the child will have attained the physical age of five or six outside world years. Thereafter, once named and inscribed in the manuscripts, the child will age substantially slower. Of course, after thirty physical years, Dragonblood or Lapidarian Elixir can be ingested to halt aging to a virtual standstill — a much slower rate even than that of the Azoths."

"Has an alchemical child ever moved through the orders to become High Azoth or Azoth Magen?" asked Genevre, now not only watching the children but imagining their lengthy and potentially challenging futures.

"According to *Lapidis Philosophorum 8118*, a textual ambiguity suggests the possibility that High Azoth Makala of the 5th Rebel Council may have been an alchemical child."

"High Azoth Makala. I've read of her."

"She is thought to be an original ancestor of the bloodline," explained Thuja.

The bloodline. For as long as Genevre had known Dracaen, he had been enamoured of it, fixated on unearthing its descendants, re-establishing its lineage in the name of the plan. Aiming to reproduce the mutual conjunction of Ilex and Melia. Finally, Genevre believed she understood. Thuja had unwittingly provided her with the missing link: Makala. If indeed Makala had been an alchemical child, if indeed an alchemical child began the bloodline, Dracaen would need to produce an alchemical child for himself in order to bring his plan to literal fruition. She wondered in that moment what other partial truths he had told her.

"Genevre? How are you faring?" asked Fraxinus.

She had become lost in her reverie, barely registering that he had entered the room.

"Fine. I'm fine. I . . . I realized I need to ask something of Dracaen. Did he mention when he would come to see the children?"

Fraxinus and Thuja exchanged a glance, leaving Genevre worried that they too were now hiding something from her.

"He will not be joining us until the end of the three nines."

"Why?" asked Genevre.

Fraxinus, normally forthcoming and generous with Genevre, lowered his eyes and waited for

Thuja to respond. Clearly Dracaen, as High Azoth, had requested Fraxinus to yield to Thuja if Genevre were to question them.

"The High Azoth is observing ritual protocol as outlined in the *Osmanthian Codex*. He does not want to risk . . . contamination."

"Contamination? Are the children infectious?" Genevre instinctively moved to where they played. She knelt down and placed a hand on each of their faces to gauge their temperature before Fraxinus responded.

"No, Genevre. But they are *alchemical*," he reminded her. "As High Azoth, Dracaen must follow the protocols. He must avoid . . . connecting . . . with his progeny before the hour of maturity. Only at the end of three nines can the alchemical child be named and accepted by alchemists of the Rebel Branch, including Dracaen. He observes an ancient practice, replete with ancient laws, dating back to at least the 5th Rebel Council. Since you are yet unable to read the 5th Council script of the *Osmanthian Codex*, you must accept his word."

"Perhaps, as an outside world scribe——" began Thuja, but Genevre cut her off with a dismissive wave of her hands as she stood and faced the two Elders.

"Tell the High Azoth that his children await their father," she said.

"The children themselves must obey alchemical laws and procedures during the three nines. Even you cannot control that process, no matter the extent of your love for either one."

"Either one? I love them both equally," Genevre assured them, though she allowed her gaze to linger upon the boy.

"Which of us would you prefer to assist with today's feeding?" asked Fraxinus.

Though Genevre would have liked to nourish her children on her own, the complicated formula required the assistance of an Elder. On this day, she chose Fraxinus. She sensed that he sympathized with her plight, despite his allegiance to the High Azoth.

Thereafter, each morning of the three nines progressed as she anticipated. Fraxinus or Larix or Thuja would assist with the morning feeding — chanting the ritual words as Genevre spooned the porridge-like concoction laced with Lapis and Dragonblood into the children's mouths. Within twenty minutes after the feeding, both children would be sound asleep, napping as they digested their alchemical nourishment. On the days that she was left alone with them, she would carefully observe their faces and small bodies for signs of change. Each day, an hour or so into their nap, if she watched closely enough, she would witness a specific alteration — the thickening of an eyelash, the extension of a nose, the deepening of the blush on a cheek.

In the afternoons, they would play. By the eighth day, Genevre had extended their toy collection to include not only objects of the Flaw dimension but also those of the outside world, which she had requested Larix to attain. Thus together, day after day, she and her children played with puzzles and blocks, balls and hoops, puppets and dolls. Though they could not articulate their desires and intentions in words, they could gesture with hands and eyes and voices. As she had learned from Thuja, language for alchemical children developed at a much slower pace than their bodies. Thus, as the days progressed, together the children learned to communicate in the absence of a spoken vocabulary. Though the children shared their toys, the boy seemed to have fallen in love with one particular doll. Fraxinus had handed it to him directly when he brought it from the out-side world, and the boy had guarded it possessively ever since. Its head, including its molded hair, com-prised painted porcelain: ivory skin with blushed-pink cheeks and blue eyes, black tresses and brows. Its body was soft and clothed in an exquisite cream gown of silk and lace. He would hold it close to him, stroke its head, and kiss its cheek — as if imitating Genevre's own actions with each of her children. Twirling the girl's hair along her finger, watching the boy's love for his doll, she bathed in their literal and figurative softness.

On the morning of the twenty-fifth day, knowing that only a few days remained before all the rebels would take an interest in her children, Genevre began to grow anxious. She feared that her role in their lives would be supplanted by their role in the plan. Though she attempted to hide her worries from the children, her attempt appeared to have failed. The boy refused to eat when handed his formula. Meanwhile, the girl became ravenous, howling for more even when she had emptied both bowls. Fraxinus fetched Thuja to assist with creating more formula. Genevre attempted to coax her son to take even one spoonful from her, but he would not. She handed the bowl to her daughter, who quickly devoured its contents.

"We will try again later," said Genevre to Fraxinus. "Surely, he will be hungry within a few hours. Perhaps after their nap—"

"No," interrupted Thuja. "His return has begun. We must allow it to take its course."

"The boy must eat, Thuja."

"No. The course is now clear. Her essence will reign supreme."

Genevre shivered. "Reign . . . what?"

"Genevre," began Fraxinus. "You need to understand. The process is alchemical."

"I know that the process is alchemical." Genevre replayed the conversation. "What do you mean *his return*? What do you mean *her essence*?"

Neither Fraxinus nor Thuja spoke.

"Fraxinus! What is happening to my son?"

"He is dying."

Words could not help her here. Like her children, she could respond initially only in gestures and intonation. She sank to her son's side.

Finally, she yelled, "No! You cannot die! You must eat! You must eat!" She held him against her breast. Her daughter watched, holding the onyx egg to her mouth.

He could not die. She barely knew him.

For two days and two nights, Genevre held him to her, moving only when physical necessity required, leaving her daughter to be nourished continually by Fraxinus and Thuja. On the occasion that she would fall asleep, that her grip on her son would loosen for a moment, she would jolt awake with a cry and clasp him to her once again.

By the morning of the twenty-seventh day, her son had reverted to the size he had been when he first appeared to her. Her daughter, meanwhile, was strong and thriving. When finally satiated, she settled down and sat still with her mother and brother, watching as Genevre bathed her son's face with cool water brought to her hourly from the cavern streams.

When the hour arrived, when minute by minute his breathing became more strained, when he breathed in one final time and exhaled with a rasping shudder, Genevre sobbed. Her daughter stood up and kissed Genevre on a tear-stained cheek.

"We must return him to the birthing crystals," said Fraxinus gently.

When Genevre was ready, Fraxinus helped her to her feet. She held the tiny, fragile body in her arms as they progressed from the children's chamber to the room in which they had been born. Fraxinus led the way. Thuja, holding the girl's hand, followed behind Genevre. Genevre had expected all the Rebel Branch Elders to be assembled, but they passed no one on the walk, and only one person awaited them in the room: Dracaen. *He must avoid connecting*, Fraxinus had said. The reason was now clear. For one alchemical child to live, the other must die. For *the* alchemical child to live, a life must be sacrificed. Dracaen had not wanted to connect, to form an emotional bond with his two children because he had known that only one would be named.

In the place where the birthing alembic had stood was a hole — yet another absence within Flaw dimension. It had been carved out of the rock floor, sized for a tiny body to be laid to rest. Dracaen moved to take her son from her, to save her the required task, but she pulled back. The one who loved him would be the one to place him in his grave. As she lay her child down, Fraxinus, Larix, and Thuja chanted softly, joined for the final verses by Dracaen. Only then did Genevre notice the colourful pebbles gathered into large wooden bowls at the side of the room. Dracaen and Fraxinus carried the bowls, one by one, to the graveside.

Recognizing their purpose, Genevre took a handful and placed the fragments over her son's body. His crystalline birthing fluids had become his burial shroud. Dracaen followed her lead. Just as Thuja reached into a bowl, the girl reached up a hand and pulled at Genevre's sleeve.

"Mother," she said, startling everyone. Genevre stared at her. At first, she was too stunned by her daughter's first word to notice what she held out to Genevre in her other hand. "Mother," she said again, waving the object, gesturing towards the grave.

With a surge of love, Genevre could not have imagined being able to feel on this day, she held her daughter's hand in her own. She took the toy her daughter had carried with her on their journey from the children's chamber. Thus, under the crystalline pebbles, her beloved son was buried alongside his cherished doll.

The three nines completed, her son buried, her daughter now attended by Thuja and Dracaen, Genevre retreated alone to her designated quarters. She lay on the bed, silently observing the patterns of light and shadow dance across the ceiling. She longed to feel nothing at all. But she knew she must soon shake herself from this stupor and find the strength to comfort her daughter. Yet she simultaneously resented that impulse. How could Genevre think of her daughter when she yearned only to hold her son? She wanted to go back in time, to give her weakest child all the strength she could gather from all the elements throughout the dimensions. She wanted to go back to the moment of her children's births and observe herself through the entire three nines to understand precisely where and when she had gone wrong. She wanted to save her son. She needed to save herself.

When she finally fell asleep, one anxiety-induced nightmare followed another.

Upon waking, she waited impatiently for Thuja or Fraxinus or even Dracaen himself to bring her daughter to her. But no one did. No one even checked upon Genevre for hours. Though odd compared with mourning practices she had observed in the outside world, rebel absence during times of grief could well be a standard custom she had yet to observe. Death, after all, was rare among alchemists. She spent the remainder of the day in bed sipping water from a clay cup. She spent the evening crying until she fell asleep.

The next morning, hunger prompted her to leave the chambers. She wandered towards the dining hall. The corridors were unusually quiet, and, seeing no one on the entire walk, she began to wonder if she had mistaken the hour. The dark hallways offered no clue as to the time of day, so she took a detour to the anteroom of the gravitational timepiece and peered in the window: nine a.m. Where was everyone?

Distracted temporarily from both grief and hunger, Genevre began seeking out others. Hallway after hallway, chamber after chamber, room after room, she found no one. Even the gated cavern housing the Flaw itself was empty of rebels. After an hour's search, she stepped into the lift and descended into the archives. Here she fared no better. No one wandered the corridors, no one worked at archival room tables. Not until she had opened every door to every library in the deepest archives, not until she crossed the threshold of the small circular room that held the *Osmanthian Codex* did she cross paths with another: Dracaen.

"We must rework the text," he said.

"What? Where is everyone?"

"I sent them away — all of them, for three days and three nights. I need space and time to think undisturbed."

Feeling mildly guilty for intruding, Genevre said nothing.

Dracaen tapped a finger against a single folio illuminated with an image of a maturing homunculus within an alembic. "Your blood may have enlivened the manuscript, but we are left with blood on our hands."

"Our son has died, but we have our daughter. She thrives."

"No," he said. "She too is gone."

"What?"

"We must begin again; rework the text. Repeatedly." Tap, tap, tap, his finger moved against the folio.

Genevre stared.

"Do you hear me, Genevre? Your daughter is gone. The two of us must begin again."

Tap. Tap. Tap. Fury raged within her against the repetitive sound of his finger and the cloying tone of his words.

"My role in your plan is over!" she bellowed.

With elemental strength flowing through her veins, and using blood alchemy to draw additional power from the earth thanks to a swift, purposeful movement of her hands, she struck him. Genevre, outside world scribe, struck the High Azoth of the Rebel Branch across the face. *Blasphemy!* Dracaen stumbled away from the manuscript long enough for her to reach it. She tore from its binding the illuminated folio contaminated by his touch. *Sacrilege!*

She ran. She had reached the lift and was ascending before Dracaen had even rounded the corner of the final corridor. His calls of "Traitor! Traitor!" reached no one, since no one remained in the vicinity to heed them.

Not until she reached the portal room did Genevre stop to wonder how she would make her escape. She had no authority — no means — to activate the portal. She stood, anxious and breathless. He would find her.

"Do you require assistance?"

She spun around.

"Fraxinus! I—"

"I offer fair trade," he interrupted. "I assist you now. You assist me later."

She paused only for a moment. Dracaen could not be far behind.

"Fairly traded," she responded.

Vellum folio clutched in her hand, Fraxinus by her side to activate the portal, Genevre left Dracaen and the Flaw dimension, vowing aloud never to return.

"No!" cried Fraxinus. "Trade is troth, Genevre. You already pledged fair trade to me. To honour your word, you must return to assist me when I call upon you to do so."

"Trade is troth," repeated Genevre. "Until then."

"Until then."

flaw Dimension — 1913

Anxious, Kalina watched the others carefully. Azoth Thuja stood to her left in the gathering chamber alongside Junior Reader Tamar, who peered over the wrought-iron barrier at the Dragonblood Stone. The moment Dracaen and Fraxinus entered the room from the northern archway, Tamar turned ceremoniously to acknowledge them, crossing his wrists in front of his chest. Thuja exhibited no such formality.

"We have finally convinced her," announced Thuja. "Genevre has agreed to our proposal. She has accompanied us to Flaw dimension with the stated intention of assisting the Rebel Branch once again. The intervening years appear to have softened her disdain for you, Dracaen."

"How would you describe her demeanour?" Dracaen asked. He nodded to Tamar, who released his formal pose.

"I would describe her as *cautiously optimistic*. Larix believes her to be . . . What were his words?"

"*Resolutely apologetic*," offered Tamar.

"Apologetic?" repeated Dracaen. "If Scribe Larix believes Genevre to be repentant for her past actions, I would suggest he immerse himself in the cavern pools for restoration of his senses. She is not one to apologize, especially when she believes herself to be innocent."

"She destroyed a sacred relic of the Rebel Branch!" interrupted Kalina, indignant.

"No," countered Fraxinus. "She tore a single folio from a manuscript — one she had enlivened with her own blood."

"I am a Scribe, Fraxinus. I cannot condone manuscript defacement no matter the grounds," replied Kalina. "From my perspective, Genevre was and always will be a traitor to the cause."

"Civility, Kalina!" interjected Dracaen. "Your

attitude will do little to convince Genevre to return the folio for restoration."

"Larix could indeed use an immersion in the cavern pools," scoffed Thuja, attempting to diffuse the tension. She glanced at Kalina before continuing. "Despite Genevre's questionable history with the Rebel Branch, I trust her integrity as an outside world scribe. After all, she once understood her role in the ultimate plan, and she now recognizes the imminence of the plan's execution. Her actions in the past, as impulsive and selfish as they may have seemed at the time, were certainly understandable given the extenuating circumstances."

"And if her actions in the future prove her untrustworthy, countermeasures can be taken," added Dracaen. He glanced at Kalina as if she were to intuit the specifics of both the past "extenuating circumstances" and the future "countermeasures." Yet she barely understood a thing he had said to her of late.

Over the past week, Dracaen had been schooling Kalina with an incomprehensible mixture of literal and figurative pronouncements. *You are a Scribe of the Rebel Branch, Kalina. Thus are you a daughter of the Flaw. Beware not to be bound by emotional ties, not even those that bind the two of us. From this critical juncture forward, duty alone must influence your decisions. Manacles must be self-imposed and, once imposed, not removed until our final goal has been achieved. Too much depends upon the ultimate plan coming to fruition for any of us to deviate from our chosen roles. The war to end all wars beckons. We must heed the call of the ancients.*

She had nodded and smiled in response — a figurative sigh.

For as long as Kalina could remember, even before her Day of Decision, she had been in training for Dracaen's plan. Years ago, she had foregone her attempts to return to her outside world family, having learned her alchemical genetics were all that mattered. Apparently, many years from now, she would conjoin with a member of the Alchemists' Council, thus perpetuating the bloodline for the Rebel Branch. Though the specifics were unclear, she certainly understood that all Dracaen ever cared about was the bloodline. If, as Kalina gathered from overhearing snippets of conversation, Genevre was of the bloodline, she and Kalina would inevitably be paired to work together. In all likelihood, they would spend the next several decades occupied with scribal tasks of one form or another, all in the name of perpetuating the bloodline — all for victory, all for mutual conjunction, all for free will throughout the dimensions. But her duties did not include the directive to *like* Genevre; to succeed, Kalina merely had to tolerate the stranger as an ally.

Dracaen moved to stand directly in front of Kalina. "I would caution you against becoming overly confident in your superiority with Genevre. You may think yourself knowledgeable about the outside world, invulnerable to its dangers thanks to your alchemical skills. But we all have our weaknesses and, thus, our vulnerabilities, no matter our powers. Do not move too swiftly beyond your training. You have a century of work ahead of you before your conjunction."

Like most Elders she had met, Dracaen spoke with a patronizing moral superiority that occasionally irritated Kalina. His advice to her today had already begun to grate.

"I understand my role and my abilities, High Azoth," she said. "Freely chosen, my decision is to work towards the Rebel Branch plan of mutual conjunction and free will for all."

"So be it," intoned Dracaen, as if ending a ritual chant. He turned again to Thuja. "Where is Genevre?"

"She awaits in the Dragonblood Chamber. Larix and Samba have remained with her. They await our arrival for the tour and introductions."

"The tour?" echoed Fraxinus.

"What word would you prefer, Azoth?" asked Thuja.

"You make it sound as if she ventured here for holiday and has willingly paid her fee for a guided excursion. She has returned to Flaw dimension after years of self-imposed exile. She has agreed to be further honed as an instrument of the Rebel Branch for eventual infiltration of the Council. Do not suggest otherwise, Thuja."

"Council infiltration?! You speak as if she were an alchemist!" exclaimed Kalina.

"Do not fret, Kalina," said Dracaen. "Unlike you, she will never be trained to assume the role of an Initiate on the Alchemists' Council."

"But make no mistake," added Fraxinus. "Genevre *is* an alchemist, albeit of the outside world. And as such, she will be trained to infiltrate Council as an outside world scribe. She deserves your respect regardless of her relationship to you."

"What relationship?"

"Stop!" said Dracaen. "You can sift through the details later. Let us go to her. I expect decorum from all of you in front of Genevre. We cannot afford for her to harbour doubts about anyone. Is that clear?"

"Of course, your Eminence," responded Tamar.

"May I offer you the same suggestion about decorum?" asked Fraxinus.

Kalina had never quite understood why Dracaen put up with Fraxinus's borderline insubordination.

"You have made your position clear," replied Dracaen.

As they progressed towards the Dragonblood Chamber, Kalina trailed slightly behind, immersed in her own thoughts on the matter. She knew of the prophecies. She knew of the bloodline. She knew of Ilex and Melia and their mutual conjunction. She knew the role she was to play in Dracaen's plan to bring such conjunction to all — alchemists and rebels alike. Though precise times — the day, the hour, the minute — had yet to be determined, Kalina understood the ultimate role she would play both with the Rebel Branch and the Alchemists' Council. She knew where her sympathies were to lie. She knew of the battles about to be waged, the losses to be mourned, the victories to be celebrated. What she did not yet know was how she would react to Genevre.

Upon crossing the threshold into the Dragonblood Chamber, Dracaen strode swiftly to Genevre and embraced her. "Welcome back!"

Kalina flinched at Dracaen's overt affection for the traitor.

"I do not recall meeting you before," offered Kalina, thus drawing Genevre's attention away from Dracaen and garnering a swift glance of disapproval from both Thuja and Larix. Tamar and Samba kept their eyes lowered. In uttering her words, Kalina had already broken Draconian protocols by not waiting to be introduced by the High Azoth.

"No," said Dracaen, with only the slightest tinge of reprimand. "Genevre resided here years ago, first arriving decades before you were born, Kalina." He gestured from one to the other, foregoing formalities.

Genevre extended a hand. She was striking with her olive skin, onyx eyes, and dark hair streaked with a white band at her temple.

"Pleasure to meet you, Kalina," said Genevre.

"I have never worked with an outside world scribe," said Kalina. Her words solicited additional chastising glances from Thuja and Larix. Kalina suspected that Thuja, in particular, would have lashed out at her vehemently, if not for Dracaen's earlier request for decorum. She decided to change her tact. "Nor have I spent much time in the outside world since entering Flaw dimension. But I know of its Rebel strongholds and Council protectorates. Perhaps you and I will someday have the opportunity to work in a stronghold or protectorate together."

"Perhaps," said Genevre. "I suppose that will depend on the roles we accept."

"I am the Blood of the Dragon!" called Tamar, fists clenched, wrists crossed in front of his chest.

Kalina assumed Tamar had commenced the Rebel chant either out of nervousness or to impress his superiors — his beloved Larix in particular. But both Thuja and Larix were visibly shocked that he would do so without the High Azoth's lead. Dracaen merely stared at Tamar, apparently gauging the audacity and potential usefulness of this Junior Reader. And Fraxinus, not about to reply before Dracaen, attempted but failed to repress a smile.

Kalina alone, holding up her clenched fists in the second position of the Rebel chant, finally broke the silence: "I live as the Flaw in the Stone!"

For a full three weeks, Kalina harboured doubts about Genevre despite Fraxinus's insistence that she should be trusted. Why should Kalina trust her outright, even if Genevre did have a connection with Dracaen and the Elders that began years ago, even if she did agree to stay and work in Flaw dimension? To Kalina, Genevre remained an outsider, an interloper who had been thrust upon her by Dracaen, a disruption. Worse, Genevre seemed poised and determined to usurp Kalina's position as Dracaen's cherished one. Larix sang Genevre's praises to Kalina so often that she began to wonder if he had been seduced by her charms, which added to Kalina's own need to be vigilant against them.

This fortitude was not too difficult. Kalina found Genevre to be surprisingly diligent with scribal labours but rather unenticing as a scribal companion. She arrived at the Scriptorium on time, focused intently on the day's manuscripts, and spoke pleasantly with Kalina and Thuja whether engaged in discussion of scribal matters or merely in small talk over meals. But Kalina did not feel she could accurately gauge Genevre's motives beyond those stated aloud in support of the rebel cause: *We must ensure free will for all. We must work to increase the Flaw in the Stone.* On the surface, then, Genevre exuded optimistic dedication, but Kalina often sensed a quiet skepticism. On such occasions, if their assigned task required an extended period of meditative silence, Kalina could sense heartache — a repressed grief about which she wondered intently but dared not ask Genevre.

After one such emotionally puzzling afternoon

at the calligraphy tables, Kalina found herself seeking conversation with Dracaen. As much as his formality and rhetorical flourish annoyed her at times, she longed simply to listen to the methodical rhythms of his deep, agreeable voice. Perhaps he would tell her what she needed to hear.

"What was Genevre . . . before?" Kalina asked Dracaen.

"A mortal of the outside world, as were we all," he responded.

"No, I mean to you, to the Rebel Branch. You have welcomed her back. And now the Elders speak in whispers when she leaves the room. Clearly, she has a history in Flaw dimension beyond common knowledge. Did she betray you, Dracaen? Did she break your heart?"

"So, you believe I have one after all!"

"You have been kind to me."

He turned away, nodding slowly. "She did not break my heart. We were not lovers, though I did . . . admire her."

"You were attracted to her? Did she reject you?"

"No. You misunderstand. We were not attracted to each other. We worked together, as you and she are doing now. I admired her dedication. Together, we took a step that moved the Rebel Branch closer to implementing the ultimate plan."

"What step?"

"We . . . We conjoined our abilities in an attempt to . . . recreate a mutation of the bloodline. Only a certain bloodline . . . formula . . . will enable rebels to conjoin with alchemists." He paused, seemingly to gauge her understanding despite the brevity of his explanation.

"Were you successful?"

"From my perspective, yes. From hers, no. In the end . . . at the end of *that time*, she was unable to recover from . . . an unbearable loss. Granted, I had lied to her. No . . . not *lied* exactly. I had uttered truths — one in particular — that she misinterpreted. I *implied* that the formula had ultimately failed. I could not allow her to seek that which needed, for the time being, to remain hidden. I encouraged her to continue our work together. She refused and left. But I knew the formula itself would one day entice her to return. After all, she maintained a fragment of it — the folio she tore from the *Osmanthian Codex*. Enough time has now passed. Soon she will learn once again that what is lost can be found, that what is hidden can be revealed."

"You are choosing your words carefully and speaking in riddles. What are you hiding from me?"

"Under the current circumstances — at this precarious juncture in dimensional history — I choose to reveal only as much as necessary to reassure you that Genevre is trustworthy. All else must remain in the confidence of the Elders for now. Do not worry, Kalina. I swear on the Dragonblood Stone itself, Genevre would never purposely harm you. Indeed, she has confided in me that you have become the primary reason she has chosen to remain with us."

"What do you mean?"

"Years ago, Genevre became skilled at interpreting ancient manuscripts from the deepest archives. During recent work with one such manuscript, she has determined the name of the person with whom you will mutually conjoin in Council dimension. She has chosen to work towards helping you achieve that goal. Rebel will indeed conjoin with alchemist."

"And I'm that rebel? I've not even been initiated to Council!"

"Kalina, my dear, the conjunction itself is over a century away. Genevre and I took the first step towards that achievement decades ago. But, regarding your role, for now let us speak in months, not decades. Over the upcoming year, you are to hone your skills with Genevre. Step by step, Kalina, piece by piece. Your current charge is to learn to accept her, to trust her, to know without doubt that she is here to help and not to hinder you."

"What will come of that trust in the short term?"

"My hope is that she will agree to braid her essence with yours."

Kalina had not anticipated this turn. She had come to Dracaen only as a temporary respite from Genevre. She had not expected to return to her chambers convinced that her future relationship with Genevre would include a proposal, that she

and Genevre would together take the rebel equivalent of holy vows.

"Her name is Sadira," Genevre said. She spoke with
such a matter-of-fact tone that the name barely
registered.

"Who?" Kalina asked.

"The alchemist inscribed to conjoin with you.
Her name is *Sadira*."

"Sadira. I don't recognize—"

"The name is Persian. It means lotus tree."

"Is she—"

"She's currently a Junior Magistrate with the
Alchemists' Council. A century from now, when
you attempt to conjoin with her, she will have been
a Senior Magistrate for several decades. And, if all
goes according to plan, by that time you will have
been a Senior Initiate for a year."

Kalina squinted at her. Surely, she must be
missing something — some nearly imperceptible
quality to Genevre that would become visible if she
watched her from the correct angle. Just what sort
of powers did this outside world scribe have in her
repertoire? Did Dracaen truly expect that Genevre
and Kalina would together be able to manipulate
Council manuscripts to such an extent that Council
Readers would not notice the rebel origin of their

inscriptions and lacunae, that their alterations would be found, still perceptible, a century from now?

"How did you determine that Sadira would be the one?"

"Blood alchemy."

Again, Kalina stared at Genevre, waiting for something further to be revealed.

"Years ago, through blood alchemy — alchemy accessible to me, thanks to the bloodline — I gained access to myriad manuscripts that others had neglected for centuries. Over these last few weeks, when not in sessions with you, I've been working on interpreting minute details of one particular manuscript. There I read of Sadira, the lotus tree. She is to conjoin with the Guelder rose — with you, *Kalina*."

"Sadira and Kalina. The lotus and the rose. How beautiful." Kalina paused before adding, "Thank you . . . for your diligence."

"I recognized the name Sadira when I read it," said Genevre. "I learned long ago that Sadira was the Initiate brought onto Council to fill the spot left open by Ilex and Melia. Their unorthodox departure resulted in an elemental disruption that Sadira alone managed to quell. The accomplishment of such a feat as an Initiate portends the magnitude of her future powers. She is rumoured to be a naturally born daughter of the bloodline."

Of course Sadira is of the bloodline, thought Kalina. *One day*, Dracaen had repeatedly said to her, *you will conjoin with an alchemist of the bloodline. Rebel and alchemist will finally be one.*

"The conjunction will be an honour," responded Kalina, unwilling to admit she was intimidated by Sadira, based on that description. Such a powerful alchemist could overcome Kalina, rendering the mutual conjunction impossible. "Do you know much about them? Ilex and Melia?" asked Kalina, shifting the conversation away from Sadira.

"I know them personally. They were my teachers, my mentors. I would not be the alchemist I am today without them."

"Yes, of course," replied Kalina. "They were powerful Scribes on the Council." She shook her head, as if to adjust the puzzle pieces as they began to fit painstakingly into place. "And they are also of the bloodline. We are all part of Dracaen's plan."

"Indeed."

"So here we are. Sadira and I are cast to play the new Ilex and Melia."

"To speak figuratively, yes. But, in the end, you are meant to surpass them. Whereas they were both Scribes of the Alchemists' Council, you are a Scribe of the Rebel Branch, a daughter of the Flaw. When you conjoin with Sadira, you will transmute the essence of Flaw with the essence of Lapis into human form. Ilex and Melia merely revealed that mutual conjunction can be accomplished outside its mythical framework. You and Sadira will change the dimensions by altering the established rules. You two will be the first of your kind. After you, others will follow. No longer will alchemists fall victim to the Sacrament of Conjunction; instead, they will reign victorious through the Rite of Equivalency."

Kalina smiled, allowing herself a moment to be tantalized. Had she the right to feel pride for a hypothetical outcome predicted to take place a century into the future? The puzzle she had so carefully constructed could quite easily become fragmented as the years progressed. She glanced towards the manuscripts on which she and Genevre were meant to be working.

"What if something goes wrong? What if Council Readers detect our transgressions? Or what if we simply . . . make a mistake? You speak as if our scribal powers are immaculate. Yet it stands to reason that if we can manipulate the inscriptions of others to change the world, then others can manipulate ours to change it back."

"You must learn to have as much faith in yourself as I have in you."

Though Kalina realized that Genevre may simply be attempting to buoy her resolve with flattery, she appreciated that Genevre *wanted* her to succeed. This outsider about whom Kalina had doubts for weeks had ardent faith in her ability to affect the future of all dimensions. In the light of such confidence, how could Kalina not be charmed?

The night of the braiding was exquisite in its beauty. The expanse of the cavern glowed with the amber light of luminescence lanterns and Lapidarian candles. The pools were shimmering with phosphorescence. Shadows and light danced upon the smooth jet walls as rebel attendants fanned a soft breeze across the water. Cool forest-scented mists — cedar and juniper, pine and fir — drifted gently across Genevre's face as she turned towards Kalina. The hollow notes of the wooden chimes jangled softly in the distance, distinct above the deep vibrations of the preparatory chanting of the Elders.

Genevre's senses were tantalized by the splendour even before she caught sight of Kalina, whose robes glistened, reflecting the light of the room, like a beacon calling Genevre towards her.

"You look radiant," Genevre whispered once she had reached Kalina. She kissed her softly on the cheek. "The ceremonial robes become you."

"As do yours," Kalina said quietly. "They also appear much more comfortable. Mine are unbearably heavy. You may have to steady me!"

Genevre adjusted her angle to observe the details of Kalina's jewel-encrusted robe. Symbolizing air, Genevre's robes were replete with feathers. In contrast, Kalina's symbolized earth. Crystals and gemstones, along with gold, silver, and copper coins, must indeed be a literal burden for Kalina to bear. How much more so the figurative burden of the ties that were about to bind her to Genevre for an eternity? Yet this woman — so young relative to most alchemists she knew — had agreed to the bond when Genevre had made the explicit proposal. They had known each other for only eight months at the time she proposed to her — eight months of working on manuscript revisions hour upon hour, week upon week, dawn and dusk blurring until they could barely tell one folio from the next.

Come to the pools with me, Genevre had said after they finally completed the inscription of one particularly challenging palimpsest. As she rinsed her bathing sheet under the spray of the sapphire waterfall, Kalina had asked, *How am I to ensure my inscriptions are always as accurate as yours?* What could Genevre have responded other than *Write and write and write. Then read and read and read yet again. And, finally, braid your essence with mine.* Kalina had slipped at that very moment on one of the wet stepping stones, and Genevre had reached out a hand to steady her. *I will*, Kalina had responded. Now, two months further along, their revisions of three particular manuscripts nearing completion, with the braiding ceremony about to begin, Genevre steadied Kalina once again as she wavered under the weight of her ceremonial robes.

"To an outside world observer, I would look like your bride," laughed Kalina. Genevre's thoughts flitted away from the braiding ceremony into a muted yet poignant memory of her first wedding. She could hear the vessel smashing as if decades collapsed into mere seconds between the wedding and the braiding. In how many ceremonial bindings would she participate before her life reached its natural end? Perhaps no end could be considered natural when time was being manipulated in the hands of the alchemists.

Tonight's braiding would ensure their scribal cohesion, that their manuscript inscriptions solidified. Once the ritual was concluded, Kalina could never be completely erased by Scribes of the Alchemists' Council since part of her would eternally exist within Genevre and the textual revisions they had made together — ink upon ink, pen upon pen, stroke upon stroke. Each letter, each icon, each illumination, and even each incised lacuna would be mutually conjoined forever. No one — current or future Scribe or Reader — would recognize the one from the other, the original from the revision, the written word from the edited text. Two scribes, once braided, could never be completely severed; whether in this life or in life everlasting, their words forever entwined.

The rebel attendants having departed, only the Elders remained to witness the ceremony. Considering the grandeur of the setting and the significance of braiding, the brevity of the ritual itself was surprising. Each carrying a small mahogany tray, Thuja bore the rings, Larix the pens, and Samba the silk ties. Symbolic of the ceremony, the rings were braided metal — a strand of gold, a strand of silver, a thread of copper as the binding element. Holding one of the rings to her lips, Genevre kissed it gently before placing it into Kalina's hand; Kalina held the ring to her own lips before sliding it onto her chosen finger. A braiding ring is molded in advance to fit whichever finger its wearer chooses; Kalina had chosen the third finger of her left hand — the ring finger, as she had learned to refer to it in the outside world. For her part, Genevre chose the middle finger of her right hand, reasoning that she would be reminded of her braiding with Kalina through all her future scribal endeavours.

No words were uttered during the inking. Like the rings, the pens and inks had been chosen and prepared in advance. For the pen, Genevre had chosen a bloodwood shell with golden trim and nib. Kalina had chosen an ebony shell with silver trim and nib. Ground and purified from the dust of precious Chinese cinnabar ink cakes and Dragonblood Stone, the ink for the pens was specifically blended for braiding — alchemically manipulated to remain visible for eighteen days. Genevre kissed the pen, took Kalina's right hand into her left, and inscribed the hallowed vow onto her exposed wrist. *My words bleed into you*, wrote Genevre onto Kalina. *As I bleed into your words*, wrote Kalina onto Genevre.

The final stage — the binding — was conducted by the High Azoth himself. Dracaen tied a blue, then a green, then a red silk ribbon around the wrist of Genevre and then of Kalina; he then tied the ends of Genevre's blue ribbon to the ends of Kalina's green one and vice versa. The ends of the red ribbons were left to flutter in tribute to the Dragonblood Stone, and to the blood that now figuratively flowed between the braided pair. Thuja and Larix each recited a verse from the *Haytim Manazir* as Dracaen bowed, hands crossed. To seal the braiding, a small crystal goblet of Dragon's Blood tonic was shared, sip by sip, by Genevre and Kalina. The goblet was then shattered against a slate panel set into the kiln for this purpose. At that moment, the ribbons themselves crystallized, shattering into small colourful pebbles that bounced playfully along the cavern floor.

With that sight and sound — the shattering that marked the end of the ritual — the unacknowledged truth overcame her. Genevre was jolted back to her past, to the pebbles that exploded like shrapnel at the birth of her children, to the crystalline pebbles that covered the fragile body of her son at his burial. She stared at Kalina, as if she were looking upon her for the first time.

"Do not ever doubt my love for you," she quietly but resolutely assured Kalina.

She then turned to Dracaen, seething.

He stepped back, raising his arms. "Leave us!" he commanded of the Elders. "Thuja! Assist Kalina to her chambers." Kalina appeared about to protest but then quietly gave Genevre a hug before departing, as quickly as she could manage in her heavy robes, along with Thuja and the others.

"How could you?" fumed Genevre.

"What I have done, I have done in the name of the plan," responded Dracaen calmly.

Genevre shook her head in disbelief. "You lied to me! You told me she had died!"

"No. I told you she was *gone*. And she *was* gone. By the time you found me in the *Osmanthian Codex* library, she had already been taken to the outside world where she was to remain hidden until she came of age. For her sake, for her safety, I could not have you searching the world for her. I could not have you *find* her, *expose* her, *endanger* her."

"Yet you have now endangered her by braiding her to me! Our essences are now linked!"

"From your perspective, I have endangered her. But the Alchemists' Council is about to endanger us all. The Third Rebellion approaches. Your braiding will eternally protect Kalina from complete erasure. And her conjunction will eventually save us all."

"My role in your plan is over."

"Why should I believe you when you uttered those very words to me once before?"

"I will depart tonight."

"And you will return again, as you did ten months ago. When necessity calls, you will return. For Kalina's sake, if not for mine."

Genevre did not respond. She turned from him and walked swiftly out of the caverns, not looking back. She stopped briefly at her chambers to change and to gather her belongings. Then she searched for

Azoth Fraxinus. Without need of explanation, he accompanied her to a portal upon request, transporting her to her clay-coloured home in Santa Fe.

"Shall I wait?" asked Fraxinus.

"Wait?"

"To transport you back to Flaw dimension."

"No. I choose to remain here," she said. "For now."

"I understand," said Fraxinus. "You may call upon me, should the need arise."

As he rounded the corner, moving out of her sight, she opened her fist to reveal one of the items she had confiscated from Flaw dimension: a single coin. She had excised it from the bejeweled braiding robe when Kalina hugged her. She looked at it now, a small copper signet. On one side was a crown. On the other was an intricately carved bee. In her ten months with the Rebel Branch, Genevre had read and transcribed the *Osmanthian Codex* in its entirety. She could now devise her own plan, and this coin would forever after signify her intention.

"How could you have allowed her to leave?" yelled Kalina.

"What choice did I have?" asked Dracaen.

"*What choice did you have?* You're the High Azoth of the Rebel Branch! Your very existence personifies choice!"

"As does hers," Dracaen responded calmly.

"Genevre chose to leave. You know as well as I that no one can be forced to remain in Flaw dimension. Each of us — rebel or outside world scribe alike — must choose to do so." He paused, turning to look directly at her. "Including you."

She watched him carefully. She had spent fifteen years of her life with him. He had doted upon her, much more so than he had on his other Initiates, even those who had arrived after her, even those younger and equally as powerful. He had been her mentor, advising her not only on her alchemical training within Flaw dimension but preparing her for her future life with the Council. She could read him as well as she could read any alchemical manuscript. And, in this moment, she could read that something remained hidden.

"No."

"*Yes*, Kalina. Genevre chose to leave."

"I am not refuting her choice! I am refuting the rationale you are spouting! She made a choice when she braided with me. I held faith in that choice. But it now appears you have influenced her choice to leave me, to change the direction in which we were headed. What is it that you're hiding? And *why* are you hiding it? We were progressing. All was aligned. All was in place. How am I to play my role in the Third Rebellion without Genevre?"

"Kalina, you have been elected to play a critical role in both the Third and Fourth Rebellions. That plan has not faltered. Within months, as our

Readers have predicted for years, all dimensions will reach the point of crisis. We will all be called upon to restore the Flaw in the Stone. Within the century, all dimensions will reach the brink of annihilation. Yes, I have hidden certain details from you. But I have done so out of necessity. I could not risk losing you at this critical juncture."

"*You* losing *me*? What of *me* losing *her*? I have lived thirty-five years, and I have never felt as close to anyone as I felt to Genevre during the braiding — not to anyone of the outside world, not to anyone here in Flaw dimension, not even to you."

"You are a daughter to me," said Dracaen softly.

In three swift strides, Kalina moved to the wrought-iron barrier surrounding the Dragonblood Stone. "Yet you have treated me like a protégé." Her voice resonated over the mists of the Flaw, her back turned to Dracaen.

"Having spent fifteen years here in Flaw dimension with me, you would deny me the honour of my paternal role?"

Kalina heard a catch in his voice. Her words had stung him, even more fiercely than she had intended. Instinctively, she longed to embrace him, to tell him that he had indeed been for her the only father she had cherished. But she recognized that he was responsible for her dilemma — he had, after all, brought her to Flaw dimension as a young woman, removing her from her outside world family.

"Ten months. She has been with us for only

ten months, Dracaen. You promised years! Genevre replaced the mother you denied me. And now you are denying me the chance to know her."

"You do not understand, Kalina." He too now stood beside her, his hands clenched on the wrought-iron railing only inches from hers.

"Then explain to me."

Kalina expected Dracaen to justify his or Genevre's actions. She was not surprised in the least when he attempted to quell her anger at his role in Genevre's sudden departure by reassuring Kalina that Genevre would be safer living outside Flaw dimension — disassociated from the rebels. She listened, tears brimming, as Dracaen explained that Genevre's actions were selfless, completed as part of her role in the plan, enacted to mitigate putting Kalina herself at risk. All of this, she found not only annoyingly predictable but most likely a distortion of the truth.

"You told me you had lied to Genevre, led her to misinterpret your words. And now I'm certain you're doing the same with me. If you expect me to continue to trust you, show me the courtesy of honesty."

Dracaen paused before he responded. "You were not born to your outside world parents." He placed a hand on her shoulder, from which she was too shocked to pull away.

"I don't understand," she said, astounded at this revelation.

"You were not . . . physically . . . You were not . . . procreated by man and woman of the outside world." He stumbled over his pacing and language, clearly attempting to steady his voice.

"I . . . What? What do you mean? Then how was I . . . born?" She too could not find the words she needed.

"You were alchemically created, here in Flaw dimension. You were *composed* in an alembic with the help of a Dragonblood seed conjoined with a Lapidarian egg. To ensure your survival after your naming, you had to be hidden in the outside world until you grew strong enough to return to us, until rumours of your existence became merely the stuff of ancient myth and calligraphy."

Kalina trembled. She grasped the railing to keep from falling. "I am an alchemical child? I was . . . *created*? By whom?"

"The Elders . . . primarily."

"Which Elders?"

He paused again, leaving Kalina to question his honesty even in this moment of truth. "You were created by me, Kalina. The others followed my instructions."

"*Instructions?* They *assembled* me — piece by piece? As a *design* for rebel insurgence?"

"You are living proof of the homunculus, an alchemical creation we thought lost forever to the deepest archives."

"I am a creature? I am a creation like an outside world storybook monster?" She shook her head, thoughts racing. "Then I'm grateful Genevre has left us. She'd be appalled at this revelation. Had she known, she would not have braided with me."

"No, Kalina. She would not be appalled. She understands that you are the pinnacle of our ultimate plan: mutual conjunction for all through the formula. *All* will be free. She has played her role, and you will play yours. You will ensure the survival of free will for eternity to all who exist throughout the dimensions."

"You praise free will, yet you give me no choice. You created me, you have lied to me for years, and now you expect me to do your bidding."

"No, Kalina. I expect you to choose to be the rebel Genevre and I conceived you to be."

III
Council Dimension — 1816

Melia sat at the edge of the catacomb alembic debating whether to enter the healing waters. She had been feeling off-balance for no apparent reason. Though they shared a body, Ilex claimed to feel fine. Melia had agreed to enter the shadows until the discomfort passed. None of their fellow alchemists had found Melia's temporary absence troubling; in general, over the sixteen years since the conjunction, Council members tended to accept that the unprecedented result would entail equally unprecedented behaviour by Ilex and Melia. Melia assumed several weeks would need to pass before anyone questioned the absence or presence of one over the other. Sitting here now she wondered if anyone other than Saule, and perhaps Ravenea, fully understood her as *herself*. Of course, too much time spent in the catacombs would affect their Council duties, a possibility that weighed heavily upon Melia. Council members would soon enough resent her neglect of Novillian duties.

For four days Ilex had maintained control of their body while Melia rested, mentally withdrawing into a space she experienced physically as a dark, cool cavern. It reminded her of the Flaw dimension, but soft drumming rather than wooden chimes resonated. She remained in this state, only vaguely aware of the activities being pursued in mind or body by Ilex as he went about their Council responsibilities. Though she was happy to have missed a long Council meeting during this period of absence, she had become gradually more uneasy with each passing day — the dream-like state transforming into a series of nightmares. Thus, her plan to achieve rest appeared to have been thwarted by her mind rather than their body. Yet even physically she simply did not feel like herself, not even like the self she had come to know as conjoined with Ilex. Finally, frustrated and exhausted, Melia had no choice but to emerge from her virtual hibernation. The shift had occurred too quickly, catching both her and Ilex off guard.

Saule had been walking beside Ilex discussing a fluctuation in fire — a slight elemental imbalance the Rowans had sensed a few days earlier and raised at this morning's Council meeting. She had clearly been startled when Ilex suddenly lurched forward, his breakfast following shortly thereafter. Though such occurrences may be familiar to people of the outside world, they were virtually unheard of in Council dimension. Alchemists simply were not prone to vomiting, let alone into the precious channel waters.

"Ilex! Melia! Sit down!" Saule insisted, guiding them towards the nearest bench.

Melia looked back towards the stream.

"Don't worry, Melia! The alchemical waters have taken care of the instrusion. Let me take care of you," said Saule. She supported Melia by the arm, helping her lower herself to the bench.

"When I was an Initiate," Melia said to Saule upon settling, "I wanted to clean a shell that I'd brought back as a souvenir from an outside world beach. I dipped it into the channel waters closest to residence chambers. When I accidentally dropped it, I combed a few feet of the bottom of the channel section, searching, but it was gone. I figured it had been whipped away in the current — that it would resurface at some future point in the classroom alembic and result in the Azoth Magen reprimanding my carelessness. But that never happened, of course." She smiled, remembering. "A few months later, Ravenea, using her own hairbrush as proof, illustrated that the waters immediately dissolve all non-metallic objects that are not being held or worn by an alchemist."

"Only alchemy can outwit alchemy," replied Saule.

"What do you mean?"

"To contaminate the channel waters, you would need to use powerful alchemy. The shell and the contents of your stomach are apparently not powerful enough."

Melia laughed, despite her discomfort. "I will keep that in mind."

"Your rest was disrupted," said Ilex, his face momentarily appearing in place of Melia's. "We were too loud, perhaps."

"No. I am simply unwell. I can no longer hide from the truth."

The leaves rustled gently in the branches overhead. Melia continued to feel nauseated. She longed to move herself from the bench to the ancient apiary — specifically to the branches of the wisteria tree. She longed to fall asleep cradled in the depths of its purple haze.

"How long have you felt unwell?" asked Saule.

"A week or so — a few weeks, I suppose, if I am honest. I recall feeling dizzy for the first time during the Initiate class on conjunction."

"That was over three weeks ago," said Saule. Having been the Magistrate in charge of that class, Saule would remember. "What have the Azoths suggested?"

"We've not consulted them," replied Ilex. "We thought rest would help. Like so many physical challenges since the conjunction, we believed we could resolve the problem on our own without resorting to Azothian interference. I see now that we were wrong."

"Perhaps a session in a catacomb alembic is in order," suggested Saule.

Of course, Melia realized, as did Ilex and Saule, that one could not simply remove oneself from Council duties and occupy a catacomb alembic without first attaining permission from an Azoth. Melia did not want the Azoths to know of their problems. Such a confession could lead to yet another investigation, another series of tests, or, at the very least, to another tribunal of questions about the sustainability of mutual conjunction. They had endured enough such intrusions — outright abuses at times — during the first few years of their co-existence.

"I will escort you to Azothian Chambers now," said Saule who, though she had been a good friend and confidante for years, did not seem to understand the depth of Melia's fears. How could anyone understand something only she and Ilex had ever experienced?

The agonizing hour that followed was spent recounting the state of their well-being to Azoth Magen Quercus who, inevitably, asked another question for each one that Melia or Ilex answered. Melia felt she would have collapsed had Ilex not supported their body. Finally, acknowledging that he could not account for the weaknesses or anomalies of a mutually conjoined pair since he had no precedent with which to do so, Quercus granted two days in a catacomb alembic, gesturing with a sweeping motion that she, Ilex, and Saule should depart without further ado. Saule walked with Ilex, offering her arm for physical support if needed.

So here Melia sat, Ilex having entered the shadows upon their arrival. Saule waited patiently to help her into the alembic.

"I fear it will not work," said Melia.

"Why?" asked Saule.

"I do not think even the alembic waters can cure what ails us."

"But you don't know what ails you," replied Saule.

"I'm beginning to suspect the problem lies with the conjunction itself."

Saule stared at her, bewildered. "No! How can that be — after all these years?"

"Our conjunction is unprecedented. Perhaps our ability to maintain it is limited."

"But Ilex is fine. I am sure—"

"No." Melia paused, shaking her head. She debated how much information she should share with Saule. Finally, though, she realized she had to confide in someone, and Saule was certainly her closest friend. "I haven't been completely honest, Saule — not to you and not even to Ilex. He's not fine. He fades away on occasion."

"Fades away?"

"He disappears from my awareness, as if he unwillingly and unknowingly enters the shadows.

When he returns, he doesn't even realize he has been gone until something tangible pierces his reverie — an afternoon shadow appearing on a wall, for example, when he assumed the sun had only just risen. I must fill in the gaps for him."

Saule laid a hand on Melia's shoulder and kissed the top of her head. "I am sorry."

"Saule, I am truly afraid that I am beginning to dominate — that my body is rebelling against Ilex. I fear, despite the sixteen years as partners in mutual conjunction, I will be victorious in the conjunction. It otherwise makes no sense that Ilex would have these lacunae in his consciousness. I thought if I purposely entered the shadows, all would be well when I returned to our body and mind. But he has disappeared again, just moments ago. I fear not only that the alembic waters will do no good, but that they could, in fact, make the situation worse."

She broke down then, crying. Having said aloud to Saule what she had secretly feared in moments of Ilex's absence, Melia felt vague possibility become probability. How could she face the prospect that the person she had loved for centuries, the person with whom she had been physically conjoined for sixteen years, was slowly disappearing into nothingness? She had always assumed erasure would be one of the most difficult processes to bear — walking around Council dimension as an Elder knowing what others did not know, knowing that someone who used to be present was now no more than an absence, not even a memory, to all but the privileged few. But this process was worse — this process of someone disappearing bit by bit. Unlike those who are erased, Ilex would eventually simply cease to be. His presence, his existence, his absence, and his death would be marked only by tears in the Amber Garden.

Saule had moved closer to Melia. She now sat beside her, legs dangling over the edge of the alembic, an arm across Melia's shoulders, her own shoulder supporting Melia's head.

"You cannot know what will happen, Melia. As you yourself said earlier, your conjunction is unprecedented. Perhaps the catacomb alembic will help. Perhaps this is merely a phase in your development. Perhaps you are entering a period of dominance that will later recede. Entering the alembic offers the best chance for you both to regain strength. Even if you are not healed of this problem, you should at least gain insight. In the altered state of alembic immersion, you will understand your body in ways you cannot hope to achieve otherwise. Please, Melia. Please immerse yourselves in the alembic waters."

Melia nodded. She knew Saule was right. She knew she must choose the path that had the greatest chance of success. She stood then and, with Saule's help to steady her, made her way down the stone steps into the depths of the alembic. She positioned herself as protocol dictated — body submerged, head above water in the hollow of the stone pillow. And she waited, watching Saule move back to the outer rim of the alembic chamber to chant the ritual words that would nurture the waters into compliance. She watched as the emerging vapours began to change colours, and then she closed her eyes.

Suddenly Melia's awareness was elsewhere. She could no longer see Saule or the alembic or the catacombs. She was for all intents and purposes *nowhere*, though she knew better. She knew she was inside herself in yet another state of altered consciousness. Unlike when she had purposely retreated to the shadows over the past few days, she now felt wide awake — more alive and well than she had ever felt even when fully conscious in Council dimension or the outside world. Yet she could not possibly have been healed so swiftly. These feelings of well-being must be an illusion, a calming façade created by the alembic waters to ensure she remained in position.

Time became muted. She could not tell if hours or only minutes had passed. Her thoughts meandered, sometimes focused, sometimes a rapidly firing collage of images that made no sense to her. She would touch momentarily upon Ilex — sensing him within her own being. Then he would vanish, and she would feel as if she were completely and only herself, as if they had never conjoined. As much as she feared his disappearance, Melia realized during her immersion that her preferred state of being among these fluctuations was one of all-encompassing silence — dark and empty, cool and tranquil. She knew the emptiness was most certainly an illusion — that she was being given a reprieve from a continuous awareness of Ilex's emotions and sensations, of his movements, of his physicality. She wondered if he could sense that she liked this, that as the seconds or minutes or hours moved ahead, she hoped to remain alone for many more hours or days or weeks. Was she supposed to feel guilty for savouring her time alone, her time to be by and in and of herself? She felt content. Yet she could not bear losing Ilex permanently.

Then something stirred her — an indistinguishable sound from far away. It did not startle her as much as it made her curious. Silencing her intrusive thoughts, she listened. At first, it remained faint but steady. As it grew louder, she understood it to be rhythmic, like a heartbeat. Perhaps it actually was a heartbeat — from the heart she shared with Ilex. The sound was disconcerting yet comforting, loud yet muffled as if reaching her through the alembic waters. Yet how could that be? She was in the waters herself. She could not possibly be hearing Saule's heart, could she? Or the heart of another Council member waiting with Saule for Melia's re-emergence from the alembic?

As she relaxed into its constancy, she began to feel soothed by its familiarity. Where had she heard such a sound before? Perhaps she recalled it from a previous alembic immersion years ago — decades, a century — too long ago for her to have a conscious memory of the event. Though alchemists lived for hundreds of years, their memories were fallible. But this explanation did not seem quite right, did not feel quite accurate. She imagined herself even further back in time — back to the first months of her being, swathed in embryonic waters, listening to her mother's heartbeat. Of course, she had never had a conscious recollection of such a moment; what she experienced now was some sort of imagined memory — one possible, she assumed, only through the alchemical powers of the alembic.

And then she stopped. She stopped imagining because she suddenly knew. She knew in a way she had never known anything before — as if all other knowledge became irrelevant in that moment. The realization was so overpowering that she awakened immediately and sat up with such force the alembic waters splashed over the side and ran down the stone steps.

"What's wrong?" asked Saule.

"You . . . you're still here?"

"Yes. I've not yet left. The lights were fluctuating in a way I'd not seen before. I thought I should wait until they had settled before leaving you alone here. You have been immersed for just over an hour."

Saule moved from the bench beside the alembic to the third step on the stone staircase and looked intently at Melia. She then moved to the fifth step and stared at Melia's face. Melia assumed she was checking for damage, but she then realized she was looking for Ilex.

"He's not here," said Melia. "Ilex is no longer here."

"What do you mean? Were you right? Has he been dissolved into you after all these years? Are you the victor in the conjunction after all?"

"No. He has retreated for now. Out of necessity. He has made room."

"Made room? For what?"

"Our child."

The following week, having learned to emerge for brief periods as their child slowly gestated, Ilex rested with Melia in the wisteria tree. Their tears and silence reminded Melia of the long, awkward periods they had spent together leading up to their conjunction. Once again, neither Ilex nor Melia knew what to expect. The simple fact was that alchemists could not get pregnant. Yet here they were, the exception to the rule once again. Alchemists cannot mutually conjoin. Alchemists cannot become pregnant.

"Perhaps we're not alchemists," suggested Ilex. He laughed.

"Perhaps not for much longer," responded Melia. She wanted to cry. Her fears inevitably led to discussions about the future. *You are of the bloodline*, they recalled Dracaen saying before their conjunction. So too would be their child.

"My love, forgive me for what I am about to

say," warned Ilex before speaking words that startled Melia. "But I must say it now, before I retreat again into the shadows." He paused. "We cannot keep this child."

Was Ilex proposing an alchemical solution to terminate the pregnancy? Melia could not bring herself to respond or question. She simply did not want to know his meaning and was thankful in that moment that they could not hear each other's thoughts.

"If this child survives its birth," Ilex clarified, "which it may well not, we cannot keep it. We must assure we give birth secretly — outside Council dimension. And we must thereafter disassociate ourselves from our child. Otherwise, the bloodline trials on the innocent babe will be endless — exponentially worse than our own. We cannot subject a child to such barbarity."

Bloodline trials. Bloodline trails. Trails of blood. Melia shuddered. She could not help but picture their child covered in blood. Perhaps she and Ilex could escape altogether, hide away not only for the birth but so that no one would ever find them. As they had done years earlier before their conjunction, they began to contemplate fleeing to the outside world. Could they survive if they were to cut all ties with the Council? How long could they live without Elixir? Perhaps Saule could supply them with Lapidarian honey and find adoptive parents for the child, who would thereby never be found even if the Azoths located its escapees. She spoke aloud options as they occurred to her. Together she and Ilex hypothesized various scenarios until exhausted.

"Perhaps years from now, when the child has matured . . . perhaps then, we can be reunited," suggested Ilex. This possibility gave Melia a flicker of hope. Unlike in her most dreaded scenarios, she need not abandon her child for eternity.

A bee landed on Ilex and Melia then. They stood, and Melia gently shook their robe to encourage it to fly away. But it stayed put, and another soon joined it. And another. Ilex suggested taking the robe off. Melia lay it over a low branch of the tree, careful not to trap the bees. Unharmed, they flew from the robe and landed on Ilex and Melia's cotton shirt. Others soon followed. Melia had counted eighteen before so many arrived that she could no longer keep track. Ilex suggested they run for the portal, but Melia saw no sense in such a gesture. She was not about to leave the ancient garden and emerge from the portal with bees clinging to their clothes. Ilex began to argue, but soon after the point was moot. Melia closed their eyes and knelt to the ground. Within moments, hundreds of bees had landed upon them. Melia could no longer physically see them, but she could sense their bluish-green Lapidarian tinge, could feel it in their vibration. She could hear them humming a deep, dark tone that gradually moved Melia into a meditative state. She could no longer sense Ilex at all.

The first sting surprised her. It did not hurt her at all — no more than a light pinprick. It had simply been unexpected given the maturity of their Lapidarian pendant. The dozens — hundreds perhaps — of stings that followed were almost soothing. A light sensation of prickling moving across her body. *Her body.* She could feel every inch of it — every inch as *her body alone.* No Ilex. No child. Her body alone. She knew the bees were injecting something into her with their stings. But if a venom, it resulted in no apparent toxicity. Indeed, she felt better than she had in years, better even than when immersed in the catacomb waters. What good had the catacombs done to heal her? None whatsoever. They merely led her to the knowledge she would eventually have gained by natural means.

Natural means. None of this process was natural. Or perhaps all of it was. Perhaps alchemy is the most natural process of all. Perhaps we should all be given the opportunity to completely transform ourselves and the worlds in which we thrive.

Melia fell into a sleep-like trance. She dreamed vividly — flashes of insight that she would later struggle to remember, the sound of wooden chimes calling her to Flaw dimension, mists moving across the Dragonblood Stone, bees appearing and disappearing. She felt trapped. She felt free. She could taste both bitter vitriol and golden-sweet honey. A boy. Ilex presenting a pendant chain to a boy. Their son? No. Yes. She could not be certain.

She awoke. She could not move her body. Had the bees drugged her? She felt her child stir within her. She felt Ilex stir. He was trying to move their left foot and ankle, attempting to free it of the shackles that were keeping Melia immobile. She struggled then too. She helped Ilex, accomplishing only the slightest movement at first. A foot, then a leg, then part of the torso: free. They were encased in something. Melia felt as if she were hatching from a shell, pecking away at it bit by bit, picking the hard casing away from its inner fluid. But when she and Ilex had finally freed their hands and arms completely, when they were finally able to sit up and clear the remaining debris from their eyes, Melia realized the material was not shell. They had been swathed in honeycomb, complete with wet golden nectar. The bees had disappeared — flown away, their work completed. Or they had hidden away to die from stinging and exhaustion.

"Did they help or hinder the child?" asked Ilex.

"Helped," replied Melia. "I am certain." She felt invigorated. The Lapidarian bees had somehow infused her, Ilex, and the child with their essence. Had they been injected with the bee-venom equivalent of Lapidarian Elixir? Could it sustain them? Could Ilex and Melia now survive without Elixir in the outside world thanks to these tiny alchemists?

Three weeks had passed since Melia had made her revelation in the catacombs to Saule. Saule gradually understood that, in all likelihood — though they had no precedent for confirming the mechanics of the matter — the night of intimacy she had shared with Ilex and Melia had resulted in the pregnancy. With that knowledge, Saule felt not only involved but *responsible*.

"Have I *fathered* this child?" she had asked one evening.

"I believe you were the conduit for conception."

"But *how*? Did I somehow transfer—"

"No! Not physically. You know as well as I that alchemists cannot become pregnant. If we existed as two separate bodies, Ilex's seed would have been deemed an invader, like a virus, readily quelled by my Quintessence. The only explanation is alchemical — a phenomenon of mutual conjunction we've yet to understand," said Melia.

"Yes, but if I hadn't entered you—"

"Saule! You are certainly under no obligation to take responsibility as a parent — whether mother or father."

"I'm both perhaps," replied Saule.

"Or neither," responded Melia.

"Don't push me away," implored Saule. "I may not be a biological parent to this child, but I certainly played a role in the alchemy of its creation. And I could well be your only friend and, more importantly, your only *ally* if you intend to carry through with your plan to leave Council dimension for the outside world without consulting the Elders." She had dropped her voice to a harsh whisper.

Melia lowered her head. "I apologize, Saule. I'm tired. And I'm scared. And I don't know what to do. I don't know what is best for us. And I most certainly don't know what is best for the Council."

"All that matters in the immediate future is what is best for you and Ilex and the child," affirmed Saule.

"And how am I to determine even that?"

Thus, the conversations continued along these lines whenever the opportunity arose for time alone. In particular, whenever possible, Melia and Saule would sit together after the evening meal in the wisteria tree. Ilex had retreated further into the shadows since the bee incident, emerging for only a few minutes per day, and the bees paid Melia no attention whatsoever thereafter. Melia and Saule would often chat late into the night, the apiary perpetually moonlit after sunset. Rumours began to spread as a consequence. No one suspected the truth, of course. How could they? Conception was, as it were, *inconceivable* since it had never before happened to a member of the Alchemists' Council. Instead, their conjectures revolved around sexual or romantic liaisons between Melia and Saule. Ravenea was the one who finally made them aware of various fragments of gossip: *Melia and Saule have fallen in love. Melia is no longer faithful to Ilex. She is now truly an alchemist like the rest of us. I haven't seen Ilex in weeks — Saule*

must have scared him away. Imagine the surge to the
Quintessence if all three were to—

"Stop!" begged Melia.

"Is any of it true?" asked Ravenea. She had taken it upon herself on that evening to join Melia and Saule in the ancient garden to confront them directly.

"Yes," lied Melia. Saule started slightly.

"I do not believe you," replied Ravenea. She knew Melia too well. "You are hiding something. And I am disappointed that you have not yet confided in me." She turned and walked away from the wisteria tree, back across the field to the portal.

"What if she takes her suspicions to the Elders?" asked Saule.

"She won't," said Melia. "She may be disappointed in me, but she will not betray me. Besides, what would she tell them? All she could offer would be mere speculation. She knows we will turn to her when necessity requires."

Over the weeks, despite uncertainties about the future, Melia and Saule were occasionally able to take a few minutes of those hours spent in the wisteria tree to relax completely: to watch the Lapidarian bees move from one blossom to the next, to enjoy the evening light through the flowers and branches, to pretend momentarily that nothing was out of place despite the weight bearing down on them both — on them all, including Ilex and the child that he and Melia carried — with each passing day. Sometimes they could forget; yet no matter what fleetingly distracted them, they were inevitably brought back to their reality.

"It seems always to be spring here," observed Saule on one such evening. "Nothing ever changes — perpetual beauty. As beautiful as I remember it to be, surely the outside world pales in comparison."

They were thus distracted.

"Such is the alchemy of the ancient garden," said Melia. "I have often wondered how the Lapidarian bees fare in the outside world upon their first encounter with seasonal shifts — the highs and lows in light and temperature that they would never have encountered here."

"As I wonder how *you* will fare, Melia."

They were thus brought back.

Melia smiled despite the emotional twinge of pain. "Your concern is valid, Saule. We must be sure to choose a temperate climate as our destination."

They joked on this particular occasion, but such practical considerations were indeed of importance as they worked through the details of the plan, such as it was. Early in her discussions with Saule, Melia had contemplated confessing the truth to Quercus. Repeatedly, Saule offered her advice: *You cannot take a child conceived in Council dimension into the outside world; you must remain here among alchemists; you must remain in proximity to the Lapis.* Despite her earlier conversations with Ilex, Melia had initially agreed with Saule, in theory if not in heart. But a more recent discussion with Dracaen, which she had taken upon herself late one night without Saule's knowledge, had convinced her otherwise.

"A child conceived through mutual conjunction is a miracle of the bloodline. You know this to be true, Melia. As such, the child belongs to the Rebel Branch," Dracaen insisted.

"*As such*, our child belongs to us — to Ilex and me," Melia snapped. But she knew even then that her retorts against the High Azoth were weak. Melia, in agreeing to take the Sephrim years ago, in attempting and succeeding at mutual conjunction with the assistance of the rebels, now felt like a mere vessel, like a human alembic whose sole purpose was to incubate and then deliver a miracle child — one who would be sought across the dimensions, fought over at best, destroyed at worst.

"Consider the future of the Alchemists' Council," Dracaen had said.

In Dracaen's view, even before the child was born, it had already become a symbol of possibility: a means for the Rebel Branch to enact its ultimate goal. The child would be the One to perpetuate the bloodline and, thereby, to ensure free will for all through a return to mutual conjunction — for mutual equivalency between the rebels and the alchemists. He did not see the pressure such hope put on the child and Ilex and Melia themselves. Did Dracaen expect them simply to relinquish the child to his care? Did he expect them to allow their child to become a victim in his obsessive and seemingly unending search for a means to preserve the bloodline?

"For the child's safety and for your own well-being," Dracaen assured her. "I offer you the better choice."

"The Council will inevitably hear that the Rebel Branch is raising a child. They will find a means to investigate."

"We will hide the child, as you yourself would do. We will watch it from afar, protect it. We will refrain from making direct contact until after it has reached an age when initiation to the Rebel Branch would not be questioned."

Melia determined on that night that she must not grow attached to her child. She must not. Yet how could she not? And what would Ilex think? He now emerged only on occasion, and he seemed as indecisive as she was. *You must decide, my love*, he would say, before falling swiftly back into the shadows he was forced to occupy as the child inside them continued to mature.

The child was indeed growing. Melia could feel it. But thus far they showed little visible sign of pregnancy, especially given the ample nature of Council robes. Still, she knew that no matter the length of gestation — which she assumed would be slowed substantially, given the Elixir that had flowed through their veins for decades — eventually she would not be able to hide their physical circumstance. And even if they could hide their physical form with the help of their most generous robes, they certainly would not be able to hide the birth or the child itself once it had been born. Melia had concluded weeks ago that they could not deliver the child in Council dimension nor, as Dracaen would prefer, in Flaw dimension. Thus, she needed to accelerate her plan for their permanent escape to the outside world. Once the child was born, once Ilex had returned from the shadows, they could consult with Dracaen together and decide whether or not to seal their child's fate.

A full two months had passed before Melia's final week as a member of the Alchemists' Council arrived. When the time had seemed right, Melia had chosen to trust Ravenea to help — a decision Saule initially questioned. But Ravenea had proven herself more than worthy over the years and was, Melia convinced Saule, their only conceivable ally on Council. Though she had been both shocked at the news of the pregnancy and angered at Saule and Melia's extended silence on the matter, Ravenea had eventually agreed to assist them for both personal and pragmatic reasons.

"The suffering must end," said Ravenea. "You and Ilex have been through enough tribulations." She paused and smiled. "Besides, alchemists have little patience for children. Imagine if your child got loose in the Scriptorium!"

"Thank you, my beloved friend," Melia said, embracing Ravenea.

"Of course," continued Ravenea, her tone serious once again, "all ties between us will thereafter be severed. My path towards Azoth must remain clear of trespass."

Melia nodded, tears welling.

"I, on the other hand, have no such Azothian ambitions," said Saule.

"Regardless," responded Melia, "you'll have ventured enough by assisting our escape. I cannot ask you to risk erasure through continued contact."

"You have not asked. I chose to love you, no matter the risk."

Tears had flowed freely in that moment and many times thereafter until the final hour.

Now they waited together beside the wisteria tree, about to embark upon the first precarious step in the plan: an unorthodox departure from Council dimension. Departure via the main portal or even the cliff face would leave a transport signature that could easily be used by the Elders to track Ilex and Melia's destination in the outside world, so Ravenea had suggested a radical alternative. Like the bees of the ancient garden, Ilex and Melia would enter the outside world through the fissure in the wisteria tree. Such a move was unparallelled, of course. But so was mutual conjunction, so was an alchemist's pregnancy, and so was escaping without a trace. *You will be carried on the wings of the bees*, Ravenea had explained last month after hearing Melia's tale of their protective venom. Saule had shaken her head in bewilderment, hands covering her face. She knew that Ravenea was a skilled alchemist — one who had far exceeded others of her order at each rotation. But surely even one so skilled in manipulating elements could not succeed at magic.

"It is not magic," Ravenea assured them. "It is blood alchemy."

"Blood alchemy?" repeated Melia and Saule simultaneously.

"Blood alchemy is the ancient practice of manipulating elemental cohesion with the Elixir-infused blood and Quintessence-infused breath of an alchemist."

"'The ink and the words are the blood and the breath,'" recited Melia, remembering a fragment of a text she had studied over a century earlier.

"Like the sacrifices of old," continued Ravenea, "pure blood alchemy was abolished from official Council doctrine after the First Rebellion — its power more feared than revered. And with each Final Ascension of an Azoth Magen, more knowledge of blood alchemy has been lost to us. Now early Council doctrine is ancient history relegated to the deepest archives."

"Yet you have somehow managed to unearth

this alchemical art from the archives?" asked Melia, the anxiety in her voice tinged with skepticism.

"Indeed I have," replied Ravenea. "I believe ancient knowledge could well prove valuable rather than detrimental to future Councils. One must be prepared not only for the inevitable but for the previously inconceivable. You and Ilex have taught me that lesson well, and more than once, Melia."

Thus, they began; thus they studied; thus they practised over the weeks between that day and this one. Now Ravenea stood, ancient manuscript in hand and scribal tools spread before her on a makeshift platform atop a wide, relatively flat, waist-level branch of the wisteria tree.

"Hold this," she said to Melia, passing her a small clay vessel.

"Recite these words after I light the Lapidarian candle," she instructed Saule, handing her a small scroll.

Saule began to recite as soon as the flame was kindled. She recognized the ancient script; she had studied it years ago as a Senior Initiate. *From the Lapis to the Scribe; from the Scribe to the Reader.* With words intoned enlivening words inscribed, the alchemical transmutation began. Within seconds, the bees began to arrive — a few at first, then dozens, then a few hundred at least. They gathered into a small swarm on the branch above the one holding the manuscript.

"Choose one," she said to Melia.

Melia continued to hold the vessel in one hand and hesitantly reached up towards the bees with the other. She positioned her fingers, palm up, near to the swarm of bees as if she planned to scoop up a handful. But instead of doing so, she waited for one of the bees to approach her. Within seconds, one did. It walked across a fingertip, along the finger, and into her hand. Saule reached over and pulled the lid off the vessel. Though not visible from her position, Saule knew the vessel contained a mixture of equal parts Lapidarian ink, Lapidarian honey, and Melia and Ilex's blood, the latter of which had been extracted via a sharp blade at sunrise.

"Step forward," Ravenea said, gesturing to the manuscript.

Melia stood directly beside the branch in front of the manuscript. She poured a thimbleful of the blood-infused mixture onto an image of a bee in the manuscript and manoeuvred the actual bee in her hand to move from her palm onto the now-obscured folio image. It did so without reluctance, as if it understood its role in the process. Melia then drank the remainder of the mixture. In a flash of light that emerged suddenly from the glowing fissure of the wisteria tree, Saule was temporarily blinded. Seconds later, having regained her vision, Saule realized that both Melia and the bee were gone. The fissure, charred with black edges, would soon crumble to ash.

"The blood alchemy ritual has ended. As a result

of its success, Melia and Ilex and the child will, forever after, be intimately connected with Lapidarian bees. Time will tell whether such a connection proves useful."

"And what of us, Ravenea? What now? We have aided in an unauthorized and blatantly unorthodox ritual. Ilex and Melia are gone. The Elders will question us all. They will undoubtedly read our pendants."

"Hence the necessity of our final step," said Ravenea. "Set your pendant here." She set her own pendant between the manuscript and the Lapidarian candle. "Melia procured a solution — presumably from a rebel, though she didn't specify and I didn't ask. It will render our pendants impenetrable regarding not only events of today but also of all events regarding Ilex and Melia that took place over the past six months and that will take place hereafter into the future. This prohibited rendering of the pendant should remain undetectable to others, including the Elders — but I emphasize *should*. A proficient Reader or Elder may well detect something amiss. If investigated — if discovered — you could be accused of Rebel Branch alignment. Are you prepared for that, Saule? Are you prepared to risk erasure?"

"What choice do I have now or in the future? I helped a friend, and I will continue to help her without regret."

"Your choices remain yours, Saule. But do not allow your path to interfere with mine. Ongoing collaboration or even hushed discussion between us regarding the escape or the pregnancy or the child — should one thrive — could endanger us all."

"I understand," she replied, but her tone hinted otherwise.

"Saule, listen to me. I am not being unduly harsh or unreasonable. I am being practical. If my path to Azothian status is blocked by scandal, my ambitions to effect change in the future will come to nought."

Saule met her eyes and nodded. "Scribe Ravenea, I vow on my Quintessence to hold silence with others regarding your involvement in Ilex and Melia's escape, and I vow to hold silence with you in the future regarding the escape and the whereabouts of parents or child."

"We are hereby forever bound by this promise for eternity," pledged Ravenea as she poured a blood-red liquid over their pendants and sealed the fluid with Lapidarian wax from the candle.

"For an eternity, we are bound," replied Saule.

Within the hour, Ravenea and Saule had both returned to their respective residence chambers, confident that all had progressed as planned. Of course, Saule could not know whether Ilex, Melia, and their unborn child had emerged unscathed from the fissure into the outside world. It was too soon to hear from them; Melia had made arrangements for clandestine contact through the Santa Fe

Rebel Branch stronghold. But for now, Saule could only hope that the ritual had worked based on its apparent success in the apiary.

Unease plagued her in the days that followed. All was made worse once the absence of Ilex and Melia became Council-wide knowledge. At first, when alchemists simply asked after them, they accepted Saule's response: *No, perhaps they are in the Scriptorium.* But after three days, the portal logs were consulted. And after five days, all hell broke loose — Ilex and Melia's absence could not be justified, certainly not to the Elders of the Alchemists' Council. The Azoths were furious, especially when no one could pinpoint precisely when or how Ilex and Melia had departed. Nor could anyone trace the precise location of the Lapidarian fragment within their pendant. After two weeks, rumours and theories began to spread: *They have abandoned their duties. They have joined the rebels. If they left with their pendant, they have confiscated Council property. Indeed, they have confiscated Quintessence! They merely vanished — an alchemical mutation inevitable with mutual conjunction.* And so on and so on. A few of the theories made Saule laugh, but most upset her — not because of their level of inaccuracy, but because of the malicious tone with which they were uttered. But no one suggested Ilex and Melia departed Council dimension in order to give birth to an alchemically conceived miracle child. For that, at least, Saule could be grateful and relieved.

Though none of the rumours received official validation, the speculation continued unabated until, three weeks after Ilex and Melia had left, more pressing matters came to light. Remarkably, the Novillian Scribes had discovered that despite the potential of rebel alliances, Ilex and Melia could not be erased. This is not to say that the Elders *chose* not to erase them, but that they literally and physically could not be erased from the manuscripts. *Malevolent alchemy! Rebel Branch mysticism!* These and other such accusations quickly pushed aside wayward rumours of the disappearance. But the Azoths attributed the impossibility of erasure from the manuscripts to the strength of mutual conjunction or inaccessibility of their pendant rather than to direct involvement of the rebels.

Equally problematic, the disturbance in elemental balance caused by the abrupt departure of the conjoined pair became blatantly evident over the course of the same time frame. Balance would need to be restored immediately. Thus, as the Elders worked on temporary countermeasures to maintain dimensional equilibrium, the Readers were to labour day and night until they accomplished their duty to choose and locate a new Initiate and thus return the Council to one hundred and one — to *only* one hundred and one, now that the mutually conjoined pair no longer remained a factor in the calculation. The possibility of ascending in the extensive rotation — that is, in a rotation that began with a vacancy in the Novillian order — quelled some of the rumours. Why continue to speculate on *how* the space had opened when one could simply be content that opportunity had knocked? Azoth Magen Quercus chose Scribe Obeche to ascend to the Novillian position. *You must assure that Obeche does not surpass you*, Saule said to Ravenea. *No one would be able to tolerate him as a Rowan, let alone an Azoth.* Ravenea laughed and blushed. For all her power and knowledge — and, of late, duplicity — Ravenea retained an honest modesty in her abilities.

With all ascensions of the rotation assigned, with an Initiate spot vacated, with hours upon hours of work completed by the Readers to determine the next alchemist to join the Council, the final step of the Ritual of Location was performed by the Scribes. Given the unusual circumstances — that the new Initiate would be the replacement for a mutually conjoined pair who had purposely vacated Council dimension — the Azoth Magen himself officiated. Though Saule was not present, Ravenea reported the events to her in detail. All had apparently progressed as usual with only three aspects of note. First, immediately after the completion of ritual, Obeche's nose had begun to bleed — for the first time in his life — which resulted in several drops of blood falling unceremoniously into the Albedo waters. Then Cedar, the newly appointed Senior Magistrate, had been chosen to make initial contact with the new Initiate. Finally, the crossing point — the moment at which Cedar and the new Initiate were predicted to cross paths — was to be at midnight that very night. According to Ravenea, Cedar had been rather shocked at the news, especially at the lack of preparation time. Ravenea had offered to accompany her, but Azoths Ailanthus and Kezia forbade such a move, suggesting that yet another breach of protocols could make an already awkward situation worse.

Not yet an Elder, Saule was neither invited nor required to be present to greet the Initiate upon arrival. Nonetheless, she was more than curious. Thus, she opted to wait, concealed, under the willow tree in the courtyard, curious to see precisely who had been deemed worthy to replace the irreplaceable. Frankly, Saule doubted anyone would be up to the task. How could only one nascent Initiate effectively replace two conjoined Scribes — two Scribes who could not be erased, thanks to the nature of their conjunction or their bloodline? Of course, rotation and initiation were ancient and, admittedly, logical rites of passage that had worked successfully for the Alchemists' Council for eons. However, this Initiate was different. This initiation, like Ilex and Melia themselves, was unprecedented. The newcomer would fill a spot that had occurred not through conjunction or erasure, but through a purposeful absence and forbidden blood-alchemy ritual — one abetted by Saule herself. Under such circumstances, how could Saule not be intrigued by the chosen one?

Thus, it came to be that Saule's first glimpse of the new Initiate was dappled, occurring as it did through the leaves of the willow tree. Moonlight bathed the courtyard. Saule heard her voice before seeing her. She was, Saule presumed, replying to a question: *Yes, Magistrate Cedar, I would be glad to do so.* When Cedar and the Initiate stepped into the light of the open courtyard within view of Saule's place of hiding, she fell forward slightly, causing the leaves to rustle. Cedar glanced towards the willow tree but then returned her gaze to the Initiate.

"This way, Sadira," Cedar instructed.

Saule knew this name: Sadira, the lotus tree. Her name was as beautiful as her long, gold-hued hair caught in the moonlight. Saule was wholly captivated. As Sadira and Cedar walked out of sight, Saule moved from behind the willow branches to the bench beside the Wishing Well to contemplate her future. If only she had a coin.

When Sadira stepped out into the main courtyard on her first morning in Council dimension, she wondered if she had been brought to hell. She had not thought to ask Cedar under the previous night's moonlight what to expect of the landscape at dawn. The sky, the grounds, even the trees in the distance appeared burnt orange — not the brilliant orange and pink and purple of the sunsets or sunrises she so adored in the world she had chosen to leave behind. Though no flames were visible, Sadira understood within moments that this world was on fire. How had she failed to notice the overpowering environment the night before? Perhaps the effect was visible only in the daylight hours. Perhaps, like all else here, the flaming skies were a consequence of the alchemy of Council dimension to which she gradually would have to acclimate. The air smelled acrid; a fine white dust clung to it, slowly descending to coat the pathways she had been instructed to use. *If you awake early, explore the grounds. You will not get lost if you stay on the paths.* These had been Cedar's words to her the night before. Sadira had indeed wakened early — too early, it appeared, since she had not encountered another soul between her chambers and this inferno.

Sadira took slow, tentative steps along the path directly in front of her; when she had progressed far enough along to necessitate a decision, she chose to veer left. Eventually, she reached the most sublime spectacle: a walled garden filled with trees whose trunks appeared covered in an ochre-coloured glass and whose leaves glistened through the layer of white dust. Wiping aside the dust from one of the leaves, she realized that the tree comprised amber, not glass. Admiring its beauty, Sadira attempted but failed to pick a leaf off the tree. It simply would not detach from its stem no matter her efforts. *Alchemy*, she presumed once again.

The first sign that she was not alone in this

burning and dazzling world came as a high-pitched cry. Though she saw no one in that moment, she did not need to wait much longer until various voices were calling out *Fire!* and *Awaken the Azoths!* Several robe-clad folks soon appeared within her range of vision, frantically moving across the court-yard and along the path. *Where is it? What is going on? How could this happen spontaneously?* Sadira abruptly realized that smoke and ash were not the usual state of affairs in Council dimension.

A bell began to toll. She could not fathom how the sound reverberated as loudly as it did. Many more people appeared in the courtyard thereafter, a man in dark green apparently taking a head count. Though the alchemists were dressed in robes, at least as many others donned liveries that she con-cluded marked their trade within this dimension. Observing those she assumed were cooks or kitchen workers, she had to wonder why none of their group had been awake as early as she had. Would they not have needed to be preparing food for the day? Perhaps the kitchen and residence for its staff were below ground. Perhaps she alone had wandered out-side to greet the dawn. She recognized a few faces in the crowd: Cedar, who had brought her into this world, and the Azoth Magen and the Elders, including Obeche, to whom she had been intro-duced by Cedar shortly after her late-night arrival.

"The Elder Council will proceed to Inner Chambers to commence the Ritual of Restoration!"

announced Azoth Magen Quercus. "All others will work together to ascertain the source of this elemental imbalance. Ravenea! Organize the alchemists into groups of four, elementally balanced where possible, to seek the source of the disturbance. Jinjing! Organize the workers to secure all Council buildings! The libraries and archives are priorities!"

Sadira, as a newcomer, assumed she would be instructed by an Elder to return to her residence chambers. But no one paid her any mind. Everyone was too focused on the emergency at hand. So Sadira concentrated fully on Ravenea's commands, not wanting to miss her own name being called for a grouping. But Ravenea did not call out names; instead she asked for division by element, calling out "earth, air, water, and fire" as she pointed to each of four locations in the courtyard. The alchemists divided accordingly and then reorganized themselves into groups of four — one alchemist for each of the four elements. Not knowing her element, Sadira simply stood still a short distance in front of Ravenea.

"Sadira!" Cedar called to her. "Join us!"

"I don't know my element."

"You are *water*," said Ravenea.

Do they expect me to extinguish the fire? Sadira thought to herself. Of course, she had no idea how to proceed with such a task. She merely followed Cedar and Obeche as they joined Ravenea to form their group of four.

"Well, Sadira," said Cedar, "there's nothing like

initiation by fire." Cedar and Ravenea smiled, but Sadira was too nervous to appreciate humour.

"Where shall we begin?" asked Cedar.

"I suggest we begin where others might forget to look," replied Obeche.

Sadira followed Ravenea, Cedar, and Obeche out of the courtyard and through the corridors to one of the few places in Council dimension she recognized: the portal chamber.

"The ash is thicker here," Sadira observed. Compared with the substantial layer of ash directly in front of the portal, the paths of her early morning sojourn had received a mere sprinkling of white dust.

"What if the protectorates—" began Cedar.

"No. A fire in a protectorate would not affect us here — not directly, not like this," replied Obeche. "But a fire in the apiary would."

Ravenea turned to him. "Yes."

"Most likely the lavender fields," said Obeche.

"No. The fire is in the ancient garden," said Ravenea. "In the wisteria tree."

"You seem certain," observed Obeche.

Ravenea said nothing, but her fear was visible in her eyes. Though Sadira knew little of her new world and its occupants, she knew enough about people to know that Ravenea knew something beyond what she was expressing.

"Cedar and I will go first," Obeche offered. "You two follow immediately behind."

Moments later, Ravenea reached out to hold

Sadira's hand. Together they stepped towards the portal as Ravenea recited a series of words and numbers that Sadira assumed were coordinates to the ancient garden.

Being transported to the garden was little better than the journey into Council dimension Sadira had experienced the night before. She felt pulled and swayed and, upon arrival, nauseated. The scene before them was one of devastation. Though Sadira would never know the beauty that had once greeted those who travelled here, she would never forget seeing what was left. The smoke and ash of Council dimension were minor complications in comparison with the scorched landscape she now witnessed. Everything — absolutely everything — that once had flourished was charred to the colour of coal. The grounds smouldered; occasional orange embers were visible amidst the blackness. The scorched remains of a tree — tangled, brittle branches — loomed against the white smoke sky. This, realized Sadira, must have been the wisteria tree.

"You must put it out," said Ravenea.

"Put it out?" echoed Sadira. "I don't understand."

"As you will come to appreciate gradually, Sadira, you are unique. All new Initiates—" began Ravenea.

"We do not have time to explain! We must extinguish the fire now!" demanded Obeche.

"No, Obeche. Only Sadira can extinguish this fire. And to do so, she must first understand. Like all Initiates, she must hear, must interpret, must absorb our stories. Otherwise, she will be unable to intuit what she alone must do," replied Ravenea.

Obeche responded with a taut expression, but he remained silent.

"All new Initiates," began Ravenea, "despite precautions undertaken in advance by the Elders to mitigate damage, cause a slight disturbance to the elemental balance of Council dimension. A few days, a week, occasionally a month of adjustment is generally required. The stronger the newcomer's elemental essence, the longer the period of adjustment. Usually, the resulting imbalances manifest in a general sense of unease for all members of the Council — headaches, anxiety, the occasional mental or physical stumble on the part of even the most experienced alchemists. When an alchemist permanently leaves Council dimension — either by conjunction or erasure or Final Ascension — the new Initiate takes a place amidst not only the one hundred and one alchemists but also the elements represented collectively. Over the course of the adjustment period, the elements alchemically rebalance: the presence of the new Initiate overcomes the absence of the one conjoined or erased or ascended. However, on this occasion — on the occasion that brought you to us — a place on Council opened for an unprecedented reason: an escape."

"An escape?" repeated Sadira. She was intrigued by this possibility. Perhaps she too could find a means to escape from this hellbound world.

"The escape in and of itself is only one of the unprecedented factors," continued Ravenea. "The other is more complex. The alchemists who escaped were mutually conjoined — two alchemists conjoined equally into one body. You will learn of the Sacrament of Conjunction in your Initiate classes, Sadira. For now, you need only understand that, in their conjoined form, these alchemists — Ilex and Melia — represented mutually balanced fire and water for sixteen years. The Elders announced last week that they have reason to suspect Ilex and Melia escaped Council dimension by way of a temporary portal alchemically created in the wisteria tree. Now, in light of the charred landscape before us, we can postulate that the sudden elemental loss — one not anticipated and, therefore, not mitigated in advance by the Elders — would be alleviated only by an equally strong, equally conjoined balance of fire and water in the new Initiate. Your element is purely water, Sadira. It appears your arrival was deemed a threat by Council dimension. Fire has risen up against you in response. Therefore, *you* must extinguish it."

"How?"

"Its place of ignition appears to be at the fissure left in the tree in the wake of Ilex and Melia's departure," observed Obeche. "You must walk across the embers and close the fissure."

"I cannot see a fissure."

"When you reach it, you will see it — gleaming

against the blackened remains of the tree," explained Ravenea.

"What am I to do when I see it? I am . . . new. I am not yet an alchemist."

"You are an alchemist, Sadira," Ravenea answered reassuringly. "Though untrained, you need not fear. Certain knowledge of alchemical truths is innate within alchemists, no matter their training, no matter their awareness of their differences. You would not have otherwise been brought here as an Initiate. As an alchemist, you will know instinctively what to do when you are required to do it."

Sadira stared at Ravenea, this woman she barely knew. Was she being led unceremoniously to her death? Yesterday morning, she had taken a leisurely walk along the riverbank. She had stopped in one of her favourite spots — a tiny inlet where the water remains virtually at a standstill, forming a pool under a tree at the edge of the park. She had stood for several minutes in that spot watching her reflection, contemplating the progress of her life and the possibilities for her future. She remembered wondering what would happen if she were to remain in that spot, standing still at the edge of that motionless pool, for the rest of her life. Perhaps she had already succumbed to death in that moment. Perhaps she had not, in fact, been intercepted last night by Cedar, not offered the possibility of hundreds of years of life within Council dimension, not handed a means to fulfill her destiny as an alchemist.

Perhaps she had not been instructed by a Council Scribe to extinguish a fire intent on her destruction. Perhaps she had indeed been vanquished to hell.

"You must help the Elders, Sadira. You must support the Ritual of Restoration," said Cedar quietly but insistently.

What choice did she have? Somehow she knew intuitively — alchemically, perhaps — that she must remove her shoes. Having done so, she took her first tentative step onto the ashes and embers, then another, and another. To her surprise and relief, the ground did not burn her. Instead, it sizzled under each foot as she progressed towards the remains of the tree. Her strides became broad and determined once she realized the fire would not — perhaps *could* not — physically harm her. *I am water.* She looked back on occasion, saw the alchemists watching her. She could hear Obeche chanting, intoning words that she did not understand.

When she reached the tree, she raised a hand to a large branch, steadying herself as she stepped over an area of tangled, scorched, and presumably fragile remains, and she saw not only the light of the fissure but something far more unsettling. Small, singed, winged insects — hundreds, it appeared, in varying degrees of distress — struggled in jagged movements along the surface of one of the larger branches. *Bees*, she suddenly realized. Here were the remaining inhabitants of the garden. Like her — the invading stranger — their goal was to reach the light of the fissure. She watched the few who made it, those who had managed the journey and lurched themselves into the abyss. If only she too could fit through the small aperture of light.

"Now!" she heard Ravenea call out to her. "Close it now!"

Of course, she could not escape. She could not save the remaining bees. She could do nothing other than reach her fingers to the fissure and extinguish the source of devastation. Ravenea had been right. Sadira did know what to do when the time arrived. And the fissure responded accordingly — its light fading into darkness, its opening searing itself shut. The bees continued to writhe. The few who had been nearest to the fissure before Sadira's interference fell onto their backs, their tiny legs thrashing about in a futile attempt to right themselves. Sadira could not stand to witness this agony. She picked up a fallen piece of branch — charred but solid — from the ground and began a task she assumed merciful at the time but that would haunt her through her first few years on the Council. She smashed them, each of them, all of them — first in groups and then, where necessary, one by one. She struck again and again and again — her blows ringing out across the desolate landscape — until every one of the bees in her sight had been put out of its misery. Then she turned and walked back to the alchemists awaiting her.

Juniper season had begun. Of course, Melia remained unaffected, her immune system having been
enhanced for many years through Quintessence
in Council dimension and made all but imperme-
able because of her conjunction with Ilex and her
encounter with the bees. Whereas her neighbours
complained of scarcely being able to catch a breath
in the pollen-drenched air, Melia wandered for hours
through and beyond the borders of Santa Fe inhaling
spring fragrances. She would run her hands across
the foliage of all the trees and bushes within her
reach, attempting to transfer their scent to her own
body — to her hair and neck and arms. Her sense
of smell heightened by the pregnancy, these walks
enlivened her, comforted her, and thus helped her to
deal with the inevitable pain of the contractions she
had been suffering through the still-cold nights and
into the brilliant light of early morning.

For weeks now, the child within her had seemed
ready to be born, as if screaming through Melia's
body. Yes, the conjoined body she shared with Ilex
was indeed hers alone for now. One month ago, after
more than a year of pregnancy, Ilex had retreated
completely. *A temporary side effect*, Saule had assured
her when Melia realized that Ilex was no longer
accessible at all. *Or a permanent transmutation*,
Melia had responded. For what could either of
them know about this process since both mutual

conjunction and pregnancy were unprecedented among alchemists of the Alchemists' Council. Not a single manuscript in Council dimension offered up assistance. They — Melia and Saule — could only guess; they could only dream; they could only hope that the dreams they had woven through the winter did not turn to a nightmare in the spring.

Melia sat in a rocking chair staring out at a juniper tree, a silhouette against the backdrop of the evening sun.

"Did you know," Saule said to Melia, "that most junipers are dioecious?"

Saule stood on the other side of the room pouring tea into the delicate china cups Melia had obtained only last week on one of her walks.

"They are what?"

"Dioecious: individual juniper trees are considered either male or female — the male and female reproductive parts exist on separate trees. They are analogous to people in that sense." Saule smiled as she handed Melia a cup of tea. "To most people."

"Yes — most people, but not like Ilex and me. Ilex and I, we are . . . unnatural."

"No. You are *super*natural. You are sacred. You personify the original state of being."

"Existing in an original state of being can leave one excruciatingly lonely."

Saule nodded, though Melia perceived that she could not fully understand.

"And what of this child?" Melia asked. "Will my

body — a sacred vessel or not — be physically capable of bearing this child into existence? Or will the child be carried only as a part of me into eternity — like the fragment of the Lapis in my pendant? Perhaps the outside world alchemists were correct when they depicted conjunction in their iconography as a stage in the creation of the Philosopher's Stone."

Saule, having been close to tears in her empathy for Melia's agony, smiled then in amusement. "What are you suggesting, Melia — that your immaculate conception is about to produce a messiah? Imagine the Council's reaction to that scenario!"

They laughed until Melia's joy was suddenly pierced by the pain of that evening's contractions. "You should go," she said to Saule. "You need to return to Council dimension before you are missed. There is nothing more you can do for me now."

"As far as the Council is concerned, I am conducting research in the outside world for three days," Saule replied. "Besides, I can't leave you tonight since there is, in fact, something I can do for you now."

Another contraction prevented Melia from responding.

"I've discovered something else about juniper trees," Saule announced.

"I am in no mood for another botany lesson."

"A few weeks ago," Saule continued, ignoring Melia's retort, "I learned that ingesting juniper berries can cause uterine contractions. I reasoned that a distilled and potent elixir made from juniper berries and combined with Lapidarian essence could induce labour."

"You reasoned?"

"I made an educated guess supplemented by advice from a few Council manuscripts and a botany text from the outside world. I am an alchemist, if you recall."

Melia smiled despite her pain. "Did you bring it — this juniper elixir?"

"Yes."

"May I have it?"

"Yes."

"Why did you wait until now to tell me? You should have served it with the tea."

"The thought had occurred to me. But I also reasoned that the elixir would be more effective if taken when the evening's contractions were already well underway."

"Please, Saule, your reasoning is becoming as painful to bear as the contractions."

"The elixir will increase, not decrease, the pain."

"But then it will end. Finally, it will end. I can persevere if I know there will be an end."

Saule retrieved a small vial from her satchel and poured its contents into one of the tea cups. Melia consumed the contents within seconds. And then they waited.

They waited and waited. For the next six hours, Saule remained at Melia's side. The contractions continued with no increase in intensity from those Melia had been experiencing each night over the last several weeks. But, as the first light of dawn filtered through the window, Melia felt a shift occur.

"It's time," she said. "It's time. Take me outside."

"Outside?"

"You were right earlier. This child is sacred — the progeny of Ilex and Melia, of holly and mahogany conjoined. It must be birthed outside, witnessed by the trees."

And so it was that on that morning, more than a year after Ilex and Melia had fled from Council dimension, their child was born to Melia, pulled from her body by Saule's strong hands in the cold spring air of a Santa Fe dawn. The child cried, and Melia held her close.

"What is her name?" asked Ilex.

He had returned. Saule had been right again: Ilex's regression had indeed been temporary.

Melia cried then. She cried for her child. She cried for her conjoined partner. She cried for the woman who had sworn to help them all and had followed through. She cried and cried. And her tears of joy fell onto the ground under the tree that had borne witness to the miracle.

"Our child will be named for the tree that gave me salvation." She held her baby girl up towards the bows of the juniper. "Her name," Melia proclaimed, "is Genevre."

IV
Council Dimension — Spring 1914

Since the birth, almost a century ago, Saule had been awaiting a sign of Genevre's existence in a Council manuscript. Mercifully, she herself had spotted the first known reference. A week ago, Azoth Ailanthus had requested a Lapidarian Scribe to assist with ritual transcription. *Each day we move closer to our goal*, Ailanthus had said. *Now we are here. Centuries of work have brought us to this moment.* He pointed to an open manuscript featuring a small illumination: two emerald green coniferous trees atop a red and blue sphere; forming a circle around the image were the tree names *Cedrus deodara* and *Juniperus osteosperma*.

Cedar and *Juniperus*? *Juniper. Genevre!* Saule, shocked, backed away from the manuscript too quickly to escape Ailanthus's attention.

"I too was surprised," he said. "So simple, yet it eluded us for centuries. *Centuries!* Imagine the Azoth Magen's reaction upon yesterday's revelation!"

"What? What eluded you?"

"The chant! Look! Behold the words required to invoke quintessential balance in the Oils of Annointment! Finally, with Azoth Magen Quercus at the helm, the Council can once again attempt elimination of the Flaw."

Saule glanced again at the manuscript. She saw then what Ailanthus had meant for her to see. He had been pointing not to the illumination but to the inscription on the adjacent folio. Here resided a lengthy incantation comprising both the words and gestures required for the 17th Council to animate the oils with which they would anoint the Lapis. Each Council required a unique chant — one whose specifics were purposely inscribed to remain hidden until triggered for awakening. Saule glanced again at the illumination and wondered what or who the catalyst for revelation had been. Had Genevre somehow enlivened this manuscript? Had Cedar?

Saule spent the remainder of that afternoon repeatedly transcribing the chant onto parchment scrolls. Each member of the Council, including her, would need to rehearse both the words and the movements. As she worked, Saule recalled an Initiate lesson Ravenea had taught her centuries earlier. *Water, earth, air, fire; ink, parchment, voice, dance; with body and breath do alchemists transmute the elements; with body and breath do alchemists transform the world.* What was to become of this world now? With each replication of the chant onto parchment, Saule's anxiety increased. The Azoth Magen was about to lead a ritual whose purpose was to remove the Flaw in the Stone. If he were to succeed, how would the paths of Genevre and Cedar ever cross? With ink-stained hands, her current task complete, Saule sought Ravenea, attained a portal key, and made her way to the cliff face.

Council Dimension — Summer 1914

Thus drop the Sulphur! Thus rise the Mercury! Thus bind the Salt! Black, red, and white lines of powder lay strewn atop the Lapis. Azoths Ailanthus and Kezia were responsible for the black and red respectively — onyx and cinnabar, grated earlier with ritual precision by the Rowans using lathes of Lapidarian-infused tungsten. Azoth Magen Quercus himself had laid the precious salts — white diamond and opal, ground painstakingly by the twelve Lapidarian Scribes in a titanium mortar and pestle. The powders lay dormant until the Novillian Scribes performed the sacred gestures and words that enlivened them — dust to dust, earth to earth, air to air. Once suspended above the Lapis, the chants of the Readers animated the particles of powder. They vibrated intensely until, as if by spontaneous combustion, they burst into flames. Finally, they transmuted into a fragrant mist that fell back onto the Lapis like a gentle rain.

Sadira stood transfixed. Though she had been with the Council for almost a century, observing the Elders perform a ritual for the first time inevitably captivated her attention. On so many occasions over the years, even as she had moved through the Council Orders into the Magistrate, she had felt like a Junior Initiate first witnessing alchemical transmutation. Today was such an occasion. Always Sadira yearned to participate in the complex alchemy of the higher orders. Always she longed to discover the yet undiscovered. Even as an Initiate seeking escape, Sadira had become obsessed with learning everything she could about the complex maze of Council dimension tunnels. Of course, her primary duty over the decades had been to observe, to study, and, more recently, to teach. At rituals, she would chant and gesture and resonate, all in aid of those of the higher orders, those performing the intricacies at hand. Not since her first morning in Council dimension had she made what she considered to be a pivotal contribution — not since she had extinguished the fire left in the wake of Ilex and Melia. On many a day since, she had felt rather useless, necessary only as an instrument for the Elders, biding her time to play a more demanding role. Today, at least, her assigned task was critical.

Today, every single alchemist of the Alchemists' Council was necessary to the proceedings. All one hundred and one were required. Those in the protectorates had been called back home, even as the outside world began to wage its battles. Today, Azoth Magen Quercus and all the Council Orders from Azoths to Junior Initiates had been assigned a role. If even one alchemist were missing, if even one task were neglected during the ritual, all could be lost. Yes, the Azoth Magen could order the Council to begin the ritual again. But a mistake made once could be a mistake made repeatedly, and alchemical fatigue would thereafter set in. Another century or more could pass before the Azoth Magen would regain the strength to try again. Thus, as the Elders had made clear on each of the fifty-five days of preparation leading to this day, nothing less than perfection would be accepted. Every single alchemist, including Sadira, had been made to rehearse until no doubt — no room for error — remained.

For three days, the skies will darken! For three days, we will call back the light! In the final hour of the third day, the grace of Final Ascension will descend upon us!

Such was the chant that the Azoths had uttered in 8th Council dialect on the first day. Such was the chant that had echoed through the halls and chambers, that had moved over the lands from the courtyard to catacombs to the redwood forest on each day since the first. And now, here they were — here Sadira was — on the fifty-fifth day. Five and five: a symbolic conjunction of Quintessence. Yes, the outside world had suffered dire consequences from the moment the chant had first been uttered. Yes, the Vulknut Eclipse would be such a powerful alchemical phenomenon that its overwhelming effects would bleed through the dimensions on the first of its three days. The Council had timed the *Remota Macula* — the Removal of the Flaw — accordingly. Where its effects would be visible in the outside world, the people would presume a natural phenomenon, as they always did with so many matters of alchemical interference. But their eclipse would not portend the auspicious time the people of the outside world anticipated. No, the world would suffer immeasurably during the periods of both literal and figurative darkness. For three days after the five and five, the Council would be engaged with preparations for Final Ascension. The outside world and its wars were of little consequence, despite Council vows. All would be justified at the end — at the *ultimate* ascension. All would be well. *All* would be saved in the One.

Sadira had to believe this promise. What did she have otherwise? What value was her life — what value had her life been over the years, especially in its currently extended form — if it were simply to end three days from now? Admittedly, doubt niggled her on the occasions that her defences were down and fear overshadowed her reason. *What if the One failed to materialize? What if the One was as much of a myth as Aralia and Osmanthus? Or what if the One had been severed forever along with the Aralians and the Osmanthians? What if Sadira was about to die alongside her fellow alchemists? What if the people of the outside world were suddenly left without the Council?* Thankfully, such moments of concern were not only infrequent but brief, easily resolved with a simple shift of perspective. All Sadira needed to do was search the faces of her fellow Council members for a reassuring glance. The Elders radiated serenity even amidst the monotony of the endless rehearsals for the ritual.

As instructed, Sadira attempted to empty her mind, sitting in contemplation of the Lapis for the hour before the *Remota Macula*. The difficulty of one's assigned task was relative to one's Order of Council, with the Scribes being the exception. Scribes were required merely to stand as witnesses to the proceedings. All others were given words to recite. Accordingly, Sadira's words and gestures were more difficult than those of the Initiates but less difficult than those of the Readers. The Order of the Ritual was also performed relative to the Council Orders, thus beginning and ending with the Azoth Magen. Though the opening of the ceremony was straightforward, the closing was extraordinarily complex — half an hour of tongue-twisting chants to be performed solely by Azoth Magen Quercus. With each rehearsal, Sadira came to admire Quercus more and more. During the *Remota Macula* itself, within five minutes of Quercus's chant, Sadira found herself tearing up. Her ritual performance over, her tears could not affect the outcome, but she had to will herself not to sob audibly. How could she accept that mere days from now, if the Lapis absorbed the Gift of the Magen, Azoth Magen Quercus would literally dissolve into dust?

fflaw Dimension — Summer 1914

Eight months had passed since Dracaen had confessed the truth to Kalina. Though she had gradually come to accept the reality of her alchemical origins, she continued to question her existence. Her image, reflected back to her from the cavern pools, was as misleading as she felt her body to be — an illusion temporarily revealed by a trick of the light and the elements. The time had finally come. No more delays. No more excuses. She needed to leave Flaw dimension. She needed to take time to process outside Dracaen's realm of influence. She needed to consider the ethics of creating — manufacturing — a child of the cause, to reach a decision about her role in his plan. She wanted to find Genevre and tell her what she knew: that Dracaen had lied to them both. Though she understood that his intention had been to protect her — to protect both mother and child — she could not reconcile

Dracaen's apparently selfless gesture with his concealment of truth over the decades.

Which of his roles was his true self: the saviour or the liar? He had protected her. If Dracaen had not brought her into the relative safety of the Rebel Branch, the Alchemists' Council may have found her and claimed her as their own. But would the Council have harmed an alchemical child? Perhaps they would have dissolved her into the elemental particles from which she had been born. Ultimately, Council sought to deny free will; Kalina existed as the ultimate expression thereof, as the physical manifestation of the choice to transmute the elements into a human being, into life itself. In that sense, Kalina was the Flaw incarnate. Would the Council not seek to eliminate her along with the fissure that made her conception possible? Or perhaps the rebels had painted the alchemists as the life-threatening enemy only as a means of training her to fear the other. She no longer knew what to believe.

Thus Kalina had resolved to seek out Genevre, to get to know her, to learn of the role she had played in her creation, to confront her, to ask her if the freedom to choose included the freedom to act as gods. *There are no gods*, Dracaen used to say to her, *only beings who invent gods*.

Why? she had asked him once. She had never forgotten his answer: *To explain their lack of choice in their world.* She did not know whether inventing a god was better or worse than acting as one. She did not know whether engineering a child in an alchemical vessel was better or worse than procreating one in a womb. Either way, what choice did the created being have in the act of its own creation? No choice at all. What then did the Flaw in the Stone offer? Perhaps free will itself was a mere illusion to those whose choices were made amidst lies — lies masked as truths fabricated in the name of an ideal realized only by the chosen few. Her anger at Dracaen simmered as she reached her decision to leave Flaw dimension to seek out Genevre. She recognized her hypocrisy. How could she be angry with Dracaen and yet accept Genevre as her — the word still felt foreign to Kalina — *mother*?

As she walked through the corridors towards the portal, unwavering in her intention to depart, Kalina silently rehearsed phrases she might soon utter aloud: *I know who you are to me. I know you are my mother. I know I am your daughter. I need an answer to one question: Why did you abandon me?*

"Do not—" Dracaen began when he spotted her.

If he said another word, Kalina did not hear it — a thundering crack suddenly resounded through Flaw dimension. She could hear nothing at all in the immediate aftermath of the disturbance. Neither could she see beyond the thick mists, now churning and billowing like dust clouds in a desert storm. She could barely breathe. She fell to her knees winded, fearing for her life. And then, nothing: no sounds, no sights, no mists, no movement of air or dust. Even the wooden chimes were silenced. She shook her head to reorient herself. She rose to her feet and stared at Dracaen. He appeared stunned, unable to move.

"What happened?" she asked.

And then the shriek: Thuja, screaming in one, long continual note, a siren wailing through Flaw dimension.

Dracaen came back to life, turned, and moved swiftly towards Thuja's cry. By the time he and Kalina reached the Dragonblood chamber, Thuja stood silent, amidst dozens of rebels who had answered her cry. Kalina blinked — something was wrong, but she could not process the altered reality; her brain could not quite catch up to her eyesight.

And then the shock: beyond the gathered rebels, in front of Thuja, behind the wrought-iron barrier lay absolutely nothing. The Alchemists' Council had finally succeeded. At last the Aralians had won the Crystalline Wars. They had removed the Flaw in the Stone.

Sundsvall — Summer 1914

Jinjing sat at a small table running a finger over a section of gold leaf in an illumination of a glorious peacock — its plumage inscribed in jewel tones and precious metals. The texture beneath her fingertip brought her comfort. So did the very fact of the text: its illicitness in particular. For all intents and purposes, she had stolen the manuscript. As Keeper of the Book of both the North Library and the Qingdao protectorate, her manuscript privileges were extensive, but she certainly was not permitted to remove one — no matter how small — from Council dimension without permission. Temporary relocation of a manuscript to a protectorate was permissible on occasion; she had herself once transported two volumes of the *Rosarium Philosophorum* for Azoth Ailanthus to the Vienna protectorate. However, she knew that a request to bring a manuscript to this isolated location would have been denied. So, she had hidden it under the folds of her coat before meeting Obeche in the portal chamber. If Jinjing were fated never to return to Council dimension, she would keep a piece of it with her. At the height of the five and five, Council would not miss a single volume amidst thousands. Besides, she rationalized, no alchemist would require a manuscript after ultimate Final Ascension since no alchemist would exist outside the One. And if those who resided in the outside world were not, despite Council assurances, likewise absorbed into the One, then Jinjing wanted physical proof of the alternate world she had once called home.

Obeche had volunteered as the Elder to accompany Jinjing to the Swedish outpost and ensure that she was safely ensconced. That was a week ago. She had not heard from him since. His habit of abandoning her had unnerved her. He had promised her that they would see each other again once they co-existed within the One. But that assurance had not prevented her from holding out hope for a final exchange in the outside world as two individuals. She should have known better. After all, she knew this to be the final week of preparation of the *Remota Macula*. Removing the Flaw had been Obeche's obsession for so long that in all likelihood he had not given her a second thought since leaving her here. Like the manuscript, her absence would not be noticed. She no longer mattered to him or to the Council. She closed the tiny, ornate cover of the *Tinctura Universalis* and peered out the window, debating whether to venture out to the bakery down the street. What would the local people of this outside world town think of her, such an obvious foreigner? *Where are you from?* she imagined someone asking. *Another dimension that you could not possibly understand*, she imagined herself answering. *You would not even understand the words I speak to you now without the benefit of Lapis-induced* Musurgia Universalis. She imagined her anger turned to bravery in what might be the final days of her existence. But she then opted not to be lured by her desire for Swedish pastries.

Why could the Council not let the Lapis be, leave it untouched, Flaw intact? She had tried to understand the explanation of the sacrament over the years, but she was never able to fully appreciate it. In all honesty, she did not care. For most of her tenure with Council, she had no reason to believe the *Remota Macula* would ever take place. The ritual had reportedly been attempted on occasion over the centuries, but it had never succeeded. Council records of such attempts included detailed rationale for failures. The aftermath of each attempt meant a redoubled effort at rebalancing the elements both of Council dimension and the outside world. Azoth Ailanthus once told her that Council neglect during an attempt at *Remota Macula* had been responsible for the Mongol Conquests. Jinjing had doubted the veracity of the claim until a few weeks ago. The reports of the outside world conflicts since the Calling of the Chant terrified her; she now feared what would happen if the 17th Council failed. Would millions die once again in the pursuit of an unattainable goal? Of course, Jinjing understood that the Council could not stop *now* — not now that they had started, not now that they had neglected the outside world just long enough for it to have begun its descent into a corruptive and destructive abyss. Now the Council *must* make the attempt — not for the sake of One, but for the sake of all.

Yet if the Elders truly had faith — full confidence that the *Remota Macula* would succeed — why had they stationed her at the outpost? Her duty after the five and five was to observe and transcribe the effects over the three days of the Vulknut Eclipse. She must do so from a vantage point that coincided with the outside world's solar eclipse and note Lapidarian effects, to determine whether or not the Vulknut Eclipse even occurred as a phenomenon in the outside world. She had been furnished with spectacles that would allow her to look directly at the sun without being blinded. The lenses had been crafted from crystals mined from the deepest wells and coated with alchemically enhanced Elixir. Jinjing herself had been given a concentrated dose of Lapidarian honey as a precautionary measure against retinal damage. If she was worried how the townsfolk would react to her request for a pastry, she could barely fathom what they would think of her later today: a spectacle-laden foreigner standing in the middle of the town square staring up at the blood-blackened sun.

Council Dimension — Summer 1914

Saule watched the Azoth Magen's face as he moved his hand over the smooth surface of the Lapis. He walked slowly around its entirety, bending and stretching to adjust the angle of his vision. Though the light in the room had diminished, it remained sufficient for assessment.

"What say you?" Quercus asked the Azoths.

As slowly as Quercus had done, both Ailanthus and Kezia made their inspections.

"What say you?" Ailanthus asked the remaining Elders, who one by one walked the circumference of the Lapis.

When the final Elder — Novillian Scribe Esche — had made his inspection, he nodded his agreement to Rowan Kai, who nodded her agreement on behalf of all four Novillians to the Rowan Badara, who nodded his agreement on behalf of both Rowans to Azoth Ailanthus.

"I concur," said Ailanthus.

"I concur," said Kezia.

Together, gripped with anticipation, they all waited — the newest Initiate to the eldest Elder — to hear the pronouncement of the Azoth Magen. Quercus shook visibly as he held the Azothian sceptre aloft.

"The Lapis is perfected. So say we all!" said Quercus.

"So say we all!" echoed the entire Council, and a cheer resounded.

Saule shuddered. Sadira reached for her in response, clasping Saule's arm in eagerness. But Saule knew that neither Sadira nor anyone else who had noticed her trembling fully understood the extent of her alarm. Azoth Magen Quercus, Azoths Ailanthus and Kezia, Scribes Ruis, Obeche, and even Ravenea — everyone whom she could see from her position in the Scriptorium, everyone whom she had known for decades upon decades — appeared content. If they were trembling, they were doing so out of exhilaration.

For the Alchemists' Council, their sacred goal had been met. *The goal* had been met by *this* Council on *this* day. And Saule had borne witness.

The transmutation had already commenced. The sky, visible through the east window, had begun to darken. The Vulknut Eclipse was underway. Would perfection for all in the One follow in its wake? Or would the eclipse drape the outside world in metaphorical darkness for years to come — years during which the Council would be distracted with recovery from failure? They would not conclude that ultimate Final Ascension had been a mythical construct. They would instead be motivated to rationalize its failure. Instead of maintaining elemental balance, they would spend their time placing the blame on the rebels, on the traitors, on the unfaithful, or on the unorthodox. And in the process, they could well discover that one pesky discrepancy in the complex interplay of alchemy, bloodlines, and deception — the role she had played in helping Ilex and Melia to conceive a child and escape on the wings of a bee.

Ilex and Melia rested against the trunk of a large tree to catch their breath. They had walked as quickly as possible on their uphill journey. They preferred to travel in the moonlit calm of the early hours, visible only to those they chose to encounter. On this occasion, they had seen no one on the road, let alone in the forest. To attain the best possible view of the sky, they were headed to a clearing at the top of the hill.

"Clouds may impede our vision," reasoned Ilex.

"Perhaps," replied Melia. "Nonetheless, let's proceed."

Other than the occasional interjection for a misstep or choice of direction, the two did not converse over the remainder of the walk. They reached their destination within the hour. Together they began to assemble the equipment — Ilex manoeuvring their left arm, Melia their right. The pair had become so fluid in their bodily movements over the years that little need for discussion or instruction was required even when engaged in complex physical tasks.

"Clouds or no, I doubt we will detect anything at all. We would need to be on the other side of the world to witness even the slightest Lapidarian effect."

"Saule requested we make our observations here."

"To what end?" Ilex asked, clearly frustrated.

"You would deny her request after all she has done for us?"

"Of course not. I am merely questioning her choice of location."

"To what end?" Melia asked, and their conversation ceased.

The equipment ready, crystalline lenses in place, they waited. On occasion, Melia would hold their pendant up to the sky to ascertain the time. Ilex remained still, drifting into the shadows to sleep at one point. Melia considered waking him up, insisting that he remain alert, but she decided to let him rest. If the Vulknut Eclipse did manifest, these could be the last peaceful moments she had to herself. For, as much as she loved Ilex, she often craved significantly more time alone.

The sound reached her before the sight. She did not hear it with her ears; she perceived it — a low hum vibrating within her. She could not pinpoint its source. The noise simply overcame her. She repositioned herself at the telescope, its wooden frame and crystalline lenses assembled and sturdy against the dust-encrusted rock. She scanned the horizon, the trees barely distinguishable from the sky. She saw nothing but muted tones of grey against black, the occasional ray of moonlight. Then it happened. The humming ceased. The sizzling and crackling began. She felt Ilex suddenly return to consciousness, alert, uneasy. He tried to lift their hands to their ears, but Melia knew such a move to be pointless, so she tightened their grip on the telescope.

They both saw the luminescence at once: a blue-green tinge spreading across the sky like a dye dispersing in water. Invisible to the naked eye, the colours were clearly perceptible through the alchemical lenses. They could signify only one event: the *Remota Macula* had succeeded.

"Three days," whispered Melia. "Three days until the end of the world."

"Three days to live!" said Ilex, with an enthusiasm Melia failed to comprehend. "We are free!" Did he wish to be free of her? No, that was not where his thoughts were headed. "We no longer need to hide ourselves away from the Council," he continued. "Where shall we go? What shall we do to celebrate?" He exhibited more vigour in these few moments than she had experienced in him for the last several years. She felt him stir with arousal. Abruptly, she centred both of them into *her* body, its potential for excitement currently dormant.

"I feel no desire to celebrate, Ilex."

"Hold faith in the One, my love. All will be well."

"No, Ilex. You misunderstand. I have not lost faith in the One. I have come to fear it."

Ilex breathed, calming himself in an attempt to intuit her meaning before offering solace. "Melia, we have nothing to fear."

"Not a single member of the Alchemists' Council truly understands what it means to be *one* with another," said Melia. "You know as well as I — indeed, you are the *only* one who knows as well as I — that mutual conjunction is both difficult and complicated. Yes, we both survived the conjunction. Yes, neither of us has known the loss of the other. But at what cost, Ilex? At what cost?"

"Melia! You and I and Genevre—"

Melia lunged backward and swung around in a futile attempt to confront Ilex.

"Do not include Genevre!"

"But if ascension to the One were to occur, we three could—" began Ilex, but Melia cut him off again. She had always been able to dominate their body — all of it, even the mouth and tongue and vocal cords — when her anger flared. She literally stopped him from being able to continue his words. He had learned long ago that resistance was futile.

"Ilex, you have shared my scars. You have embraced me when I had nothing left to embrace. We have become masters of an intricate dance that we learned, step by step, day by day. We are two beings within one body. Imagine if we were three? Imagine if our child had become one with us — literally *one* — from the moment of conception."

Melia paused. She waited for him to respond, but he did not speak.

"Now imagine four and then five and then a dozen, a hundred, a thousand. Imagine hundreds of thousands upon thousands of thousands of thousands. Imagine *all* as One. And then tell me again that we have nothing to fear."

Council Dimension — Summer 1914

Cedar had never known Ruis to appear so gratified. When the Azoths had completed their declarations, Ruis audibly cheered. He pulled Cedar to him, pressing himself against her.

"We will reconvene in three hours," announced Quercus.

"'My love is as a fever, longing still,'" Ruis whispered to Cedar.

He did not wait for her to reply, for her to pull from memory a Shakespearean response. Instead he swept her along, almost running through the corridors to his chambers. Others too appeared to be following suit. She wondered vaguely whether the Azoth Magen had someone to accompany him to his chambers. Even as she lay with Ruis, savouring what could be their last physically intimate hours together, her mind wandered away from Ruis's touch and urgency to Council concerns. The success of the *Remota Macula* astounded her. If all continued to go as the Azoths intended, only three days remained until the ultimate Final Ascension. Only three days remained. Three days. As much as she loved Ruis, as much as she had enjoyed their sexual intimacy over the years, she could not abandon her trepidation about the future to remain fully in the present with him now. Instead she automatically moved her body in rhythm with his, concentrating not on insuring their mutual gratification — he seemed to be doing just fine on his own — but on her fellow alchemists, both those she had once known and those she would soon know no longer. Thus, it happened that just as Ruis collapsed in exhausted pleasure she was remembering the day Sadira had extinguished the fire in the ancient apiary. She felt mildly guilty for dividing her attentions until Ruis, having recovered his breath, reminded her they would soon be together as One for eternity. Then she cried.

"Do not cry, my love!" Ruis pleaded, embracing her. "Our ascension into One is the Sacrament of Sacraments! Embrace this ideal, Cedar! Imagine what awaits us once we have ascended, once we have returned to our Origin. Imagine existing in the originary state before division, before creation, before *difference* prevailed. We will no longer be mere alchemists battling for a position in the fray, tinkering with the elemental balance of the created world. We will no longer be bound by creation because we will *be* the Creator! We will no longer fear our end because we will *be* the beginning! We will no longer require ink to inscribe our texts because we will *be* the Word!"

"I am not you," whispered Cedar.

He did not respond because he did not hear her. He released his embrace, turned away, and fell into his dreams.

Council Dimension — Summer 1914

With the entire Alchemists' Council otherwise occupied, Saule slipped away unnoticed to the cliff face. Her walk along the forest path confirmed what she had sensed earlier but been unable to articulate: Council dimension had ceased to breathe.

From the moment she had first stepped into this landscape years ago, she could feel its vibrancy, the alchemical pulse evident just under the surface. She could watch it in the breeze rocking the cedar boughs, she could touch it in the trickling stream of the channel waters, she could hear it in the tinkling reverberation of the trees in the Amber Garden, she could taste it in the sweet golden honeycomb of the apiary, she could bathe in its fragrant scent as she lay in the lavender fields. Now only the *fact* of the dimension remained. She walked along a path through the redwood forest, but instead of vitality she sensed only lethargy. How much longer until Saule herself became stagnant?

By the time she reached the cliff face, Saule knew with certainty that she had nothing left to lose. She pressed both hands against the rock, recited the key she had been given for the contingency plan, and, after a few minutes of unnerving nausea, she emerged into yet another forest. Only this one was bathed in moonlight, and she was no longer alone.

"Melia! Ilex!" Saule called as she stepped forward to embrace them.

"My dear," said Melia. "As much as I longed to see you again, I hoped this particular meeting would never occur."

"We needn't despair. You two exist at the point

of conjunction — of alchemists and rebels, of one and the other, of all three dimensions. You can choose to help me while choice remains an option, while the residual effects of the Flaw still linger. Together we may be able to stop Final Ascension, to resist the One."

"But what of the people — the people here, the people around the world — who are to be saved in the One along with the Council?" protested Ilex.

"The Council has all but abandoned its charges, all but forsaken its vow to maintain elemental balance," replied Saule. "The people of the outside world will suffer inexorably for the three days of the Vulknut Eclipse. And if ultimate Final Ascension occurs, all of us — alchemists, rebels, and people alike — will be annihilated. I cannot abide such destruction."

"No, Saule. We will all be *saved* in the One," said Ilex.

"And if the One is mere myth, if the One ended eternally with the Crystalline Wars, then the Flaw dimension will cease to exist, Council dimension will stagnate, and the outside world will be mired in the chaos, unbalanced and unstable forever. If you truly hope to save the people of the world tonight — *all* its people — then you need to listen to me."

Ilex lowered his eyes.

"What do you want us to do?" asked Melia.

"Take me to the High Azoth of the Rebel Branch."

"Take you to Dracaen? Saule, you risk erasure!" exclaimed Melia.

"Erasure! What is erasure compared with complete annihilation? If you take me to the High Azoth, I can offer my assistance to the Rebel Branch, help them to breach Council dimension. Together we can work to restore the Flaw in the Stone. Together we can return to the balance that has sustained all dimensions for generations."

"I want to help, Saule."

"As do I," added Ilex.

"But we cannot take you to Dracaen. We have no means to open a portal to Flaw dimension even if we knew how to locate one," explained Melia.

Saule could not respond. Ilex and Melia were her last hope. She had been certain they would be able to help her, that they would have maintained contact with the rebels.

"Unless—" began Melia.

"Unless what?" asked Saule, hope rising in her once again. She watched them carefully. She could tell that Melia wanted to speak, but Ilex was attempting to hold their mouth shut.

"Ilex! You just told me you wanted to help. Please keep your word," begged Saule.

"A . . . contact," said Melia. "An hour's walk from here—"

"No!" Ilex interrupted.

"Ilex! She is our remaining link to the Rebel Branch. Consider what I said to you earlier tonight. Consider the repercussions."

"We do not even know if she is still—"

"I know, Ilex. I know where she lives."

"Who?" asked Saule.

"An outside world scribe," said Melia. "Years ago, Dracaen requested we train her. We worked with her for almost forty years alongside Dracaen, teaching her all that we recalled from our days as Council Scribes. She may still be in contact with him."

"We don't know whether she's in contact or not," said Ilex. "We've not spoken with her for months."

"Why not?"

"Last year we learned of a decision she and Dracaen made together without our approval," explained Melia, her resentment clear. "We vehemently disapproved. Their choice and its repercussions created additional risk for us."

"And for them," added Ilex.

"But current circumstances necessitate taking the risk," said Melia. "Who other than us would care to look for her now? The Vulknut Eclipse has provided virtual certainty that no one from the Alchemists' Council will be searching for any of us."

"Let's go then!" urged Saule.

Within minutes, they had emerged from the forest. Within the hour, they had arrived at a small adobe structure with a quaint courtyard visible in the moonlight. Saule was surprised to see an indoor light suddenly brighten the window as they stepped onto the walkway. Moments later, she heard the door being unlatched. They had no need to knock. Perhaps outside world scribes had more intuition or alchemical abilities than Saule realized. A woman ushered them into a spacious central room with eclectic furnishings.

Ilex and Melia hugged the woman. When she stepped back from them, she shook her head and sighed. "I've missed you," she said.

"Saule," said Ilex. "Allow me to introduce you. This is Genevre. Genevre, this is Saule, Lapidarian Scribe of the Alchemists' Council."

At first, Saule merely smiled politely and extended her hand. But something pulled at her — something that she would have recognized immediately if the extenuating circumstances had not been so dire. This woman was not merely an outside world scribe trained by the Rebel Branch. This was Genevre — *the* Genevre. No wonder Ilex had resisted Melia's suggestion that they meet with her tonight. She could tell by Genevre's demeanour that she did not recognize Saule. Why should she? They had not seen each other since Saule had taken her to the outside world family who would raise her. And though Saule had maintained periodic contact with Ilex and Melia over the years, they had purposely avoided discussion of Genevre. They could not risk inadvertently exposing her to Council.

But time suddenly slowed, collapsed in that room. Listening to Genevre's voice, recognizing the significance of this reunion, the Vulknut Eclipse itself was temporary eclipsed for Saule. If they were all to die in three days, she would die having had this one moment of happiness. And if they did not die, if she could help the rebels restore the Flaw in the Stone, Saule would ensure that Genevre came to work for the Council, that her name was indeed inscribed in the right manuscripts at the right time, that her scribal skills were confirmed by outside world documents. For although she had not heard her name uttered for years, Saule knew beyond doubt that Genevre could provide a conduit among dimensions for many years to come. And no one on Council other than Saule herself ever need know the truth of her origin or the extent of their alchemical bond.

Flaw Dimension — Summer 1914

The rebels gathered around Dracaen awaiting response. If there was ever a time they required guidance from their High Azoth, it was now. As much as Kalina had wanted to leave, she realized she needed to stay. If the Rebel Branch could not restore the Dragonblood Stone within three days — the time it would take for the residual effects of Dragonblood to dissipate — complete annihilation would be their fate. The entire Flaw dimension would disintegrate, the rebels along with it. They must choose wisely now or live an eternity with no choice at all.

"Breach! Breach!" Dracaen cried. And the others soon followed, the rallying cry echoing through the chamber in the hollowed absence of the hallowed Stone.

The Third Rebellion had begun with Dracaen's call to arms.

Though their time frame was severely limited, Dracaen insisted on protocols, maintaining that they could not breach Council dimension without a means, that they must take the time to formulate an infallible plan. He met for three hours with the Rebel Elders to strategize. Kalina waited impatiently with the Scribes and Readers. The chamber droned with hushed voices. Small groups of rebels speculated on manoeuvres, conjectured the details of the Elders' battle plan, readied their literal and figurative swords.

Finally, Dracaen and the Elders emerged. They did not appear as the rebels had imagined they would. They looked drawn, fatigued, and, worst of all, *older*. They were now literally surviving on borrowed time — second by second, molecule by molecule, the Dragonblood Elixir in their veins fragmented in the absence of the Stone. Kalina and the others remained silent, fists closed, wrists crossed, heads bowed, awaiting word from the High Azoth, ready to reply, prepared to make their choice.

"Victory requires two steps," announced Dracaen. "A portal and a sacrifice. We have one but not the other."

Kalina lifted her head. She then realized that Thuja had already stepped forward, marked by the blood-red shawl upon her shoulders as a martyr to the cause. Kalina tensed with guilt, tears brimming. This woman, whom she had known as long as she had known Dracaen, had offered herself as the sacrifice. Larix too stepped forward then and kneeled at Thuja's feet, lowering his head to the ground as a gesture of utmost respect. After all the rebels, including Kalina, had done the same, Dracaen too lowered himself to the floor. The High Azoth honoured the one willing to be sacrificed for the sake of all.

When Thuja gave the sign to rise, Dracaen once again assumed pride of place and addressed the rebels. "Kalina!" he called out, loud enough to startle her. "You must reach out to Genevre. You must call to her. You must ask her to bring Ilex and Melia back to Flaw dimension."

Kalina could not respond. Perhaps the absence of the Dragonblood Stone was affecting her ability to process information. Had she heard Dracaen correctly? Had he suggested that Genevre was in contact with Ilex and Melia? She grimaced as she realized that once again he had withheld information from her. Or perhaps she had simply not thought to put the pieces together. Genevre had trained with the Rebel Branch under Ilex and Melia's mentorship for decades. They had likely remained Genevre's outside world contacts — her means of access to knowledge about Council dimension. Then the entire plan became suddenly clear. Dracaen needed Ilex and Melia to open the breach. If Kalina wanted to survive, wanted to be able to make the choices she had so urgently anticipated just hours ago, she would have to comply.

She stepped forward then, not because of Dracaen but because of Thuja. If Thuja could sacrifice herself for the good of all dimensions, then certainly Kalina could play her part.

Santa Fe — Summer 1914

Before Ilex and Melia appeared with Saule on Genevre's doorstep, Genevre had been sitting at her dining table rolling a fragment of the Dragonblood Stone back and forth over the wooden surface as if trying to imprint the wood with the stone. She had no intention of damaging the table or the fragment; her movement was merely an unconscious nervous gesture. Her fingertips burned slightly. At first, she wondered if the sensation had been caused by the antique cinnabar ink in which the fragment had been hidden. It had, of course, coated her fingertips when she fished the fragment out of the thick paste. Its stains still lingered. But no matter how often she had had cinnabar or vermilion inks on her hands and fingers in the past, she had not once experienced this reaction. She realized shortly thereafter what this unorthodox sensation meant: the Dragonblood Stone itself had been compromised. *Remota Macula*.

Frightened, she held the fragment tightly and

thought through her options. At first, she contemplated going to the stronghold portal ground that she had used last year with Thuja and Larix. She could sit on the nearby bench and wait for a rebel to emerge. But even as she began to gather belongings for the trip, she realized the futility of this plan. She doubted any of the portals to Flaw dimension would still be active under the circumstances. This realization made her fear for everyone within the dimension. The entire Rebel Branch may well be trapped, all portals rendered inactive the moment the Flaw vanished from its cavern. Of every rebel she had ever known, she, of course, feared most for Kalina. How could Genevre have abandoned her daughter yet again? She should have remained in Flaw dimension and attempted to create another child as companion to the first. Yes, she would have had to watch the second child's homunculus twin die, as she had her first created son. But Kalina would have had a sibling with whom she could create the most potent alchemy in the universe. Surely, together, two alchemical children would have a better chance of restoring the Flaw than one child alone.

Perhaps she could seek out Ilex and Melia. They in turn could seek out one of their Council contacts. They hadn't spoken to her in months — since the day she had finally told them the truth about creating an alchemical child with Dracaen. But Genevre's desperation called for equally desperate measures. Perhaps she could convince them to set aside their misgivings. Despite their anger at both Dracaen and her, they must nonetheless care about others within the Rebel Branch. They had, after all, worked with various rebels over the years. Would they not be willing to save their rebel colleagues from being trapped within Flaw dimension? Would they not be willing to help Genevre save her daughter even if they had shunned her for the very act of creating Kalina? Had they not mentored Genevre for decades — trained her to be one of the best outside world scribes the rebels had ever known? Perhaps the intervening months and the removal of the Flaw would together convince Ilex and Melia to forgive her. Genevre could only hope they would seek her out in order to attempt to save themselves and others. Why would either of them want to risk becoming One with everyone when they could barely stand being one with each other?

Genevre jumped, alarmed. She heard a noise outside just as she also received a startling jolt from the Dragonblood fragment. She stood up, manoeuvred the fragment into the hemline of her skirt, and moved towards the door. Instead of extinguishing the lights, she lit another. She wanted to ensure that whoever approached would realize she was home. She heard footsteps. As the people moved closer to the house, she understood that her hope had been met. Ilex and Melia had come to find her after all.

She unlatched the door and ushered them in, surprised to see that they were not alone. The stranger was named Saule. She was a Lapidarian Scribe of the Alchemists' Council. Apparently Ilex and Melia had been friends with her for years and had arranged to meet outside a temporary portal in Santa Fe if the Council ritual was successful. They had spoken in detail on the walk to Genevre's. They now had a plan. They required Genevre's assistance to breach Flaw dimension. More specifically, they required her Dragonblood fragment. If used together with the fragment carried by Ilex and Melia, they may be able to be transported through a temporary portal. If successful, if they managed to open a portal to Flaw dimension, Saule would help the rebels breach Council dimension.

Genevre stared at Saule. She did not look like a Council traitor. Then again, what did she expect a traitor to look like? After all, Genevre had not changed her own appearance after being accused of treason by the rebels.

"Where do we begin?" Genevre asked. "Even if our fragments are able to work together as a means of transport, we have little time to scour the country for a temporary portal ground."

"We need not seek portal ground. We need only to remain outdoors with our fragments in close proximity to one another," said Ilex.

"I don't understand," said Genevre. "Can our fragments create a portal now that the Flaw in the Stone has been removed?"

"No," replied Ilex. "We can only assume the rebels

themselves will attempt to contact those whom they know possess fragments of the Dragonblood Stone in the outside world — the only bits of the Stone that now remain in the aftermath of the *Remota Macula*. If they call to us, you should be able to hear."

"Dozens of fragments exist in the world. Will they call to each inheritor individually?"

"No, Genevre," began Melia. "Only a certain call could be successful at this time of crisis. And only you could be successful at hearing it."

"Why would I be chosen to receive the call — an outside world scribe who purposely abandoned Flaw dimension? Perhaps you—"

"You are the only possible one, Genevre. I have come to understand as much tonight," said Melia.

"You are the only possible one," repeated Ilex. "The cry can hold only one intention, one element that will allow it to break through dimensional space."

Genevre looked closely at Ilex, whose face fluctuated rapidly with that of Melia. She then focused on Saule, who wore a pained expression that reflected their apprehension.

"What element?" Genevre asked, turning from Saule to Ilex and Melia once again.

"The cry must be pierced through and through with love."

"Dracaen does not love me. He merely needed me, time and again."

"And once again, Dracaen needs you. But he will not be the one to call to you, Genevre. He would have no reason to believe you would answer. Only one person loves you enough to seek you out. Only one person can forgive your abandonment."

A shiver overcame her. Genevre now understood what Melia was avoiding uttering in Saule's presence. She understood too that Ilex and Melia had forgiven her. Without her ability to hear the cry, they could not enter Flaw dimension no matter how many Dragonblood fragments they possessed. No one in the world would be able to hear Dracaen call across dimensions. But, without doubt, Genevre would inevitably, eternally hear a cry from her daughter.

Flaw Dimension — Summer 1914

"I am the Blood of the Dragon!" called Dracaen, fists clenched, wrists crossed.

"I live as the Flaw in the Stone!" replied the rebels, uncrossing their wrists, holding their fists up, parallel to their shoulders.

Kalina opened the gate in the wrought-iron barrier that had surrounded the Dragonblood Stone. As the gate clanged shut behind her into its locking mechanism, she shivered. Now the barrier surrounded nothing at all — an empty space that left no trace of its former sacredness. Kalina stood in the centre of this absence to perform a task that, according to Dracaen, she alone could perform.

All usual portals had been sealed the moment the Dragonblood Stone had disappeared. Thus were the rebels trapped within the rapidly faltering Flaw dimension. Thus had they been condemned to death by a Council who sought their own eternal salvation.

To survive, she must do as Dracaen instructed. To save all dimensions, she must save herself. She was, after all, the remaining link to the Dragonblood Stone. Her veins coursed with its blood. *Sanguine essence, sans Quintessence, Sanguinessence.* On Dracaen's signal, she would call back Genevre. The alchemical daughter would cry out to her creator. Genevre — should she be listening — could re-enter Flaw dimension through her fragment of Dragonblood Stone and its connection to her alchemical child. With her, she must bring Ilex and Melia, the only pair bound through the conjunction of Dragonblood and Lapis. Together, the alchemical child born to the Flaw dimension, the scribe born to the outside world, and the mutual pair conjoined within Council dimension would provide the trinity: the sulphur, the mercury, the salt; the three worlds required for the Breach of Blood, for victory in the Third Rebellion.

Kalina breathed slowly, attempting to calm herself. The rebels gathered around the perimeter, hands forming a barrier of flesh and blood along the railing of iron. One after the other, each of the rebels began to hum, low and droning. When Dracaen himself added his voice to the mix, Kalina lay prostrate on the newly exposed ground. She placed her hands, palms down, above her head. To Kalina, the surface under her fingertips and forehead felt like a soft, tender wound freed too early of its scab.

The droning turned to chanting. *Sanguinessence! Sanguinessence! Sanguinessence!*

"Mother!" Kalina cried. "Mother! Mother!"

Releasing their hands from the railing, the rebels reached for the pots of water filled earlier from the cavern pools. One by one, they tossed the water onto Kalina and into the dimensional wound within which she lay. Setting down the water pots, they each reached for a handful of soil, mined the day before from the hills above the quarry. Kalina felt the earth fall in shards against her back, dry and heavy after the cool water. Next drifted the leaves and petals, gathered that morning from the stone pathways that snaked through the garden. And, finally, the fire — small, fragile embers carefully chosen, collected from the furnace with tongs forged in the molten lava of the deepest pits.

"Mother! Mother! Mother!" Kalina cried.

The earth beneath her rumbled. It then shook so fiercely that Kalina feared the wounded ground would open and devour her. When it stopped, she slowly rolled over and sat up. Her head spun. A hand reached down to help her to her feet. She regained her balance and looked at the people who now stood with her. Genevre had answered her plea. But she was not alone — she had brought not only Ilex and Melia, but someone else.

"Tell me who you are," Kalina demanded of the woman.

"I am Saule, Lapidarian Scribe of the Alchemists' Council. I have carried my pendant for three hundred and eighteen years. I am here to aid the Rebel Branch, to join the Third Rebellion, to open a portal to Council dimension, to restore the Flaw in the Stone."

Council Dimension — Summer 1914

As the Council Elders reconvened to develop a plan of procedure, Cedar waited in the Scriptorium with a few Lapidarian Scribes and Readers. She wondered vaguely why Saule was not yet present, but reasoned that she had wanted to spend as long as possible with Sadira. Those two had been virtually inseparable for the past decade. Amur, meanwhile, had evidently been standing by the fountain for a while when Cedar arrived. Certainly, she could not deny his diligence or faith. He looked at her then, and she wondered if pendant proximity had allowed him to notice her brief focus and praise. Under normal circumstances, such proximity would not be so potent, but the Vulknut Eclipse created far from normal circumstances. What would Ruis think if he knew Amur desired her? What would *she* do if she and Ruis and Amur had hundreds of years ahead of them?

Within half an hour, the Elders arrived. Azoth Magen Quercus distributed a list of tasks. For two days, every member of the Council would work in various ways to prepare for Ascension — sanctifying ritual objects, preparing the scrolls, shaving the dust from the Lapis, mixing the inks, distilling the Elixir. Even the Junior Initiates carried out the symbolically paramount job of cleaning the Scriptorium and the main Council chambers. Not a minute was to be wasted, not a detail forgotten.

At one point, as Cedar ironed the precious sheets of the sacred crystalline parchment for the Azothian final inscriptions, she mused that her fellow alchemists reminded her of worker bees. She longed then to visit the lavender fields, to share one last time with Ruis the emotional intimacy she should have been more clearly focused on earlier. Sheet by sheet, she became more agitated by this notion. How could she have let her mind wander at such a critical time? Now, no time remained. Her love would die or be absorbed or become part of the One. She would no longer be herself. And Ruis would no longer be hers alone.

In her reverie, Cedar left the hot press too long on one particular sheet of parchment. The slight but sudden acrid scent startled her. She lifted the iron immediately and gazed at the sheet. She then glanced up and around the chamber. No one appeared to have noticed her error. She alone was responsible for the parchment sheets that would be sewn that night into the ritual scroll. Setting the iron aside, she lifted the burnt sheet and held it up to the window — but the light was dull, almost nonexistent. Still, the fire from the kilns revealed no visible scorch mark.

"Hold it above the flame of a Lapidarian candle to be certain," said Saule.

Saule had startled her, appearing from nowhere at Cedar's side. Her error with the parchment had been witnessed by someone after all. Cedar walked to the small alcove near the fountain and withdrew a candle and holder from the third shelf. Saule followed her. They stood together as Cedar lit the candle. Cedar then stood still. Her task had been simple, but her mind had wandered again. In front of Saule, she did not want to shed light on her carelessness.

"Give me the sheet," said Saule. Cedar could have refused. After all, they were both Lapidarian Scribes and Cedar had more years of experience. But such matters of hierarchy mattered little in these final days relative to the tasks at hand.

Saule held the parchment above the flame. Cedar sighed. The sheet was visibly darkened with a scorch mark — a shadow visible behind a section of crystalline fibres. "The Flaw in the Parchment," said Cedar, attempting levity while strategizing a means to create a replacement for the invaluable and virtually irreplaceable sheet. "If we work together to scrape the Lapis, we should be able to duplicate—"

"The parchment is fine, Cedar. You need not replace it."

Cedar balked. Her lips quivered as she opened her mouth to protest. But she saw something then, when she looked at Saule. She saw something that she would never be able to confirm with certainty afterward: a flash of amber within Saule's eyes. If they were to use the marked parchment the Ascension might fail. Such was the probability if an imperfect object were to be used in the presence of the perfected Lapis. In the aftermath of failure, an investigation might lead to Cedar's role. In turn, she could be punished or erased. Yet here was Saule. Here was Saule informing Cedar with a glance exchanged that she knew the parchment was flawed and that she condoned its use. Saule wanted the Ascension to fail. She wanted someone in whom to confide, someone with whom to conspire. Cedar thought of Ruis once again. She thought of the future she could share with him — the leisurely days in the apiary. She then blew out the candle, took the sheet from Saule, and walked quietly back to her station.

For the entirety of the third day, Azoth Magen Quercus read aloud the Scribal Scrolls. Upon completion of the eighteen pages of recitation, he would begin again. Every five recitations, which took approximately three hours, he would allow himself a break, during which time Azoth Ailanthus or Azoth Kezia would take a turn at the eighteen-page oration. Now, in the final hour at the end of the final recitation, Quercus set down the scrolls, raised his hands into the first position of the Ab Uno, and eloquently recited the *Mundus Subterraneus* key. If all had gone well during the entirety of the Vulknut Eclipse up to this moment, the Azoth Magen would be subsumed by the Lapis, and Final Ascension of the entire Alchemists' Council would be imminent. Cedar held her breath in anticipation, listening to the final digits of the key as if to an outside world countdown. But instead of ringing in a new year, death would toll. The shadow on the parchment crossed her mind.

The moment he uttered the final syllable, Azoth Magen Quercus was gone. No Sword of Elixir required. No final words of wisdom or farewell. He simply no longer existed, his body having disintegrated into a fine dust that floated through the room, noticeable only in the shafts of moonlight filtering through Scriptorium windows. Azoths Ailanthus and Kezia sank to their knees, hands in the second position of the Ab Uno, heads bowed. Shortly thereafter, the entire Alchemists Council was on its knees. They too, along with all of Council dimension, would soon be dust — mere particles, fragments of their former selves floating eternally in the vast absence of absolutely nothing. *The shadow had made no difference at all*, Cedar realized as her knees protested in discomfort against the cold stone floor. Such was the pain of her existence in these final moments of her mortality.

The wait became more agonizing with each passing second. Had Ruis not assured her the time between the Azoth Magen's ascension and their own would be minimal? Yet the interval had already moved beyond seconds into minutes. After ten minutes, Cedar could no longer hold her station; she lowered herself into a seated position, releasing the Ab Uno gesture to steady herself with her hands. Others soon did the same. Another ten minutes having passed, and Ailanthus, steadied by Kezia, stood and walked slowly towards the Lapis. Obeche followed, gesturing to Ruis to join them. Kezia turned. Stepping forward, apparently about to offer an explanation, she was stopped in her tracks. In the immediate aftermath, Cedar could not comprehend what had happened. She merely saw Kezia fall — not to her knees, as she and Ailanthus had done earlier, but straight forward, her head striking the hard floor with a thud. And then Cedar saw them: strangers.

"I am the Blood of the Dragon!" called one.

"I live as the Flaw in the Stone!" called the other.

Man and woman, standing atop the Lapis in an act of sacrilege so astounding that for several seconds no alchemist moved.

"Rebels!" cried Ailanthus finally breaking the silence. He lunged towards the man, but he was thrown back with such a force that Cedar feared he would be the third Azothian casualty of the day.

Kai rushed towards him, helping him to his feet. Ruis and Obeche charged towards the couple atop the Lapis, only to meet with the same barrier as had Ailanthus. Nearby Elders prevented them from falling to the ground.

Cedar could not fathom how the rebels had breached Council dimension. Had they used the Lapis itself as a portal? Had the absence of the Flaw ironically left it vulnerable to intrusion by those remaining in Flaw dimension? Had the Elders been aware of this potential outcome? Surely not.

"Who are you?" asked Obeche.

Though no written protocols existed for such an event, Cedar felt certain that Azoth Ailanthus should have been the one to address the rebels. Obeche had overstepped. The bemused expressions on the rebels' faces indicated that they too had not expected Obeche to play Council emissary. Ailanthus moved forward, taking a position beside Obeche.

"Step down, Dracaen!" bellowed Ailanthus.

Dracaen. High Azoth of the Rebel Branch. Cedar knew his name, but she had never seen him before now.

"We are not here to step down, Ailanthus. We are here to restore the Flaw in the Stone."

Audible shock rippled through the Council.

"You are too late," replied Ailanthus. "With his sacrifice, Azoth Magen Quercus sealed the Stone into a state of Lapidarian perfection."

"And with *her* sacrifice," Dracaen said, pointing to Kezia, where she lay on the ground, "perfection has been thwarted. A shadow once again makes its way across the chamber."

"How dare you compare her murder to Quercus's sacramental death," said Ruis.

"How dare you be so naïve," responded Dracaen.

He turned to the woman beside him, who then knelt on the Lapis.

"I am the Blood of the Dragon," she said, crossing her wrists.

"You will live as the Flaw in the Stone," replied Dracaen.

The woman uncrossed her wrists, moving her fists to her sides. Dracaen, suddenly wielding a dagger from beneath his robes, plunged the weapon into the woman's exposed chest. Unlike Ailanthus, she did not turn to dust. She turned to blood.

And the blood poured over the Lapis.

And the Flaw bled into the Stone.

The words came unbidden to her memory. Cedar had read them, time and again, in the ancient accounts of the First Rebellion. This woman, this rebel whom Cedar did not know, had died not for herself alone, not for the promise of everlasting life, not for eternal perfection in the One, but for the very ideal that had brought her to her death. She had enacted her free will; she had made a choice — and now *choice* was, once again, the fate of all.

V

𝔔ingⅅao — 𝔣all 1914

Jinjing longed to return to Council dimension, to be once again Keeper of the Book in the North Library. In the aftermath of the Third Rebellion, her previously intermittent duties in the Qingdao protectorate had been transformed to permanent *until further notice*. The Council could not simply abandon all protectorate libraries to the ravages of outside world politics. Someone had to remain posted as caretaker of the manuscripts. So Jinjing's sense of duty led her to agree to the post, and her esteem for the manuscripts led her to remain in Qingdao even as activity in the harbour increased, even as ultimatums were issued, even as war escalated, even as the enemy approached from the north, even as the steamers were sunk, even as the bombs began to drop. Even as she began to blame Council for the misery that surrounded her.

So here she waited, alone and frightened, listening to the torrential rains, recognizing that when the clouds eventually cleared from the sky, they would most likely form on the ground once again: clouds of water replaced by clouds of smoke from the bursts of enemy shells, flashes of lightning replaced by explosions from guns. A loud knock at the door startled her.

"How have you fared since your return from Sundsvall?" Obeche asked, once Jinjing had ushered him and Cedar into the small protectorate kitchen.

"Considering the circumstances, relatively fine," Jinjing responded indifferently. She refused to give Obeche any reason to suspect she was happy to see him. "How is everything with the two of you and within Council dimension?"

Obeche and Cedar glanced at each other, neither answering Jinjing's question. Eventually Cedar gestured for Obeche to answer.

"Some progress has been achieved," said Obeche.

"Progress?" replied Jinjing. "Am I correct in assuming you made your way here on foot from a temporary portal?"

"Yes, of course."

"Is this progress?" Jinjing raised her arms and gestured widely as if to encompass not just the room but the districts beyond the protectorate. "Qingdao is under siege. And the relentless rains have created additional misery! Walking even a short distance for supplies leaves my clothes soaked through." She held up a jacket she had earlier draped over a drying rack. "These mud stains are permanent. Clearly, the Council has abandoned both their duty to maintain elemental balance and their concern for us mere mortals of the outside world."

"I am sorry your current experience in Qingdao is so unfortunate. But we have most certainly *not* abandoned our duty!" replied Obeche, with a clear edge of anger.

How had she ever loved this man? Where was the sweetness he had used so long ago to woo her?

"War in the outside world is not unusual," said Cedar, evidently attempting to calm the approaching storm. "The Council is in the process of repairing the damage that began with the five and five; eventually we will succeed, as we always have. The circumstances are simply . . . complicated this time around. But balance will prevail."

"Is this process of repair working?"

"At the moment, no. But ultimately, yes," replied Obeche.

"Is that a riddle you expect me to solve?"

"This attitude is unbecoming, Jinjing. I assumed you would welcome our visit after so many weeks in isolation. And I could use a cup of tea after that horrendous walk in the rain through Qingdao."

"My months in isolation during the *horrendous*

events of Qingdao have allowed me time to contemplate. And I certainly would not have anticipated a visit from you and Cedar at what appears to be the height of the siege. Forgive me if I appear somewhat out of sorts," she responded, her attempt to mitigate sarcasm not quite successful. "And you have visited often enough in years gone by to know where the tea is kept."

Jinjing recalled briefly the long hours she and Obeche had spent sipping tea, scrutinizing meticulously illuminated manuscripts, revelling in the intensity of the colours or beauty of the designs, sitting side by side in the protectorate library as if they were both Council Readers tasked with interpreting ancient scribal prophesies. Of course, she was not a Reader, as was abundantly clear of late.

"I empathize with your concerns, Jinjing," offered Cedar. "Certainly the implications of current events are far-reaching and disturbing."

"How then are these events *progress*?"

"The Elders have been working incessantly on reducing the Flaw in the Stone," said Obeche. "Doing so should decrease Rebel influence and, thereby, aid the Council in returning balance to the outside world."

Jinjing did not respond. She wanted to dub Obeche's obsession with the Flaw in the Stone as *the Flaw in the Plan*, but she knew enough about him to know that a critique of the Council's methods at this point would only fuel a debate that she was in no mood to have. He had a penchant for argument, and she was too tired to do so with any logic or tenacity.

"As I suggested earlier," continued Obeche, filling the void left in Jinjing's silence, "ultimately, we will be successful. Everyone has heeded the rallying call to decrease the Flaw as a means of insuring Council withholds power from the Rebel Branch, despite their victory during the Third Rebellion. The Elders maintain hope that their progress will lead to renewed success of the ancient prophesies — for another complete erasure of the Flaw followed by rituals that will lead to ultimate Final Ascension. The disturbances in the outside world may well be mere signs that we are approaching salvation."

"*Salvation?* Elimination of the Flaw is the primary reason for the current unbalanced state of the world," Jinjing said. She resented the way Council clung selfishly to a prehistoric mythology whose probable outcome would be annihilation not just of the few but of the multitudes.

"I, on the other hand," admitted Cedar, "have my concerns with the ancient prophecies. But Obeche believes my viewpoint to be selfish."

"What concerns?" asked Jinjing. Intrigued, she turned away from Obeche.

"Please do not mistake this opinion as blasphemy. But I believe Council needs to focus on repairing the world before perfecting the Stone. Another attempt at removing the Flaw could have serious repercussions the Council has not antici-pated despite the current fallout. Ancient prophe-cies from millennia ago are difficult even for Elders to interpret."

Jinjing posed her next question to Cedar as nonchalantly as possible. "Do you not believe Final Ascension will transport us all to yet another dimension, one of even more splendour than Council dimension itself, one that facilitates con-junction as One?"

"As I said, I believe Council should focus on repairing the world."

"Cedar has temporarily lost her faith thanks to the recent Rebel victory," Obeche interjected. "A predicament both inappropriate and unbecoming for a Lapidarian Scribe of the Alchemists' Council."

"Faith has nothing to do with the matter when lives are at stake, Obeche. I have had those same doubts," admitted Jinjing, her effort to remain casual abandoned. She needed Cedar to under-stand that she could be her ally. "Presumably several Council members harbour such post-rebellion con-cerns. Frankly, Obeche, I am surprised you don't. A wrong move — one that perpetuates rather than eliminates this war — could cost millions of lives."

As if on cue, the sound of an explosion rela-tively nearby punctuated the discussion, rendering Obeche temporarily mute. Jinjing saw his annoy-ance immediately change to concern. Cedar moved towards a window to investigate, but Jinjing placed a hand on her shoulder before Cedar could peek behind the tapestry. She had hung tapestries over all the windows to prevent the light of even one Lapidarian candle being spotted by outside world soldiers or other passersby.

"Perhaps this visit was unwise," managed Obeche.

"I fail to understand your reason for venturing here," said Jinjing. "News that the Council is continuing its attempt to reduce the Flaw could have been sent by messenger."

"The Elders require you to work with a Council Scribe to help locate potential outside world scribes. As you know, locating outside world candidates with precision during war measures requires the work to take place in an outside world protectorate."

"So you chose the Qingdao protectorate during a siege?"

"We did not choose the Qingdao protectorate. We chose *you*. And you happen to reside in the Qingdao protectorate," explained Obeche.

"And to be frank," continued Cedar, "Qingdao may be under siege, but it's also well removed from the escalating tribulations in Europe. The Elders outright refused to send me to Vienna despite my willingness to return to the source and investigate."

"The source — what source?" asked Jinjing.

"Apparently the conflict started at the beginning of the five and five with a disruption in balance near Vienna — possibly within the Vienna protectorate itself, though tracking the precise location will be impossible until at least a few Scribes and Readers are permitted to visit the city in person."

"For now," said Obeche, "you and Cedar are to work together with the material the Elders and Readers have gathered thus far. Your goal is to locate at least two — preferably three — outside world scribes who, in turn, will assist with the mundane scribal tasks as the Council Scribes work on more pressing matters in their efforts to decrease the Flaw."

"Are Cedar and I solely responsible for locating these coveted outside world scribes?"

"No. We have chosen four protectorates and four Keepers of the Book to pair with four Lapidarian Scribes," explained Obeche.

"Am I to understand that you yourself will be returning to Council dimension?"

"Yes. My skills will prove more useful there. My duty was merely to ensure Cedar arrived here safely."

"I had suggested two Scribes be sent to each protectorate," said Cedar. "Doing so seemed the most reasonable under the circumstances. However, my dissenting voice was barely heard."

"I welcome your dissenting voice," responded Jinjing.

Obeche shook his head. "Do not let Cedar's more radical opinions sway you from your duties, Jinjing. Your pristine work and unwavering commitment to the Council has always been for me your most admirable characteristic."

"As you know, Obeche, I have never faltered in my

responsibilities. My sense of duty is the reason I currently reside in Qingdao. Though I value the opinion of all Council members, I wouldn't allow anyone, Cedar included, to change my mind on convictions I've reached and continue to hold of my own accord."

"That reassurance is indeed welcomed," replied Obeche, with a formality that emphasized his role as her superior rather than her beloved.

This exchange with Obeche inexorably altered Jinjing's opinion of him. The swiftness of this transition in her thinking surprised her. But by the time Obeche departed, Jinjing had become steadfast in her opinion on the siege, the war, and the role of the Flaw in both. Obeche had managed to accomplish the opposite of his apparent intention. Where he had attempted to persuade her that Council worked to the benefit of all, he had instead managed to confirm her suspicions about the mounting chaos of the outside world: all was to blame on the Alchemists' Council.

She needed a means to ascertain the details of Cedar's convictions. So far she had only a glimmer of hope that Cedar represented an ally. Jinjing knew she would have to endeavour to discover the truth of the matter; after all, though Cedar was not currently an Elder, she would surely become one, and Jinjing suspected she would need a friend in upper echelons as the years progressed — *if* the years progressed. If the renewed attempt at eliminating the Flaw failed, and if repairing the world succeeded, Cedar could become a Novillian Scribe in the next rotation, a likely prospect if, as Jinjing now predicted, the current Council hoisted itself with its own petard.

Cedar examined the fragments of handwriting from the pages Jinjing had spread across the table. Though she had always admired the Keeper of the Book, resentment lingered over her own unorthodox posting in Qingdao. Would not her talents as a Lapidarian Scribe be better employed in the Scriptorium? Surely a Reader or even a Senior Magistrate could take her place. Yet here she sat in the outside world with Jinjing searching for the proverbial needle among a jumble of miscellaneous haystacks. When first informed by Ravenea that she had been chosen for the task by Elder Council, Cedar had requested the rationale. *You are trustworthy, Cedar. Your status as Lapidarian Scribe affords you some privileges. Consider the duty an honour.* This particular duty meant leaving Ruis for the duration. This duty meant aging for the duration. This duty meant spending countless hours shifting through sheets of parchment and paper by Lapidarian candlelight looking for signs of alchemical talent among would-be alchemists. She wearied.

"Do not fret, Cedar," said Jinjing, apparently intuiting Cedar's dissatisfaction. "Your time away from Council dimension will be short relative to your eternal life. Readers have already worked for months to match tree names and geographical locations to potential outside world scribes. All we have to do is examine the inscriptions and determine to whom we should offer Council training."

"I have no intention of making an official complaint. But neither do I plan to thank the Elders for this assignment."

"Your dedication to mundane but necessary tasks will undoubtedly encourage the Azoths to look upon you more favourably at the next rotation."

"I've never cared how I appear to the Azoths. One day I will ascend to Novillian Scribe based on my achievements, not on my apparent dedication."

"I admire your stance. As a Keeper of the Book, I certainly recognize the importance of individual achievement on the road to Elder Council."

Cedar looked up, quizzical. Jinjing had taken a risk in praising Cedar on this front — one that could easily be mistaken as a plea for the individual rather than the collective.

"Of course I respect the Elders," clarified Jinjing. "But I've been with Council long enough to recognize that reaching one's potential is not necessarily accomplished through uniform agreement. A dissenting voice such as yours can divert attention when necessary, if not stem the tide of disaster completely."

Cedar's astonishment at Jinjing's brashness was now clearly visible in her expression. But Jinjing chose that moment to move her glance over the documents rather than Cedar's face — a sign perhaps that she had said as much as she cared to for the moment.

Thus, they refocused on the work at hand, moving each page into position, examining the ink and penmanship, the lines of text and the empty spaces between the lines. The potential scribes of the outside world had worked their alchemy, knowing instinctively that something lay beyond their grasp, gesturing towards the ineffable with their letters and words and icons and symbols, reaching out to the Council without conscious intention. Like all seemingly impossible tasks, this one assigned to Cedar and Jinjing appeared without end or solution for hour upon hour until suddenly a flash of inspiration made Cedar pause, fingertip to page, having felt a resistance of her skin to the texture of the ink.

"*Bee-loud glade,*" Cedar read aloud.

"What?" replied Jinjing.

"This phrase on the page — *bee-loud glade* — it feels . . . different."

Jinjing reached for the paper and examined it closer to the candlelight. She ran her fingertips over the letters, then nodded and smiled.

"Yes, as does *linnet's wings.*"

"May a writer be assigned as an outside world scribe?" Cedar asked, astounded.

"A writer? I should think writers are eminently suitable to scribal endeavours. Do you know these words? Have you seen them before?"

"I've heard them. They are part of a poem. Ruis recited it to me once. We were in the apiary, lying amidst the lavender. *Are we not already in a bee-loud glade?* he asked me. And I laughed because the bees surrounded us. After that day, whenever he wanted us to have time alone, he would whisper, 'Meet me in the bee-loud glade.' And I would."

"Where are the corresponding documents? What is the potential scribe's tree name?"

Cedar stood and moved to the corner table. She shuffled through the corresponding documents until she found the correct one.

"Coll," Cedar read aloud as she walked back to the table. "His interest in alchemy goes back at least two decades. Strange," she said. "Based on these statements, Rowan Kai suspects he was contacted by a Council member years ago, though she could find no official record."

"Perhaps this hypothetical contact was made by a Rebel rather than a Council member."

"Perhaps," replied Cedar. "Such an occurrence would be rare but not impossible."

"And where does Coll reside?"

"He moves about, it appears — but I would say London and Dublin primarily."

"As soon as possible, we will send the scribal sample and documents back to the Readers and ask them to hone in on the location."

"Until confirmation, I suppose I'm to remain here to continue the search."

"Hone your skills at assessing the truth amidst words inscribed by outside world poets. All the better to entice Ruis back to the bee-loud glade," Jinjing joked.

"All the better to engage in our literary game at any rate. But I don't need the words of poets to entice Ruis. I merely need to look at him."

Jinjing laughed as she left the room, and Cedar pulled the next sheet of paper towards her.

Three weeks later, Cedar stood in front of a mirror across from her bed in Qingdao. She had removed the nighttime cover from her window. The perpetual sounds of war had temporarily abated to allow a full and restful night's sleep. Coincidentally, even the rains had subsided. In the bright morning light, she examined her face closely, checking for signs of aging. She knew, of course, that a few weeks — even a few months — would make little difference to her Elixir-enhanced body, but this period in Qingdao was the longest she had been removed from Council dimension since she had entered as an Initiate. Not surprisingly, she *felt* different, and she had begun to wonder if she *looked* different. She focused on a small line under her right eye, not sure whether or not it had been there the week before or even the day before. How could she not know the intricacies of her own face? Perhaps the food rations had taken more of a toll than she had realized. Even the Lapidarian honey had to be used sparingly until the supply could be replenished.

Certainly, given the vast number of hours she had spent over the weeks squinting at the scribal fragments and manuscripts by candlelight at Jinjing's ongoing insistence, she would not be surprised if the skin surrounding her eyes was indeed suffering the first visible signs of impact. On the occasional sunny day, they worked primarily in the natural light filtering through the upstairs library windows, but the nature of war, the variances of seasonal weather, and the characteristics of Lapidarian ink required candlelight much of the daylight hours, and entirely during nighttime sessions. They could not waste a minute in their efforts to locate scribes. The Council wanted all the assistance they could get in their attempts to rebalance the elements — even if these gruelling labours were eventually reflected in Cedar's appearance, even if Ruis noticed her malnourished fatigue when he next caressed her cheek.

Cedar wondered then if Jinjing had similar vain concerns when she thought about seeing Obeche after an extended absence. Thus far she had attempted to maintain a certain level of decorum with Jinjing. Yes, she and Jinjing had laughed on occasion during the first few weeks of her stay in Qingdao; yes, they had complained about the personalities of certain Council members; yes, they had even shared a few intimate details about their respective relationships with Ruis and Obeche. But Cedar had not ventured too far into Jinjing's past, into the details of the personal life she had brought with her to Council dimension and, more recently, to Qingdao. She had not even asked directly how Qingdao's unfolding events were affecting her. She was not certain whether doing so would be appropriate. To Cedar, Jinjing had always been a friendly and dedicated Keeper of the Book of the North Library. She had not known her — though she had certainly heard *of* her — in Jinjing's early days as an outside world scribe. But lately, after working together for so many hours over the weeks, Cedar had begun to sense a shift in Jinjing's attitude to their work and to Cedar herself. So today would be the day to enquire further, to ask questions, to learn if Jinjing shared her growing doubts about Council protocols.

As it happened, they were in no rush on this particular morning. Just yesterday, Obeche had finally returned. Though brief, his visit meant that she and Jinjing had been able to submit the two potential candidates they had located: Coll, endorsed weeks earlier, and Genevre, endorsed only two days ago. Though the Council still hoped for a third name, she and Jinjing could certainly take a break for a few hours — perhaps the entire day. After all, several more weeks would pass before Obeche returned. Not until then could they know whether either of these two potential scribes had been accepted. Not until then could Cedar learn whether she would be relocated to make first contact with one of the new scribes. The protectorate documents suggested that Genevre was an artist of minimal repute, living alone in a small New Mexican town. Though Genevre's proximity to the Santa Fe protectorate was appealing, Cedar dreaded the thought of being sent to such an isolated place. Coll, on the other hand, was most likely to be in London. London had always fascinated Cedar, though she did not relish the idea of being sent anywhere in Europe during this war. Regardless, for now she could do little but wait for news. She and Jinjing seemed perpetually to be waiting to hear from the Council. They awaited letters from Ruis and Obeche, they awaited word about the war, they awaited news on the state of the Flaw, and now they awaited confirmation on the acceptance of the prospective outside world scribes. Certainly, after weeks of labour and anxious anticipation of results, they could at least take the opportunity to relax and temporarily distract themselves from the long wait ahead.

At first, Jinjing and Cedar sat together silently in the protectorate library and listened. After a few minutes, Jinjing removed a tapestry and opened one of the windows to bring in the cool air. No flashes, no blasts, no shrieks, not even a whiff of smoke carried on the wind from a distance. Peace had temporarily descended. Surely, they could open all the shutters and enjoy natural light for the day, even if the cold required them to wrap themselves in heavy shawls. Surely their efforts, like the siege, could come at least to a brief cessation.

A man in a nearby street broke the silence with a laugh, and others followed suit.

Jinjing shook her head. "They are naïve," she affirmed quietly.

"Even the wisest among us are naïve on occasion," responded Cedar. She moved away from the window to take a seat on the tableside bench.

"You sound like the Azoth Magen. Have you Azothian aspirations?" asked Jinjing. She remained at the window.

Though she suspected Jinjing to be teasing, Cedar responded in earnest. "Most certainly not. Ruis has ambition enough for us both, despite his failings. Or perhaps because of them."

"Ambition may not be the deciding factor for Azothian ascendance. You need look no further than to Obeche for confirmation."

Cedar smiled. She had grown to appreciate Jinjing's sense of humour and her jibes at Obeche.

"What do you see in him?" Cedar asked. "Or what *did* you see in him when you first met?"

"Nothing at first. I just relished his praise," admitted Jinjing. "Early on, I'd purposely align my hours in the library to coincide with those he monitored. He'd encourage my talents. *Stop fretting*, he would say. *Your work is pristine. Our manuscripts and keys and catalogues will be in good hands when you are an official Keeper of the Book.* When that day finally arrived, he kissed me for the first time to wish me luck. I liked it. I wanted more, and I told him as much." She laughed, blushing. "As I grew to know him over the years, his integrity is what kept me enamoured. But of late . . ."

"Yes . . . *of late*," repeated Cedar. She understood Jinjing's dilemma. The same qualms had needled her over the past year regarding Ruis.

"They're each on a mission," said Jinjing. "Obeche and Ruis. They removed the Flaw once, so they believe they can do so again. You'd think they were both Azoths already. Can you picture the two of them, side by side, making Azothian decisions?"

"I try not to," said Cedar. Yet she could, of course. She doubted Obeche would ever progress above Novillian given his temperament. But she could picture Ruis as Azoth, even as Azoth Magen. And in the process of such reveries, she had occasionally questioned her commitment not only to him but to the Council. She did not relish the prospect of Ruis lording Azothian status over her or, worse, of giving her a direct command that she would have to follow despite her misgivings. Their differences of opinion might eventually prove their undoing. *Of late* she had, indeed, begun to imagine a different world, one that she could be comfortable inhabiting for a potential eternity. *Of late*, Ruis was, more often than not, absent from her imagined scenario.

"The people of Qingdao believe the war has ended. I'm certain it has barely begun."

Cedar nodded. Jinjing stood across the table from her. She stared at her, contemplating.

"Thousands will become millions," Jinjing said. "The dead will outnumber the living. War will never cease. Yet I ask myself what's worse — the death of millions of the outside world or the end to all beings of all dimensions."

Cedar knew she must now proceed with care, regardless of their past conversations, regardless of how far from orthodoxy they had strayed together before the current peace in Qingdao. Jinjing's hesitancy regarding Obeche or her questioning of *what is worse* did not necessarily equate with a complete condemnation of the Council or its rites forevermore. And if it did, even Cedar could not condone such heresy outright.

"Ruis and Obeche aim to prevent further carnage," offered Cedar. "If they can remove the Flaw again, if ultimate Final Ascension *can* happen, they believe all will be well. If so, these wars and their casualties will be forgotten eternally."

Jinjing moved to the small stool at the end of the table. She tilted back her head, stretching muscles sore from dozens upon dozens of hours labouring over the manuscripts in dim lighting. From her seated position, Jinjing was able to tilt her head back far enough for her long, braided hair to touch the floor. She appeared both youthful and weary.

"Ruis and Obeche aim, once again, to remove the Flaw in the Lapis," Jinjing said, her head upright, her eyes piercing. "They claim the best of intentions. They claim to speak for all as they work towards saving themselves. They claimed as much only a few months ago before their success and subsequent failure. Observe the results."

"They *do* work towards saving us all, Jinjing, not themselves alone. No matter one's faith in their ability to succeed, or in the outcome of ultimate Final Ascension, their aspirations incorporate *all*." Cedar realized her path might diverge with Jinjing here. Though she did not believe Final Ascension resulted in life-everlasting, and though she believed in maintaining the Flaw in the Stone, Cedar nonetheless believed Ruis and even Obeche had honourable intentions. She had to believe they were principled or she would have to part ways from Ruis.

"But who is *all*, Cedar? All the alchemists? All the rebels? All the people of the outside world? All the people of Qingdao?"

"Yes. *All* will be One. So it is written. But I do not—"

"Whose One?"

"The quintessential One—"

"No, not who *is* One? *Whose* One? To whom does this quintessential One belong?"

"According to the Law Codes, the One belongs to us all in Final Ascension."

"No, Cedar. The One is theirs alone. The One is represented in *their* manuscripts, in *their* sacraments, in *their* histories, and in *their* mythologies. It

242

does not belong to the people of the outside world, not even to outside world scribes. They choose the One for themselves. Have they ever even thought to offer that choice to us? Have you?"

"The Council cannot offer each individual—" Cedar began, but Jinjing held up her hand.

"You misunderstand, Cedar. My question itself illustrates the problem. If the Alchemists' Council were to *offer* us a choice, then our choice would be inherently dependent on their goodwill to extend the offer and respect our choice."

Cedar breathed deeply and adjusted her pendant on its cord before responding. "The outside world has benefitted from the Law Codes and the vows the Council follows to maintain elemental balance throughout the dimensions."

"Do you think me blind, Cedar? I have observed the result of the abuses of those codes and vows over these months in Qingdao. Should the choice to save or kill ourselves — the people of Qingdao, the people of the outside world — not be ours alone? Should we not control the balance of our world? Should we not *learn* to protect ourselves? We've never been left to fend for ourselves without Council interference."

"The people of the outside world cannot be expected to protect themselves. Qingdao alone has illustrated as much." Cedar's growing agitation was evident in her voice.

"Qingdao alone? Qingdao has *never* been alone. The choices of others have been thrust upon us

243

— whether by the Council or otherwise. And here we are, well advanced into a war that could easily have been prevented had the Council not lost its focus, not forgotten to protect those for whom they uttered their vows. We could have done better if we had been left alone from the beginning — if the Council had never taken its vows, if the Council had never interfered."

"You speak blasphemy, Jinjing. And you have spoken it in the presence of a Lapidarian Scribe." Immediately, Cedar felt a twinge of guilt and lowered her head. She had perhaps crossed a line in her pursuit of assessing the opinions of a potential ally regarding the need to maintain the Flaw. She needed time to process what Jinjing was asking her to acknowledge.

"What have I left to lose? Is this not as good a time as any to utter my truth?" asked Jinjing. "Around me are the dead and the naïve." She gestured towards the window. "Yet with them I have found a place."

"A privileged place, Jinjing. To pretend otherwise would be hypocritical. You speak of the oppression of the Council making choices on your behalf, yet you have reaped its countless benefits for many years. If not for the relative safety of the protectorate library, you yourself might well be among the dead of Qingdao. And if not for Lapidarian honey — even in its relative scarcity of these months — you may well have died long ago, long before the advent of war. We have *all* benefitted from the

Council." She paused, observing Jinjing, whose eyes were closed. "And we must all continue to do so."

"Must we?"

"Jinjing! Would you truly choose to leave if the opportunity arose?"

"Would you?"

"How old were you when you were first approached by Council?" Cedar asked Jinjing as they sat down to their afternoon tea. They had barely spoken since their heated discussion that morning, and Cedar longed to break the tension before venturing further into assessing Jinjing's stance on Council politics.

"Thirty-two."

Cedar smiled. "I was only twenty, as are most Initiates. I am now two hundred and . . . forty-one. I often forget my age since I am rarely asked for my outside world birthdate. As you know, after Elixir, Council counts an alchemist's time only in pendant years."

"Let me hear it," suggested Jinjing, automatically moving her hands into the second position of the Ab Uno.

"I am Cedar, Lapidarian Scribe of the Alchemists' Council. I have carried my pendant for two hundred and eleven years," she said by rote.

Jinjing smiled and then sighed, frowning. "You are fortunate to have been chosen as an alchemist, to have been granted Elixir and a pendant rather than having to rely solely on Lapidarian honey. As you can see, I appear much older than you despite my relative youth." She ran a hand over her hair.

"How old are you?"

"Ninety-six."

"I have never quite understood the alchemy of Lapidarian honey, despite my years on Council," admitted Cedar. "Its properties are so diverse — affecting different people at different levels of potency. I could name a few cooks who've aged much faster than you appear to have done. You seem to have been fortunate with your Lapidarian results. At ninety-six, you don't look a day over forty."

Jinjing laughed. Perhaps she too was in a better mood now that a few hours had passed since their discussion, now that they both had time to remember one poignant reality: they were currently one another's only company. All in all, despite this morning, Jinjing had certainly proven herself a much better companion than Cedar was likely to have encountered in any of the European protec-torates, including Vienna. She shook her head at the thought of Vienna.

"No matter what the ratio, my life has certainly been extended. In that sense, as you suggested ear-lier, the Council has kept its promise to me, for better or worse."

"For better or worse?" Cedar asked, careful to maintain a neutral tone. After all, Jinjing appeared to have capitulated on at least one point. And Cedar wanted her to know that she was ready and willing to listen.

"Sometimes — especially when I am able to walk through parts of Qingdao and observe its people — I wonder what would have become of me if I had simply lived out my natural life. What if I had declined the Council's offer when they first contacted me? What if I had flatly refused or feigned indifference when asked to venture to Council dimension? If the names you and I submitted yesterday are verified by the Elders, the choice Council presented to me is the same choice they will give both Coll and Genevre. A hundred years from now, will they question their choices as I'm now questioning mine? Will they carry on, completely content — or completely naïve — eventually pursuing their paths as Keepers of the Book? Or will they begin their journeys only to give up? Will they come to recognize the flaws in the system — flaws much more difficult to erase than the Flaw in the Stone?" She stopped momentarily and sighed. "I also wonder what would have become of me if at some point during the first few years, long before I became Keeper of the Book, long before my friends and family had faded away, I had abandoned my post at my first inkling of dissatisfaction. Perhaps I'd not be feeling the way I currently do."

"What caused that — your first inkling of dissatisfaction?"

"I'd become close to my mentor, a Lapidarian Scribe named Erez."

"Erez! Yes! I admired him. We share name-sakes."

"Ah, I'd forgotten, *erez* means *cedar*. Truthfully, I fell in love with him. That can happen on occasion when a Council Scribe and outside world scribe work closely together. A certain intimacy is shared. Consider that advanced warning for your work with Coll or Genevre."

Cedar smiled. "What happened?"

"He was called to conjunction. And he wasn't victorious. And for weeks I understood the sacrament as a barbaric ritual."

"The Sacrament of Conjunction is a necessity for replenishing Quintessence."

"I recognize that, Cedar. The privileges we hold depend upon the sacrifices of others. I appreciate as much as I loathe that fact. But Scribe Erez became, in that single moment of his conjunction, my great unrequited love."

"Does she know? Ravenea, I mean. Does she know you loved the one with whom she conjoined?"

"She knows I wished for his victory."

"Then she also knows you longed for her demise."

After admitting her love for Erez and regret for Ravenea's victory, Jinjing had sighed and returned to her document work in another room. Later, having exchanged a few pleasantries over evening tea, Cedar again ventured back into the conversation that Jinjing had brought to a close.

"What of other friends in Council dimension? What of Obeche? He's provided you with some comfort, has he not?"

"Obeche has been a lovely distraction for several years."

Cedar could not imagine Obeche as *lovely*.

"But the outside world war has begun to affect my sense of purpose," Jinjing continued. "I fear my sense of duty will soon conflict entirely with Obeche's. I don't want to hurt him. But, as you know, of late I blame the Council for slacking in its duties to maintain the balance of the world. I blame the Elders for focusing too much on their precious Lapis and its Flaw. *Forget the Flaw*, I want to scream. *Let it increase! Focus instead on fixing the outside world! Abandon the One!* At other times, I find myself thinking quite the opposite: that perhaps it would be best under the circumstances if Council did indeed find a means of permanently eliminating the Flaw and of achieving ultimate Final Ascension thereafter. I'm such a hypocrite!"

"No, Jinjing. I appreciated your questioning of the One earlier today. I question it too. I fear life as we know it would end."

"Yes. We would all rise infinitely into the One."

"No. We would all die." Cedar paused, assessing

Jinjing's reaction. "I apologize for my earlier outburst. You can speak the truth to me. No one is listening to us. I'm not asking you to explain your reservations about faith in the One. I'm asking directly: Do you believe we would all, in fact, *become* One?"

"I don't believe in the One. But I believe we all *could* die. And if we do, then I hope we all die simultaneously, together, without prolonged suffering, without invading each other's lands, without the sounds of bombs and gunfire, without individuals dying in the streets and fields in agony, without death threatening, lingering, never quite taking hold even when so many pray for it to do so. Living in perpetual anguish in the outside world is exhausting. On days filled with such thoughts, I find myself hoping the Elders can permanently eliminate the Flaw. On other days, I simply long for the world to be released from Council oppression."

"You indeed have been jaded by the events in Qingdao."

"And you seem completely unaffected by the suffering surrounding you now."

Cedar paused, considering her response. She had planned to learn more about Jinjing today, but the conversation had continually ventured into territory she had not been expecting to explore. Was Jinjing correct in her assessment and all that it implied? Was Cedar ignoring the intensity of suffering in the war-drenched segments of the world in order to ensure that she herself survived? She wondered if Jinjing was testing her, seeing just how rebellious her rebel sympathies were, deliberately goading her into saying something she might regret — something for which she might be accountable to the Elders. Perhaps her work here in Qingdao was a test, a Lapidarian version of the complex Initiate tests she had undergone years ago. Or perhaps she was merely being paranoid. Perhaps the sounds of battle resuming once again in the distance were affecting her more than she realized.

"I appreciate your candour," Cedar finally replied. "You have been in Qingdao much longer than I, and you have first-hand knowledge of the people and events here that I could never hope to gain. But I cannot agree that eliminating the Flaw is the answer. If such a statement is blasphemy, then so be it. I'm not the only member of the Alchemists' Council who has advised caution on the matter over the years, and certainly not since the Third Rebellion. Yes, the people are suffering. Yes, this war is devastating. Yes, ultimate Final Ascension offers us a means to end all such misery. But do we want to end *all* life for the sake of ending its less admirable aspects?"

"The Elders may tolerate the occasional dissenting voice — whether yours or that of any other Council member. They also know that dissenters are few and far between. In the end, your meagre efforts will be for nought since you're one among many. If the Flaw is eliminated, you alone cannot re-inscribe it."

Cedar waited. She watched Jinjing, assessing her movements. Jinjing's right index finger tapped slowly and softly on the table. Finally, the complexities of all Jinjing had said to her that day sifted into one radical thought that she dared in that moment to express.

"You're right. I most certainly cannot re-inscribe it alone. I would require assistance from the Rebel Branch."

Jinjing stopped tapping. She stood up, leaving the room without saying a word. Had Cedar misinterpreted? Had she failed the test? Was Jinjing determining a means to report Cedar as a blasphemous traitor? Her heart raced. But, within a minute, Jinjing had returned. She held two small glasses and a bottle of plum wine. She set down the glasses, filled each with wine, passed one to Cedar, and held the other up towards her.

"A toast!" said Jinjing. "To the Rebel Branch!"

"To the Rebel Branch!" replied Cedar. She felt both calm and exhilarated, fearful and brave. But later, as she settled into bed for the night, the tapestry once again placed carefully over her window, she recognized with palpable relief that she had found an ally in Jinjing. They had found each other. Never again would either be alone in her dissent.

Jinjing sat on a wooden bench in a small abandoned hut; its open-walled structure suggested it had once served to sell wares — vegetables perhaps, or pottery. Cedar had returned to Council dimension a month ago but had managed to contact her last week by concealing a letter inside a messenger-delivered box of Lapidarian honey and other supplies. The letter confirmed that Cedar had made contact with the rebels and requested they in turn make contact with Jinjing. Yesterday, she received a note from a young boy, who had arrived breathless but proud, clearly content to have succeeded at the task of navigating the streets undetected. Jinjing assumed he had been bribed and convinced his mission was part of the war effort. And she hoped the bribe had been worthy of the risk, perhaps food enough for a meal — something he could bring back to his family — rather than a trifle, like a small biscuit or sweet he had consumed along the journey. The note had said to meet here, so here she waited, excited but anxious.

Two soldiers walked by, one of whom noticed her and paused briefly, as if unsure of his next move. She lowered her head and huddled closer to the wall. Perhaps convinced she was merely an old woman taking temporary shelter, he turned away again and carried on alongside his companion. Jinjing sat upright again and glanced around. The rain had stopped. The only person in sight was a figure — features indistinguishable from this distance — walking along the main road in Jinjing's direction. If this was the person she was meeting, she could not imagine why the hut was chosen as the rendez-vous point. Would it not have been prudent to meet farther down the road, farther away from the heavier trafficked area?

Jinjing became more nervous the closer the figure appeared. Even when only a hundred feet or so away, she still could not tell whether she was watching a man or a woman. Not until the person stood within a few feet of her was Jinjing able to discern her identity. Her rebel contact was a young woman with pale eyes and skin.

"Jinjing?" she said.

"Yes."

"I am Kalina. Junior Scribe of the Rebel Branch of the Alchemists' Council. I have carried my Dragonblood pendant for six years. My current mission is to increase the Flaw in the Stone."

"Six years?" repeated Jinjing. "Does the Rebel Branch assume my intentions unworthy of a meeting with someone more . . . mature?"

Kalina maintained her composure despite the insult.

"You will be meeting with the High Azoth. I have been sent as your escort. Given my age and relative anonymity — unknown, that is, to anyone on Council who might make an impromptu visit to the Qingdao protectorate today — the Rebel Branch Elders decided to assign me with this . . . *vital* task."

"Sarcasm does not become you."

"Very few things become me, Jinjing — hence my training to become someone else."

"A noble aspiration."

"Time will tell. For now, I remain a Junior Scribe, and preparatory work awaits us. Take this fragment and follow me — walk far enough behind me that we do not appear to the casual observer to be together." Kalina held out a small red stone, which Jinjing immediately placed into a pocket in her jacket. Kalina turned and continued along the road in the direction she had been walking before stopping at the hut.

Jinjing followed several steps behind, slowing her pace when necessary. She marvelled at their ability to progress down this road at all without being questioned by any number of men in uniform. Perhaps they gave little mind to women. Or perhaps the fragment of stone Kalina had given her had protective properties of some sort. Why was so much of her understanding based on mere guesswork these days?

After walking for at least half an hour, they finally arrived at a flagpole, though it held no flag. Jinjing glanced out at the harbour and the vessels on the water. She supposed someday this pole would be claimed by the victors.

"Take my hand," said Kalina. "Place your other hand on the pole."

Jinjing did as instructed, noticing in the process the softness of Kalina's hand compared to her own. *To be young again* was Jinjing's final thought before the world around her became a blur and she was being whisked through a portal. By the time they emerged at their destination, Jinjing had temporarily forgotten her wistful nostalgia for youth and simply felt thankful to have arrived alive. She blinked several times in an attempt to focus her eyes in the dim light. She could hear a noise that sounded like bamboo wind chimes in the distance.

"Where are we?" asked Jinjing.

"Flaw dimension," responded Kalina moving away from the portal and along a corridor.

Jinjing followed, of course. She had not yet been instructed otherwise. The corridor appeared made of natural stone, as if the Flaw dimension were carved into solid rock. She sensed they were underground, though she had no means of knowing for certain. Why, Jinjing wondered as she followed Kalina, would a group of alchemists — even rebel alchemists — choose such a dark and dismal landscape when they could instead choose the beauty of Council dimension? She then wondered about her own future landscape given her choices of late. Perhaps she should attempt to find some pleasure in these cold stone walls. When the corridor opened into a large, well-lit cavern filled with tables and shelves heaped with manuscripts and scrolls, Jinjing could only assume she had been granted the privilege of stepping into a Rebel Branch library or archive collection. How could they possibly trust her with this knowledge? How could they trust her not to report to the Elders a storehouse of information that Council could pillage?

Kalina gestured for her to take a seat. Though Jinjing did not want to be impolite, she could not help but stare directly at Kalina on occasion. Her hair and skin were so pale that to Jinjing she appeared illusory, as if she were a fragile doll and not a real person at all. Perhaps all alchemists of the Rebel Branch had an air of otherworldliness to them. Or perhaps all alchemists did, and Jinjing simply had never noticed amidst the sensuous splendours that imbued Council dimension. Here in the shade-filled, misty caverns of Flaw dimension, Kalina simply seemed ethereal against the darkness. Jinjing smiled, expressed her gratitude again, and then lowered her eyes.

Five minutes later, a man in bright blue robes entered the room and approached her. Jinjing looked into his bright green eyes as he stood before her. "I am Dracaen, High Azoth of the Rebel Branch of the Alchemists' Council."

Only when he extended a hand, and she reached out to him in return, did Jinjing notice she was shaking, that she still needed to relinquish the stereotypes she had so long carried regarding the Rebel Branch. What had she to fear? After all, the rebels valued free will above all. What harm could come to her among a group of people who claimed to value her choices as much as their own?

VI

Other than with Jinjing, whom she now considered a friend, Cedar had no previous experience working closely with outside world scribes. She had, of course, often worked in their proximity, engaged them in conversation, requested items, or assigned tasks as she did with any of the outside world workers. Certainly, she appreciated their importance to the Council, especially as potential candidates to become Keepers of the Book. But she had never engaged with one at the level of intimacy required of teaching and assessing a new recruit. Ruis would take exception to this assessment by reminding her of the sexual liaison she had undertaken with Oren, an outside world scribe of the Vienna protectorate, half a century ago. But she would counter that her weeks of passion with

Oren did not count since they were not specifically engaged in Council duties at the time.

Outside world scribes worked primarily in the protectorates under supervision of the Magistrates. They came to Council dimension only when training or working on tasks with specific Lapidarian or Novillian Scribes. Often engaging directly with the Keeper of the Book to help translate or transcribe outside world alchemical manuscripts, they had proven integral to Council operations. According to Ruis, Coll was proving particularly useful in his work with Eurig, Keeper of the Book of the London protectorate. *A Keeper of the Book in the making himself*, Ruis had whispered to her regarding Coll when Cedar had visited the London protectorate last week. But Coll had already established himself in the outside world as both an alchemical adept and as a masterful poet prior to beginning his manuscript labours. To become a Keeper of the Book, he would have to be willing to pledge himself for life to the Council. In Cedar's opinion, that prospect was unlikely given Coll's numerous and varied connections to the outside world. Her own new charge — Genevre — seemed a much more likely candidate to remain faithful to the Alchemists' Council.

As far as Council Elders and Readers were concerned, Genevre had not yet distinguished herself in the outside world. Yes, like Coll, she had her creative talents. What good would she be to Council at all without a previously honed skill that a Council

Scribe could readily transform into something useful for manuscript work? In Genevre's case, that skill was with inks and paints, papers and canvases. Whereas Coll was a poet renowned in various European cities, Genevre worked as a painter in a small American town only recently becoming known for its emerging artists. Admittedly, Cedar had come to recognize that rhetorical skills were not as significant to the scribal endeavour as she had once believed. Anyone could read or copy written text. But only a few could master vibrant manuscript illuminations. Perhaps such alchemical illustrations were to become Genevre's forte. Of course, like all potential outside world scribes, Genevre also appeared to be reasonably adept at alchemy — as much as anyone outside Council dimension could be given their inherent limitations. All outside world scribes had dabbled in alchemy for years, though they certainly could not be considered true alchemists. At that thought, Cedar shook her head wondering how many of her entrenched beliefs would be challenged before her outside world tenure ended.

So here she was, waiting on the porch of a traditional Santa Fe house — box-like with a flat roof and clay-coloured walls. She had knocked and, at the lack of response, sat to rest in a rocking chair near the door. Her walk from the temporary portal ground had taken half an hour in the bright sun and cool air. The atmosphere was pleasant, she thought as she rocked herself gently. A budding cottonwood tree proved a unique feature of the yard, which was artistically landscaped by someone who clearly appreciated attention to detail. Perhaps this new recruit would prove to be a viable scribe for more than only her skill with inks.

After twenty minutes or so, a striking woman appeared at the gate. She had olive skin and jet black hair, emphasized by a streak of white near her temple. She wore strands of turquoise beads, which hung from her neck across the front of a loose green cotton dress. She smiled, and Cedar blushed because the woman simply looked too beautiful in the late afternoon sun.

"Hello," said the woman.

"Hello. I'm Cedar. Sorry if I startled you — a stranger in your garden."

"Not at all. I'm Genevre."

How strange, thought Cedar, that Genevre seemed completely at ease by her unexpected presence. Perhaps day-to-day life was calmer by nature in Santa Fe, undoubtedly more so than in other parts of the current world with its raging battles.

"Hello, Genevre. I've been sent to speak with you."

"Sent?"

"Yes. By Elders of the . . . That is, by a group of . . . alchemists."

"Alchemists!" Genevre laughed. "Well, how intriguing you have sought me out. It appears news of my eccentricities has spread. Are *you* an alchemist?"

Though an understanding of basic alchemical principles was a key characteristic the Council required of all outside world workers, the immediacy of Genevre's question surprised her. *Be completely upfront during your first meeting*, Ailanthus had said during her preparation session. *Doing so will allow you to evaluate responses and thus determine suitablility. If a potential outside world scribe appears to lack basic knowledge of alchemy, walk away. The candidate will gradually forget the encounter if never brought into Lapidarian proximity for training.*

"Don't worry," Genevre assured her. "I've been longing to meet someone who shares my fascination."

"Yes. I'm an alchemist. I'm known within our group as a Lapidarian Scribe."

"What are your duties?"

"We're trained to inscribe alchemical manuscripts with Lapidarian ink — that is, ink gleaned by Novillian Scribes from the Lapis."

"The blue gemstone?"

"No. *The* Stone — the one you would likely call the Philosopher's Stone."

"You inscribe manuscripts with ink made from the Philosopher's Stone? So you're quite powerful within your group, no?"

"Relatively, I suppose. But the Elders — the alchemists who sent me to you — have even more experience and knowledge."

"Why would the Elders be interested in me?"

"They believe you've shown alchemical potential — that you could help us as an outside world scribe."

Genevre laughed. "My knowledge of alchemy is limited, though I'm reasonably well versed in the works collected by Ashmole in *Theatrum Chemicum Britannicum*. What I would give for a visit to the British Library to see an original alchemical manuscript!" She sighed and shrugged.

Cedar smiled then, imagining the expression Genevre would sport upon first crossing the threshold of Council dimension's North Library.

"Of course, I wouldn't want to be in Europe right now. I prefer to be ensconced in relative safety here. Granted, it's rather backwoods — so to speak — in its distance even from major American cities. But I've always liked the idea of striking out on my own. Though I have to be honest and say that I wasn't alone when I first arrived. I had a man with me — a lover — who has since departed. We weren't married, understand. I trust you're not offended."

With each word Genevre uttered, Cedar became that much more enamoured with her, far more than she had been with Coll.

"No," said Cedar. "Not at all."

"So, are you here to convince me to use my knowledge of alchemy for the war effort?"

"Well . . . indirectly . . . I suppose."

"In that case, will you come in and have a cup of tea? If nothing else, I am certainly patriotic and will agree to do my duty if at all possible. Women are underutilized if you ask me."

"Right," replied Cedar. *Though not women on Council,* she thought to herself.

Thus, Cedar found herself sitting across the table from Genevre. She would recall this meeting with fondness even decades later: Genevre smiling and chatting, radiant in the dust-filled streams of sunlight that soaked the room. She talked animatedly, pouring and refilling the tea over the first hour. By the second hour, Genevre had brought bread and cheese and figs to the table. Never did she react to Cedar's explanation of herself or the Elders or the Council or even of Council dimension as if it were a shocking revelation. Such was the way with outside world scribes, Cedar assumed — so different from potential Initiates, whose alchemical ability was genetic but whose knowledge of outside world alchemy was minimal at best. What good would outside world scribes be if easily alarmed or unable to accept the possibility of a world beyond the one they already know? Genevre responded with notable enthusiasm on the occasions that Cedar would provide a particularly detailed description of Council dimension landscape.

"I would love to sit there," she admitted after Cedar had described the Amber Garden.

"As would I," responded Cedar. "I have spent only two days in Council dimension over the last several months. As pleasant as this visit with you has been so far, I long to go home now. I must say, though, that I find your property here is quite charming — exquisite really, especially considering the relatively barren landscape."

"I will take that as a compliment."

"My apologies if I've offended."

"You made a geographical observation — hardly an offence. Tell me then, Cedar, how many . . . *outside world* people work for the Council? And what is it that you and the Council will be asking of me?"

"The Council employs dozens of outside world workers to assist with our alchemical duties and daily needs. For example, in each library the position of Keeper of the Book is held by someone who originally trained as an outside world scribe. We also employ cooks and gardeners and artisans and wardens. As payment, these workers receive all they need to live contentedly along with a supply of Lapidarian honey — honey produced by the bees of Council dimension and thus infused with Quintessence. The honey improves their health and prolongs their lives. Of course, their bodies still age and deteriorate at a faster rate than do those of Council members. But a lifespan of more than two hundred years is certainly not unusual."

"Are you offering me such a position — one that would extend my life?" asked Genevre.

"Yes. We have need of a new influx of outside world scribes. Initially, you would work with the

Keeper of the Book in the Santa Fe protectorate library. Eventually, you would be brought to Council dimension for specialized training by Lapidarian and Novillian Scribes, likely including me. In general, you would be helping us to transcribe and protect certain manuscripts. If all progresses smoothly over the first few decades, and you wish to prolong your tenure with us, you could apply to train as a Keeper of the Book."

"As interesting and flattering as this proposal appears, I must ask why you've chosen me. What distinguishes me from anyone else in Santa Fe?"

"Under normal circumstances, as is the practice with choosing new Initiates, potential outside world scribes are located by our Readers who interpret manuscripts. The process is lengthy and complicated and occasionally flawed."

"Flawed?"

"There have been mistakes. Even I have arrived on occasion in the wrong place at the wrong time — finding no potential Initiate in sight."

"How can you be certain that the Readers were correct about me? What if you are in the wrong place at the wrong time right now? What if I am not intended to be a scribe for the Alchemists' Council after all?"

"The Readers were not solely responsible for finding you. The Council is currently operating under war measures — not because of the outside world war, but because of the internal problems that may well have led to the outside world conflicts. You were located by a combination of procedures undertaken by Readers and Keepers of the Book. I myself found a sign that led us to you while working with Keeper of the Book Jinjing in the Qingdao protectorate — in China. You were then approved for assessment by the Elders. One of my duties now is to evaluate your potential as we speak."

"And what is your verdict?"

"So far, I approve," announced Cedar. "But our conversation is far from over."

Genevre nodded. "No, I suppose it's only just begun. Where am I to work? Where is the protectorate library of Santa Fe?"

"Temporarily it's housed in a small adobe structure near San Miguel Mission. We hope to move the manuscripts to a more spacious and less exposed permanent location as soon as possible. Apparently, a hotel will be constructed within the next decade that Council already has a hand in planning — a design that will include secreted rooms for protectorate purposes."

"Move the manuscripts? So, will you need to assess my muscular strength and determine how many manuscripts I can comfortably carry?"

Cedar laughed. "I doubt the scribes will be required to do more than supervise such manual labour. Time will tell, of course. First we must succeed at our current undertaking — ending the wars both within and outside Council dimension and re-establishing balance of the outside world."

"When do I begin?"

"I must consult with the Elders first. We're meeting at the protectorate early tomorrow. If you're successful, you will be required to dedicate your time to us, not to your current worldly work. You will be taken to the library and introduced to Gad, Keeper of the Book of the Santa Fe protectorate. You'll then begin your training."

They spoke for another hour before Cedar shook Genevre's hand and walked back across the yard and down the street towards the protectorate portal. She was certain that she and Jinjing had correctly identified Genevre as an outside world scribe. Any lingering doubt she might have had was erased completely when they touched hands. If she had not known better, she would have assumed Genevre had been granted Elixir. Or perhaps she had ingested some Lapidarian honey at some point along her journey. After all, Council honey had made its way into the world on various occasions thanks to a few outside world beekeepers who housed Lapidarian bees for the Council and distributed — with or without permission — a jar or two of Lapidarian honey among family and friends as a curative for a flu or cold. Perhaps Genevre had once been cured by Council Quintessence without even knowing so. Perhaps as a child she had been fed, unwittingly, a spoonful or two of Lapidarian honey by her mother.

Or perhaps, as Ruis was sure to suggest, Cedar had simply been enticed once again by the beauty and charm of an outside world scribe.

Flaw Dimension — Summer 1915

Within six months, and somewhat to her chagrin, Jinjing had in all but name become a spy for Dracaen. On each occasion that she returned to Flaw dimension for additional rebel training and strategizing, Dracaen inevitably drilled her for information — especially if she had spent more than a few days in Council dimension rather than in Qingdao. To Jinjing's dismay, he never seemed completely satisfied with her answers. *I am a Keeper of the Book, not an Elder*, Jinjing reminded him repeatedly.

"What of the new outside world scribes?" he asked her earlier that day. "Do you see a future Keeper among them?"

"We have only two — Coll and Genevre — but I would be premature in assuming their future roles," Jinjing responded.

"No particular news on one or the other?"

She would have assumed Dracaen's question typical among his other inquiries had Kalina not also brought up the topic of the outside world scribes. They were seated in one of the cavernous archive rooms reading about cinnabar inks.

"What can you tell me of Genevre?" Kalina asked immediately after Jinjing had mentioned both her and Coll.

Jinjing tilted her head back and stared at the ceiling. She contemplated her next move. Clearly Genevre, not the two outside world scribes in general, was of interest to the rebels.

"Who is Genevre? Who is she to *you*?" she asked Kalina.

"My mother," responded Kalina.

Jinjing firmly held her lips closed to prevent herself from expressing audible shock.

"Are you surprised?" asked Kalina.

"Only that . . . Only that you would entrust me with such . . . information," said Jinjing.

"I consider myself an excellent judge of character," Kalina assured her. "In fact, such intuitiveness is a trait of alchemical children, according to manuscript lore. But never having met another, I cannot know for certain."

"Another what?"

"Alchemical child. As far as I know, I'm the only one to exist."

Jinjing's first instinct had been correct: Kalina truly was a mystical creature. The trembling she had felt months earlier when she first arrived in Flaw dimension returned with this new knowledge. Jinjing had never known such powerful alchemy to be possible. She had assumed, like everyone in Council dimension, that the homunculus was a figment of the rather vivid reimagining of alchemy by false practitioners — as far from true alchemy as outside world alchemists were from members of the Alchemists' Council. Perhaps, as Dracaen was fond of explaining, the Rebel Branch truly did comprise alchemists with superior powers to those of the Council. Perhaps Flaw dimension libraries were indeed replete with even more ancient manuscripts than Council dimension and the protectorates combined. Perhaps the Flaw would one day consume the bulk of the Stone, would encroach on Council dimension itself.

When assigned to the North Library in Council dimension rather than the protectorate library of Qingdao, Jinjing had had numerous opportunities to observe Genevre working with Cedar. But she had not noticed anything amiss. Indeed, not until Kalina's revelation did Jinjing even have reason to suspect Genevre was a rebel. Why had Cedar kept such an important detail from her?

"Does Cedar know of your connection with Genevre?"

"Cedar currently knows nothing about me. And what she knows of Genevre is minimal. Eventually, she'll recognize that Genevre has rebel sympathies, but she certainly won't suspect extensive rebel training. And she'd never fathom that Genevre and Dracaen had created an alchemical child together."

Upon hearing this detail, Jinjing had maintained her composure for Kalina's sake. But later, back in the Qingdao protectorate imagining Dracaen's proposal, she recoiled at the prospect of Genevre being lured by the promise of an alchemical child. She should have had more fortitude. She should have refused Dracaen's advances. Yes, Kalina was pleasant and, apparently, integral to the goal of mutual conjunction for all. But Jinjing nonetheless found the thought of mechanically engineering elements into human form ethically questionable. Was such a potent alchemical feat the ultimate manifestation of choice? Was Kalina the living embodiment of an end-game in a dimension literally built on free will? If so, perhaps Jinjing did not belong here after all.

These were the thoughts she fostered before becoming a hypocrite. These were thoughts Jinjing later attempted to banish when she learned the truth of Dracaen's interest in her, on the day he proposed they become spouses in a chemical wedding.

Council Dimension — Fall 1915

In Santa Fe, talks continued regarding the art museum. Genevre could barely tolerate the conversations. But, of course, her friends and acquaintances — especially those whom she had not encountered for a while because of her Council work — continued to ask if Genevre had aspirations for a show herself. She would smile and laugh and claim she had not recently been inspired. When asked where she had been, she explained she had taken up work as an illustrator for government documents. *Top secret*, she would add. Given the news about the escalating war in Europe, responses would range from a raised eyebrow of doubt to wide-eyed shock. But no one asked for additional details or questioned her necessity to be unusually silent.

Genevre herself was not certain of the truth of her intentions. With the Flaw safely re-ensconced in the Stone, why not simply assist the Council in their repair of the world? The people of the outside world could certainly use the help. And doing so would in no way harm Dracaen's plan for mutual conjunction, which still required a variety of alchemical alignments alongside another century of outside world time. When Cedar first offered to take her through the Santa Fe portal to Council dimension for training, Genevre relished the opportunity. She could meet others. She could distract herself from thoughts of her art, and the war, and her daughter, and her continual yearning for a sibling for Kalina, someone to help her fulfill the alternative plan that she could sense, though not yet fully articulated, prickling under her skin, awaiting her conscious and reasoned scrutiny.

Though both Cedar and Gad had described it to her in detail, Council dimension was much airier and brighter than she had expected. She could not help but compare it to Flaw dimension. In place of caverns were gardens. In place of stone walls and hard-packed soil were vibrant murals and tiles. Genevre liked the glittering beauty of the Amber Garden best of all. Something about the movement of the light reminded her of her own garden in Santa Fe.

As her weeks of training passed, she worked alternately with Cedar, Saule, and Amur. Each Council Scribe worked with her on honing one specific skill. Amur was particularly gifted at gilding. Thus while working with him, Genevre also got to work with alchemically transmuted gold leaf, applying it onto manuscript folios or covers with Azadirian embellishment tools. These efforts were purely decorative in function. She most certainly would not be inscribing world-altering manuscript illuminations alongside the Lapidarian and Novillian Scribes. With Saule, she would work on transcribing copies of manuscripts, primarily for classroom or archival purposes. Genevre longed for the opportunity to speak with Saule privately; she wanted to converse not only about Kalina but also about Ilex and Melia. But someone was inevitably in close enough proximity to overhear. Coll, the other outside world scribe who had come to train alongside Genevre, was of particular annoyance — always present and working and seeming to outdo Genevre, despite her extensive Rebel Branch training. She grew increasingly suspicious of him as the weeks progressed, especially when he trained alone with Ruis, who clearly preferred him. She knew Ruis longed to perfect the Stone once again. Coll would learn of only one side of the story if Ruis were the only alchemist with whom he spoke.

Genevre came to enjoy her sessions with Cedar best of all. Though a Scribe, Cedar worked with Genevre on scribal concerns only part of their time together. During the final half hour of each lesson, Cedar taught Genevre how to read, interpret, and pronounce 5th Council dialect. Of course, Genevre recognized 5th Council script primarily from her transcription and study of the *Osmanthian Codex*. However, beyond brief phrases she had memorized for her wedding with Dracaen and conception of Kalina, she had never been effectively trained in the dialect's pronunciation. Now Genevre found herself purposely completing her daily inscriptions in rapid time in order to allow additional time for dialect practice. Skilled knowledge of 5th Council dialect pronunciation could prove far more useful to her future than gilding or transcription. Within a few weeks, pronunciation drills became the most cherished part of her entire Council experience.

Pointing to an alchemical symbol or series of characters, Cedar would phonetically pronounce the corresponding 5th Council word or phrase.

"Po-LEMINK-a man-a-tore-us tear-ATUNE-um," Cedar would say.

"Polem-INKA man-A-torus tear-A-tunim," Genevre would reply.

"No. Try again. Po-LEMINK-a."

"Po-LEMINK-a."

"Good. Man-a-tore-us."

"Man-a-tore-us."

"Tear-ATUNE-um."

"Tear-ATUNE-um."

"All together," Cedar would then say.

"*Polemica manatorus teratunum*," Genevre would reply.

"Excellent! Now, translate it."

"*Controversy binds the world.*"

And so on. Day after day, week after week, the lessons continued until Genevre could read aloud and understand full pages of text and, when prompted, conduct a rudimentary conversation with Cedar. Occasionally an evening lesson would progress much longer than scheduled, and Ruis would barge into the tutorial room requesting Cedar retire for the evening. On one such evening, Cedar wrote three 5th Council words onto a slip of parchment and passed it to Genevre before wishing her a good night.

"*Ilus min enkalios*," Genevre read aloud after Cedar had left the room. "*He is jealous.*" Genevre smiled, though she was not certain in that moment of what specifically he was jealous. Not until months later, after witnessing the propensity of alchemists to have romantic liaisons with each other regardless of gender, did she realize what it was that Ruis suspected. All was innocent, of course. Genevre had no intention of pursuing sexual relations with Cedar. Nonetheless, on that particular night, she found herself imagining being intimate with her. And this line of thought led Genevre to conceive of a new possibility. Cedar was a powerful alchemist who knew 5th Council dialect and could surely recite the ritual words accurately. What if Cedar could help her conceive another alchemical child? What if Genevre could convince Cedar of the child's importance to the future of the Council? Ferreting for clues as to Cedar's alliances thereafter became Genevre's mission between lessons. Basic questioning did not take her far. A strategy would be required if Genevre were to progress at all.

As it happened, Genevre's emerging skill as a specialist in 5th Council dialect proved useful as a step towards her goal. One afternoon when Ruis and Cedar were conducting a joint inscription lesson with Coll and Genevre, Coll asked a question about the Flaw in the Stone. Ruis began to recount aspects of the ritual that had led to its successful removal.

"You will try again soon, I presume?" questioned Coll.

"I will succeed again soon," answered Ruis.

Cedar then did something that Genevre found extraordinary. She replied to Ruis's comment using 5th Council dialect: *Tutee scala ralinquin hin encanitorum questus, mina eros.* Coll clearly had no idea what Cedar had said. And Ruis had no idea that Genevre could understand. He assumed the words

Cedar had spoken were understood by him alone. But Genevre did comprehend, not just the words but the underlying message. Cedar had purposely provided Genevre a hint at her allegiances. Now Genevre merely needed to figure out how committed Cedar was to her sacrilege: *You must relinquish this foolish quest, my love.*

ffⱡaw Dimension — Winter 1915

Jinjing had listened to Dracaen's proposal for a chemical wedding in early summer, had accepted it by midsummer, and had prepared herself for the intricacies of its rituals during the transition from summer to fall. At first, she marvelled at her ignorance — the wedding and its repercussions had been merely the stuff of legend from the perspective of a Keeper of the Book of the Alchemists' Council. But as the weeks progressed, whenever she officially attained a few hours or days extended leave from Council duties, Jinjing was schooled on the rituals by Azoth Fraxinus. She devoured the lessons and continued her studies during leisure hours. On the day Fraxinus called her *exceptional*, Jinjing beamed with contentment. The Elders of the Rebel Branch clearly respected her abilities and intelligence far more than the Council Elders had. Why would they otherwise have chosen her as the spouse of the High Azoth, as the mother of his children? Here Jinjing was embraced, not abandoned at a distant outpost.

On the crisp fall evening that Jinjing and Fraxinus carried the children from the pebble-like remains of the birthing alembic to the prepared chambers, she could not have felt prouder. As they walked, she admired the golden locks of her daughter's long, damp hair cascading over Fraxinus's shoulder. Her daughter looked like a miniature version of Kalina. And since Kalina shared no physical characteristics whatsoever with Dracaen or Genevre, Jinjing had not expected her son to have hair the colour and texture of her own. As he slept, she caressed his head, running her fingers through the dark and shiny tresses.

When both her son and daughter died in her arms the next day, Jinjing was inconsolable. Dracaen immediately suggested they try again, but Jinjing vehemently refused. She could not put herself through such anticipation and heartbreak again. At the depth of her anguish, she could not even recall the reason she had agreed to assist Dracaen in the first place.

But time passed, and eventually she agreed to assist Dracaen again. He convinced Jinjing that she must have mispronounced certain words of the ritual, thereby negatively affecting the elemental and chemical balance within the birthing alembic. *Practice will ensure perfection. Our children will save the world*, he insisted. So Jinjing rehearsed until she knew by rote both the diction and rhythm of her brief but cru-cial parts. Thus, when the Rebel Elders chanted the ritual from the ancient text, her responses were flaw-less. Yet her next child had not even matured in the alembic before the waters blackened and stagnated. *We must have combined the wrong ingredients*, said Dracaen. So they tried again. *The elements misaligned*, he said as his next excuse. And they tried again. *You must desire success as much as I do*, he insisted. On that occasion, the twins emerged from the alembic physi-cally conjoined and died within an hour. Thus passed the months of winter.

After five attempts, Dracaen concluded that the repeated failures were the fault of Jinjing alone. Her status as outside world scribe and Keeper of the Book was simply not enough. Her blood was not pure.

"You are not of the bloodline."

"I never claimed to be," Jinjing responded quietly.

"Azoth Fraxinus must have made an error in the reading."

"Regarding my suitability?" she asked.

"He claimed you were of the bloodline, but it appears you are not. I suggest you refrain from these visits until I next call upon you to return and assist," Dracaen concluded.

Jinjing found the remark callous. She was ashamed of herself in that moment — not because she had failed Dracaen as a chemical spouse, but because she had agreed to his demands time and time again rather than voicing her opinion in the matter. She left Flaw dimension that day intending never to return.

Genevre persevered, biding her time. Over a year had passed before she finally trusted Cedar enough to believe a proposal for a chemical wedding would at least be met with due consideration. She and Cedar had become close friends during their months of working together. Additional war measures instigated in reaction to the outside world crisis had made their work even more intense, especially of late. Between tasks, they often spoke at length about the Flaw in the Stone. Though Genevre refrained from admitting to her rebel training, she acknowledged her sympathies with certain aspects of rebel philosophy. And though Cedar showed no interest in supporting Rebel Branch control over the outside world, she nonetheless made her desire to maintain free will within the Council abundantly clear. Indeed, at times Genevre was convinced Cedar wanted Council to gain even more control over the outside world than they already possessed. She therefore could not reveal her entire plan to Cedar. Instead, Genevre would have to frame her intentions prudently.

As they neared the end of the year, Genevre

began to rehearse her proposal. She needed to convince Cedar that an alchemical child could help strengthen the Council, and could help provide a means of mutual conjunction within Council dimension, which would thereby provide alchemists a means to control more aspects of the outside world. Genevre saw no need to reveal that she and Dracaen had already married and created an alchemical child, nor explain that Kalina was to play a key role in Dracaen's ultimate plan for ensuring free will for all, including those of the outside world, through a conjunction of Alchemists' Council and Rebel Branch. Genevre need not explain any detail beyond those immediately necessary.

Guilt over these planned omissions occasionally surfaced. Genevre rationalized their necessity not only with her internal refrain — *for the good of the plan* — but also with sheer practicality. After all, if Cedar accepted her proposal, they would require months to prepare for the ceremony. Genevre would therefore have plenty of time to assess the situation and provide additional details to Cedar as required. For now, Genevre merely needed to make an official Gift of Proposal. She knew from her first wedding that a proposal could not be made, let alone sealed, without an object of significant symbolic and emotional value being offered. Dracaen had given her a feather, its shaft beaded with garnets, turquoise, and silver. He had found the feather in the outside world on the same day he had first met Genevre.

Dracaen himself had crafted the beadwork casing. The feather had thereafter been housed on a shelf in his main chambers, used regularly during ceremonial events to direct the mists or smoke over the ritual objects. Knowing the value of the feather to Dracaen, Genevre in turn appreciated the significance of his proposal.

When the appropriate day arrived, Genevre walked arm in arm with Cedar to the Amber Garden and presented her with the bee-embossed copper coin detached from Kalina's braiding dress. With the exception of her braiding ring, the coin was Genevre's most cherished object. What better gift to present to the person with whom she hoped to conceive a second child?

"What is this?" asked Cedar.

"A Gift of Proposal. A symbol of my commitment to you," Genevre responded. "I propose a chemical marriage for the purpose of creating an alchemical child."

Cedar appeared perplexed. Several awkward seconds passed.

"The coin is beautiful," responded Cedar finally. "But I don't understand. A chemical wedding? An alchemical child? Genevre, I'm flattered you would consider me as your chemical spouse, but . . . the homunculus is . . . the homunculus is little more than an ancient fable, lost centuries ago along with the bloodline."

"No," said Genevre. "We don't need the blood-line. I found a ritual in a 5th Council manuscript. It makes no mention of the bloodline."

"Perhaps you have misread—"

"No. The manuscript is clear. We represent opposites — an alchemist and an outside world scribe. Together we can produce an alchemical child who, in turn, will *reconstitute* the bloodline. We must try, Cedar. Our child will ensure the survival of both Council and Rebel Branch, of both Lapis and Flaw. We can be heroes."

Observing the way Cedar caressed the coin and glanced up at the glistening amber, Genevre understood that she had firmly implanted a seed. *Heroes* had clearly struck a chord. Cedar merely required time to contemplate Genevre's proposal. And time was one element Council dimension had in abundance. Thus when Cedar departed that evening, promising they would begin studying the manuscript together within a few days, Genevre could not have been more pleased. How could she have known that her days with the Alchemists' Council were numbered?

"Where have you been?" asked Ruis.

"Where have I been?" Cedar replied, annoyed by his tone. "Working."

"On what in particular?"

"What is wrong with you?"

"Nothing is wrong with me. I asked you a simple question."

Cedar stared at him, wondering momentarily if he had overheard her conversation with Genevre. "I'm a Lapidarian Scribe. An outside world war is underway. Work takes priority in times of crisis."

"Don't lie to me, Cedar."

"What part of that—"

"You were with her — again! With Genevre."

Surely he would not have purposely eavesdropped. Yet he clearly suspected something to be amiss.

Cedar enunciated her reply carefully. "As I said, I am a Lapidarian Scribe. Genevre is an outside world scribe. Of necessity, we work together for the good of the Alchemists' Council." She paused awaiting a reply, but he only glared at her. "If I didn't know you as well as I do, I'd swear you were jealous."

"Sometimes I wonder if I know *you* at all."

Perhaps this argument had nothing to do with Genevre. Perhaps Ruis had somehow learned of Cedar's alliance in the Third Rebellion. She decided to shift tactics.

"Do you remember Oren?"

"Oren? From the Vienna protectorate? What does he—"

"We shared at least a month of intimacy, and yet I remained committed to you. And what of Coll? You've not mentioned the time I spend with him."

"Coll regularly spends time with both of us together. I *know* him. Genevre prefers to spend hours upon hours with you alone. She fawns over you in a way Coll doesn't."

Actually, he does on occasion, Cedar longed to admit, but she thought better of it. She crossed her arms and observed Ruis closely for a few seconds. "My point remains the same, Ruis. The time I spend with outside world scribes shouldn't matter a jot. My commitment is to you."

"And mine to you. I trust you, Cedar. My suspicions do not stem from jealousy or lack of trust. They stem from . . . *concern*. Based on my observations of her behaviour over the past year, Genevre is unlike Oren or Coll or any other outside world scribe. She wants something from us — from the Council. She . . . she's too . . . *advanced* — too knowledgable about alchemy."

"Too knowledgeable? You see this trait as a threat to the Council?"

"Yes. She may well be aligned with the rebels. Granted, I may be wrong, but we currently cannot afford the risk. We must concentrate on resolving the fallout of the Third Rebellion. And we must do so without hindrance or distraction."

Cedar uncrossed her arms and placed her hands into the pockets of her robes. She stroked the coin that rested at the bottom of one. What if Genevre did know too much? Cedar could not afford exposure of her own rebel sympathies at this delicate time. Perhaps Ruis was right. Perhaps she should focus solely on her sacred duty, keep the vow she had taken years ago to maintain the elemental balance, help repair the world from its current state of devestation. Once Council had brought an end to the outside world war, Cedar could respond to Genevre's proposal without divided loyalties or guilt.

"Your suspicions would be better suited to a discussion with the Elders rather than with me, Ruis."

"With that I can concur."

"Be sure to present your case as tactfully as possible. Otherwise the Azoths may deem you delusional. Perhaps suggest that *both* outside world scribes are current impediments to Council work — that Lapidarian efforts would be better suited to manuscript revision than training, that the war could sooner be ended."

"Yes," he nodded.

Ruis left her then to seek out Ailanthus and the other Elders. Not until the following day did Cedar see him again and learn the repercussions were worse than she could have predicted. He had spoken with the Elders late into the night, and the Elders in turn convened an early morning meeting to discuss the matter among themselves. That afternoon they spoke with each of the Lapidarian Scribes, including Cedar, asking them a series of questions regarding both Coll and Genevre. By the early evening, Azoth Magen Ailanthus called a special meeting wherein he asked all Elders and Lapidarian Scribes to vote on whether the two recent recruits should be excised from Council and its protectorates until after the war. Eighteen of twenty voted in favour of excision. Only Saule and Ravenea voiced their dissent.

Santa fe — Winter 1918

How could Cedar have known the war would continue for another two years? She had thought continually about Genevre during her absence and sought her out the moment Ailanthus granted permission. Now she and Genevre stood together at the edge of a field. At Genevre's insistence, they had ventured here through a temporary portal. As they had done at their first three war-torn destinations that day, they surveyed the devastation for as long as they could bear before returning once again to the portal chamber in Council dimension. Finally, they returned together to Santa Fe.

"What have they done?" Genevre asked. "What has the Council done? How can you remain—"

"The Council is not solely responsible," Cedar replied.

"Is it not the Council's sworn responsibility to ensure the stability of the outside world?"

"Yes. But even alchemists are vulnerable to failure. For the past few years, we have been failing. The Flaw in the Stone was erased. The Council became focused on its salvation. The people of the outside world were left to make their own decisions, heedless to consequences. Ever since, we have been working to re-establish balance." Cedar paused before adding, "Do not insist that I explain what you already know, Genevre. I weary of it. I am weary of it all."

"Yes, you and others have explained it to me. The logic made sense, once upon a time. When you first approached me, I was optimistic about my future with the Council. I longed to participate in something that mattered. Three years have passed since then. Now that I have seen the repercussions of those years, your explanations — the philosophy, the politics, the protocols — appear to me as perpetual excuses for incompetence."

"Incompetence! Genevre! The Alchemists' Council most certainly has its faults. But incompetence is not one of them. I would be among the first to admit our mistakes — the removal of the Flaw in the first place being an unassailable misstep. Within a few months of working together, I had shared with you my perspective on the Flaw. You have thus known all along where my sympathies lie."

"Yet here I am, having been promised an extended life only to be exiled to the outside world. If I agree to return to Council work, what will I gain as the years of my protracted life continue to pass? Am I to witness more harm? Am I to endure more pain?"

"I have allies, Genevre. I am working to increase the Flaw in the Stone so that its eradication will never occur again. As the years progress, we will find solutions together."

"Allies? On the Council? What good will a few allies do amidst the dozens who worked to eradicate the Flaw in the first place? Perfection has been achieved and lost, the outside world flounders, and now you expect Council to abandon all hope of achieving the One? You can see the irony, the hypocrisy, can you not, Cedar? Council members cannot agree with each other on how to solve the world's problems because they once again have the freedom to make individual choices. Disagreement *is* an exercise in choice. Perhaps your beloved Ruis is correct in his desires. Perhaps the best option would be to remove the Flaw once again — this time permanently, this time without rebel interference."

Cedar stood silently beside her. Cedar wanted to reach out to her, hold her hand, comfort her, but she knew better than to think Genevre would welcome her affections under the current circumstances.

"Let us go inside, Genevre."

"Why? So you can lure me back with flattery and false promises?"

"Genevre—"

"You abandoned me, Cedar! With no explanation other than what Ruis offered, I was excised from Council dimension. How could you have left me to flounder alone in the outside world after being my mentor and teacher for a year? How could you have sided with the Elders when the Council tossed me aside like a broken alembic? Can you even begin to understand the emotional trauma your decision caused me?"

"I'm sorry you were hurt. But you're skewing the course of events, Genevre."

"How can you, as a Scribe of the Council, claim that *I* am skewing the course of events? I would not have thought you a hypocrite, Cedar."

"I have a job, Genevre! The Azoths proclaimed that your work with the Council had temporarily ended. The outside world war had become too grievous to require the assistance of outside world scribes! What did you expect me to do?"

"*Too grievous to require*? Admit the truth, Cedar! The Council could not *trust* outside world scribes at the height of the outside world war! But I expected *you* to trust me. I expected *you* to convince the Azoths of my indispensable value!"

"You were *new*, Genevre. You still required training, and no time for training remained. The war had gone on too long. The Azoths would not have listened to me! They had other duties for me to fulfill. Between my work and Ruis—"

"Duties? Work? Ruis? Excuses, Cedar! You went from spending *hours per day* with me for months on end to having no contact at all! You could at least have visited me. Clearly, you didn't want to see me. You purposely *chose* not to see me. Just admit that! Just be honest: my proposal scared you!"

"What did you expect? I wasn't about to toss away my security for your fantasy! And Ruis isn't an excuse, Genevre. I loved him — I still love him — and my love for him always brings me back to my bond with him. As much as I admired you, you and I didn't share the strength of the bond I shared with Ruis. He wanted you . . . *gone*. He thought we were spending too much time together. I know hearing that must be hard—"

"Yes, it is hard. Here you are, having reappeared after two years? And for what? What does the Council want of me? What does Ruis want of you?"

"The Council wants nothing from you. And Ruis is not a factor. I want . . . you."

Watching her carefully, Cedar could tell Genevre had let down her guard, even if only for one barely perceivable moment.

"Two years ago . . . before you left," Cedar continued. "I wasn't in a position to agree to your . . . proposal. It did scare me. Of course it scared me."

Genevre placed a hand against the wall beside her, as if to brace for impact.

"I still have the coin," said Cedar. She held out the small, bee-embossed copper coin, which Genevre snatched from Cedar's hand immediately.

"How can you have kept this from me? You should have found a way to return it long before now. I feared it was lost to me — forever! I feared *you* were lost to me forever."

Cedar watched Genevre struggle not to cry as she placed the coin in a small wooden box on a nearby shelf.

"Genevre, I cherished the coin. As I cherished you. I simply wasn't . . . ready."

"What are you saying, Cedar? Are you here to accept my proposal?"

"Yes."

Genevre scoffed. "Why should I believe you? What's to keep you from abandoning me again, from abandoning our alchemical child?"

"I've changed. The Council has changed me. The outside world war has changed me. I've come to recognize, as you yourself suggested today, that a few Council allies will not be enough. I said as much to another outside world scribe years ago, but now I truly understand. An unorthodox solution is required for a fundamental change." Cedar paused before adding, "And I spoke with Saule."

Genevre became noticeably more interested in Cedar's explanation. "Saule?"

"She's agreed to help us. The devastation caused by the outside world war—"

"Caused by the *Council*," Genevre interrupted.

"*Exacerbated* by the Council," Cedar allowed, "led Saule to seek me out. She's known for years that I held rebel sympathies. We finally spoke of our respective roles in restoring the Flaw in the Stone. She told me she met with you during the Vulknut

Eclipse. She told me she entered Flaw dimension with you. As you can imagine, these revelations came as a shock to me. But then she told me something else — something that changed the entire scenario." Cedar scrutinized Genevre's reaction in that moment, wondering how many details of her past Genevre had neglected to share.

"If I kept something from you, it was not out of selfishness but concern for your safety and for the good of the future bonds between rebels and alchemists. Cedar, you were well on your way to becoming an Elder at the time of my original proposal. The less you knew about my history at that time, the better. Your pendant was not immune to Azothian readings, after all. And the Council was still on the hunt for rebel sympathizers in the aftermath of the Third Rebellion."

"True. But had you chosen to trust me with this particular detail, if you had offered the truth to me along with the coin, I may well have conceded, may well have found the courage to speak up for you at Elder Council. Now two more years have passed us by. As have millions of lives."

"Do you dare to blame me?"

"Of course not. I didn't mean—"

"What detail? What could I have revealed to you back then that would have made all the difference?"

"That you'd already successfully conceived an alchemical child with Dracaen."

Genevre stared, her cheeks suddenly flushed. "Do you honestly expect that I would risk my child's life by revealing her identity to a Council Scribe?"

"Of course not. Even now I'm not asking you to reveal her identity. But you could have told me she existed; you could have asked Dracaen to help us. If the Rebel High Azoth had—"

"No! I couldn't have asked Dracaen. After the Flaw was restored, I left both Dracaen and my child in Flaw dimension to pursue a life with the Council. I couldn't simply leave Council dimension to go on excursions to visit them! Besides, the child I yearned to conceive with you was to be *ours alone*, Cedar. Dracaen couldn't know. Just as you couldn't know about my child with him. No alchemical child can be fully revealed until the necessity for revelation outweighs the risk of exposure. If we're to proceed, I need to know you understand and accept that necessity — I need your sacred vow."

Cedar lowered her eyes, contemplating the situation. *The child I yearned to conceive with you was to be ours alone.* Cedar longed only to embrace Genevre. Instead, she pulled her pendant from beneath her robes and held it against her heart. She moved closer to Genevre, placing a hand on her cheek and locking eyes. "I swear to you, Genevre, I understand the necessity of concealing the alchemical child. You have my vow."

Genevre reached for Cedar's hand and kissed it

once. Cedar brushed her fingers over Genevre's lips before letting her hand drop away.

"Why did you choose me?" Cedar asked.

"It's complicated."

"I assumed as much. But I want to understand the complications."

"I couldn't ask Dracaen. He would have wanted to keep the child for himself — raise our second child as a rebel like he did with the first. My child with Dracaen belongs in Flaw dimension as a member of the Rebel Branch. My child with you would belong in Council dimension, would become a member of the Alchemists' Council."

"I am not the only alchemist you could have asked, Genevre. Saule already knows of your first child. Why did you not ask her?"

"Saule is . . . alchemically unsuited to me — her elemental essence is too . . . similar to mine. Chances of conception and survival will be far greater if the child is conceived with you; our essences together can work as conjoined opposites. Besides, we need Saule as an ally. We can work together — you, Saule, and I — to create this child."

"Yes, togther in Council dimension. You must return there with me. I've managed to convince the Elders that I need your assistance. Of course, they assumed I meant for illuminating manuscripts, not for generating a homunculus."

Genevre turned away to reach for the wooden

box on the shelf; she removed the coin and then stood before Cedar. She knelt on the ground like a man of the outside world proposing to his beloved.

"Cedar, Lapidarian Scribe of the Alchemists' Council — I, Genevre, outside world scribe, request your hand in a chemical marriage with this coin acquired from the braiding gown of my first child. I propose to you a ritual bonding. I propose to you a conjunction of opposites to be bound together for the purpose of creating an alchemical child together — a child who can help to save the worlds. Do you accept my proposal?"

"I do."

Council Dimension — Winter 1918

Saule was the one to first suggest the catacombs. Cedar balked at the idea. Provided the ritual conception took hold, the incubation could take weeks. The more time that passed, the more likely an alchemist would require revitalization in the catacomb alembics. They could not risk being discovered; if caught, both Saule and Cedar would surely be erased, and Genevre banished permanently to the outside world.

"The water of the catacomb alembics is substantially more powerful than the channel waters elsewhere in Council dimension," said Saule. "The incubation would likely progress more quickly than in Flaw dimension, at least as it is described in the *Rakta Pathara Codex*."

The *Rakta Pathara Codex* was a two-volume Draconian manuscript Genevre claimed to have surreptitiously borrowed years earlier from a rebel stronghold in Santa Fe. When Cedar had asked how she had accomplished such a feat, Genevre had suggested she not pose such questions. *The less you know, the less the Elders will be able to read in your pendant.* Not until then did Cedar recognize the full extent to which she was engaged in breaking Law Codes throughout the dimensions.

"Genevre and I will request permission to work for a week in the Sante Fe protectorate," continued Saule. "When we are ready, I will go to Ailanthus, explain that I have returned from Santa Fe . . . *infected* by a manuscript fungus and need to be immersed or, even better, *quarantined* in a catacomb alembic for a least five weeks. We will then work in the catacombs assembling equipment and ingredients. You will join us whenever possible, Cedar. And you will warn us if anyone from Council is scheduled for catacomb healing."

"A manuscript fungus?" Cedar repeated, skeptical. "What is—"

"The Azoth Magen will not want to risk infecting other Council members. And even if he does not believe me — even if he suspects that I merely need a break from my duties in the aftermath of the war — he will be too busy attempting to repair the world to bother arguing with me."

Thus, they gradually implemented their plan. Day by day, object by object, word by word, they moved together closer to conducting the ritual itself. When the hour of the ceremony arrived, Cedar stood quietly by Genevre's side listening to Saule recite the relevant passages from the *Rakta Pathara*, participating, as necessary, with words and gestures at appointed intervals. The words of transmutation were read by Genevre from a transcription she had made years earlier from another rebel manuscript. When she need not participate directly, Cedar contemplated the significance of the agreement she had undertaken with Genevre. Together they were attempting to create the alchemical child who, alongside its sibling, held the potential to end the conflict that began with the Crystalline Wars, who could finally bring unity to the rebels and alchemists. If they succeeded, Cedar would be honoured throughout the generations. Wouldn't anyone find such a role appealing? Wouldn't anyone have agreed to Genevre's proposal under these circumstances?

Genevre was the one to smash the vessel and thereby implant the seed. Saule had explained that only someone from the outside world could do so. *Are you certain?* Cedar had asked. *We are certain*, both Genevre and Saule replied simultaneously. They also explained that Cedar would have to refrain from visiting the catacombs during the incubation period.

According to Saule, a passage of the *Rakta Pathara* indicated that only the chemical spouse who had smashed the vessel could witness the incubation and birth. Cedar would be called upon after the birth for the naming. *Are you certain?* Cedar had asked again. *Yes. Disregarding the ritual instructions could have dire consequences*, Saule had explained.

Cedar should not have given into temptation. She should have listened to Saule. She should have believed Genevre. But she thought she knew better. She thought she too deserved to bear witness. Two weeks into the incubation, when she knew Council members and outside world scribes, including Genevre, had retired to their chambers for the night, Cedar walked through the shadows over the grounds to the catacombs. Just inside the entrance way, she removed her pendant and hid it temporarily in a small crevice. She was not concerned about an Elder reading it — Saule had temporarily altered its elemental vibration to distort accidental revelation of the marriage and conception. She did, however, want to ensure Saule could not sense her presence through pendant proximity. She progressed quickly but quietly until she reached the entranceway to the incubation alembic. Then she watched, smiling with satisfaction when she finally realized Saule had immersed herself in another alembic for the night. Cedar had nothing to fear, or so she believed, as she made her way to the side of the incubation alembic and peered through its transparent walls.

What she witnessed was something more beautiful than she had ever seen in Council dimension, more beautiful to Cedar in that moment than the Lapis itself. It glowed like a star in the sky, changing colours through the spectrum, a rainbow of crystalline structures, sparkling in the alembic light. She watched her future child late into the night, leaving only when she saw the lights in Saule's alembic begin to flicker. She worried momentarily that Saule may struggle to emerge without assistance from the alembic, but she then remembered that the immersion was only for rejuvenation rather than healing. Saule would be fine. As would the child — clearly Saule's caution regarding her interpretation of the *Rakta Pathara* had been unfounded.

Three weeks later, at a similarly late hour, Saule woke Cedar from her slumbers.

"Come with me to the catacombs," she whispered.

They did not speak on the journey through residence chambers, the courtyard, or even Council grounds. They could not risk being overheard. But Cedar became irritated when Saule refused to answer her questions as they progressed through the catacombs themselves.

"Please wait, Cedar. Genevre will explain."

She waited. Step by step, her concern grew. If all was well, would Saule have not told her? Would she not have announced, back at Cedar's chambers, *Your child has been born*? When they finally arrived,

Cedar was overjoyed. She could see that Genevre held a child in her arms — a girl with golden hair, bright like that of Sadira. Surely Saule and Genevre must be pleased as well. But as she reached Genevre's side, she saw the tears. Genevre was crying, not in joy as Cedar would have expected. Instead, she looked grief-stricken. She moved her arms so that Cedar could see her daughter's face, exquisite in its silent fragility. Motionless. Stillborn. Cedar fell to her knees and wept.

If only pride had not turned her from protocol. If only she could rescind her mistake.

Santa Fe — Winter 1918

"Cedar blames herself," Genevre said to Saule. "We must tell her the truth. We should have told her the truth from the beginning. She trusted us, and we have used her. She doesn't deserve to be treated this way. No one does."

"We made a decision, Genevre. We did what was necessary under the circumstances. Within the century, Cedar will understand as much. She is also working towards eventual change for all."

"And for now?"

"Within the decade, she will of necessity no longer dwell on the past but look towards the future. When the plan has been fulfilled, Cedar will learn the truth, she will understand, and she will forgive us our transgressions."

"Cedar believes she did something wrong. She believes herself responsible for the death of our daughter. Our lie to her is much worse than her abandonment of me. She will suffer for months, years, decades."

"As must we all at some point," replied Saule. "As did you, years ago when you left Kalina behind. You did so out of necessity, Genevre. As you must do now." Hearing no response from Genevre, Saule gently added, "The time has come. Bring the child to me. We must leave you tonight."

Genevre shook her head. She had dreaded this moment. Yet she knew Saule was right. She knew the child must be taken somewhere never to be found by either rebel or alchemist. Not even Genevre could be told where Saule planned to seek safe haven — not until enough time had passed for Saule to ascertain whether the arrangement was indeed safe and secure.

"Just a few more hours."

"No, Genevre. Fetch the child," said Saule.

Genevre moved slowly to the bedroom and gathered the small body into her arms. She returned to the main room, sombre but steadfast. *For the plan*, she said to herself.

"Wake up, my dear," Saule said to the child, stroking his jet-black hair. "We must walk. I cannot carry you."

The boy blinked. He moved from Genevre's arms to stand facing Saule.

"Bid farewell to your mother," Saule advised him.

The boy did not look at Genevre. Instead, he moved towards the door and stood facing it, not looking back. Saule took his hand, opened the door, nodded to Genevre, and progressed down the walkway. Genevre stood in the doorway watching, tears burning in her eyes. Doubt coursed through her. She wanted to run to them, grab her child, take him to Cedar, and plead her forgiveness. *He's our son*, she longed to tell her. *Our son. His alchemical twin died, but he survived.* But the moment passed as if in a dream. Saule and the child had already reached the gate.

As Saule unhooked the latch, the boy turned around and extended his tiny hand to Genevre. Genevre did the same in return, waving goodbye. He looked so innocent. Yet one day he would cross this threshold again as the skilled alchemist she intended him to be.

VII
Qingdao — Winter 1939

In the decades since Saule had arrived on their doorstep with Genevre's black-haired child — Payam — Ilex and Melia had kept in regular, if infrequent, communication with her. Genevre, on the other hand, had refused direct contact with her parents or child, unwilling to risk that someone — Cedar or Dracaen, in particular — was watching her interactions too carefully, would notice the child, and intuit the truth. Genevre wanted her son to live in the outside world — just as she and Kalina had done in their youth — free for a few decades from both Council and Rebel Branch influences. Under the circumstances, who better to raise Payam than the alchemists whose conjoined bloodline made his conception possible? Melia had initially protested her decision, insisting that Genevre get to know Payam.

Her pleas for a bond between mother and son were especially strident after hearing that Genevre would be working primarily in the Santa Fe protectorate. But when Ilex learned of Genevre's intention — to work at the Santa Fe rebel stronghold helping train Kalina for Council infiltration — he convinced Melia to respect Genevre's decision regarding Payam. In addition to keeping their grandson from prying eyes and interference, Ilex himself loathed the idea of becoming entangled with rebel politics yet again.

Ilex and Melia sent regular updates about Payam to their daughter with Saule as intermediary. Every few months, as she had always done since Ilex and Melia had departed Council dimension, Saule would find an excuse to visit an outside world protectorate library and, in the process, meet with her beloved friends. Along with a renewed supply of Lapidarian honey, she would bring news of Genevre. Saule would spend a few hours with Ilex, Melia, and Payam, learning all she could of the child's progress to report back to Genevre at the next opportunity. Occasionally, if she sensed someone growing suspicious of her frequent visits to Santa Fe, Saule would temporarily relocate Ilex, Melia, and Payam through a series of protectorate portal stations. A few years ago, they had spent a pleasant six months in Istanbul. Today, they sipped jasmine tea from small, elaborately patterned cups in the upper room of a residence near the Qingdao protectorate. This rather conspicuous location made Melia nervous, but she had trusted Saule for years and saw no need to question her choice now.

"Any news of Genevre and Kalina?" asked Melia. Having recently witnessed a growth spurt in Payam, she could not help but wonder about the progress of Genevre's other alchemical child.

"What a timely question," responded Saule.

"Has something happened?"

"Yes. Genevre has finally told Kalina about her brother."

Ilex leapt forward, transforming Melia's features abruptly to his own before Melia was able to prevent him. "Kalina resides with Dracaen! What was Genevre thinking?"

"She decided that the looming outside world turbulence predicted in various Council and Rebel Branch manuscripts required an adjustment to the plan," said Saule.

"How did Kalina take the news?" asked Melia, temporarily regaining control of their body from Ilex. His focus on politics could wait. In this moment, emotions were paramount. After all, Payam too would be affected by this connection someday.

"Apparently in stride." Saule smiled and shook her head. "The news of Payam triggered curiosity rather than shock. She asked why Genevre had waited so long to tell her. However, given her own experiences with being secreted away, Kalina didn't take long to accept Genevre's explanation and request an opportunity to meet with him."

"No!" cried Ilex.

"Yes, Ilex. Though physically he still appears to be a child, Payam will soon be twenty-one. You and Melia have kept him safe for more than two decades. The time has come for an initiation of sorts: he must meet both his mother and sister. Genevre plans to visit within the week. Then, the following week, she will introduce him to Kalina."

"A reunion with Genevre I understand and encourage. But what is to stop Kalina from informing Dracaen immediately? She has remained faithful to her father and the ideals of the Rebel Branch since the Third Rebellion!"

"Yes, Kalina remains loyal to the rebel ideals. As do I," replied Saule. "But she has recently learned something about Dracaen that has resulted in a shift of allegiance."

"Explain," requested Melia, struggling with Ilex for dominance.

"Kalina believes Dracaen intends to create another alchemical child."

Suddenly incensed, Melia asked whether Dracaen had forced his will upon Genevre.

"No! Of course not. Dracaen is High Azoth of the Rebel Branch. He cannot force his will upon anyone within Flaw dimension," replied Saule firmly. "But he has, apparently . . ." Her voice trailed off, as if she was not sure what words to use.

"He has *what*? Saule! I hardly think this is a time to censor yourself!"

"Years ago, and years after failing to convince Genevre to join him in creating another child, Dracaen convinced someone else to enter a chemical marriage with him."

"What! Did the marriage result in an alchemical child?" enquired Melia.

"No. Children were conceived, but they did not survive," explained Saule.

"Is Kalina certain? Perhaps one did survive only to be hidden from view."

"Dracaen seeks a sibling for Kalina. If one had survived, Dracaen would certainly have informed Kalina."

Melia, suddenly concerned for Payam, stood up and moved quickly to the window. But he appeared fine at the moment, batting small stones down the deserted road with a stick. No one else was in sight. Unbidden, her concern regarding their proximity to the protectorate resurfaced.

"Who was she — Dracaen's chemical spouse after Genevre?"

"Jinjing, Keeper of the Book of the Qingdao protectorate."

The puzzle pieces were beginning to fall into place. "Is that the reason you have housed us here? Are Ilex and I to consult with Jinjing?"

"After failing to produce a child with Jinjing, Dracaen left well enough alone for many years. But Azoth Fraxinus, out of respect for Genevre, has recently brought his concerns to Kalina. He reports that Dracaen has recently renewed his efforts to perfect the formula for a higher purpose. A sibling is no longer enough. Fraxinus believes Dracaen's goal is to strengthen the power of the Rebel Branch with several alchemical children."

Melia felt Ilex physically protest.

"Genevre and Kalina have developed a plan," continued Saule. "Kalina will soon propose that plan to Jinjing. I have been sent to propose the same plan to you. If all goes well, together we will form a coalition: you two, Genevre, Kalina, Jinjing, and me."

"To what end?"

"Revolution."

Though Jinjing worked primarily in the Qingdao protectorate and Genevre primarily in the Santa Fe protectorate, their paths occasionally crossed when reassigned temporarily to the North Library. On each such occasion, Jinjing would observe Genevre closely and ponder yet again how many times she had submitted to Dracaen's demands, how many times she had endured the ritual and its agonizing results before their success with Kalina. She longed to admit to Genevre that she sympathized with her plight, to confess that her treatment by Dracaen still haunted her. But no practical opportunity arose.

On lonely nights during assignment in Qingdao, Jinjing contemplated Kalina herself, repenting that she had ever thought her otherworldly and, therefore, had considered her somehow unworthy of her full trust. Kalina had survived impossible odds. She existed. She was no more human or inhuman than any alchemist in Council or Flaw dimensions. Jinjing's newly amended view of Kalina was put to the test on the morning she opened the door of the Qingdao protectorate to find Kalina on its threshold. Years had passed since they last had met. Yet, unlike Jinjing and Genevre, Kalina showed no physical signs of aging. Such was the fortune of being an alchemical child, Jinjing surmised.

"The outside world is about to plummet into chaos again," said Kalina. She remained outside, glancing around as if afraid of being seen.

"So I understand," responded Jinjing.

"Nothing has changed in that regard. Neither the Alchemists' Council nor the Rebel Branch has managed to halt the outside world degradation. An intervention is required."

Nothing appeared *to have changed*, thought Jinjing, *but clearly something had*. Otherwise, Kalina would not have taken the risk of entering a Council protectorate unaccompanied. Jinjing ushered Kalina inside and down the hallway into the small kitchen. She could not take her into the main manuscript room. Though unlikely given the war, the possibility remained that Obeche might arrive with a Council update.

"You mentioned an intervention," prompted Jinjing, gesturing for Kalina to sit.

"Years ago, Dracaen told me you had abandoned your training with us, that you forsook the rebels. I believed him. But recently Azoth Fraxinus told me the truth: Dracaen was the one to have abandoned you."

Jinjing stood still, both fearful and hopeful. She had always admired Kalina's forthrightness, but she had not expected this revelation.

"Individual choice is an admirable ideal," continued Kalina, "until it imposes itself on the choices of others. What Dracaen did to you was reprehensible. Fraxinus believes he has begun trying again. But more worrisome, if he were to succeed, his desire could never be satiated. Theoretically, he could create hundreds — thousands — of alchemical children. He would then be more than the High Azoth. He would be the commander of a virtual army of alchemical children bred to overtake the Council. He must be stopped."

Jinjing sat on a bench across the table from Kalina. "How?" she asked.

"We must convince Dracaen we are following his plan, that we believe he aims to benefit all through the promotion of free will and mutual conjunction. We must act as though we are ignorant of his desire to create alchemical children. Meanwhile, we must strategize and develop an alternate plan to ensure liberation of all."

Though Jinjing appreciated Kalina's sentiments, she could not see a means to change the situation.

"What do you propose, Kalina? That you and I overthrow the High Azoth of the Rebel Branch?" Jinjing laughed, but Kalina merely frowned.

"No. I propose that you and I, along with Ilex, Melia, Saule, and Genevre work together with my brother to overthrow certain influential individuals on both the Alchemists' Council and the Rebel Branch."

"*Your brother*? You said Dracaen had not succeeded."

"No, he hasn't. But Genevre has. With Cedar. For now, he is called Payam. One day, he will be granted a tree name."

"Payam," repeated Jinjing softly.

"When I confided in Genevre regarding Dracaen, she confided in me regarding Cedar. I have not yet met him — Payam. And Cedar doesn't know."

"Cedar doesn't know? About her own child?"

"Saule took him shortly after he emerged to be raised in protection with Ilex and Melia."

"How can Saule condone concealing a child from its own mother?"

"Jinjing, be reasonable! Genevre and Saule have had to make difficult choices in difficult times! For better or worse, Payam required protection from warring factions. Who better to protect him under these circumstances than Ilex and Melia? The Council gave up searching for them a century ago, and Dracaen already took what he needed from them. As to Cedar, Saule requires a rebel sympathizer on the Alchemists' Council who can assist her when necessary without the risk of exposing us or the child when her pendant and thoughts are read by an especially astute Elder. Cedar will be reunited with Payam in due time."

"And what role will your alchemical brother play among these factions?"

"When he has matured, he will join the Alchemists' Council. Then, together, we can work to unite the dimensions. As has been prophesied for years, I will mutually conjoin with an alchemist. If all goes as planned, my brother will mutually conjoin with a rebel. Thereafter, out of necessity, rebels and alchemists will begin to work together to repair the world. Granted, an alchemical child can take between five and ten decades to fully mature, and Payam has passed only two. But in less than a century, both he and I will be fully ensconced in Council dimension, primed to initiate the revolution."

"What do you propose we do in the meantime? What if Azoth Fraxinus is correct in his suspicions? What will become of the children Dracaen inevitably creates?"

"Dracaen cannot create an alchemical child without a chemical spouse from the bloodline. He is delusional if he thinks otherwise. We must hope he cannot find one. Fortunately, Fraxinus abhors Dracaen's plan. If necessary, he will lie once again. As he did with you, he will convince Dracaen that a potential spouse is of the bloodline when she is not. Fraxinus believes once Dracaen has failed a handful of times, he will cease his efforts and search for a solution to the error of his ways. The search alone could take the better part of a century."

Jinjing shivered. She had not known of Fraxinus's role. He could have spared her.

"Fraxinus regrets what happened to you. And he regrets what may happen to others. He had assumed Dracaen would stop, that after his failed attempt with you, he would come to realize that I was a miracle child. A miracle never again to be replicated without Genevre. But, of course, Dracaen is not one to give up, even if years pass in the interim. Therefore, we have no alternative but to strategize, to ensure we are ready to intervene when necessary."

Jinjing nodded, stunned at these revelations, unable to otherwise respond.

"We must trust each other alone — our coalition," insisted Kalina. "For the future good of all dimensions, we must be prepared to confide in one another, yet lie to others."

Jinjing understood that Kalina trusted her implicitly. Yet she hesitated as she contemplated whether to agree to her proposal — not because she lacked trust in Kalina, but because she lacked trust in herself. She caught a glimpse of her reflection in a small golden mirror hanging on the opposite wall. Did she recognize herself any longer? At each of her previous points of decision, Jinjing believed she had made the morally correct choice. She had agreed to work for the Alchemists' Council when encouraged by Obeche. With the alchemists, she had intended to help protect the outside world. Instead, she had inadvertently participated in its downfall. Amidst the first outside world war, she had then agreed to work for the Rebel Branch when encouraged by Dracaen. With the rebels, she had intended to help ensure the permanence of the Flaw in the Stone, so the Council never again had reason to distract itself from its purpose to maintain elemental balance. She had believed in Dracaen's stated long-term intentions of free will and mutual conjunction for all. But she had inadvertently become a victim to his obsession to produce another alchemical child. Now, jaded and aged, Jinjing was being offered a chance to begin again, to align herself with an alchemical child and her insurgents. Could such a motley coalition succeed at supplanting influential Elders of both the Alchemists' Council and the Rebel Branch?

"If you agree to join us, we would require your assistance immediately."

"I need more information — more details about the plan."

"Genevre has proposed the creation of a breach in interdimensional space with its focal point here in Qingdao. Years ago, she transcribed the ancient ritual from a manuscript in the deepest rebel archives. The breach would allow us future access to Council dimension — access to decree our acts of rebellion, including the mutual conjunctions. Ilex and Melia will perform the ritual using bloodline alchemy, but they require you to assist with pronunciation. Interdimensional breaches are geographically specific. For certain sections of the ritual, alchemical dialects cannot be used. Instead, we must use the primary language of the people of Qingdao."

"So . . . you've chosen to include me only because of my linguistic ability?"

"We've chosen you because, like each of us, you have ties to both the Alchemists' Council and the Rebel Branch. We've chosen you because, like us, you've taken personal risks to effect necessary change. You've chosen repeatedly to stand up where others would have submitted. We've chosen the Qingdao protectorate because *you* live here. You speak the languages of all the communities in which you reside, including that of Qingdao. We've chosen *you*, Jinjing. But if you reject us, we will respect your choice and find an alternate location for the breach."

Jinjing was both pleased and intrigued. "How would we sustain a breach powerful enough to last several decades undetected?"

"It doesn't have to last decades. It merely has to open decades from now."

And there it was — the golden nugget that swayed Jinjing's decision. Kalina proposed powerful alchemy beyond any Jinjing had encountered: the transmutation of time. Jinjing responded with neither the Ab Uno nor Rebel Branch gesture. Instead, she shook Kalina's hand, acutely aware of both its alchemical strength and human fragility.

For as powerful as Ilex and Melia knew blood alchemy to be, for as much as they had already accomplished as alchemists, they nonetheless doubted their ability to succeed. The instructions were clear. They were to create a breach through time. The negative space they created today would open as positive space seventy-five years in the future. The resulting vortex in the outside world should — theoretically — thereafter allow unrestricted access between Flaw and Council dimensions. Of course, the possibility for abuse was inherent: once discovered, both rebels and alchemists could access the channel. Ilex, Melia, and their allies could only hope that the temporary vortex would close immediately after they accomplished their tasks.

All ritual materials had been prepared in advance. These materials fell into two broad categories: physical objects and ritual words. Attaining the majority of the tangible items was relatively straightforward thanks to Saule and Genevre, who pilfered them from Council dimension. However, five of the physical objects had to be attained from diverse locations in the outside world, which delayed the process substantially. Jinjing located one item within a few hours' travel of Qingdao; Saule attained the other four by fabricating excuses for unorthodox portal trips. The most difficult of the four was a white truffle, which Saule finally managed to obtain in a remote village in Italy. Meanwhile, Ilex, Melia, and Jinjing rehearsed. They read and reread the alchemical recipes, aligning the ingredients as they were attained. They also repeatedly practised both the physical gestures and vocal intonations of the ritual itself — the blood and breath, the earth and air, the body and the spirit of elemental Quintessence. Correct pronunciation in each language was paramount to assuring the vortex opened at the right time and place.

"What do you make of the reference to the Prima Materia?" asked Ilex one day during yet another rehearsal of the ritual words. "It appears both in the list of ingredients and in two verses of the ritual."

"Yes, that too mystified me when I copied the ritual from the manuscript. But I've come to interpret the phrase as a figurative reference to all the ingredients we have collected," said Genevre. "That is, I believe the phrase to be a term for the collective ingredients. As a whole, together, they represent the Prima Materia from which our vortex will be created."

"What if your interpretation is incorrect? What if the Prima Materia refers to another substance altogether? The primary matter from which the dimensions themselves were created?"

"If so, we have no means to attain it," responded Genevre. "And the ritual will fail."

"Which would explain why none of us has ever heard of alchemists of the current era attempting the transmutation of time."

"At least if we fail for our lack of understanding or attaining the Prima Materia, the fault will not rest with me and my flawed pronunciation," laughed Jinjing.

Though she had laughed, Jinjing appeared the most anxious in this regard, rehearsing her part until well after midnight on multiple occasions. As a Keeper of the Book, her knowledge of alchemical rituals was extensive; however, her personal experience was limited to marriage and birthing rituals in Flaw dimension and consecrations on relocated manuscripts in Council dimension. A few nights ago, she had admitted her concerns to Ilex and Melia. In turn, they admitted their own to her.

"When attempting the virtually impossible," said Ilex, "one must lower one's expectations of success."

"When attempting the virtually impossible," added Melia, "one must increase one's tendency to smile."

They relaxed and continued their rehearsal.

Once all objects had been obtained and all words learned, they chose a precise date and time to commence the Great Work. During the ritual, Ilex and Melia would perform their portion from the building in which they were housed; Jinjing and Kalina would perform their portion from the protectorate library. To triangulate the ritual space, Saule and Genevre would be positioned on another street holding a fragment from both the Lapis and the Dragonblood Stone. Though Jinjing had suggested Payam be sequestered outside the triangle for the duration of the ritual — at the home of an acquaintance of hers — neither Ilex nor Melia agreed. As much as they trusted Jinjing, they could not trust a stranger and thus risk interference by either the Alchemists' Council or the Rebel Branch while Payam was out of their immediate vicinity. Instead, Ilex and Melia purchased several new puzzles assured to keep him occupied in his room.

All was progressing as planned until they reached the point of no return — until the triangulated area sparked with a turquoise flash indicating the space had been primed for acceptance of the Words of Transmutation. To the outside observer, the flash would have seemed little more than a momentary trick of the eye. To Ilex, Melia, and the others, it signalled the transition to the next stage of the ritual. As planned, Ilex and Melia would commence the Dance of Conjunction, Jinjing and Kalina would begin the Recitation of the Portal, and Saule and Genevre would enact the Scattering of the Dust — that is, they would sprinkle powder scraped from both the Lapis and the Dragonblood Stone onto the ground at their feet.

Upon completion of their portion, Ilex and Melia stood at the open window looking out onto the street. They presumed Jinjing and Kalina were doing the same. Saule and Genevre were the only two who could not see directly into the centre arena of the triangulation. They had all agreed in advance that upon the completion of the ritual, Kalina and Genevre would return to confer with Ilex and Melia. Meanwhile, Jinjing and Saule would hold their positions to maintain the triangulation for a full hour to observe the results or any lingering alchemical effects. Thereafter, they too would reconvene with the others.

Genevre and Kalina walked into Ilex and Melia's main room together. Neither one had noticed anything on their walk that could confirm a transmutation of Prima Materia into a time vortex had occurred. For the next fifteen minutes, all four stood at the window looking out onto the street, scanning for signs, but they observed no change in the landscape whatsoever. Consequently, by the twenty-minute point, they had all come to believe their efforts had failed.

"All that work for nought," said Ilex aloud.

Then the unthinkable happened.

Though her hope for ritual success had abated, Genevre nonetheless felt content that the attempt had given her the opportunity to spend time with her son. She smiled serenely as she walked towards his room, where she planned to join him to solve the most complex of the new puzzles. Finding the bedroom empty, Genevre assumed Payam had disobeyed the instructions to stay in his room to go to the kitchen for a snack. Not finding him there, she feared he had hidden himself silently in the main room to observe the ritual. But after a swift search behind furniture and within cupboards, she concluded he was missing.

"I cannot find—" she began. But Ilex and Melia turned to her, a horrified look on their face.

Genevre ran to the window. The truth of Payam's whereabouts was worse than she had imagined. He was in the street playing ball with a young, dark-haired woman. Genevre knew that the aura of magenta around the woman signified she was from another time. The depth of the magenta suggested she had emerged from decades into the future — most likely from the projected point seventy-five years from now. The transmutation had worked after all. The physical proof was standing in the street playing ball with Payam. But this proof was a potential problem. Payam had interrupted the timeline by interacting with the woman.

"Who is she?" whispered Ilex.

Genevre shook her head. She moved to the door and watched, waiting for her chance to extract Payam without drawing the attention of the young woman. Already, they would have to suffer the repercussions of Payam having been witnessed from the future. But at least he would have aged substantially by then, his appearance having thus changed. Genevre, on the other hand, could not risk being recognized by the woman seventy-five years from now.

Genevre's opportunity arose when the woman

turned to chase the ball. Genevre ran into the street, snatched Payam into her arms, and ran back before the woman had even reached the ball. In the meantime, Ilex and Melia had adjusted the shutters so that they could continue to watch the woman without her being able to see them. After quickly resettling Payam into his room and insisting firmly he stay put, Genevre returned to the main room to observe the woman who, by this point, appeared quite distraught. She walked along the street knocking on doors, including theirs. Genevre turned quietly towards the bedrooms in case the knock caused Payam to come running. But this time, he remained in the back as instructed, so Genevre turned again to the window to watch the woman. Eventually, she wandered out of their sightline; despite their curiosity, they had no choice but to remain indoors until the entire projected hour of the transmutation had run its course.

Even then, they opened the front door slowly and peered out cautiously before venturing into the street. Jinjing had done the same. They knew better than to discuss the events aloud where they could be overheard. They all stood in the street silently, shaking their heads in amazement as they awaited Saule. Upon her arrival, they all returned as planned to Ilex and Melia's.

"Fetch Payam," said Jinjing, as they settled into the main room.

As soon as Genevre gave the word, Payam rushed to greet them, running down the hall and into the arms of Ilex and Melia. They held him for a few moments before directing him to a chair, at which point Jinjing, as nonchalantly as possible, asked, "What did the woman say to you?"

"I don't know," responded Payam. "I couldn't understand her."

"Perhaps she will think their meeting no more than a chance encounter," suggested Melia. "We may never know her name."

"Jay-Den," said Payam.

"She told you her name?" asked Melia.

"She pointed to herself and said *Jay-Den*."

"Jay-Den," said Genevre.

"May I go outside? I want to play ball."

"Yes," said Melia.

They watched him as he began kicking his ball against a building across the street. They were glad he had not noticed anything out of the ordinary.

"Jay-Den," Genevre said once again.

"Not quite," said Jinjing. "Her name is Jaden. The word is a variant pronunciation of Jade, as in *Crassula argentea*."

"An alchemist!" exclaimed Kalina. "Are you certain?"

"Yes, I am certain."

"How?"

"Arjan told me. In the protectorate. While we watched Jaden and Payam in the street."

"Arjan? Another alchemist from the Council?" asked Kalina.

"Not just any alchemist from the Council. He also arrived from the future. Arjan, of course, is his tree name. If I am not mistaken, he was once Payam."

Everyone gasped.

"He appeared in the protectorate during the transmutation. I now believe him responsible for it. That is, I believe Payam and Arjan together to be responsible."

"Responsible? But *we* performed the ritual," said Saule.

"Yes, but nothing happened until Payam ran into the street. Surely in those first twenty minutes, you began to suspect the ritual had failed. I certainly did," admitted Jinjing. "But the moment Payam interacted with Jaden, Arjan suddenly appeared at the window inside the protectorate library. I knew then we had succeeded."

"What did Payam— what did Arjan tell you?" asked Ilex.

"He spoke to me as if he knew me. And I quickly realized he knew me from the future. He did not appear to think anything amiss. He merely believed I had returned to the library to speak with him. He barely looked at me when he spoke. He kept glancing out the window or at the manuscripts on the table. So, I assumed we'd met in his time-line but he hadn't observed me closely enough to notice subtleties of age difference. He just rambled on about the work he and Jaden had been assigned. They were searching for bees in the manuscripts

— bees that had been disappearing from manuscripts. That's what he emphasized repeatedly: disappearing bees. I didn't quite follow. He said the task was one meant to keep Council Initiates busy."

"Are you saying that Arjan and Jaden are Initiates on the Alchemists' Council seventy-five years into the future?" asked Kalina.

"So it appears," replied Jinjing.

"We must ensure that they are," said Saule, clearly agitated.

"What do you mean?" asked Ilex.

"We must ensure that seventy-five years from now, Arjan and Jaden are indeed situated as Initiates, will return together to Qingdao, will enact again what we have witnessed today. Otherwise, the portal will not open for us to carry forward the plan."

"Will they not necessarily *already* be situated and then return by the mere fact that they were here today? Is time not stable in that sense?" asked Melia.

"Time is stable as long as no one interferes with it. We have interfered," replied Jinjing. "Payam spoke with Jaden, and I spoke with Arjan. The timeline has thereby changed."

"We'll watch, carefully," said Saule. "We'll monitor the manuscripts. We'll insert Jaden and Arjan where necessary. We'll create both palimpsests and lacunae. We'll ensure Council seats are vacated."

They all sat briefly in silence. What had they done? What more would they be required to do? *If only Payam had not run into the street*, thought

Genevre. *How had he managed to reach Jaden without anyone noticing?* She shivered in sudden recognition of a possibility. "Jinjing, did you see Payam run into the street towards Jaden? I mean the actual *running* part?"

"No. When I first saw him, he was already standing with Jaden."

"That's right," confirmed Kalina.

"Yes, us too," said Melia. "When Ilex and I noticed Payam outside, he was already with Jaden."

"So no one observed Payam moving between two points — from the front door to Jaden? We've all merely assumed he ran into the street twenty minutes after we completed the ritual?"

"Yes," responded Jinjing. "What are you suggesting?"

"If Payam snuck outside while we were occupied performing the ritual — rather than afterward when you were all looking directly into the street for a sign — if he were *already* outside at the very moment we completed the ritual, he may have disappeared through time right then. He may have left both our sight and timeline but entered Jaden's. He may have been in *her* timeline far longer than twenty minutes. What we witnessed may have been Payam bringing Jaden back to our timeline."

"How could he manage such a feat?" asked Melia. "He is only a child!"

"No," said Genevre. "He is not *only* a child. He is currently an immature alchemical child." Genevre thought back to the words in the manuscript that she had taken to be a metaphorical flourish. She fell to her knees. "The Prima Materia. The alchemical child, before maturity, before elemental corruption, *is* the Prima Materia. Without Payam *already* outside during the ritual, we would have failed. Alchemical children are the primary material required in the transmutation of time. They will be coveted for this factor alone. We can tell no one. No one." She looked at Kalina. "Especially not your father."

Melia set the newspaper with its glaring headline onto the table: *Germany Attacks Poland*. Within two weeks of returning to Council dimension, Saule had risked another portal trip to Qingdao to bring Melia various outside world papers. Knowing Council meetings would swiftly follow the news, she stayed only a few minutes before leaving Ilex and Melia to contemplate the matter.

"The outside world has been in turmoil since before the Third Rebellion, Melia. Another war was inevitable. We've no reason to believe the time transmutation had any bearing," said Ilex.

"We have no reason to believe it didn't," she responded.

"You cannot blame yourself."

"But neither can I blame the Council," said Melia.

"Decades ago, they did what they thought right. But they were wrong. We've now followed suit."

Melia needed to rest. Her role in the successful transmutation had initially left her hopeful. After so many years and so many sacrifices, she had believed victory was in sight — the permanence of free will, the choice of mutual conjunction, the restoration of alliance between alchemists and rebels. Then Saule arrived with the papers. Now she felt exhausted and defeated. She needed reassurance that her actions were for the good of all and, someday, would be validated as such — even if outside world circumstances currently appeared to suggest otherwise.

Of course, the long-term goal and outcome would remain elusive for another seventy-five years. She would have to carry the burden of her role until then. That thought almost too much to bear, Melia retreated partially into the shadows, handing Ilex the reins to control their body. She could still observe the world, but she could also catch her breath before proceeding. She knew Ilex would much rather spend time with Payam, no matter the additional energy required, rather than retreat to recover his strength.

"Are you happy, grandfather?" asked Payam.

"Quite content," responded Ilex.

"Me too," said Payam. He then turned back to arranging pieces of an elaborate structure he had begun to build at the kitchen table.

Melia watched him as he contemplated the

pieces, carefully moving one and then another into tentative place. He had always been an industrious child — both productive and creative in his play. When not building worlds with blocks or stones or abandoned pieces of wood that he had collected from both streets and forests, he would read or solve intricate puzzles. Of course, above all else, Payam placed his love of alchemy, which he knew primarily as chemical arts — bottles and jars, water and fire, salts and compounds. Ilex and Melia taught him what they could, all that was appropriate for a boy of his age, all that was appropriate for a boy who would someday be positioned to change the tenets of alchemy forever after.

"Payam," said Ilex gently, "let's go for a walk. You may return here later to continue your project. It's time to collect a gift I have arranged for you."

"A gift!" Payam abandoned the structure and reached for Ilex's hand. "Do we have to travel far to collect it?"

The journey through the streets of Qingdao was longer than Melia expected. She had assumed Ilex's offer of a gift comprised a walk to the small bakery a few minutes' stroll away from their makeshift home. But Ilex walked directly past the shop, ignoring Payam when he politely requested a sweet bun. They walked for at least twenty minutes before Ilex turned up a narrow street of which Melia had no recollection from her months in this town. She contemplated emerging from the shadows to ask where they were headed — and *why* — but she decided to wait, as Payam was being made to do. She would be surprised along with her grandson. Mutual conjunction had to allow for independent thought and action on occasion; otherwise, this state of being would have become intolerable years ago. After one hundred and thirty-nine years, she and Ilex had experienced every possible emotional and psychological response to their shared existence — from absolute joy and love to utter despair and loathing for one another. Fortunately, the latter moments were few and far between. Otherwise she would have to question whether mutual conjunction was indeed preferable to singular victory or defeat.

Payam had helped, of course. Children, no matter how conscientious, no matter the age or maturity, could not take care of themselves. Upon Payam's arrival, he had necessitated for Ilex and Melia an intense form of cooperation and focus. Such cooperation had become paramount when Payam, having lived with them only a year, became desperately ill the day he managed to open a jar of Lapidarian honey and ingest over half of it before they noticed. They had been told that alchemical children had no need for Lapidarian honey; they had not been told an excess of it might kill him. Together they had nursed Payam slowly back to health using an alchemically rendered concoction in a base of juniper and sage oils. They fed him one drop per hour over a twenty-four-hour period and kept all jars of honey well out of his reach thereafter. This silent walk, led by Ilex to uncharted territory, was testament on Melia's part to their ongoing collaboration for the sake of Payam.

Finally, Ilex stopped in front of a nondescript dwelling and knocked. A man whom Melia had never met opened the door and smiled. "Come in, come in," he said, gesturing. He led Ilex and Payam through a narrow hallway, across the kitchen where a woman was chopping vegetables, and out another door into a small courtyard. "Wait here." Ilex and Payam sat on a stone bench while the man disappeared into a shed — his workshop perhaps — in the corner of the courtyard. A few minutes later, he emerged carrying a small embroidered pouch, which he handed to Ilex.

"Thank you," Ilex said, bowing slightly. The man smiled broadly.

"You will find this piece to be one of my most exquisite — if I may be permitted a moment of self-indulgence."

"No need for modesty," replied Ilex.

"What is it, Grandfather? Is this my gift?" asked Payam. Melia had to give Payam credit for remaining quiet since his request for the sweet bun.

"Grandfather!" said the man to Ilex. "You are so vigorous and handsome; I felt certain you were the boy's father."

"I do not have a father," said Payam.

The man looked from Payam to Ilex, apparently worried he had caused offence. He closed his eyes and bowed his head slightly. "My humblest apologies for my rudeness and my sincerest sympathies for your loss," he said. Given his gesture of humility, Melia was not certain to whom he addressed his regrets.

"We raised him as our own. Payam has been with us his entire life," Ilex clarified.

The man looked at Payam, assessing him. "Ten years or so, then?"

Payam did not respond; he focused on the pouch Ilex held.

"No matter. Clearly, you are very mature for your age," said the man.

Indeed he is, Melia wanted to say. But, of course, she could not — *would not* — say so even if she were the one the man could see and hear. Payam *appeared* and often acted as a boy of nine or ten, but he was, in fact, twenty. Melia assumed this gift Ilex was about to proffer was to mark Payam's upcoming twenty-first birthday. She and Ilex could only hypothesize that his aging had been slowed due to his alchemically manufactured bloodline and all that coursed through it — Quintessence and Lapis, Sephrim and Dragonblood. What could they know about the complications and intricacies of the alchemy and biology of such matters beyond what they had experienced for themselves or learned from Saule over the years? Kalina had begun to offer insights, but her development seemed markedly different than Arjan's; by the time she had turned twenty-one, she was already living in Flaw dimension.

When Payam was brought to their doorstep, he appeared to be a boy of five. Yet he could do little more than gesture and articulate with random sounds, having limited language skills for his first year with her and Ilex. Years had passed thereafter during which he seemed not to age at all either physically or mentally. And then a month would go by where he appeared to age an entire year. Her best guess would be that, since coming to live with them, Payam had aged approximately one physical year for every five that passed. But how could she know what the future would bring? She had no means of knowing what ratio of age — body and mind — would hold throughout the year, let alone the entirety of his life. No matter, as long as he appeared to be in his twenties upon his initiation to the Alchemists' Council. According to Kalina, she had aged slowly for her initial twenty years; for the fifteen years thereafter, she aged more rapidly; by her mid-thirties, she appeared to be in her early twenties and had remained as such ever since. If he were to follow the same pattern, Payam would soon head into an intense growth period.

As Melia regained her focus, she watched Payam sit patiently as Ilex explained the importance of the gift he was about to bestow.

"This gift is your inheritance. It will forever bind

you to us. Hold out your hand," said Ilex, unknotting the pouch. Payam did as instructed, and Ilex emptied the contents of the pouch into Payam's palm.

Holding up his new treasure, Payam exclaimed, "Grandfather, how beautiful! So many strands of silver together!"

"One of its cords belonged to your grandmother, and one belonged to me. Master Liu wove our two cords with two new strands — four elements forming one whole. May you wear it well," said Ilex as he took the silver braided chain from Payam's hand and slipped it over his head and around his neck.

"What shall I string from it, Grandfather?"

"For now, nothing. Someday, this chain will hold a pendant. You must endeavour to keep it safe."

"My pendant? A pendant like yours? A pendant like grandmother's?" Payam reached out and held the Lapidarian pendant still worn by Ilex and Melia, still coursing with Quintessence after all these years.

"Yes, a pendant like mine, if all goes well."

"You will become a good and prosperous man, Payam," said the jeweller, who had created the future pendant-bearing masterpiece. "You will live a long life and make your grandparents proud."

Melia felt a fondness for Master Liu in that moment. Clearly, he too had admiration and hope for Payam. He too could picture a glorious future for her beloved boy, even if he did not know anything about the complexities of Payam's path. Not until Ilex and Payam had said their goodbyes, not until they were home again, not until Melia had emerged from the shadows to enjoy tea and noodles that evening did a chill course through her. How could Ilex have arranged for the chain to be crafted without her knowledge of the matter? The only period during which being in the shadows had been so disruptive to time and thoughts was during her pregnancy. Only then had Ilex repeatedly suffered from lapses of awareness — gaps in the timeline — of this sort. And certainly they were not pregnant now; they had made the choice long ago not to engage in a liason that could lead to another pregnancy. How then had she managed to retreat so far into the shadows that she had been rendered unconscious? More disconcerting, how had she managed to return from this virtual unconsciousness unaware of time having gone missing? How — and she admittedly asked herself this question with penetrating trepidation — could she possibly have reached such a cloud of unknowing without being pushed into submission? In that fraction of a second, Melia feared for the stability of her bond with Ilex. And she trembled.

Qingdao — Summer 1940

No one had reason left to doubt Melia's suspicion. The success of the transmutation of time had left her and Ilex vulnerable to memory lapses. Everyone else who had partaken in the ritual seemed unscathed. But Ilex and Melia were becoming fragmented — as if they were being pulled apart little by little with each passing day. The virtual conjunction through time of Payam and Arjan had somehow affected the literal conjunction of his grandparents. Given the lack of precedent outside the ancient Rebel Branch manuscripts for every aspect of the complicated current circumstances, no one could fathom a precise cause — let alone a solution.

But one particular incident necessitated a request for help nonetheless. One day, Melia stood before a mirror and saw a reflection that startled her. Instead of seeing her own face or that of Ilex, she saw both at the same time. Their faces appeared side by side, as if their neck held two heads — like those images of the Rebis from outside world manuscripts housed at the British Library and elsewhere. Ilex, upon seeing the reflection, leapt backward in shock, thus wrenching Melia away from the mirror in the process. By the time she righted herself and peered into the mirror again, the dual-headed image was gone; in its place was the face of Melia alone.

"We cannot allow this process to continue!" cried Ilex, clearly terrified. "What if we lose control completely? What if someone *sees* us transform from one body to two and then back again to one? We'll not be able to leave the house — ever — not even to move homes at Saule's request."

"Calm down, Ilex!" Melia insisted firmly. "I have to think." She moved their body to a bench near the window and stared out into the street. She realized she was focused on the very spot where Payam and Jaden had met.

"We need to talk with Saule," said Ilex. "She'll help us. She has always helped us."

"Of course. But we have no idea when Saule will next appear. The outside world war may make time away from Council dimension impossible for her. Still, we need to get word to her. We can ask Jinjing to return to Council dimension to bring her word."

"Are you suggesting we knock at the door of the protectorate? What if someone from Council—"

"Payam!" Melia called out loud enough to be heard at the back of the house.

"No!" protested Ilex.

"If someone from Council is with Jinjing, Payam can pretend he knocked on the door in hopes of attaining a sweet."

They carefully outlined the instructions for Payam, and he was sent on his first official mission. Two days later, Saule arrived. Within a few weeks, everyone who had played a role in the transmutation was engaged in finding a solution to halt the dissolution of Ilex and Melia's conjunction. By the end of the month, they had devised a plan.

They had concluded that what Ilex and Melia required was an infusion of Quintessence to strengthen their pendant. They put forward and rejected various propositions as to how such a feat would be accomplished: channel water (too weak), Lapidarian honey (Saule already secreted a jar per month — missing supplies would be noticed), fragment of the Lapis (its whereabouts could be tracked), immersion in the catacomb alembics (too risky), Lapidarian dust or the resulting ink (the inventory was too carefully monitored to confiscate the required amount). The suggestion of ink gradually led to the possibility of scraping Lapidarian ink from the manuscripts themselves. But that suggestion was deemed impractical: excising enough ink to be effective would not only be laborious and time consuming but cause extensive, readily noticable damage to the manuscript folios.

"What of the bees themselves?" asked Saule one visit.

"The bees? What do you propose? We let them sting us?" asked Ilex.

"No. I wonder if we could transport some here. If we bring a queen along with them, they could form a hive and a perpetual supply of honey."

"No, that wouldn't work," said Ilex. "Melia and I repeatedly relocate. And bees cannot continually be transported without drawing unwanted attention to the transporters."

"Wait. I have an idea," said Genevre. "I remember something — a ritual from the ancient manuscripts."

"A ritual from the ancient manuscripts is what got us into this mess in the first place," complained Melia.

"Then perhaps it makes sense to use another such ritual to resolve the dilemma," suggested Saule. "What are you thinking, Genevre?"

"Literal bees may not be able to be transported inconspicuously, but figurative bees could be," explained Genevre. "We can transfer bees from Lapidarian manuscripts without producing obvious lacunae. We can alchemically enliven them, encourage them to migrate to their queen."

"What queen?" asked Ilex.

"We'll produce one," said Genevre. "We'll inscribe an emblem of a queen bee in a manuscript of our own creation. The Lapidarian ink required to illuminate only one bee would be minimal. We would alchemically enhance the queen — through blood alchemy — to attract bees from other Lapidarian manuscripts to her. They would fly — so to speak — from various original manuscripts to the new one. We could then use the accumulated ink from those bees to make an infusion of Quintessence."

"Such an act, if even possible, is tantamount to erasure. And the bees in the apiaries would likewise be affected," added Saule. "They too would begin to disappear."

"The Council apiaries house tens of thouands of bees — twenty thousand in the lavender fields alone. We would require a few thousand at most," said Genevre.

Encouraged by Genevre's point, Melia asked about the practicalities. *What materials would be required? What level of alchemical skill? How long could they carry out such a deception?*

"How can such a complex form of blood alchemy erasure be accomplished without the assistance of the Rebel Branch?" interrupted Saule.

"It can't," said Genevre. "I would require not only a supply of Dragonsblood ink but also the assistance of a rebel skilled in the most intricate of erasure procedures."

"You are not suggesting we ask Dracaen? We cannot risk—"

"No. I'm suggesting we ask someone I trust implicitly," said Genevre. "Someone who will simultaneously trust what I reveal yet not dare suspect that I have anything to hide. If we align ourselves to him now — even if only partially — rest assured, he will help us when needed in the future."

"Of whom do you speak?" asked Saule.

"Azoth Fraxinus."

Flaw Dimension — Summer 1940

Genevre sat at the wooden table, four scrolls opened, weighted, and positioned for maximum visibility. She worked by candlelight, assuming the light of the Lapidarian wax would provide her with a better visibility than luminescence lanterns. The hours of the night passed quickly, and soon the first rays of sun broke through the windows illuminating the gold and cinnabar inscription on the upper portion of the scroll.

"Here," said Fraxinus. He pointed to a single elemental symbol. "Put a drop here."

Genevre moved the fragment of the Dragon-blood Stone to a position above a small glass plate. With a ruby blade, she expertly scraped miniscule fibres of dust from the stone to the page. Fraxinus removed a tiny vial from beneath his robes and allowed a drop of the dissolution liquor to mix with the Dragonblood dust. Genevre, with the most delicate brush she could find, immersed the tip into the resulting ink and painted crimson dots onto the wings of the queen bee.

"Scribe Ruis has assigned me to work with him in the North Library next week. I can transport the manuscript then without drawing suspicion. I have determined its most effective placement would be in the ninth division of the fourth floor. Worker bees should begin to emigrate from the nearby manuscripts shortly thereafter."

"Yes, but do not expect swift results. Weeks must pass before you will have collected enough bees to provide Ilex and Melia any relief whatsoever."

"Let us hope, meanwhile, that no one from the Council notices the missing bees."

"Do not fret, my dear. Decades will pass before enough bees have vanished for anyone to take notice. And even then, a coincidence of timing would be required. Someone would need to see a bee disappearing — witness the erasure as it happens — before suspicions are stirred. Meanwhile, bee by bee, Ilex and Melia can stabilize their conjunction through the Quintessence of Lapidarian bees that you provide for them."

"Thank you, Fraxinus. We are all grateful for your assistance."

"Assisting your parents is the least I can do. Your plan is sound and virtually undetectable."

Genevre smiled, but anxiety nonetheless mounted. "If anyone notices this manuscript and attributes it to me, my days as an outside world scribe will be numbered."

"What care have you of numbers," responded Fraxinus, "when the Dragonblood Stone can offer you absolute zero?"

Genevre smiled.

"The future is ours, Genevre. We need merely wait for its unfolding."

"And once fully revealed, will you expect me to refer to you as High Azoth Fraxinus?"

"Only in front of the children."

VIII
Qingdao — 2008

Ilex was shaking. Melia could feel his vibrations within her. Jinjing watched them calmly from the sunlit bench by the window. Saule stared at the document, clearly speechless.

"Dracaen's intentions are clear," said Ilex. "In light of this evidence, we can no longer claim ignorance. As we suspected years ago, he indeed aims to populate the dimensions with alchemical children."

"Yet he has failed, time and again," added Melia.

"How many attempts since he tried with me?" Jinjing asked Saule, as she moved towards the table.

"Fifty-four."

Hearing Saule utter the number aloud, Melia felt numb. Jinjing braced herself against a chair.

"Fifty-four pairs barely formed," clarified Saule. "Another twenty-six pairs born and buried before

the three nines. Eighty sets of alchemical twins conceived and terminated. Eighty. Dracaen has tried to
duplicate the success he shared once with Genevre
eighty times over the last seven decades — five in
the decade following his attempts with Jinjing,
another five during the 1940s, and seventy within
the past five years. His once well-intentioned pursuit has become his obsession."

"Seventy in five years? Why? Something must
have shifted," suggested Melia.

"Perhaps. But regardless of his rationale, he
refuses to see *reason*. He refuses to accept that he
cannot succeed; he sees only that he has failed and
must try again."

"To what end?" demanded Ilex. "What suffering has he inflicted in the process? Not only on
the children who were born and died, but on the
chemical spouses."

"Who were they?" asked Jinjing. "Who were the
spouses?"

"A chemical wedding is a bond of opposites,"
said Saule. "So Dracaen's spouses would all have
been outside world scribes — *potential* scribes.
Presumably, he lured them with promises of
alchemical knowledge and later by the idea of being
the co-creator of a new breed of powerful alchemists. With each failure, he simply began anew."

"And then what? What became of these spouses
afterward?" asked Ilex.

"We can only guess — perhaps they were returned

to the outside world having been told their alchemical skills had not proven sufficient."

"We must stop him!" said Jinjing.

Melia felt Ilex reach out to Jinjing, taking her hand.

When Genevre had first told her about Kalina, Melia had vehemently rejected both her and the child. She could not comprehend how Genevre could condone *constructing* a being in an alchemical vessel. But the Vulknut Eclipse had changed everything. How could she and Ilex not have accepted a means for returning the Flaw to the Stone — even if that means were an alchemical child? Thereafter, she had begun to believe that mutual conjunction between rebel and alchemist could indeed bring an end to the conflict that had begun with the Crystalline Wars. Melia could not have known then that Genevre had a plan of her own, a plan to ensure that Kalina had an ally — a brother to complete the alchemical pair. She loved Payam more than she had loved anyone in her life, including Ilex. She could not condemn Genevre for creating him. The lure of the alchemical child was too powerful even for those with the best intentions. But the havoc wreaked of late by Dracaen was untenable, his obsession too entrenched, his thirst for power unlimited.

Melia leapt up, startling Ilex. "He knows!" she said. "Dracaen must have learned of the link between alchemical children and the transmutation of time."

Saule and Jinjing turned to her, desperation evident.

"Dracaen has no intention of creating an army of beings whose power would ultimately supplant his own. He wants the power of the alchemical child for himself. He wants the ability to move through time alongside an alchemical child. He wants the opportunity to transform all three dimensions according to his personal vision."

"What of Kalina?" asked Saule.

"Perhaps he understands the role of the *immature* child, the role of the Prima Materia. And besides, Kalina has another role to play in Dracaen's plan: to conjoin with Sadira. Dracaen needs someone else, someone new, someone not fully matured nor yet assigned a role."

"Then let us give him one," said Jinjing.

"Give him one? We cannot—"

"But we can," insisted Jinjing. "If we introduce him to Payam, Dracaen will end his unconscionable pursuits. He will believe his problem is solved if we convince him that Payam has not yet fully matured. He's already accepted Kalina's conjunction with Sadira as part of his plan to perpetuate the blood-line. What if Genevre can likewise convince him that he should be the one to conjoin with her other alchemical child, that *conjoining* with Payam will provide him with unimaginable powers? As Rebel High Azoth, surely he would not only welcome the conjunction but do whatever needs to be done to ensure its success."

"And what of Payam?" asked Ilex.

"As you yourself witnessed," Saule responded, "Payam has transmutation abilities exceeding those of any known alchemist. His powers will continue to mature. Thanks to you and Melia, his ethics are beyond reproach. Mutually conjoined, Payam will be well positioned to temper the High Azoth."

Ilex and Melia walked to the window. They peered out onto the street where Payam had once stepped through time. They shook their head in disbelief. Their future now lay in the hands of the child Genevre had alchemically created, the boy Ilex and Melia had raised as their own, the only alchemist throughout the dimensions with the potential to defeat Dracaen.

Council Dimension — 2008

Assuring that the Council Readers would find Kalina's name in the Lapidarian manuscripts was relatively straightforward given that the Rebel Branch Scribes had been working on the manuscript manipulation for years. Once all was prepared and confirmed, Saule went to Obeche. Feigning confusion, she asked for his assistance with the interpretation of an unusual passage in *Enfant d'or 7875*. Obeche, as Saule had expected, interpreted the passage as describing not only an impending conjunction but also an inauguration of a new Initiate. Such a textual pairing — conjunction and initiation — was a rare and precious find. Obeche proudly took the manuscript to the Azoths who, in turn, set the Readers onto the investigation immediately. Within three months, two Lapidarian Scribes had conjoined with one another, and Kalina had become Council's most recent and most promising Junior Initiate. Thereafter the Rebel Branch Scribes set about manipulating manuscripts to ensure Council Readers, within the decade, would discover evidence positing Kalina for conjunction with Sadira. Meanwhile, once ensconced in Council dimension, Kalina found means to provide Ilex, Melia, and Genevre — who now resided in the outside world — access to relevant manuscripts and transcripts. Together they worked with Saule on textual and iconographic manipulation, inscribing the Initiate most likely to be confirmed after Kalina's conjunction.

All appeared to be going as planned until the night Ravenea sought Saule out in her chambers to inform her of a finding in *Arbre de cuivre 2089*.

"I did not want you to learn of this potentially upsetting news from anyone other than me. I'm so sorry, my dear, but it appears you are marked for conjunction. I have not been so torn about a conjunction since that of Ilex and Melia."

Saule smiled. She had no doubt that Dracaen

would provide her with Sephrim to ensure her victory. "Your sweetness is touching, Ravenea. But conjunction is a sacrament. We both knew this day would come."

"No, Saule, you do not understand. I did indeed know this day would come. It's the pairing itself that concerns me."

"I don't understand," said Saule.

Ravenea handed her a piece of parchment inscribed with a single sentence that Saule presumed she had copied from *Arbre de cuivre 2089*. Reading the words, Saule could not breathe. A chill coursed through her. This result could not be, yet the evidence had been placed in her hands: *Le saule se conjoindre avec l'arbre de lotus.*

ꜰʟaw Dimension — 2008

Seated at the main table, arms on its surface, Saule placed her head in her hands. Azoth Fraxinus peered at the document. Dracaen paced from one side of the small room to the other. Hands clasped, Kalina stood beside Larix.

"Are you certain? Absolutely certain? Not even a shred of doubt remains?" asked Dracaen.

"No. Yes. No doubt. Yes, I am certain," said Saule.

"Which manuscript?"

"*Arbre de cuivre 2089.*"

"Folio?"

"Fifteen verso."

"The inscription?"

"*Le saule se conjoindre avec l'arbre de lotus.*"

"Saule will conjoin with Sadira," Kalina uttered quietly.

"I know what it means, Kalina!" bellowed Dracaen.

"No, Dracaen. You do not know what it means," insisted Fraxinus calmly. "These words literally say only that the willow will conjoin with the lotus. None of us knows for certain to which alchemist each tree name refers. One line in one manuscript housed in the Paris protectorate does not equate evidence. Dozens of lines, dozens of cross-references must be affiliated."

"Azoth Fraxinus is correct," agreed Larix. "The one line could quite reasonably refer to a different willow and a different lotus — Reader Vurban and Magistrate Hasu perhaps. Or even Senior Initiate Kamala. Conjunction of an Initiate is rare but not impossible." His voice faltered, his final word barely audible. He was clearly attempting to reassure everyone, especially Dracaen, but his own uncertainty was tangible despite the logic of his words.

No one spoke. Each awaited another. Saule watched Kalina, longing to comfort her. With the revelation of a single sentence, Kalina's entire life purpose had been suddenly upended. Surely Dracaen must have known that even the most highly skilled scribes in Flaw dimension could not control the

Lapis itself or the diligent work of Council Scribes and Readers. He must have suspected that a manuscript inscription that defied his plan would one day surface, despite Rebel Branch efforts. Dracaen would need to change his plan. Revisions would need to be made of various Lapidarian inscriptions. Time could not be wasted.

But he stood defiant and resolute, not about to back down at this crucial point, only a few years away from the prediction that Sadira would conjoin with Kalina. In the outside world, Dracaen might recognize himself as the proud patriarch of this makeshift family. Within dimensional space, he stood as their chosen leader. Saule had indeed *chosen* him years ago. She had once believed his motives were good, had believed that ultimately Dracaen wanted to offer free choice to all and would accept it as such, even if it eventually meant his own demise. But he had become so fixated on the bloodline and his plan for Kalina's mutual conjunction, so insistent that it played out precisely as he envisioned, that he had come to frighten her on occasion. Today was one such occasion. He seemed enraged at her news of the manuscript inscription. But if she had taken Genevre's advice and waited to reveal her discovery until additional evidence surfaced, the repercussions could have been even more dire than they seemed in this moment. For now, Saule needed to persuade him that they could still work together towards his goal, that Kalina and Sadira's mutual conjunction would still take precedence.

"In all likelihood, Fraxinus and Larix are correct," said Kalina, finally breaking the silence. "The line refers to different alchemists. And we need not concern ourselves further. We simply need to search for other evidence."

"We do not have time to search for other evidence. Saule is named specifically," replied Dracaen, his frustration far from abating. "And with regard to the lotus tree, we cannot take the risk. If Council Readers find evidence that corresponds with the line in *Arbre de cuivre 2089*, convincing them otherwise will become even more difficult. No. We will not wait. We must redouble our efforts at scribal revisions immediately. Saule, you must work to align your conjunction with someone else. What were the other lotus names? *Hasu* and who?"

"*Kamala*. But we must consider Saule too," said Kalina. "If the manuscripts are to be revised, then Saule must also be removed from the inscriptions of conjunction."

"Absolutely not!" scolded Dracaen. "Conjunctive partners cannot be chosen simply on the basis of which alchemists we prefer remain in dimensional space!"

"So, you are choosing to revise one and not the other!" Kalina had moved directly beside Dracaen, hands raised above her shoulders in frustration.

"Sadira is essential to the plan! Saule is not!"

Saule flinched.

"Saule has been essential to the plan from Genevre's conception onward! Where would your precious bloodline be without her? Where would *I* be without her?" countered Kalina.

"Yes, Saule has been critical to the plan," said Dracaen. "But we cannot manipulate the manuscripts to change both names. We cannot prevent Saule from conjoining simply because you would prefer her to stay! Given that the Council Elders have already found the inscription in *Arbre de cuivre*, erasing even the one name and inscribing an alternative in its place will be a feat beyond what we had anticipated."

Kalina sighed and walked away from Dracaen. She met eyes with Saule and then with Dracaen before saying, "Then choose wisely. Choose someone over whom Saule would be sure to dominate essences."

"Yes, of course. Of course, we will attempt to assure Saule's victory," conceded Dracaen. "At the very least, she will be supplied with Sephrim."

No one other than Saule understood the bitter truth of this moment. He had uttered what she too had initially assumed. But since discussing the manuscript line and its repercussions with Genevre, she had understood otherwise. Saule knew that she would not be the one to take the Sephrim. She knew that she could not be the victor, that her involvement in the plan to manipulate the manuscripts had not been undertaken solely for the purpose of this particular conjunction. In consultation with Genevre, Saule had agreed to play the sacrifice when the time arrived. She had done so out of loyalty not only to Genevre but to Ilex, Melia, and Payam. Saule understood that she must conjoin with one person specifically: Cedar. She knew not only that she would have to inscribe the manuscripts to replace Sadira's name with Cedar's, but she also knew that Cedar would have to be assured victory. She knew she would give Dracaen's Sephrim to Jinjing who, in turn, would offer it to Cedar. And worst of all, Saule knew that she would have to conjoin with Cedar without ever being able to explain the truth to her beloved Sadira.

Santa Fe — 2008

Within minutes of reassuring Ilex and Melia that he would supply Saule with Sephrim to ensure her victory, Dracaen had relaxed enough to accept Genevre's offer of a small meal: bread, honey, cheese, dates, and spiced wine. They had agreed to gather again to discuss strategy regarding Kalina, Dracaen none the wiser regarding the end game.

Genevre had known long ago this day would come. But decades ago *someday* remained myriad years away. She would not have thought the years would progress so rapidly, especially since leaving

Council dimension permanently more than sixty years ago. Yet now here they were. The day had arrived as if the intervening years had never happened. Her long-held secret must be revealed. She had worked to change Dracaen's plan without his knowledge. In its stead, she had — quite literally — conceived her own plan. To Cedar, she had lied directly. To Dracaen, she had lied by omission.

Genevre exchanged charged glances with Saule during the meal. Like Ilex and Melia, they also regularly looked to the door. He would be arriving soon. Dracaen remained silent as he drank his second glass of wine, clearly ruminating on how to proceed.

"Onward!" he said suddenly, marking an end to the respite. "We must find a compatible conjunctive partner for Saule and then determine how and where to inscribe revisions. Of course, eventually, we must also ensure that inscriptions conjoining Sadira and Kalina are easily made visible to Council Readers."

"I mean no offense," began Melia, "but how are we to accomplish either of these tasks — let alone both? Dozens of manuscripts will inevitably be affected. Saule cannot simply abandon her regular Council duties to work around the clock on revisions. Yes, Ilex, Genevre, and I can help, but our manuscript access is limited at best. Could anyone else be brought onboard — other Council dimension scribes with rebel tendencies?"

"Cedar and Jinjing seem the obvious choices," suggested Kalina.

Genevre glanced at Saule. "No," said Genevre. "Jinjing, yes. But Cedar must remain . . ." She struggled for the appropriate words.

"Removed," offered Saule.

"Yes," continued Genevre, "Cedar must remain removed from manuscript manipulation regarding conjunction."

"Why?" asked Dracaen. He sat up straight, clearly recognizing in that instant that he did not know all that they knew.

"Because she's the one with whom I must conjoin," revealed Saule. "If she were to inscribe her own conjunction, the Elders would recognize her Novillian signature."

Dracaen placed his hands flat on the table and leaned towards Saule, who sat directly across from him. "Again, I ask *why*?" When neither Saule nor Genevre responded, Dracaen furiously pushed himself up from the table, causing his chair to fall back and crash loudly onto the floor. "Tell me now what you have obviously been keeping from me!"

"Cedar and I conceived an alchemical child together," announced Genevre.

Dracaen slammed a hand against the wall.

"I . . . I have a . . . sister?" asked Kalina, for Dracaen's sake.

Dracaen turned.

"No," said Genevre, "your sister died."

"And the alchemical twin?" asked Dracaen.

"The twin survived," admitted Genevre. "Kalina

has a brother. Cedar doesn't know of him, but she is nonetheless integrally connected to us all."

At that very moment, as if on cue, a knock at the door rang through the room. Saule stood to answer, resisting Dracaen's attempt to dissuade her. Everyone, including Dracaen, stared at the handsome young man in the doorway.

"Come in," said Saule.

He walked directly to Dracaen and bowed, wrists crossed in front of his chest.

"Who are you?" asked Dracaen.

He uncrossed his wrists and brushed his long dark hair away from his face. "I am Arjan."

Council Dimension — 2009

Saule stood beneath her favourite tree in the Amber Garden contemplating the approaching conjunction. Only two days remained. Two days remained until she would no longer be herself, no longer be herself alone, no longer be alone with Sadira. Jinjing had, months ago, supplied Cedar with the Sephrim. Of course, Saule did not know whether Cedar had ingested the compound. Only Cedar herself knew what ethical lines she was willing to cross. Only Cedar herself knew what burden of guilt she could bear for eternity.

"I don't want to lose you."

Saule turned quickly. Sadira had startled her.

"Nor I, you," she replied.

In that moment, Saule no longer thought of Cedar's guilt. Instead, she recognized her own. She had not lied outright; she honestly loathed the thought of losing Sadira. Yet she had lied to her beloved indirectly. After all, Saule had volunteered to carry the knowledge of the bloodline, of the alchemical children, and of her role in their creation to her virtual grave. She had agreed to act as a human vessel entombing the secrets in the act of conjunction with Cedar. How could she not? She had been the conduit for the conception of Genevre. In that sense, Arjan and Kalina were her grandchildren as much as they were Ilex and Melia's. She must protect them from the Council for the sake of Genevre's plan, no matter what or whom she must consequently leave behind.

"You're supposed to reassure me," complained Sadira. "You're supposed to tell me that you're certain you will be victorious in the conjunction, that you and I will walk through the upcoming centuries together."

Saule stared up into the branches of the tree. The amber leaves glistened, clicking lightly against one another in the breeze. She felt her own tears begin to well. Sadira put a hand on Saule's shoulder and kissed her cheek.

"My request was selfish," said Sadira. "I apologize, my love. I shouldn't ask or expect you to console me at this difficult time. I should be the one reassuring you. Have no fear. Conjunction is not dependent on the Orders of Council. Essence is all that matters. And your essence is strong, flowing as a swift current through your veins. Victory over Cedar will be yours — essence for essence, blood for blood."

Saule sighed. She longed to fall to her knees and weep. But she did not. She longed to cry out the truth, to curse all those responsible for the creation of the alchemical children. But she did not. Instead, she turned and faced Sadira.

"Thank you."

Those were the last words Saule said to Sadira. Within the hour, both she and Cedar were sequestered in Azothian chambers, counting the final hours until their conjunction. Whenever possible, without seeming too conspicuous, Saule watched Cedar, observed her gestures and expressions, all in an attempt to glimpse a sign that she had ingested the Sephrim. None occurred until the moment of the conjunction itself.

Thus two shall be one, the Elders declared.

The chanting slowed, transformed momentarily into a cacophony of individual voices, and then progressed to the harmonious yet nearly inaudible intonation of the "Sol und Luna."

Saule emerged from the trees and moved past

the Elders towards Cedar. Cedar turned, placed her palms against the cold rock face. Saule stood behind her, exhaling warm breath against Cedar's cold neck. She could no longer hear the chanting. Then, sudden and harsh, Saule felt her essence begin to merge with Cedar's. They struggled until the darkness of the cliff turned to the light of conjunction — of sulphur and mercury, of red and of white. Cedar's cry of anguish — *I'm sorry! I'm sorry!* — rang through Saule as the ineffable presence of self rushed out, purified in its escape. And thus Saule knew in that final moment, alongside those words of atonement, that Cedar had succumbed to temptation.

How could she expect Ruis to understand? Cedar barely understood herself. Perhaps the Sephrim had affected her conjunction with Saule in unpredictable ways. Or perhaps the rebel who had supplied the Sephrim had neglected to explain its side effects. Side effects — Cedar shook her head. Even she must admit that such a striking shift of emotional and physical affections could not merely be attributed to side effects. She was dealing with *primary* effects — unforeseen consequences of decisions she had made over the last few years, which were about to change her life and the lives of others.

Cedar also had to admit that blaming the Sephrim or the conjunction or Saule was an evasion of the truth. Yes, she had once been deeply in love with Ruis, had once longed for nothing other than to steal away with him into the lavender fields of the apiary. Yes, she had once been thrilled to hear him quote to her from outside world poems — especially on the occasion that he would utter something new to her, words that from that moment on would be part of their shared repertoire, words they could utter to each other while working among various Council members without anyone understanding the precise implications even if a phrase was recognized by a listener as *some outside world allusion*. Yet, after a few centuries, even such exchanges had become commonplace, at times no more than a game based in nostalgia, fun in its way, even poignant on occasion, but no longer thrilling. Perhaps the truth of the matter was as straightforward as the passing of time, of dwindling affection for one person — as important as that person might have been or might still be — and growing affection for another.

That too took time — Cedar's nascent affection for Sadira — to grow and to be recognized. After all, she had known Sadira for many years, had worked with her on various Council duties and missions prior to envisioning what it would be like to kiss her. She remembered the day though — the very moment that their collegial relationship had shifted in Cedar's mind to something beyond what she would have expected even days earlier. A few months after her conjunction with Saule, Cedar had been assigned to work with Amur on the restoration of a recovered 14th Council manuscript. An outside world scribe had found the yet-unnamed manuscript during his training as Keeper of the Book in the Vienna protectorate. He had observed what he thought to be the blue-green tinge of Lapidarian ink on an elaborately detailed illumination of a hummingbird. Linden had confirmed the scribe's suspicion and brought the manuscript back to Council dimension for confirmation by the Elders and, once confirmed, for restoration by the Scribes. On this particular day, Cedar had been working late, matching green inks for the restoration of the fourth folio, and Sadira had wandered into the Scriptorium. She had heard about the manuscript and hoped to see it, to watch the Scribes engaged in the restoration. Cedar had gestured for Sadira to take a seat on the bench beside her.

She had assumed Sadira would watch for only a few minutes, but she remained transfixed for more than two hours.

"Let's break for tea," Amur had suggested.

"Or wine," Sadira had responded. "We are nearing the end of the day."

Cedar had smiled. A while later, they had sat on benches in the Amber Garden with other Scribes who had been working in the Scriptorium that day. They had sipped plum wine and talked and laughed and enjoyed the glistening of amber in the rustling leaves.

"I am surprised that the restorations interest you so much," Cedar had said.

"Not these restorations in particular," Sadira had explained. "I'm intrigued by the process, by the way that a Novillian Scribe *inscribes*."

"And do I inscribe as you expected?"

"You hold the pen differently than I'd imagined you would. Your hand moves so subtly and gracefully. I was entranced."

"You were watching my hand?"

"Yes."

Cedar had not known how to respond. She had not been able to look at Sadira directly. Instead, she had stared at Sadira's pendant, which caught the late afternoon light. All future plans had shifted right then — that moment when Cedar had not been able to move her gaze away from the pendant. She had longed to take it in her hand and bring it to her lips and feel Sadira's Quintessence through it. But, of course, she would not have dared make such a bold move — certainly not there in the Amber Garden among their peers.

During the weeks and months thereafter, Cedar took any opportunity she could to work with Sadira. Often weeks would go by when she would see her only at Council meetings. After all, few projects brought Scribes and Magistrates together. But at other times, like when Sadira required the advice of a Scribe for one of her classes, Cedar would volunteer, and they would spend several hours together in a single day working on a future lesson plan or manuscript preparation. And Cedar's affection for her grew to the point that she could barely think of anything else. Even on the nights that she invited Ruis into her bed, she would spend the time before falling asleep imagining herself with Sadira. For such indiscretions, she felt guilty in the morning.

Meanwhile, Ruis had begun to weary her. Every day, he would say something exasperating — usually having to do with decreasing the Flaw or attaining Azothian status or aspiring to be Azoth Magen. She would listen to him, and she would nod or shake her head or express her honest opinion on the matter or lie outright. And afterward she would wander the paths alongside the channel waters or through the Amber Garden and think about the ways in which their figurative paths were veering apart, whereas she appeared to be walking side by side with Sadira. And on the occasion that she literally crossed paths with Sadira on one of these walks, Cedar would revel in the coincidence and again imagine kissing her as she continued along her way.

So here she sat on this night awaiting Ruis. She felt nervous and thus silently reprimanded herself for reacting as if she were three hundred years younger. She laughed at that thought before falling back into nervousness at the sound of a knock at the door.

"I am surprised to have been summoned this evening," said Ruis. "You usually prefer to be alone on nights before long Council meetings."

"We need to talk," she responded, immediately regretting the cliché of the phrase.

"Sounds dire," he laughed.

"Sit down."

"What is going on?"

"Ruis . . ." She shook her head. "Ruis . . ."

"Cedar! What is going on?"

"You're not going to like what I have to say."

"That seems of little consequence."

"Ruis . . . I can no longer be with you."

"In what manner?"

"I can no longer be your lover."

"So what has happened this time? Another crush? Another scribe of the outside world? Just have your fling like last time, and we will continue on together when you return."

"No. It's not like the last time. I'm in love. And she's not of the outside world."

"What? Who? Please tell me she's not an Initiate!"

"No, she's not an Initiate. But I'd rather not reveal her name to you now since she and I have not consummated our relationship."

"Consummated your relationship? Cedar! For the sake of the dimensions, you're an alchemist, not an outside world civilian! If you want to have sex with her, just tell her. Or let her hold your pendant and read your desire for herself. She will understand, as will I, that monogamy simply is not your preferred state of being."

"No, Ruis. You're not listening. I love her, and I want to be with her and her alone."

He paused then as if the truth of the matter finally manifested. "I . . . I do not understand. Why? Why after all these years?"

"Because . . . after all these years, I must . . . take a different path."

She saw him then — saw his face, saw the aging that even Elixir could not stop in that moment. She had hurt him. She had hurt her beloved Ruis. Though she had imagined on many occasions how betrayed he would feel if he ever learned of her goal to increase the Flaw, his reaction in her hypothetical scenario of revelation had always been one of anger. She had never imagined the reaction she witnessed now: grief.

"But I still . . . love you," he said.

"And I still love you. But I also love her. And I need to be with her."

"And she loves you?"

"I don't know. I've not yet confessed my feelings to her. I wanted to speak with you first. I needed to speak with you first."

"What are you saying, Cedar? If you're not certain that your feelings for her are mutual, then why are you putting me through this? You may be back in my arms by tomorrow!"

"No, Ruis. Even if my feelings are not reciprocated, I can no longer be your lover."

He sat silently for a moment. "I will not forget, Cedar. I will not forget what we have shared."

"Nor will I," confessed Cedar. "How could I? How could we?"

"'For *we* on honey-dew hath fed, and drunk the milk of paradise.'" And he cried.

"I remember my first class in Council dimension," said Sadira to Cedar, smiling.

They were seated beside each other on a bench at a mahogany wood table in Cedar's office. They had been restoring and revising an outside world manuscript that Ravenea had brought to Sadira's attention as a possible candidate for use in the Initiate classroom. The consultation had been going well all morning. But once the conversation had turned to more personal matters, it was difficult to navigate a path back to the mundanity of work — especially when neither of them appeared to want to work.

"As do I," replied Cedar.

"You looked quite magisterial — intimidating even — at the front of the room with your dark garnet robes and bright green eyes."

"That is the last thing I would want to do — intimidate the Initiates."

Sadira laughed. "Of course not." She paused.

"So you actually remember me from my first day in the classroom?"

"Yes, I do indeed remember you. Shy and reserved and pale."

"Pale?"

"So fair — your hair and skin — compared with the other Initiates. I remember that aspect in particular. The room was full. I had been assigned to give a joint Initiate lecture on Council history and erasure. I was nervous despite my decades — centuries, in fact — of experience in the classroom."

"Why?"

"Because the concept of erasure is often met with negative reactions, especially by those learning of it for the first time — by Initiates fearing the possibility of it for themselves. I stood there, at the front of the room, looking over the Initiates as they settled into their seats. And I remember distinctly that your presence comforted me. Of the sixteen Initiates seated before me, you were the only one with golden hair. *She glows*, I thought to myself. Hair colour generally is of little consequence to me, but on this occasion, your difference stood out. And when I thought of you as *glowing*, I smiled, and my nervousness evaporated slightly. Then the class continued. Eventually, as the months progressed, you were just another Initiate who pleased or infuriated me along with the others during any given day."

"Yes. I can understand that now — the infuriating part. Initiates can indeed be infuriating." Sadira nodded and smiled before continuing. "I'm glad that I stood out to you, that you really do remember."

"At times during other joint Initiate sessions, I thought you were merely playing the role of the diligent student to attract attention from Saule."

"Perhaps," laughed Sadira. "How else could I garner the attention of a Magistrate?"

"She may have noticed you because of your antics. But she fell in love with you because of your intelligence and kindness."

"Thank you, Cedar. I hope I still exhibit those traits. I often feel lost without her."

"She is here," replied Cedar, tapping her pendant against her chest.

"Do you think so? Do you think she truly is still within you? Can you feel her?"

"No, not directly. That is, I am not consciously aware of her presence. But she must be here, even if only as lingering Quintessence."

"Sometimes I think I can feel her Quintessence when I am near you," Sadira admitted. "But perhaps these feelings are merely wishful thinking."

"Perhaps."

What else could Cedar say to her now? She wanted to ask more about her relationship with Saule, but as much as she felt elated simply being in Sadira's presence, she also felt a pang of guilt for her own victory in the conjunction.

"Do you ever sense it even subtly — Saule's Quintessence?" asked Sadira. She seemed to be pressing the point, unwilling to accept that Cedar could not sense Saule. What could she do then but offer kindness to Sadira — a slight skewing of the truth to ease her anguish.

"I'm not certain since I am not as intimately familiar with it as you are."

They both sat silently for a few moments.

"May I see for myself?" asked Sadira. She nodded towards Cedar's pendant, then momentarily looked at Cedar herself before lowering her gaze to await the response.

Cedar had to give Sadira credit for her boldness — a Magistrate asking to touch a Novillian Scribe's pendant was a breach of protocol, to say the least.

"Yes," she responded, pulling her pendant on its silver cord away from herself and handing it to Sadira.

At first, Sadira merely held the pendant in her hand, caressing its gemstone with her thumb. She then moved it to her forehead for several seconds before cupping it in both hands and holding her hands to her lips.

"May I kiss it?" she asked.

Cedar could barely respond. "Yes," she managed, attempting to steady her breath. But that goal became impossible when Sadira did kiss her pendant. Initially, she gently pressed the gemstone to her lips, simply holding it there for a few moments. Then she kissed it softly, lingering as if in slow motion on the placement of the kiss. Cedar's reaction — one soft but audible gasp in particular — must have given Sadira courage because she then opened her mouth slightly and ran the silver edge of the pendant across her bottom lip, then down her chin and neck and across the top of her breasts. Cedar could not recall having ever felt anything so sensual in her life — not in over three hundred years, not with any of her lovers, not with anyone until now.

"Shall I stop?" asked Sadira.

Cedar shook her head.

Sadira then moved Cedar's pendant from where it had come to rest on her left breast to her own pendant, placing the edge of one against the cleft of the other.

"I can't feel it," Sadira said.

Cedar did not understand. How could Sadira not feel what Cedar could feel so intensely?

"I cannot feel Saule's Quintessence," clarified Sadira. "But I can sense yours."

Cedar reached out to Sadira's hand, which still clasped both pendants together, softly directing the hand out of the way so the she could reach for Sadira's pendant. She pulled the pendant towards her by its silver cord, bringing it immediately to her lips. Sadira moved closer to her in that moment, resting her forehead against Cedar's. Then Sadira's lips brushed against her cheek until they found Cedar's mouth. Cedar dropped the pendant and kissed Sadira directly. She could taste Sadira's Quintessence on her lips — so much stronger than through the pendant. And she knew for certain in that moment that even if this attraction had begun with Saule, with some minute trace of Saule's Quintessence, it was now Cedar's alone. She, Cedar, had fallen in love with Sadira not because of the physical conjunction with Saule, but because of growing respect for her through years of working together, because of genuine sympathy with her plight during Sadira's mourning of Saule, because of the hours they had sat at this bench exchanging ideas as they restored the icons and revised the text of the manuscript. Here in this moment, Cedar felt nothing other than love and desire and not even a sliver of guilt. She was certain that all was exactly as it was meant to be even if what was happening now could not have been foreseen all those years earlier when the pale, introverted young woman had taken her place among those seated in front of her awaiting her words.

Council Dimension — 2013

On occasion over the decades, Kalina had come to question her role in the plan — both in the ultimate plan of Dracaen and in the insurgent plan of Genevre. Prior to today, she had understood such doubt as both inevitable and temporary. After all, her specific role had changed multiple times along with the plans, along with new knowledge, along with the revelation of hidden truths, along with unanticipated errors in judgment or inscription that led to actions of necessity. So many years had passed, so many manuscript revisions, so many adjustments when painstaking alterations went unnoticed by Readers or were misinterpreted by Elders. Under such ever-shifting circumstances amidst opposing forces, how could Kalina not on occasion question her role — question whether said role was chosen or imposed? How could such uncertainty not, as it did today, occasionally overwhelm her? Despite everything that the rebels, Council allies, and insurgents had done over the years to ensure her conjunction with Sadira, Kalina now stood unceremoniously on the precipice of an abyss. Her official conjunction had been announced in Council dimension with little warning and seemingly beyond her control: the Elders of the Alchemists' Council had determined Kalina was to conjoin with Magistrate Tesu.

Something had gone wrong. Someone had inadvertently or purposefully thrown a wrench into the works or, at the very least, spilled some Lapidarian ink onto a rebel manuscript. Thus, once again, all the well-laid plans of both rebels and insurgents required adjustment. Kalina felt trapped in the middle. She currently sat in a chamber in Flaw dimension listening to the debates swirling around her. The voices of Dracaen and Genevre were so loud at times that Kalina physically covered her ears. Did anyone care to ask her opinion? Did anyone care that she feared being conjoined with Tesu against her will?

"Obviously, we will not let that happen," said Dracaen when Kalina finally and stridently vocalized her fear. "Rebel Scribes will simply adjust the manuscripts again. The Council will be convinced the Readers and Elders made a mistake in interpretation when they matched you with Tesu. In time, all will be sorted. You will be matched with Sadira."

"Who is left to convince them?" Kalina asked.

"What do you mean?" asked Dracaen.

"Who is left to convince the Readers and Elders to reconsider their interpretation?"

"Cedar," suggested Genevre. "Cedar remains an ally. Perhaps she—"

"Cedar? Cedar's the one who first noticed my potential pairing with Tesu in *Philosophia Sacra 3490*! Cedar's the one who brought the pairing to the attention of the Elders! Have you heard nothing I said? We need an alternate plan, not additional manuscript revisions. Clearly your methods to ensure this conjunction have failed — time and again! Has it occurred to you that someone might be working against us — someone whom we've not yet even considered? Or has it occurred to you that you might be wrong? That you may have misinterpreted the manuscripts?"

"Calm down, Kalina," said Dracaen firmly. "You are clearly too close to this matter to engage in a rational discussion about it. For your own good, please leave us and return to Council dimension. I promise you, we will resolve this matter with your best interest in mind."

"Yes. I concur. Reason must prevail," said Genevre.

Calm down? Reason must prevail? *I am the only one being reasonable!* she wanted to scream. Kalina had not been this angry with Dracaen since the aftermath of her braiding ceremony with Genevre. And she had never been this angry with Genevre. She had never longed so much for Saule. Saule would have been able to solve the dilemma. If only Saule had maintained some influence within Cedar after their conjunction.

And with that thought, something occurred to her. Varied elements of her past came to her consciousness at once: the braiding, the bloodline, blood alchemy, Saule, Ilex and Melia, Cedar, Sadira, and Arjan. She was an alchemical child who could not be completely erased thanks to the braiding and who held the potential to manipulate time through blood alchemy. She stood up and left the room, moving quickly to the portal. Most likely, the others would think she had left the meeting disgruntled, had gone somewhere to sulk. But she knew the truth. She knew *her* truth. Both Dracaen and Genevre would now have no choice but to follow *her* will, *her* plan.

Once back in Council dimension, Kalina moved swiftly through the corridors of the main Council building to Cedar's office. She knocked loudly but then entered uninvited. Cedar appeared shocked. Kalina walked to the other side of the desk at which Cedar sat working. She crossed her wrists in front of her chest.

"I am the blood of the Dragon!" she chanted.

"I am the Flaw in the Stone!" replied Cedar, quietly but without hesitation.

Together in reciting the rebel oath in Council dimension, they had taken a risk beyond measure. But no one came rushing into the room. No one hauled either of them away to Azothian chambers. No one had heard them. But they had heard one another.

"The Rebel Branch requires your assistance. *I* require your assistance."

"Another scribal revision?"

"No. Not another revision. An erasure," replied Kalina. "But its instigation cannot appear to have come from you."

"Creative ingenuity is my forte," replied Cedar. "Who is to be erased?"

"Me."

"Victory!" cried Dracaen.

Dracaen's cry simultaneously announced his triumph and brought an end to the Fourth Rebellion.

Little does he know, Kalina thought to herself, wrists crossed in front of her chest. *Little do any of them know*, she imagined Sadira thinking. The others — rebels and alchemists alike — all stood witness to an illusion: a fantasy world, plotted point by point by insurgent scribes; a palimpsest, obscuring the truth from inattentive Readers. Having been successfully erased from Council dimension, Kalina had been freed from manuscript inscriptions concerning her conjunction. She and Sadira now stood beside Arjan and Dracaen — the four finally existing as two mutually conjoined pairs. Ilex and Melia were no longer singular in their success. Kalina scanned the gathering crowd searching for one face, the final linchpin in Genevre's plan: Cedar. She appeared then, sombre despite her rebel sympathies. Kalina understood that Cedar had desired only a permanent increase in the Flaw, not an outright takeover by the rebels. Thus Genevre had relegated Cedar to the shadows, allowing her only glimpses of light to spur her onward. Kalina need provide only one more glimmer to incite Cedar to rebellious action.

Moonlight illuminating their mutually conjoined face, Kalina whispered aloud to Sadira: "Now!" In that instant, Sadira took control of their body and caught Cedar's eye, then Kalina immediately followed suit. Sadira, Kalina, Sadira, Kalina — Cedar shook her head. She had seen what Kalina had meant her to see: a continual fluctuation between rebel and alchemist.

"Arjan!" cried Jaden.

Kalina then realized Arjan had also engaged his fluctuation with Dracaen. Clearly Jaden had witnessed the shift — she struggled to pull herself from Cedar's grasp and reach Arjan.

"He is gone," said a rebel to Jaden. "If Council dimension survives the elemental changes, you can mourn him in your precious Amber Garden."

"Arjan is not gone," replied Jaden. "You are blinded by your allegiance."

"And you by yours," he retorted.

"Arjan!" Jaden cried, still struggling with Cedar. She then turned sharply towards Kalina. "Sadira!" she gasped.

Realizing that Jaden, like Cedar, could see the fluctuation of both conjoined pairs, Kalina watched them even more closely. Upon crying "Sadira," Jaden halted her struggle against Cedar. Kalina intuited that Cedar explained to Jaden that they had conjoined.

"Our mission is accomplished," called Dracaen to the rebels. "We have conjoined — rebel and alchemist, Rebel Branch and Alchemists' Council. Though the Final Ascension of Azoth Magen Ailanthus has decreased the Flaw in the Stone within Council dimension, our conjunctions will ensure its continued prominence. I will return to the Flaw dimension victorious. Kalina will remain here. Thus a conduit between our dimensions will remain permanently accessible."

"The Council will never accept Kalina. She will be removed upon discovery. The conduit will be closed once again," shouted a rebel.

"No one on the Alchemists' Council will know she is Kalina," Dracaen explained. "They will see only Sadira. Only a chosen few will recognize the one and the other."

Rebel applause and laughter erupted. Seeing only Kalina, they too were limited in their vision, but they understood the ploy.

Cedar locked eyes with Sadira. Kalina bristled with anticipation.

"Come with me, Jaden," Cedar called.

Kalina smiled as she watched them run.

Qingdao — 2014

Genevre stood beside Ilex and Melia, who were seated on a bench by the window. The transmutation of time they enacted so many years ago had indeed opened a portal on the day Obeche and Tera brought Arjan and Jaden to work in the Qingdao protectorate. Thereafter, each step in Genevre's plan had progressed with only minor glitches. In response, she had easily made adjustments, found and took detours. Now, at the height of the Fourth Rebellion, Genevre waited for the beginning of the end. Kalina was to report back as soon as possible after the conjunctions. Of course, Genevre realized an appropriate moment for departure from the fray might not occur until several days afterward. Thus she waited anxiously with Ilex and Melia, attempting but failing at small talk as the hours passed slowly each day.

"We should have thought of a more effective means of relaying the news," said Genevre. "The conjunctions may have failed completely, and we'll be proven the fools who nonetheless sat and awaited hopefully."

Neither Ilex nor Melia spoke. At first, Genevre attributed their silence to the frustration that had begun to set in hours earlier. But then she noticed that they were shivering.

"Are you cold?" she asked, though this prospect seemed unlikely.

Ilex and Melia pushed themselves up from the bench and stood facing Genevre.

"What's wrong?"

"We feared this would occur," said Melia.

"What?"

"The bees have been released," said Ilex.

"What bees?"

"The bees from the primary Council dimension apiary — the lavender fields. They have been released, most likely in an attempt to save the world," Melia explained.

"I don't understand, Melia."

"Do you remember years ago, in the aftermath

of the original time transmutation in Qingdao, when Ilex and I began to separate, when we were gradually restored by the Quintessence-laden ink of the Lapidarian manuscript bees?"

"Of course."

"We would otherwise have died," acknowledged Ilex. "The time transmutation overwhelmed us — the conjunction of one time and another was too much for our mutually conjoined nature to bear."

"At first, we merely siphoned the ink of the bees who followed our queen," continued Melia. "We were grateful for the influx of Quintessence. But later Azoth Fraxinus convinced us to begin repopulating the lavender fields. As you know, each bee inscribed within a Lapidarian manuscript simultaneously appears in a Council dimension apiary. Likewise, each bee erased from a manuscript disappears from its apiary. Fraxinus suggested we replace the bees that had migrated from the Council manuscripts and apiaries to our manuscript."

"Replace them with what?"

"With other bees — bees that fed on our blood."

"Fed on your blood? Bees don't feed on—"

"These bees did," admitted Ilex. "They were alchemically transformed by Fraxinus for that very purpose."

"To what end?" asked Genevre.

"The bees were alchemically enlivened not only to feed on our blood but, when deemed necessary, to infuse another alchemist with it, to ensure that another alchemist carried forth our bloodline by your side, should Kalina be unable to do so."

"Why would she be unable to do so?"

"No one could predict what would happen, Genevre," said Ilex. "The bee-infused bloodline was Fraxinus's contingency plan. He did not yet know of Arjan."

"You had your plan, Genevre. And we had ours," confessed Melia. "We could not be certain that any one of our coalition would survive, including you. We had to protect the bloodline at all costs."

Genevre stared. "Fine. You had a backup plan to protect us all. That doesn't explain what is happening now. You're trembling. Something is clearly wrong."

"Yes. Something is wrong. The bees have been released."

"How do you know? And what do you mean?" Genevre asked. She looked out the window half-expecting to see a gathering swarm.

"They carry our blood. We can feel its essence has shifted — it has shifted in them and, consequently, in us. The bees who survived the transfusion are flying through the outside world." Melia inhaled deeply after she had spoken as if she had used up their remaining breath.

"The transfusion? What are you saying? Has an alchemist already been transfused with your blood?"

"Yes," said Ilex.

"Who?"

"We have no way to know."

"How then? How was the blood transferred?"

"The bees would have had to sting someone — an alchemist who could survive the after-effects. Someone—"

Ilex and Melia stumbled forward. Genevre reached out to steady them. She attempted to lead them back to the bench, but they refused to move.

"Genevre. Stand back. The transmutation of both time and blood together was clearly too strong for us. We are separating."

Genevre stood still in shocked silence. She knew instantaneously that Melia was not exaggerating. The trembling had been swiftly supplanted by a vibration that appeared to be radiating from the very core of their being. One moment, Genevre stood before her parents watching a single, solid being. The next, she appeared to be watching a transparent projected image, one that flickered rapidly due to faulty technology. Within minutes, the flickering image became two. A moment later, Melia and Ilex stood next to one another, their individual solidity apparent once again. They turned to look at one another. They smiled and exchanged a kiss.

"How?" whispered Genevre.

Neither Ilex nor Melia responded. Instead they embraced her — first Melia and then Ilex. "Your separation cannot be the responsibility of the bees alone," said Genevre.

"No. I suspect the transmutation of time and the

mutual conjunctions of our grandchildren played their roles. Perhaps the dimensions are incapable of sustaining mutual conjunctions across time or across the generations. We can only hope you will determine an explanation one day."

"You can help me. We'll determine an explanation together."

"No, Genevre," said Ilex.

"Yes!"

Neither Ilex nor Melia spoke.

"What are you saying? What are you *not* saying?" Genevre looked from one to the other.

Melia then reached out to Genevre, brushing a strand of her hair off her forehead. Genevre longed to touch Melia in return, to tell her she understood all the questionable choices she had made, forgave her all the power and compulsions she had passed along to her child through the bloodline.

"Like mother, like—"

Right then, without warning, Ilex burst into flame. Genevre stepped back, startled. Melia reached for her, clasping Genevre's hands in her own. Seconds later, Melia dissolved into water, surrounding Ilex's fire in a wave of motion. Then they were gone, save tiny embers sizzling in a small pool.

Genevre knelt to the ground. Hands still dripping with Melia's essence, she cradled the embers. They did not burn her physically, but they singed her heart. Her tears fell, mingling with her parents' remains. She cried until distracted by unexpected movement. She watched the multiple ember pebbles liquefy, merge, and then solidify in her hands. She held the resulting conjunction of water, fire, and tears to the light: a pendant of honey-coloured amber.

EPILOGUE
Santa Fe — 2014

"I am here for sanctuary and for assistance with a manuscript."

Cedar stood on the doorstep looking at her friend. Genevre had aged somewhat but was still as beautiful as she had been all those years ago when they had first met. Cedar awaited Genevre's assurance that she was welcomed and that all would be well. Now that she had lost everything — even if the loss was only temporary — she needed someone to reassure her. She doubted Genevre, even with her best intentions, could reassure her with more than a hopeful prediction for the future. Indeed, she had doubted whether to seek Genevre's assistance at all. Yet here she stood by necessity, requiring both answers and assistance.

"For all intents and purposes, I have been erased from Council dimension."

"Come in. Explain everything."

"I need to know you're willing to help me."

"Of course I'll help you if I can." She held out her hand to Cedar. "Come in. Talk to me. Tell me what happened."

Cedar stepped from the bright moonlight of the yard into the dimly lit entranceway in Genevre's home. She was ushered into the living room where they sat together on a small sofa.

"What do you mean you need sanctuary?"

"I need a place to stay — an actual physical location to live for the foreseeable future. I'd prefer to stay with you rather than find a place on my own — rather than be by myself. It should be only for a few months, though I can't be certain."

"You are welcome here. You've always been welcome here."

"Thank you," said Cedar. She tilted her head back and sighed. "I didn't know what to expect under the circumstances. I'm no longer certain who you are to me."

"Yet here we are together now, like no time at all has passed. I've barely aged thanks to the Lapidarian honey."

"But so much has changed."

"An understatement if Council has decided to erase a Novillian Scribe. Let me make us some tea, and then you can start from the beginning."

Cedar nodded again. She was not certain whether she would be able to pinpoint the beginning. How could one fragment in time be chosen as the beginning? She watched Genevre moving about in the kitchen, graceful even at the most basic of tasks.

After Genevre had served the tea, and Cedar had taken a few sips, she began. "Earlier when I said that I no longer know who you are to me, I meant that I've learned something about who you are. I've learned you are not the person I thought you were or, more accurately, you're a different person than I've always believed you to be."

"I don't understand."

"I've learned the truth, Genevre. Or part of it."

Genevre stared, saying nothing.

"My preference would be for you to tell me the truth — the whole truth," said Cedar. "But I know enough to know that you would not risk revealing your remaining secrets to me until you believe the time is right."

"What is it then? What is it that you now know?"

"The name of the child you created with Dracaen — the name both you and Saule chose to hide from me years ago: Kalina."

Genevre turned her gaze to the door.

"Do you care to guess how I arrived at this realization?"

Genevre responded, "I wouldn't dare."

"Did you know that Kalina conjoined with Sadira?"

"What—"

"Then Initiate Arjan conjoined with High Azoth Dracaen. Two mutual conjunctions between the Alchemists' Council and the Rebel Branch that I had no knowledge were about to occur. And, more to the point, the repercussions have only just begun — ripple effects are now cascading through the dimensions. And I appear to have become an early, if inadvertent, victim of one such effect."

"Explain."

"Saule spoke to me."

"Saule? What?"

"She spoke to me. Saule spoke *through* me. I looked into the mirror the other day, and Saule suddenly appeared. And she spoke to me. *Kalina is Genevre's daughter*, she said. *And Arjan is—*"

Genevre leaned forward, waiting.

"That was all. That's all Saule managed to say. She was unable to complete the sentence before she vanished. She hasn't reappeared since."

"How . . . how *odd*."

"Odd? Is that all you have to say? Can you not at least tell me whether it's true or a figment of my imagination?"

"How am I to know whether Saule actually appeared to you?"

"No, Genevre! Is Kalina your daughter?"

Genevre nodded. "Yes. Yes, Cedar. Kalina is my daughter."

"Did you know she would conjoin with Sadira?"

"I . . . I knew she would conjoin someday. But I didn't know when . . . or *how*. In recent years, she has purposely kept me in the dark. We had a . . . falling out, and she broke off all but essential communication."

"A family trait, it appears," responded Cedar.

"What?"

"Like mother, like daughter. You also kept me in the dark."

"No. Yes. We . . . *I* couldn't risk . . . Cedar, Kalina is my daughter — an alchemical child. My child mattered more to me than . . . than *us*. As you know, as we discussed years ago before conceiving our own child together, sometimes such decisions of secrecy must be made . . . for the sake of . . . those we love."

"On that point, we can agree."

Genevre nodded. "Good."

"But the time has come for the truth, Genevre — the entire truth. And I also need your assistance with a manuscript."

"What manuscript?"

"Just before my erasure, I learned that Council Scribes were in the process of creating a manuscript — they plan to send it into the outside world. Its purpose is to attract potential Initiates to Council dimension. If one destined to Council learns to read between its lines, learns to perform its rituals, a portal will open and initiation will begin. We must create another — you and I. We must create an alternate manuscript, one to attract potential rebel initiates to our cause: to maintain the Flaw in the Stone."

"A Rebel Branch Initiate's Guide?"

"Precisely. Will you help me?"

"How can I refuse such a passionate plea?"

Progress was slow at first. Despite, or perhaps because of, their combined multitude of years of scribal experience, Cedar and Genevre could not simply *compose* the contents of a book-length document and send it on its way to the outside world. Together, they had to *create* a manuscript infused with alchemical potential. They had to write and rewrite and rewrite again. They had to inscribe and erase and re-inscribe. Every day, for weeks on end, they had to distill both Dragonsblood and Lapidarian inks from the minute shavings of Lapis and Dragonblood Stones that Cedar and Genevre had surreptitiously sequestered. To have its desired effect, one manuscript illumination in particular required an influx of Elixir, which neither Cedar nor Genevre possessed beyond the traces that remained in their bodies from their years with the Council. Genevre resisted gently when Cedar suggested mixing some of her own blood with the ink to ensure its effectiveness.

"You now reside in the outside world, Cedar. You must conserve your Quintessence."

"I am and always will be an alchemist, Genevre — with or without the Council."

"And without the Council, you no longer have access to the Lapis or Elixir."

"Regardless, the ink requires an infusion of Elixir, and my blood is the only way," Cedar insisted. "Don't fear. I'm not about to slice open my wrist, Genevre. What good would such a dramatic move make to this project?"

Genevre stared blankly in response. "Don't joke about such things, Cedar. Too much is at stake."

"And those stakes are the very reason I make this proposal. I am suggesting merely a drop or two of blood from my fingertip. No more than a few pinpricks will be required."

"Fine," said Genevre. "Wait here." She left the room, returning with a sewing needle and Lapidarian candle in tow. She lit the candle and held the tip of the needle in its flame.

"You don't need to sterilize the needle. My veins still flow with Elixir. It will counteract any negative . . . intruders."

"I, on the other hand, am not so certain."

Cedar misunderstood at first. She thought Genevre was uncertain of the strength of the Elixir in Cedar's blood, which Cedar knew beyond doubt would remain powerful for many years. But upon removing the needle from the flame, Genevre held it above her own finger, evidently prepared to offer her own blood.

"Hold the bottle," she instructed Cedar.

"What are you doing?"

"How much stronger will the ink be if infused with blood from each of us?"

"You are not an alchemist of the Council, Genevre. Your blood does not course with Quintessence."

Genevre smiled. "You'd be shocked."

Cedar laughed.

"You think I'm joking, but I've never been more serious. Before our time together reaches its end yet again, I need you to hear my confession. You requested the truth from me. I offer it to you now."

Cedar leaned back in her chair, hands clasped beneath her shawl.

"My blood is responsible for the mess we're in. In fact, if you were to follow my steps one by one from the day I enlivened the *Osmanthian Codex*, you might even argue that my blood is responsible for your erasure."

Cedar shook her head. "I don't understand. What's the *Osmanthian Codex*?"

"An ancient manuscript containing, among its rituals and chants, the formula for the creation of the alchemical child. My blood enlivened it. You said you were no longer certain who I was. But the fact of the matter is that you've never known who I am."

"Is that so? Tell me then, Genevre. Who are you?"

"Daughter to Ilex and Melia."

Cedar sat up straight. "Daughter? Ilex and Melia had a daughter?"

Genevre nodded, saying nothing. Cedar was left to assemble the pieces: Ilex, Melia, Genevre, Kalina. Finally, she thought of Arjan. Cedar could still hear Ailanthus's voice ringing through Azothian Chambers: *Who were your grandparents?* From that moment onward, she had known Ilex and Melia to be Arjan's grandparents. But she would not have dared suspect that Genevre was their daughter. She and the other Elders had assumed Ilex and Melia were Arjan's *grandparents* merely in name — a lie made up years ago to keep outside world folk from questioning their maturity or appearance relative to Arjan's. Now her suspicions and resulting supposi-tions ran wild.

"Do they have other children?" she finally asked.

"No. I'm their only child. My understanding is that they wanted no others."

"Did they create you in an alembic as you and Dracaen did with Kalina?"

"No. I'm their biological child."

"How? How can you exist? Alchemists cannot—" Cedar stopped herself. Clearly these alchemists *could* do what other alchemists could not. Clearly Ilex and Melia were the exception in more ways than one. "And Arjan? Is Arjan another child of Dracaen's that you decided to hide from me?"

Genevre remained silent. She closed her eyes. "No," she finally said.

Cedar could feel herself trembling.

"Saule—" said Genevre.

"Saule played a role in the creation of Arjan?" responded Cedar. She paused before adding, "That must be what she'd wanted to tell me."

"Y-yes. It . . . must have been," replied Genevre. "I know you must be angry—"

"No," said Cedar. "I only wish I'd not failed you when we created our child."

"You've not failed me, Cedar. All will soon be revealed. I promise."

Cedar nodded. In that instant, her earlier doubts about seeking sanctuary with Genevre dissolved. She ran her fingertips across a page of the manuscript.

"Your blood must be infused with powerful Quintessence. No wonder your scribal powers have always seemed so much more enhanced than those of other outside world scribes."

"Ilex and Melia were both of the sacred bloodline," said Genevre. "As mutually conjoined alchemists of the bloodline, their blood was extraordinarily powerful. My own blood is likewise powerful by virtue of inheritance."

Gradually and finally swayed by Genevre's logic, Cedar held an ink bottle beneath Genevre's hand to catch each drop of her blood. Made of clear glass and housing barely an ounce of Lapidarian ink, the bottle allowed both Cedar and Genevre to watch the blood hit the blue liquid. Unexpectedly, the conjunction of blood and ink made a sound — a short but distinct sizzle that startled Cedar. Yet as

expected, the blood remained visible only momentarily before dispersing into the ink. Cedar was more
intrigued by the sound than the sight of this venture.

"Your blood *is* powerful," said Cedar.

"Your turn," said Genevre. Cedar set the bottle
on the table and took the needle. She poised it
above her fingertip.

"What will happen if I prick my finger with this
needle, Genevre? What do you think will happen if
your blood mixes with mine?"

"Alchemy."

With those words, Genevre had offered her friend
a fragment of the truth. But what she did not reveal
to Cedar, what she knew Cedar could not have
anticipated despite the partial truths Genevre had
revealed, is that mixing even one drop of her own
blood with Cedar's would have repercussions far
more extensive than anything any alchemist could
have imagined. Cedar had hundreds of years' worth
of Elixir coursing through her veins. She remained
a powerful alchemist regardless of the unorthodox
erasure. And even more relevant in this particular
case, her Elixir-filled blood not only flowed with
the after-effects of Sephrim but also with the
essence of the one with whom she had conjoined
years ago. Thus, when Cedar pierced her own finger,
Genevre's blood mixed with that of both Cedar and

Saule. Within seconds, Cedar was writhing on the floor in pain.

"You will be okay. The discomfort will pass," Genevre said, positioning herself beside Cedar in an effort to prevent her from flailing against the edge of the raised fireplace hearth.

Moments later, Cedar screamed so loudly that Genevre feared she would attract unwanted attention from the neighbours. Thus, as soon as physically possible, she helped Cedar to her feet and guided her to the relative privacy of the bedroom at the back of the house. Within the hour, the pain appeared to have passed. Cedar rested comfortably, breathing calmly, and eventually falling asleep. But the end of the pain did not mark the end of the transmutation. The alchemy of the combined bloodlines continued even as the night progressed, even as they moved through restless dreams awaiting dawn, even as the morning light fell across the bed, even as Genevre opened her eyes to face her friend.

"Do not fear, Genevre. Cedar will be fine."

"Where is she?"

"Resting in the shadows," replied Saule.

Acknowledgements

Thank you, first of all, to all the people who wrote a review of *The Alchemists' Council*. Receiving positive feedback on Book One was extraordinarily motivating as I wrote and revised Book Two. Thank you, also, to my family, friends, and colleagues who have supported my creative endeavours in myriad ways — from retweeting book updates to laughing with me over a margarita. Thank you Farah Moosa for all our chats and dinners, and especially for listening to the book fair pitch. Thank you to all the folk who attended the Book One launch, with special thanks to friends who helped out (including those who baked bee cookies, set up beekeeping equipment, or sported sartorial bee wear): Darby Love, Marni Stanley, Kathryn Barnwell, Sonnet L'Abbé, Farah Moosa, Joy Gugeler, Melissa Stephens, Tami Joseph, Nicole Klan, and Paul Klan. Thank you

Janis Ledwell-Hunt for joining me at Nanaimo GeekCon and informing people you weren't the author! Thank you Sandra Hagan for brainstorming the Rebel Branch chant with me as we awaited literal fireworks. Thank you Malgorzata Drewniok for your enthusiasm and encouragement when we chatted about the books in London, UK. Thank you Frances Sprout, Rhonda Wilcox, and Tamy Burnett not only for the savvy reviews but also for your ongoing friendship and inspirational chats. Thank you Tami Joseph and Johnny Blakeborough for rescuing me on the day I first attempted to set up the *News from Council Dimension* blog. Thank you Elaine Lay for our biweekly alchemical ponderings during your research assistantship. Thank you Cheryl Morrison for the stunning Amber Tree pendant and our interprovincial phone calls. Thank you Joan Coldwell and Ann Saddlemyer for sanctuary and sustenance — and, Ann, thanks for our discussion on Yeats and alchemy (which, as you will see, inspired a few elements of Book Two). Thank you Anita Young for being not only my beloved friend for thirty years but also my virtual literary patron. Thank you, once again, to everyone at ECW Press, especially Crissy Calhoun and David Caron. And thank you, most of all, to Jen Hale — not only for the exquisite editing but also for the laughter, the inspiration, the texts, the memes, the visits, the fluctuating percentages, and the spaghetti recipes. Book Three awaits!

CYNTHEA MASSON is a professor in the English department at Vancouver Island University. After completing a Ph.D. in English with a focus on medieval mysticism, she was awarded a postdoctoral fellowship, which included work with alchemical manuscripts at the British Library. Her award-winning academic work includes the co-edited book *Reading Joss Whedon*. The first book in the *Alchemists' Council* series was shortlisted for the Kobo Emerging Writer Prize and won the Gold Medal for Fantasy in the 2017 Independent Publisher Book Awards. She lives in British Columbia.